Pas

TITLES BY MERCEDES LACKEY
available from DAW Books:

THE NOVELS OF VALDEMAR:

THE HERALDS OF VALDEMAR
ARROWS OF THE QUEEN
ARROW'S FLIGHT
ARROW'S FALL

THE LAST HERALD-MAGE
MAGIC'S PAWN
MAGIC'S PROMISE
MAGIC'S PRICE

THE MAGE WINDS
WINDS OF FATE
WINDS OF CHANGE
WINDS OF FURY

THE MAGE STORMS
STORM WARNING
STORM RISING
STORM BREAKING

VOWS AND HONOR
THE OATHBOUND
OATHBREAKERS
OATHBLOOD

THE COLLEGIUM CHRONICLES
FOUNDATION
INTRIGUES
CHANGES
REDOUBT
BASTION

THE HERALD SPY
CLOSER TO HOME
CLOSER TO THE HEART
CLOSER TO THE CHEST

FAMILY SPIES
THE HILLS HAVE SPIES
EYE SPY
SPY, SPY AGAIN

BY THE SWORD
BRIGHTLY BURNING
TAKE A THIEF

EXILE'S HONOR
EXILE'S VALOR

VALDEMAR ANTHOLOGIES:
SWORD OF ICE
SUN IN GLORY
CROSSROADS
MOVING TARGETS

CHANGING THE WORLD
FINDING THE WAY
UNDER THE VALE
NO TRUE WAY
CRUCIBLE
TEMPEST
PATHWAYS
CHOICES
SEASONS
PASSAGES

Written with **LARRY DIXON:**

THE MAGE WARS
THE BLACK GRYPHON
THE WHITE GRYPHON
THE SILVER GRYPHON

DARIAN'S TALE
OWLFLIGHT
OWLSIGHT
OWLKNIGHT

OTHER NOVELS:

GWENHWYFAR
THE BLACK SWAN

THE DRAGON JOUSTERS
JOUST
ALTA
SANCTUARY
AERIE

THE ELEMENTAL MASTERS
THE SERPENT'S SHADOW
THE GATES OF SLEEP
PHOENIX AND ASHES
THE WIZARD OF LONDON
RESERVED FOR THE CAT
UNNATURAL ISSUE
HOME FROM THE SEA
STEADFAST
BLOOD RED
FROM A HIGH TOWER
A STUDY IN SABLE
A SCANDAL IN BATTERSEA
THE BARTERED BRIDES
THE CASE OF THE SPELLBOUND
CHILD
JOLENE

Anthologies:
ELEMENTAL MAGIC
ELEMENTARY

And don't miss THE VALDEMAR COMPANION
edited by John Helfers and Denise Little

Passages

All-New Tales of Valdemar

Edited by
Mercedes Lackey

DAW BOOKS, INC.

DONALD A. WOLLHEIM, FOUNDER

1745 Broadway, New York, NY 10019

ELIZABETH R. WOLLHEIM
SHEILA E. GILBERT
PUBLISHERS
www.dawbooks.com

First Printing, November 2020
1 2 3 4 5 6 7 8 9

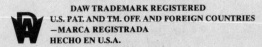

DAW TRADEMARK REGISTERED
U.S. PAT. AND TM. OFF. AND FOREIGN COUNTRIES
—MARCA REGISTRADA
HECHO EN U.S.A.

PRINTED IN THE U.S.A.

Contents

Roads Less Traveled
Charlotte E. English   1

A Ruler's Gift
Anthea Sharp   16

Rising to the Occasion
Jennifer Brozek   36

A Nursery of Raccoons
Elisabeth Waters   47

Tables Turned
Kristin Schwengel   65

Expected Consequences
Elizabeth A. Vaughan   77

Burrowing Owl, Hidden No More
Dayle A. Dermatis   95

The Dream Seeker
Paige L. Christie   117

Shadows and Reflections
Louisa Swann   132

Flying the Nest
  Michele Lang   153

Snowbound
  Brigid Collins   171

The More Things Change, the More They Change More
  Fiona Patton   187

The Choice Makes the Chosen
  Stephanie D. Shaver   205

Trial by Reflection
  Terry O'Brien   227

Theory and Practice
  Angela Penrose   242

Tools of the Trade
  Phaedra Weldon   257

The Border Within
  Brenda Cooper   282

Temper
  Mercedes Lackey   299

The Hawkbrothers' Ways
  Larry Dixon   319

About the Authors   323
About the Editor   329

Roads Less Traveled
Charlotte E. English

:I can see you, you know.:

Uselessly, Rosia tucked herself deeper into the thicket in which she had taken refuge, as though doing so might turn her invisible if she only wished hard enough.

The dulcet voice went on, inexorable. *:You look nice!:*

A choked sound emerged from the girl, comprising disgust and—in spite of herself—laughter, albeit without much mirth. Nice? She looked *nice*? After weeks on the road, wending ever deeper into the wilds of the Pelagir Hills; without money even to *eat* half the time, let alone bathe; dressed in ragged garments that were now hopelessly soiled and torn and had never been *nice* even when new.

:Perhaps it isn't the way you look so much as the way you smell,: conceded her pursuer, the words coming somehow from inside her own head. She might conclude she had gone mad and was talking to herself, save that the bright white horse, with its silvery bridle and its bells and its wide, friendly eyes, had been following her for hours; and every observation made, in those mellow tones, was accompanied by some hopeful movement. This time, it was a nuzzling at the branches of Rosia's friendly thicket. One clear blue eye peeped in.

"That's even worse," Rosia said. "If I could only get away from my *own* smell, I would."

A pause followed. Rosia received the impression that the horse was thinking.

:*No, you're right,*: came the reply. :*It isn't a vision or a scent but a . . . feeling. You* feel *nice.*:

Rosia, exhausted and hungry and despairing, swallowed a sob. "Why won't you go away?"

:*Because I'm lonely.*:

"So? Find another friend."

:*But I like you.*:

"Who wouldn't," Rosia muttered, clenching her fists. "When I've been so friendly."

:*I am your Companion,*: said the horse. :*That is the best friend anybody could have.*:

"I don't need a companion." *And I don't deserve one,* Rosia thought.

The horse lay down on the other side of the thicket, clearly prepared to wait all day if necessary. :*I am here anyway, my Chosen.*:

Rosia briefly thought of running away, but the horse would only follow. "Why are you so stubborn?" she said instead, hating the whining quality of the question. She was an *adult*—or nearly, anyway. Adults didn't whine.

The horse lipped at a scrubby thread of grass. :*I am your Companion.*:

"You said that already."

Rosia received a sense of warm amusement, like . . . a giggle. Her *Companion*, if she was such, was too young for sober dignity. :*For some reason, I got the idea you weren't listening,*: she said. :*My name is Lilan.*:

Rosia sat up as far as she was able, ignoring the tangle of thorns in her hair, and folded her arms.

:*And you are . . . ?:* prompted Lilan.

"Rosia," the name ungraciously muttered under her breath. "Peddler." *Thief.* "And a girl who talks to horses, looks like."

:*I am not a horse,*: said Lilan patiently. :*A Companion is something else altogether.*:

"I know what you are. You think I haven't seen Heralds?" Rosia had no intention of telling this peculiar creature what kinds of feelings she'd witnessed at the passage of Valdemar's Chosen. In their immaculate Whites, with their Companions at their sides, they'd blown through Rosia's life like a fresh, bright wind, untouchably distant. Unfathomably magnificent.

Not that any of them had ever stopped to talk to the likes of her, not even when her parents were alive. Peddlers were beneath such folk. She and Ma and Pa had passed Heralds on the road sometimes, that was all.

:Well, then, you know why I am here.: Lilan settled herself more comfortably, as placid as a summer lake, and if a horse—*Companion*—was capable of smiling, she was smiling now.

"You must be confused," said Rosia.

:Not in the least. You are my Chosen, and when you're feeling better, we shall be off on our way to Haven.:

"You picked wrong. Go find someone else."

:Why do you say that?: Lilan asked the question in a spirit of gentle enquiry, as though mildly curious.

Rosia bit her lip. "Heralds are s'posed to be good people."

:And you are not?:

"I'm not." She heaved the boundless sigh of a wearied spirit and added, in a smaller voice, "I wasn't so bad, before . . ."

:Before?: prompted Lilan.

Rosia tightly closed her lips.

Lilan, unconcerned, fell silent. Rosia peeped through the thorns and saw the Companion, eyes closed, lightly dozing. Or so it seemed.

"Before Ma died," Rosia said. "And then Pa, and . . ."

It was her turn to fall into a silence, though hers was of a brooding quality.

:Why don't you tell me what happened?: Lilan said. *:Once I know how awful you are, I'm sure I'll be off like a shot.:*

Rosia shrank into herself, appalled at the thought of confessing aloud to—anybody, least of all a stranger. Least of all a . . . horse. Companion. "I can't. It's too hard."

:Don't start with the hard part,: Lilan suggested. *:The trick is to start at the beginning.:*

* * *

The Pelagir Hills loomed ahead, dark and uninviting. Heavy old boughs hung over the road, casting long shadows, despite the day being rather young yet. Fall had that way about it sometimes; winter lurked just behind, and sometimes you could really feel it.

Rosia felt it keenly today.

She'd meant to plunge straight into the forest without stopping. That was how you did things that were scary: quickly, without pausing to think. But her feet had betrayed her, or perhaps it was her heart that had failed. The *darkness* under those trees daunted her. Even the road this far northwest did not much deserve the name, being a crumbling dirt track that hosted few travelers.

And then there were the stories . . .

Fever had taken her ma, not long since and her pa soon after. There hadn't been much left in their packs by then, and there hadn't been money enough for a donkey or a pony in years. Still, Rosia had never known what it was to go truly hungry—until Pa had gone. Then she'd learned.

She was hungry now. Not the light, ordinary hunger of the well-fed, but an urgent need for sustenance that tore at her insides and weakened her knees. She had sold most of Ma's ribbons and Pa's trinkets for medicine; and when that failed to save either of them, she had been forced to sell everything else for food. Now there was nothing left, not for food, not for new supplies to sell in some fresh town farther up the road. If she didn't do *something,* she would starve.

Something had presented itself. Her last coin had gone to purchase a loaf—stale but edible—from a baker a village or two back. In passing, she'd heard talk.

"Them Pelagirs, you wanta watch yersel' up there," the baker said in his gruff, deep voice to the customer after her—a man with the look (and smell) of a trapper about him. "Dangerous parts."

But the trapper had laughed. "S'alright for them as knows 'em. I'm off to get me a Firebird. Heard tell there's a few of 'em not too deep in."

"Can't say as I know anything 'bout that," answered the baker, cautious-like. "Wouldn't think it worth the danger, meself."

"Ain't much that could kill me," said the trapper cheerfully, and tipped what there was of his hat. "And for that kind o' money, I'm game to try. Good day to ye."

That kind of money?

Firebirds.

Not for nothing was Rosia a peddler's daughter. She knew well what a Firebird would fetch. A single feather would be enough . . .

" 'Scuse me," she said, turning back to the baker. "Are we near the Pelagirs here?"

"Aye, but you don't wanta go up that way," the baker replied. "Nasty place. Be lucky to come out alive."

Clutching the last piece of food she was likely to see in a while, with her pockets empty of coin and her packs empty of goods, Rosia knew she would be lucky to come out of the *week* alive. Her fingers tightened on the loaf. "Please, could you tell me the way?"

The baker had done so, if reluctantly, and now here she stood on the very edge. Hesitating.

It was the pain in her stomach that decided her. She took a step, and another—and then with a great rush of desperate energy, she plunged deep into the forest and didn't look back.

She did not, of course, stumble over a Firebird feather just lying there under the trees. Nothing so easy could come of so risky a venture.

But nor was she disappointed of her aim.

Mouthfuls of her precious bread sustained her for a day or two's wandering under the thick boughs, bolstered here and there with handfuls of berries, or an occasional mushroom. Ma and Pa had known a bit about foraging, learned during the leaner times. Rosia kept her wits about her, listened and watched for the dangers the villagers had been eager to warn each other about. Wild beasts of all kinds, they said. Some of them . . . different. Not as they should be.

The stories used words like *magic*. There used to be a lot of it, out in the Hills, and some of it lingered still.

Rosia was no careless child, not after a lifetime of wandering the roads with Ma and Pa. Even so, when the *wild beasts* of the Pelagirs found her, they caught her unawares.

She'd paused to gather a mushroom, a fat specimen with a broad cap. It was the sort with the meaty texture, one Pa had taught her to look out for, and her empty stomach growled in anticipation of sinking her teeth into it.

There had been nothing to warn her; no snap of a twig, no soft footfalls, no snarling menace. Just a sudden *rush* of movement, a loud rustling, as something leaped from the depths of a thicket; and then Rosia was down in the earth, the wind knocked out of her, and a weight on her chest pinned her where she lay.

A low, awful growling reverberated around the clearing.

The beast was some sort of feline, though larger than any Rosia had seen before. Its sleek coat was dappled with spots, and jaunty tufts adorned the tips of its ears. There was nothing jaunty about those eyes, though: topaz-gold, and fierce. The cat had bared every one of its ivory teeth; Rosia had no trouble imagining just how easily they would rip through her.

:You probably blundered into her territory,: Lilan said, carelessly interrupting Rosia's story. *:She may have had one or two young still lingering in the lair.:*

"Don't stop me," Rosia begged. "We're getting to the hard part."

:I am sorry, my Chosen. I am listening.:

Several agonizing moments passed. Rosia, her eyes squeezed shut to block out the sight of her imminent destruction, held her breath, expecting every second to be torn to pieces.

But then the weight lifted off her chest, and the

growling stopped. Faintly, Rosia heard the soft sounds of a large feline padding away.

She opened her eyes.

The cat had vanished into the undergrowth. Rosia was alone and—cautiously, she flexed her limbs and ran a hand over her torso—unharmed.

She sat up—and froze, for she was not alone after all.

It wasn't the cat. Another person watched her, half-hidden behind the gnarled trunk of a great, old evergreen tree. Shadows hid the details, but Rosia was almost certain the person was a girl, and not that much older than she was herself.

"She wasn't going to eat you," the girl said. "She just wanted you to leave. But there's plenty out here that will hurt you." She lifted one skinny arm and pointed. "The road is that way."

Her voice was cracked and dusty and . . . thin, as though it hadn't been used in a long time. Nonetheless, Rosia heard the words plainly enough.

"Wait," she said, when the girl began to slip away. "How do you know all that?"

"She told me," said the girl, and she withdrew.

Rosia sat in stunned silence for a moment, thinking that over. The cat had *talked* to this girl?

"Wait!" she called again, but no reply came.

Hastily, Rosia scrambled to her feet and took off after the girl who could talk to the beasts of the Pelagirs.

:*Animal Mindspeech,*: Lilan offered wisely. :*You run into it, now and then.*:

"*Lilan,*" protested Rosia.

:*Sorry.*:

The girl with the Animal Mindspeech lived in the Pelagirs entirely, Rosia discovered, for she had a dwelling there.

It wasn't much. She had doubtless built it herself, out of fallen boughs and branches and the like. So cunningly was it tucked between two craggy old trees, and camouflaged by the undergrowth, that Rosia would have walked straight past without noticing it at all. She was just in time to witness her quarry disappearing into a gap between the branches—and when she followed, she found a little arched entryway there.

"Hello?" she called.

No one answered her. But a fiery glow emanating from somewhere within intrigued her sufficiently to forget whatever manners Ma had tried to teach her, and she went inside. "Hello—" she called again. "I just want to thank you, and—and to ask you—"

There she stopped, for the glow had a source: a Firebird.

The graceful creature sat atop a perch near the "roof" of the dwelling—such as it was. A network of branches hung up there, all tangled together and covered with foliage. The Firebird sat with its sharp claws hooked over a lower-hanging branch and its glorious tail spilling halfway to the ground. Crimson and orange and gold and purple met Rosia's eyes in a spectacular display of color, and the bird radiated the ruddy glow of a burning sunset.

What was more, the Firebird had shed some of those feathers. More than a few. The floor—rough-spun matting worked from forest reeds—was covered in at least half a dozen of them.

"She was sick," said the girl, from somewhere Rosia couldn't see. "But she's well now."

"She's so beautiful," said Rosia, with awe.

"Yes, she is, and now go, please."

"Are you . . . do you live out here alone?"

"I'm never alone."

"I mean without . . . humans."

A soft laugh answered her, scornful. The message was clear without words: *What use have I for humans?*

"I see," said Rosia. "Thank you for helping me."

"You didn't need help."

Rosia withdrew. But she didn't leave right away. She stayed.

Later, she could not have said what prompted her to do so. She hoped it was curiosity or, better yet, concern for the Pelagir girl. She hoped it wasn't a calculated plan.

:This is the hard part, isn't it?: said Lilan, when Rosia's tale slowed to a halt.

Rosia swallowed. "Yes."

:I think I can guess what happened.:

"You can?"

:You took a feather.:

Rosia hung her head. "I did."

It wasn't the largest of them, not by a long shot. The feather she took was only a small one, about as long as her thumb. And there were seven more that she didn't take—she'd counted.

But that didn't change anything about what she had done. She had waited until the girl had gone away, and she had crept back into her forest-hut and taken one of the Firebird's feathers.

She had done so with her heart beating so fast, she thought it might burst. Fear of the Firebird had done that; what if she objected to her feathers being taken? What if she somehow told the girl before Rosia could get away, and Rosia was caught?

Rosia the peddler's daughter—Rosia the *thief*—had scarpered out of there as fast as she could go, her stolen feather clutched tightly in her fist, and she had not stopped running until her shaking legs would carry her no farther.

Then she had collapsed, shaking, into the mud, and sat there for some time.

She'd stolen something. She was a thief.

People had thrown that word at her pa before and her ma. At *her,* though she was a child. They had the look of pickpockets about them, some said: shabby attire, and the road-weary look of people who never stopped walking. People who could filch something today, and by tomorrow they'd be too far away to fear the consequences.

Ma had always brushed off such remarks, but Rosia could see that they hurt Pa. She'd ferociously resented

the people who could say such things, who could believe
so ill of strangers just because of the way they looked.

Her parents never stole. No matter how difficult the
winters sometimes got.

Rosia would never steal anything either. *Never.*

She had been so sure of that, once.

Well, never had not lasted very long.

She should take the feather back. Right now, before
it was missed.

But that was no good. The Firebird had seen her take
it, probably, and she would tell the girl what Rosia had
done. There was no undoing her deed *now.* It was too late.

And she needed the feather. There was no getting
around that, either. The emptiness in her stomach and
the weakness in her body had prompted her to do it; the
coin she could get from one tiny feather would get her
through the winter. Probably several winters.

"And that's when you showed up," Rosia finished.

:*Well, that explains why I had to delve into the Pelagirs to find you. Though I still don't understand why you
ran away.:*

"At first, I thought the girl sent you."

:*Aha.:*

"Then I realized what you were . . ."

:*And ran all the harder.:*

"Yes." Rosia sniffed, and she swallowed an incipient
tear. "Now you know why."

:*Are you ever going to come out of those bushes?:*
Lilan asked.

Rosia stifled a vague desire to remain there until she
starved to death; that would solve the problem, for sure,
though it wouldn't make amends to the girl with the
Firebird.

But that wasn't something a grown-up would do.

Finally she sighed, and she shoved her way free of the
thicket. She emerged rather scratched, but hale enough,
and presented herself to the Companion.

:*I definitely like the look of you,:* said Lilan, snuffling
Rosia all over with her enormous, warm nose.

"Even after . . . that story?" Rosia squirmed, though one hand crept up to smooth Lilan's velvety ears.

Lilan appeared to think it over. *:It is a tale of deepest iniquity,:* she said. *:No doubt about it.:*

"I know," said Rosia sadly—and only then did she notice the twinkle in Lilan's ice-blue eyes and the warmth that attended the words.

:I've heard nothing to change my mind,: said Lilan firmly. *:You are my Chosen.:*

"I can't be."

:You know that they have food in Haven? Quite a lot of it.:

Rosia's stomach growled at the prospect. "Don't taunt me," she sighed. "I can't go with you. You can't have a *thief* as a Herald."

:You're sure about that, are you?: said Lilan.

Rosia nodded.

:How about a reformed thief?:

Mutely, Rosia shook her head.

:Hm. Well, that's disappointing. I had better get back to Haven and start again. Maybe you'll let me walk with you as far as the road?:

A tear came, one stubborn droplet Rosia could not swallow. "Of course," she said with false heartiness, and fell into step with the Companion.

By then she had been traveling steadily back the way she'd come for some time, and the road was not so far away. She and Lilan covered the distance in a silence Rosia could not find the words to break.

Once they got to the road, Lilan nuzzled Rosia one last time. *:Thank you. Watch yourself out here. People can be as dangerous as wild beasts, you know.:*

With these words, she trotted gracefully away, leaving Rosia standing alone in the road.

Despite her protests, Rosia had not expected that the Companion would truly abandon her. She trudged back in the direction of the nearest village in a state of near despair, her spirits lower than at any time since—well, since Ma and Pa had gone. Her feet hurt in her threadbare shoes, and the morsels of nature's fare she had scrounged up in the forests would not ward off the hunger for long. She had no coin, and winter was coming.

The feather, tucked securely away inside a pocket, seemed to be burning a hole there. Rosia felt it almost as a physical weight, her hope and her despair, the two opposites somehow bound up in the one tiny thing.

It wouldn't do to sell it in the village; she would not get a fraction of its fair price. But she did not know how far she could go before she collapsed, from hunger or weariness or both. Nor had she any great familiarity with the area; how far away *was* the nearest town?

No matter. She would go as far as she could, sell the feather for as much as she could get, and . . . go on. Find somewhere to weather the winter. In the spring, she could fill up Pa's packs again with salable goods and take to the roads. Someday, it would be as though she had never stolen the feather at all.

She knew, even as she formed her plan, that this would never be true.

Such were the conflicting reflections occupying her troubled mind as she trudged southward. Her preoccupation rendered her oblivious, or more so than she ought to be out there on her own. Then again, what did it matter if she *was* robbed? It was no more than she deserved, and she had nothing worth stealing anyway.

The sound of hoofbeats on the approach jolted her at last out of these dismal ideas. Her head came up; in spite of herself, a surge of hope swept away all her despair. Lilan had come back after all.

But in another moment, she knew herself mistaken. There was a Companion coming up the road ahead, but it was not Lilan. This Companion had her Chosen with her: a woman, much older than Rosia, with gray threaded through her dark hair. She was on foot, for some reason; her Companion trotted sedately beside her. Rosia instinctively fixed her eyes upon the dirt before her feet, but not before she had caught the Herald's cheery greeting.

"G'afternoon," mumbled Rosia, moving over to the side of the road.

She waited there for the Herald and her Companion to pass—fortunate pair!—but instead the hoofbeats paused.

"Going far?" asked the Herald.

Rosia risked a glance up. She was being inspected, with what intention she could not fathom. The Herald's look remained friendly enough, however. "I . . . don't know," said Rosia, and then thought. "How far's it to a town?"

"A long way," came the dispiriting answer. "Farther than you can walk in that state, I'd wager."

A wave of weariness swept over Rosia, so profound as to set her swaying on her trembling legs. "Thanks," she said shortly, and she would have moved off except she did not think she could manage to do so without falling down.

"Steady," said the Herald. She caught Rosia in strong hands and set her aright again.

Rosia nodded her thanks, her thoughts too busy and her spirits too low for further speech. She would have to beg; there was no help for it. Swallowing her pride, she began with: "Please. Could you spare—"

She stopped, for the Herald had begun idly juggling two or three small objects. To Rosia's confusion, she recognized them. One was a pale, smooth pebble her Pa had given Rosia, a common thing, with no value to anyone else. He had collected it from the bank of a river, shortly before the fever. Another was Ma's blue hair ribbon, a threadbare thing now, but Rosia had made a treasure of that, too.

"You—you—how did you get those?" Rosia gasped.

"You should keep a closer watch on your pockets," the Herald said with a wink.

Rosia gaped.

"Especially when you've valuables about you," she went on, and produced Rosia's Firebird feather.

"But—" Rosia struggled to find words. "But—Heralds don't steal."

"That's true," said the Herald. "But I was pretty light-fingered when I was your age. Had to be, or I'd have starved." She grinned, and offered Rosia's three treasures back to her.

Rosia gathered them up with shaking hands and stuffed them back into the now dubious safety of her pockets. "I don't understand. How—"

"How can I be a Herald if I was once a thief?" She wasn't smiling now; she looked Rosia over with a kind of warm sympathy. "Heralds aren't Chosen for what we did in the past. We're Chosen for what we'll do in the future. You're Rosia?"

Rosia nodded, wordless.

"My name is Danna. I heard you were in some kind of trouble."

"Heard . . ." Rosia's head turned, for there were the hoofbeats again, and this time it *was* Lilan: bells ringing, coat shining, her white mane flying in the breeze. Seeing Rosia, she snorted—the sound a mixture of exasperation and, according to the feelings swamping Rosia's mind, relief.

Danna nodded in the Companion's direction. "She looked us up on purpose. Lucky for you we weren't too far away."

"Lucky for me?" Rosia repeated numbly.

Danna nodded. "We're going to need you at the Collegium, but Lilan is right. You're in no condition to make it that far without help."

"I can't go to the Collegium," said Rosia automatically.

"Mm. And why is that?"

"Heralds are—good people."

"Good people, yes," said Danna briskly. "Not perfect people. Were you planning to continue thieving?"

"*Never*," said Rosia vehemently. "But that—I never should've—"

Danna smiled, but it was to Lilan she spoke. "She *is* stubborn, isn't she?"

Lilan snorted again, and nudged Rosia with her nose—quite hard. :*Stop fighting it, Chosen. Don't you know that Companions never Choose wrong?*:

Danna rolled her eyes, apparently at Lilan's comment. "Come on, Rosia. I'd *really* like to get a good meal into you. If you starve to death now, Lilan will never forgive any of us."

Rosia was thinking. "I can't," she concluded, and she put out a hand to smooth Lilan's ears when the Companion groaned. "Unless I . . . can we take the feather back?"

Danna's response was to rummage in one of her Companion's saddlepacks. "Aha," she murmured, and emerged with a quantity of dried meat in hand. This she gave to Rosia. "Eat," she commanded. "Then up on Lilan's back. We'll make a fine procession into the Pelagirs, won't we?"

Rosia fell upon the meat and dispatched it in seconds, despite its toughness. "Thank you," she said, and she wrapped her arms around Lilan's neck. Another tear escaped, but not from grief or despair. This one came from an overflowing heart and a profound gratitude.

She'd never be alone again. And maybe she hadn't disgraced her ma and pa. Maybe, if they were here, they would even be proud of her.

Danna bestowed a comforting pat upon Rosia's shoulder. "Don't thank me," she said drily. "You might end up riding Circuit up here someday, and then you'll be wishing you'd stuck with a life of larceny."

Rosia, hauling herself gracelessly onto her Companion's back, gave an eloquent shudder. "Not a chance."

A Ruler's Gift
Anthea Sharp

Summer dust softened the road and turned the distant mountains to hazy blue shadows as Healer Tarek Strand traveled toward home.

Home in a strictly geographical sense, that was. The home of his heart lay behind him at the Collegium in Haven, a few days journey along the East Trade Road. Ahead, the track to Strand Keep unfurled through carefully tended fields. He'd known, in a distant corner of his mind, that someday he'd have to return to his birthright.

That day was now upon him, and sooner than he'd wanted.

The late afternoon sun cast his shadow as a spindly rider beside him as his mount crested the rise that marked the boundary of his father's lands.

In the distance rose the tower of Strand Keep, blocky gray stone that held memories of a hard upbringing and little joy. Tarek pulled his horse to a stop, regarding the collection of buildings clustered at the base of the tower. It wasn't an easy life, that of a border lord pushed against the boundary of Hardorn, and Tarek had to admit that his father had successfully managed his lands for decades.

But at what cost?

With a sigh, he nudged his mount into motion again. *I am here as a Healer*, he reminded himself. Not as the heir to the keep. If all went well, he'd be back on the road, headed the opposite direction, in less than a week. Back to Haven, back to his budding romance with Bard Shandara Tem, and the comfort of the Collegium, where he belonged.

A handful of years earlier, he would've scoffed openly if anyone had told him he'd end up a Healer. Lord Strand had brought his children up secure in the knowledge that the powers possessed by Heralds and their ilk—Bards and Healers included—were negligible at best and base trickery at worst.

"We've no need of such charlatans within the walls of Strand Keep," Tarek's father had said the few times Lady Strand had broached the idea of having a Healer come tend a serious injury, or a Bard visit to bring news and play them the most recent songs of the kingdom.

It was surprising that Lord Strand had unbent enough to send for Tarek now, although the ties of kinship would account for it.

Tarek patted the inner pocket where he'd tucked the letter from his mother. He'd read it enough times to know the short missive by heart.

> *Dearest Tarek,*
>
>   *I shall skip the pleasantries and inform you that your father has fallen ill. We would like you to come as soon as you may. It will be good to see you.*
> > > > > > > > *Love,*
> > > > > > > > *Mother*

His mother and younger sister, Elen, had come to Haven last year to help celebrate Tarek's graduation to full Healer. That his father had chosen to stay at Strand Keep had been no surprise. The one time Lord Strand had gone to Haven, when Tarek was first enrolled in the Collegium, the border lord had disliked nearly everything about the city and school.

It was too busy, too undisciplined, too overdecorated. That, plus Lord Strand's open disdain for the Gifts, meant he would never understand his son's choices. Tarek was anticipating an uncomfortable reunion ahead— but if he could help his father back to full health, surely that would change Lord Strand's mind about the value of Healing.

A small dust cloud rose on the road ahead; a rider, coming from the keep. Tarek squinted, trying to see who it might be, although he strongly suspected it was his sister. He nudged his mount into a faster pace.

Sure enough, within a few minutes he could make out the figure of Elen atop her favorite chestnut gelding. She was riding at a decent trot, but not a panic-stricken pace. Tarek waved, and she lifted her hand, sending him a jaunty greeting in return.

Her expression when she reached him, however, was somber.

"Hello, Tare," she said. "It took you long enough."

"I came as soon as I got word," he said. "Haven's not that close, you know."

She frowned, then glanced at the looming tower of the keep. "I was thinking I'd come fetch you over a fort-night ago, but Mother said she'd already written."

Elen had wanted him home weeks ago? Concern sparked through him. It didn't take that long for mes-sages to travel through Valdemar. Certainly it should only have been a matter of days for word to reach Haven from Strand Keep.

Tarek briefly touched his pocket. "Yet I just received Mother's letter. Did you think I'd simply ignored her summons?"

"I wasn't sure why you didn't come." Elen's expres-sion turned grim. "Father's not well. Not at all."

"What happened?"

"There wasn't an accident or anything," she said. "But starting this spring, he began to . . . slow down, I guess."

"He's getting older—and he's always driven himself hard."

"Himself, and everyone around him." Elen shook her head. "I was the first to realize there was a change, actually. I started taking on things he was letting slide. Maybe I shouldn't have, but I kept thinking he'd get better."

"What kinds of things? How did you notice?" Dust clogged Tarek's throat, and he tightened his grip on the reins. Worrisome, indeed, to hear that Lord Strand's illness had been proceeding for months.

"I started acting as his secretary two years ago," Elen said. "After Mr. Dellin passed. It was supposed to be temporary, but Father said I was doing a fair enough job that he saw no point in hiring someone new to take over—at least not until you returned. You were supposed to be coming home from the Collegium and resuming your duties as heir, remember?"

Tarek grimaced. "Things changed."

He hadn't meant to become a Healer, after all; but his Gift had insisted, and the path under his feet had changed. Now he wasn't sure where it was leading him.

"I don't think Father understands." Elen shot him a look. "He's expecting you to return and take over Strand Keep."

"I know." Tarek's thoughts skittered away from what that meant—and from the inevitable choice ahead.

Healer. Or Lord of Strand Keep.

Can't I do both? he wanted to shout. But that wasn't how life worked, no matter how much he might want it to.

"Anyway," Elen said, "a few months ago I started doing more of the keep's business: meeting with farmers, hearing grievances, consulting with the garrison commander when Father didn't have the energy."

Tarek glanced at his sister. In his mind, she was still half a child, although she was only two years his junior. He forced himself to take a harder look. Though her cheeks were still round, her features had matured. Her hair still bore streaks of honey-gold, but it had darkened from the shining blonde of childhood. And her gray eyes no longer held the open inquisitiveness of a youth, but the beginnings of wisdom brought by experience.

His baby sister had become a woman.

Apparently a very capable one, if Lord Strand had approved of her work as his secretary, however temporary.

The shadow of the tower fell across the road, the lowering sun painting the fields red-gold, and Tarek shifted in the saddle. They'd be at the stables soon, and he was more than ready to get off his horse. Though perhaps not quite as ready for what came after.

"What are Father's symptoms?" he asked.

"Most days he has no appetite. He sleeps a lot, and recently he doesn't even get out of bed."

Tarek gave her a sharp look. "That's not good."

The man who'd threatened beatings if his children weren't up at first light, ready to work, now spent days abed? Misgiving moved coldly through Tarek, a shiver touching his shoulders.

"You're a full Healer now, though." Elen glanced at him anxiously, and suddenly she looked like his baby sister once more. "You can fix whatever's wrong, can't you?"

Tarek straightened. "I'll do everything I can to help Father back to full health."

He had no other choice.

A short time later, standing beside Lord Strand's bed, Tarek's earlier fears came roaring back. The man who lay before him, apparently asleep, was a shadow of his former robust self.

"Sit down." His mother pushed a chair up behind Tarek. "I'll fetch tea."

He glanced at her, noting the weariness in her face, the dark smudges beneath her eyes. Lady Strand looked as though she, too, was in need of a great deal more rest than she'd been getting.

"Are you sick as well?" he asked, his heart squeezing with anxiety.

"Just tired." She gave him a wan smile. "Your father's had a few difficult nights."

"Difficult, how?" He glanced at Lord Strand's pale skin, the gaunt hollows of his cheeks.

His mother let out a sigh. "It's hard for him to get comfortable. His belly pains him."

"Stomach trouble?" That was more than Elen had said.

"Sometimes. Other times he can't catch his breath, or his limbs ache."

That made the diagnosis harder, and Tarek frowned, wishing his mentor, Master Adrun, were there. But the Master Healer's place was in the Collegium, not out with his new graduates, holding their hands. Even if, as in Tarek's case, their education had been a bit rushed.

"Sit with me," Tarek said, turning to his mother. "I can get my own tea later."

He grabbed a second chair from against the wall and set it down near the head of his father's bed, then sat. Muscles sore from riding protested, and he mentally shook his head. His father would scoff if he knew how a few long days in the saddle had affected Tarek.

Books are no substitute for hard work. The echo of Lord Strand's voice threaded through Tarek's memories. *A real education is gained through experience, not study.*

"Father," Tarek said, gently taking the thin hand lying atop the smooth linen coverlet. "It's me, Tarek."

There was no response, and he glanced at his mother.

"He may wake soon," she said softly. "If not, you can try again first thing tomorrow. Mornings are often better."

"I'd like to use my Gift to try and sense what's wrong," Tarek said, then hesitated. "I'd rather do it with his permission."

"Will it hurt?" His mother gave him an anxious look.

"No. An initial exploration, without attempting Healing, will be painless. But he wouldn't like knowing it was done without his knowledge."

To put it mildly. Lord Strand's aversion to the Gifts was strong.

But hopefully, if Tarek's father experienced the power of Healing firsthand, he would change his mind. At least a little. It would be best if he were fully conscious during the entire process, however, from the diagnosis through Healing and recovery.

"Father." Tarek leaned forward. "Please wake up."

Lord Strand's eyelids fluttered, and a moment later

he opened his eyes. Just a little, but Tarek could see the gleam of annoyance in their dark depths.

"What is it?" Lord Strand's usual gruff voice was diminished, creaky now rather than commanding. He blinked, then opened his eyes all the way. "Tarek—thought it was you. Just in time. You're the new Lord Strand when I go."

Tarek's mother pulled in a quick breath of denial, and Tarek shook his head.

"That's years in the future," he said. "We'll get you Healed and back on your feet in no time."

Then later—much later—he'd break the news to his father that he couldn't be the Lord of Strand Keep.

"Healing, bah." Lord Strand grimaced. "Too late for me."

"I don't think so. Will you let me try?"

For a tense moment, Lord Strand glared at him. Tarek's breath hitched at the thought his father might deny him—might stubbornly cling to the belief he was dying and thus make it true. Then Lord Strand sighed, the spark of anger fading from his expression.

"Very well," he said. "But don't say I didn't warn you."

Tarek nodded and closed his eyes. One of his first lessons had been how to shield himself, so that he didn't experience the aches and small injuries of every person around him. It hadn't been easy, probably because he'd come to his Gift so late. But he'd learned.

Now, he opened himself to let his Healing flow, and nearly jerked back at the illness he sensed in Lord Strand's body.

By the stars! His father was terribly sick, his body so compromised that . . .

No. Tarek's mind shied from the thought.

He'd been given the Gift of Healing for a reason— and surely that reason was embodied in the man now lying before him. Tarek's duty, his calling, was to save Lord Strand's life.

"Well?" His father gave Tarek a knowing look. "Bad, isn't it?"

Tarek's lips tightened. "Not good, at any rate. Why didn't you send for me sooner?"

"Wouldn't have changed things."

"Yes, it would!" With effort, Tarek forced himself back to a semblance of calm. "You have an internal sickness that responds well to Healing, if treated early. Now, though . . ."

"Incurable," Lord Strand said with grim satisfaction. "At least now you're home where you belong."

Tarek glanced away, a mix of grief and rage swamping him. Did Lord Strand really intend to die simply to prove a point?

"I'm still going to try to Heal you," Tarek said, returning his attention to his father. "Starting now."

Lord Strand's eyebrows twitched up, but he said nothing, as if inviting Tarek to do his worst.

Or his best.

Tarek took a deep breath, then closed his eyes again, sending Healing energy into his father's body. Ignoring the smaller problems, mainly to do with circulation, he concentrated on the sullen red smolder of illness crouching in Lord Strand's belly and lungs. Carefully, Tarek tried to flow a touch of brightness into the most diseased areas, encouraging his father's body to continue fighting.

"Does it hurt?" Lady Strand asked her husband.

"I don't feel anything," he said wearily. "Tarek's just sitting there taking a nap."

Tarek refused to rise to the bait, instead continuing the delicate work of shoring up the most battered of his patient's defenses. He was mindful, too, of not sapping his own strength too greatly. This was going to be a long, difficult Healing.

If it even worked at all.

Finally, he opened his eyes and looked at his father. "You'll need to eat and drink—far more than it seems you've been doing. Bone-rich broths, at the very least. Tisanes and plenty of water."

Lord Strand made a sound deep in his throat, but he didn't argue.

"I'll send to the kitchens," Tarek's mother said, rising and moving to the door.

She spoke to the servant in the hallway outside, her soft tones soothing to Tarek, even though he couldn't quite hear her words. He watched his patient, who, with a sigh, closed his eyes. By the time Tarek's mother returned to Lord Strand's bed, he'd fallen asleep.

"Can you cure him?" she asked softly.

"I hope so." Though his father's condition was far worse than he'd anticipated. Exhaling, he glanced at his mother. "Why didn't you send for me sooner?"

Her gaze went from him to her husband, who seemed to be resting well enough, though the Healing had clearly sapped his waning strength. Gently, Tarek slipped his hand out of his father's sleep-softened grasp.

"I did send for you," Lady Strand said softly. "I wrote that letter and dispatched it weeks ago, without your father's knowledge—or so I thought."

"Then why did I just receive it?"

She let out a sad sigh. "Your father intercepted it. He only told me this recently, declaring that *he* would be the judge of when you were summoned. I suppose he finally decided it was time."

"Does he *want* to die?" Tarek clenched his hands into fists and glanced at his father's sleeping face. Lord Strand looked so worn and vulnerable, it was difficult to reconcile the sight with Tarek's memories of the robust and abrasive ruler of the keep.

"Your father . . ." His mother hesitated, staring at the wall a moment before looking back at him. "He's been master of Strand Keep for decades. When you didn't leave the Collegium as expected, it was a blow. He was anticipating stepping back, helping you learn to govern as you took your place as the new Lord Strand."

"He never mentioned as much to me." Tarek frowned, guilt tickling his throat. "But I couldn't have come back sooner. I had to finish my training as a Healer. In fact, I'm still not done. Once Father's feeling better, I must return to Haven."

"Oh, Tarek." His mother squeezed his arm. "Can't you be done with all that? Your father needs you here."

What about what I need? Tarek left the question unspoken, though it burned through him. Where, truly, did he belong?

Once, he'd thought he could do both, be a Lord and a Healer, but that seemed naïve, now—the hopeful wishings of a younger man afraid to face the choices ahead.

He couldn't stay at Strand Keep.

But, under the circumstances, how could he leave?

After gaining his mother's reassurance that she'd stay with her husband and make sure he ate and drank when he awoke, Tarek went in search of his own supper.

He wasn't surprised to find Elen seated at the scarred wooden table in the great hall—a room that seemed not so large to his eyes, now that he'd seen much grander in Haven and even the Palace itself. His sister had a plate of bread and stew at one elbow and was going through a stack of papers before her.

A faint frown drew her brows together, and she looked far more serious that he could ever recall. Instead of interrupting her, he strode to the heavy wooden chair next to where she sat and leaned his arms across the high back. A quick glance showed that she was going over accounts—from one of the farms, judging by the list of harvest weights for onions and grain.

"Hello," she said, glancing up at him. "Cook kept dinner warming in the kitchen. I figured you'd be hungry after your long days of travel."

"I am, and not only from the journey. Healing is hard work."

She tilted her head. "Get a plate, and come tell me about Father."

Tarek headed for the kitchen. He couldn't resist scooping up a few mouthfuls of the delicious-smelling stew and taking a bite of hearth bread as he went to rejoin his sister.

Elen pushed the papers to the side. "Is he as sick as I think?"

"Worse," Tarek said grimly, taking a seat. "I don't know why he waited so long to summon me."

"Father's stubborn, you know that. Besides, by prolonging his illness, he's vindicated. If you can't heal him, then the Gifts are a sham, like he's always thought."

Tarek stared at his sister. "But . . . then he'll die."

She gave him a tight-lipped look in return. "As long as he's right. He's wanted you to come back and run Strand Keep for some time now. This way, he'll get that wish, too."

"Even if he's not here to see it?" Anguish flashed through Tarek. Despite Lord Strand's flaws, he was their father. Tarek couldn't imagine the world without him striding about, making gruff and critical pronouncements even as he ruled the keep with a steady hand.

"It's hard to argue with Father," Elen said. "Even when he's being an utter fool."

"I'm going to Heal him." Determination made Tarek's voice hard. "Whether he wants it or not."

His sister twitched one eyebrow up, but didn't argue. "As long as you don't hurt yourself in the process."

"I'll be careful. But make sure I eat." Suiting action to words, he took another bite of stew.

"Speaking of eating, Belinda's expecting," Elen said.

"Again? Will that make three, now?"

"You can't even keep track of your nieces and nephews." Elen shook her head at him. "You ought to go see her soon. You haven't met Mira yet, although she's two, and I'm sure Bennet doesn't remember you at all."

"I know." Tarek set his spoon down. He'd neglected family, one of the cornerstones of the borderlands, in order to follow his Gift. Was the trade worth it? Was he being too selfish?

"When are you getting married?" he asked, turning to Elen.

"Is that all you think women are good for?" She gave him a look tinged with exasperation. "I thought a Collegium education was supposed to broaden the mind."

"It did," he protested. Though, to his chagrin, he apparently still had some entrenched beliefs when it came to his own family. "I'm sorry—I didn't mean that the way it came out."

"I hope not. Just because Belinda got married as soon as she could in order to get out of Strand Keep doesn't mean it's the right path for me."

"I think she loves her husband," Tarek said, defending their older sister.

Elen gave a dismissive wave of her hand. "Of course—but she didn't waste any time moving away. Even if it's just a farmholding an hour's ride away."

"Still—is there anyone you're interested in?"

"I'm too busy." She nodded to the papers she'd set aside. "In fact, I need to get back to this, and I'm sure you're tired. I had the maid make up the bed in your old room."

It was a not-so-subtle dismissal, as well as a clear indicator that Elen had no intention of discussing her love life with her big brother. He hid his amusement at how much like their father she suddenly sounded.

"You're right." He grabbed his empty plate. "I've had a long day. See you tomorrow."

He rose, groaning as his aching muscles protested. Several tiring days of Healing lay before him, but at least he wouldn't have to sit in the saddle while he worked. It was a small blessing, but he'd still count it.

At first, it seemed impossible. Every time Tarek succeeded in beating back the sickness intent on devouring his father's insides, it seemed to return overnight. By day three they were both exhausted. At day five, Tarek was nearing the edge of his resources, and he was beginning to wonder if he could, in fact, save Lord Strand.

"Fight it, Father," he said despairingly, a full week after he'd arrived. "I can't Heal you by myself."

Morning light straggled through the half-open curtains, illuminating his father's haggard features. Tarek was in his usual chair drawn up beside his father's bed. As sunlight touched the edge of the blankets, Tarek studied his patient. Lord Strand's eyes were sunken, his cheeks gaunt, and Tarek feared he didn't look much better, himself.

Master Adrun had warned Tarek not to overextend himself when Healing—a lesson he'd learned when he'd first discovered his Gift and spent too much of his own energy to save a dying friend.

"Your Gift is not an endless river," the Master Healer had said. "Rather, think of it as a well that must take time to replenish. If you draw too much water too quickly, you risk running dry."

"Then what?" Tarek had asked, afraid he already knew the answer.

"Your own life would be imperiled. You must learn to use your Gift wisely."

Now, those words echoing through him, Tarek folded his hand over his father's.

"Help me," he said softly. "We can save you—but we have to do it together."

Tarek's father looked up at him, his gaze weary. "I am tired of being Lord Strand. You must run the keep."

"You don't have to die in order to step back!"

Lord Strand blinked. "If I survive, do you promise to assume your rightful place as Lord of Strand Keep?"

There it was—the impossible choice. Tarek screwed his eyes closed, as if that would shut out the decision he must make. Give up everything he'd worked for at the Collegium, in order to save his father.

Sacrifice his dreams, his future, and remain at Strand Keep. It was nearly as bad as sacrificing his life's energy to Heal the man.

What would such an existence hold? Managing the keep and surrounding lands was no longer the pinnacle of Tarek's aspirations. Perhaps he might be able to carve out a little time to Heal the local populace, but he certainly wouldn't be able to help many. Not with the heavy duties of Lord Strand weighing upon him, day and night.

After all, look at how busy his sister was . . .

He opened his eyes at the obvious solution, hope

untangling the tight knot in his lungs. Maybe there was a pathway out, after all.

"I promise that the right heir to Strand Keep will take over," he replied. "But in return, you must help fight this sickness."

Lord Strand pulled in a breath, then let it out in a wavering sigh. "Good."

It wasn't much of an agreement, but it was all Tarek was going to get.

And, as he'd hoped, his father had heard what he wanted to.

"Start by drinking all your broth." Tarek picked up the earthenware cup from the tray on the bedside table, and held it to his father's lips.

Without protest, Lord Strand drank, though he had to pause midway through to rest. Once he'd finished, Tarek begin another session of Healing. The sickness seemed to retreat a little faster, and not rush back in quite so violently, but perhaps that was just Tarek's hope coloring his perceptions.

Three days later, however, the improvement in Lord Strand was clear. As Tarek prepared to leave the bedroom after their afternoon session, his mother came in with a pitcher of cool water.

She glanced at her husband, then at Tarek.

"He seems . . . better," she said softly.

"Of course I am," her husband said, opening his eyes. "Now that everything's settled with Tarek."

Lady Strand gave Tarek a questioning look. "You're staying?"

"I told Father that he could step back as Lord Strand, if that's what he wants."

"It is. Stop talking about me as if I'm not here." Despite his words, however, Tarek's father sounded more tired than imperious.

"Belinda's about to have her third child," Tarek's mother said. "Both your father and I would like time to spend with our grandchildren before they're grown and gone. And he's worked so hard his whole life, it's time for him to ease up. Did you know he started a second flower garden?"

"Herbs," Lord Strand said testily. "For the kitchen."

His wife sent him a fond look. "Very well, herbs—of the most colorful and blossom-laden variety."

His father, growing flowers? Dandling grandchildren on his knee?

It was difficult for Tarek to picture. But not impossible. People changed, after all—his own life was proof enough of that.

"Rest," he said, giving his father a stern look. "We'll speak more of this later."

First, though, Tarek needed to talk with Elen. He hoped she'd agree to the bargain he'd made, or he was in deep trouble.

He found his sister, as he'd suspected, working at the table in the great hall. Although he spent most of his days tending their father, he'd noted her schedule.

Mornings, she seemed to be out and about, paying calls on the farmers and tenants or overseeing other business. After lunch, she received visitors and consulted with the castle staff. And the rest of the afternoon saw her immersed in paperwork, sometimes late into the night. More than once, he'd stumbled to bed while her lantern still burned.

"Elen," he said, rounding the table. "Join me for a walk around the keep?"

She cocked her head at him, questions in her eyes. "Do you have the time?"

"Yes." Despite his weariness, he managed a smile. "Father is finally on the mend."

"That's a relief." She closed the ledger book she'd been studying, then stretched out her arms. "I could use a break."

"You work hard," he observed.

"So do you." She pushed back her chair and stood. "My energy goes into Father, yours into Strand

Keep," he said wryly as they walked to the door. "Maybe you need a secretary of your own."

She sent him a sharp look. "You said Father's recovering."

"He is." Tarek waited until they stepped out of the hall, away from any listening ears.

The late afternoon air carried the scent of warm stone with a faint undertone of manure from the stables. It was a familiar smell, and for a moment, homesickness gripped him. Not longing for Strand Keep itself, but for the simpler days of his childhood, when he'd known his place in the world as surely as the sun traveled across the sky.

"But?" his sister asked as they rounded the corner of the keep into Lady Strand's prized rose garden.

"Father told me he's ready to lay aside the mantle of Lord Strand," Tarek said. "You've probably sensed as much."

Elen's brow creased. "He's made no secret of the fact that he wants you to run the keep. Now that you're home, I'll help you settle into the duties—"

"I'm not staying."

She blinked at him. "You can't be Lord Strand from the Collegium."

"I won't be Lord Strand." He halted and met her gaze. "You will."

Her lips parted and for a moment she had no words. Then she collected herself and shook her head. "You can't be serious. You're the heir."

"I'm absolutely serious," Tarek said with a faint smile. "You've done an excellent job running Strand Keep during Father's illness and probably for months beforehand."

"But . . . I'm the youngest child. And a girl—"

"I thought you had a broader mind than that." He gently threw her previous words back at her. "Besides, you're not a girl. You're a very capable woman who's been acting as Lord of the keep in all but name for some time now."

"I . . ." She blew out a breath and turned to study the daisies blooming cheerfully beside the path.

Worry trickled into Tarek's chest. He'd gambled that his sister would be glad to continue overseeing the keep—especially if she was finally recognized for the work she'd been doing. But what if he'd been wrong?

"Do you not want to rule Strand Keep?" he asked, his lungs tight.

She didn't speak for a long moment. It was all he could do to stand there, waiting for her answer while his thoughts stumbled hopelessly about, seeking another way out.

"I do want it," she finally said, then folded her arms about herself. "But what if I fail? It's a huge responsibility."

He let out a pent-up breath and set his hands on her shoulders.

"One you've carried well. I'm impressed by you, little sister." He grinned at her. "Besides, whatever Father says to the contrary, we both know he won't be able to completely remove himself from the business of running Strand Keep. A lifetime of behavior doesn't transform magically overnight."

Which, he reflected, *I ought to keep in mind.* His father wasn't going to suddenly extol Tarek's virtues as a gifted Healer or shout about the truth of the Gifts from the top of the keep's tower. A grudging acceptance was the best Tarek could hope for.

Elen's lips twitched into a crooked smile, and she lifted her chin. "You're right. We can't teach a dog to meow or a cat to bark."

It was one of their father's favorite sayings; but it wasn't always true. Things changed. People changed, albeit slowly.

"So you'll do it?" he asked. "You'll become the new Lord Strand?"

She nodded slowly. "I will."

"Thank the stars!" He pulled her into a quick embrace, which she returned with wiry strength.

When she stepped back, she was grinning. "When shall we break the news to him?"

Tarek glanced up at the sky. "He's at his best in the mornings. Tomorrow?"

"Tomorrow, it is."

When Tarek and Elen stepped into their father's room the next morning, their mother gave them a quick, assessing glance. Tarek wondered how much she'd guessed of his plans. She sat in her usual chair beside her husband's bed, and Lord Strand was awake, propped up against the pillows.

Tarek was glad to note the brightness in his eyes, the faint wash of color in his cheeks. His father was, indeed, on the road to recovery.

After their good-morning greetings, Lord Strand turned his gaze on Elen.

"What news of the keep?" he asked. "Have you begun showing your brother the account books? Introducing him to the farmholders?"

"There's no need." Tarek stepped to his sister's side. "Father, I won't be staying."

"Nonsense." His father glared at him. "You promised to remain here as the new Lord Strand."

"No." Tarek kept his voice calm, despite his racing heart. "I promised that the right person would take over running Strand Keep."

"You are that person." Lord Strand's voice was fierce. "It's your birthright."

Tarek swallowed, but he held his father's gaze. "It *was* my birthright—but Healing took its place."

There. The words were out in the open, and they hadn't been so terrible to speak, after all. Despite the shocked expression on his father's face, the world hadn't cracked asunder, the sun hadn't plummeted from the sky.

Lord Strand stared at him a moment more, then glowered at his wife. "We never should have sent him to Haven. It ruined him."

Gently, Lady Strand covered his hand with her own. "Tarek isn't ruined. He saved your life."

"He's abandoning—"

"I am not abandoning my duties," Tarek said, his voice strong. "I don't want to take over running Strand Keep, but you don't have to keep doing so, either."

Tarek's mother looked up, the hint of a smile on her lips as she glanced from him to Elen.

"Well, who else—" Tarek's father began, but Elen knelt beside the bed and set her hand on his arm.

"I can do it," she said simply. "I'll be the next Lord Strand."

Their father jerked his head back and stared at her. For once, the garrulous old man seemed at an utter loss for words. He didn't, however, seem completely opposed to the idea.

"You always said education is no substitute for experience," Tarek reminded him dryly. "Elen will make a far better Lord Strand than I. She's been running the keep for some time now. Surely you must have realized that."

Slowly, his father gazed up at him.

"Don't you want it?" he asked. "Think of what you're giving up."

"I'm not giving it up, I'm giving it over to someone better suited. Don't you want what's best for your holdings?"

"He's right," Lady Strand said to her husband. "Both our children have shown great talent. Just not in the ways we expected. Tarek has a Gift for Healing. And Elen will be an excellent ruler for Strand Keep."

Their father scowled but didn't argue, and Tarek knew that the matter was settled.

It took another fortnight for Tarek to feel comfortable leaving his father. By that time, Lord Strand had declared himself perfectly well and had started stomping about, blustering and telling Elen what to do. She mostly listened, but sometimes she bluntly told him no, which Tarek was glad to see. It might take a while longer, but already the balance of power at Strand Keep was settling on his sister's capable shoulders.

As he'd expected, his father made a few grudging re-marks about how Tarek's Healing Gift had "come in useful" and left it at that. His mother, in a quiet mo-ment, had pressed Tarek's hand and, tears in her eyes, thanked him for saving Lord Strand's life.

"He'll never admit it," she said.

"I know." But Tarek also knew that he had, indeed, saved his father.

In the end, it was enough.

Rising to the Occasion
Jennifer Brozek

Tressa worked the bread dough from a sticky mess into a smooth, elastic ball. Her hands and fingers knew their work as if born to it. For five years she'd apprenticed to Mariah, head baker at the Rise & Shine Bakery in Haven. It was only in the last three years that she'd been allowed to produce pastries and other baked goods for sale—starting with simple pastries, moving up to more difficult bread, and now filled pies.

As her hands kneaded and stretched the dough, intuiting how much more she would need to work it before allowing it to rest, she listened to the customer who'd just entered.

"Good early morning, Mariah."

It was Herald Arden. Tressa smiled as she eavesdropped on the conversation, already anticipating what was to come. She'd made the cheese biscuits with extra care, hoping the handsome Herald would come in.

"Good morning, Herald. Can I get you something special, or have you come for your usual?"

"A little of both. I need to pick up a half dozen savory pasties for a day trip, but I can't start the day without your special cheese biscuits. If I don't have them at least twice a week, I fade away."

"Thank you so much. We all appreciate your compliments."

Tressa's smile became a grin. She was the only one

who made the cheese biscuits these days. Ever since Herald Arden declared them his favorite in the whole of Haven . . . *"No . . . the whole of Valdemar . . ."* she'd made certain to make them the best she could. She did this every morning, and today her work was rewarded.

Someday, she would tell him that she made them and thought of him when she did. The jingling of the bell announced his departure. She'd missed his good-bye in her daydream.

"I have to have one of those cheese biscuits or I'm going to fade away . . ." Soren, another apprentice baker, declared with a wave of his sudsy hand. "Oh, please, Baker Mariah . . ."

Mariah *hmph*ed at him as she bustled into the back. "You should be so lucky to get the same reaction." Pointing a finger at Inga, the youngest and newest apprentice, she asked, "Why does Herald Arden come back week after week for his cheese biscuits?"

Inga froze in her restocking of shelves. She glanced at Tressa, eyes wide. "Uh, because he likes them . . . or who makes them?"

Tressa felt her cheeks burn at the faint praise.

"No." Mariah's voice was flat and hard. "We aren't the only bakery near the palace with good cheese biscuits. There are prettier bakers than lovely Tressa here." The baker turned her keen gaze on Tressa. "Why does the Herald return here week after week?"

Tressa knew what Mariah wanted . . . the lesson that was kneaded into them every day of every week of every month of their apprenticeship. "Because I make them with the same quality ingredients, the same attention to detail, and the same care to my work every single day. I have integrity as a baker and a person. It shows in my baked goods."

"Exactly. Quality, care, honesty, and attention to detail. We work to the best standard every single day because that is what our product and our customers deserve—whether they be royalty, Heralds, or common folk. Each one gets the same baking. . . . And why?" This time she pointed at Soren.

He answered by rote but kept his voice light. Mocking the lesson would have dire consequences. "Because it's our baking reputation that counts. We do our best in everything we do. Not just baking. Cleaning, too. Our skill. Our quality. Our goods. All of it can be trusted."

Tressa mouthed *"Our skill. Our quality. Our goods."* as Soren spoke them.

"Exactly. We bake to the best of our ability because that is our job. We stand on the honor of our character. We don't skimp on the ingredients. We don't slack on the work. We don't say "Good enough." We do our best every single day. We are the best we can be because that is our job. Our customers trust us, and because of that, they trust what we bake." Mariah eyed Inga. "*That* is why Herald Arden comes to Rise & Shine for his cheese biscuits."

"Yes, ma'am."

Tressa felt Mariah loom over her shoulder and eye the dough balls she was putting on the tray to proof.

The older woman nodded with a soft grunt of approval. "Soon you'll match me. But not yet, girl. Not yet. I still have a few tricks to teach you."

There was no need to answer her boss, even though Tressa felt the swell of pride that came with Mariah's rare compliments. Still, one of these days, she was going to tell that handsome Herald who really did the baking he enjoyed so often.

"I need you to close down the shop today and do the final clean," Mariah said without preamble. "Inga got called home. Her mam is sick. You and Soren will pick up her duties."

Tressa wrinkled her nose at the thought as she wiped down the wooden counter she'd been working on. Closing down the shop was a good couple of hours of cleaning. It was a top down clean . . . starting with the baking racks and ending with the floor and trash.

"None of that, now . . ." Mariah said with a kind smile. "A shop like this could all be yours someday. Will be. But until you make enough of a reputation to have apprentices of your own, you'll be doing all your own cleaning—opening and closing. Long hours. Also, it's a good reminder of where you've come from. Especially after this morning."

Tressa glanced up, saw the twinkle in the older woman's eyes, and scowled. She felt the heat of her flush in her cheeks. "I won't let his compliments go to my head. I make every biscuit the same."

Mariah cawed laughter. "Yeah, like every biscuit will be eaten by him!" She sobered. "But that's the trick of it. Never forget this lesson."

Tressa tilted her head, not quite understanding.

"You make every single biscuit as if that handsome Herald *will* eat it. At the time, it doesn't matter to you if he does or not. It's the *potential* that drives you to do your best. It's how you should bake everything here. As if that one particular man is your sole customer. If you continue to bake everything as if it will be eaten by someone you love—" she glanced at Tressa's cheeks, "—or at least admire . . . keep that integrity in everything you do, and you will never go wrong."

Tressa blinked at the realization. It was so simple, so obvious—and yet it had taken too many years to suddenly realize what had been right before her face. Her eyes wide, she nodded. "Yes, ma'am."

"Now, clean up. Soren will take the extra to the Temple after you take what you want." The baker tossed her apron to the counter and walked out.

Tressa glanced at the leftovers and chose two things: a pasty and a cheese biscuit—*just like what Herald Arden chose*—and put them aside. She was glad Mariah had already left. She didn't think she could handle anymore teasing today. Especially since it was true.

One thing about this apprenticeship, though, she hadn't gone hungry since she'd started it. For that, she was grateful. She lived in a tiny room in a boarding house with an indifferent landlady. After her parents died, she'd made do with whatever she could to keep her alive. It was pure luck that Mariah had seen her eyeing the stale bread meant for the slop before she'd succumbed to her stomach's rumblings. She'd given Tressa a fresh meat pie, then directed her to the Temple.

The next week, Tressa had returned to the shop and begged for work. She didn't think the baker would give it to her, and the best she could hope for was a fresh biscuit. But she'd been wrong. Mariah had offered something more: the apprenticeship. With that, Tressa's life had changed for the better.

Mariah was the first person in a long time who cared who she was, what she did, and how she did it. It made Tressa work that much harder when she remembered what her life had once been like.

With a sigh, she got to work. As always, she started with putting the excess bread, pastries, and other baked goods in the basket for Soren to take when he finished his chores. It had taken her a full year of apprenticeship to realize that Mariah knew almost exactly what she sold each day and made enough to donate to the local church each night to help feed the poor. They'd never talked about it, but Tressa figured it was one way Mariah gave back to the community that served her well.

It had been a long time since she'd closed down the shop for the day. Her back complained at the extra work, but Tressa continued to do her best. For three reasons: Mariah would notice if the shop wasn't up to her standards in the morning; Because someday she would have a shop of her own, and she might not have an apprentice to take on the grunt work in the beginning; And, finally, if she did a bad job, both Soren and Inga would know it. Mariah would make an example of her. That was something she did not want to happen.

She finished mopping the floor and opened the back door, then stopped. Soren was still out there, though she thought he'd left some time ago. He stood in the alleyway, looking around as he lifted the large basket they used to carry the leftovers to the Temple, gesturing it toward passersby. She almost called out to him, but she stepped back as he looked around with a shifty expression she'd never seen on his face.

A woman in poor but well mended clothing came up and talked to him. While Tressa watched, Soren showed the woman a loaf of bread. She nodded, handed over a coin, and took the bread. Soren gave her a small bow and turned to come back into the shop.

He stopped as he saw Tressa watching him. They stared at each other. Tressa's mind whirled. Had Soren just sold the leftovers to someone on the street? The leftovers meant to feed the poor? She stepped back into the shop and waited.

Soren dumped the crumbs from the basket into the alleyway, then sauntered on in. "I thought you'd gone home."

"I thought you'd gone to the Temple." Tressa eyed the empty basket he put on the counter.

"Well, you know . . ."

"No. I don't. What were you doing?"

Soren looked away. "Wasn't hurting no one. Just providing a service they need."

"Those goods were meant to feed the poor."

"My customers *are* poor. But they still have their pride. They don't want to take from people who can't even afford to pay a little." Soren offered open hands, a plea to understand and accept.

"But they are . . . *you* are . . . doing just that. I can't believe you. That basket was meant for the poor that the Temple feeds. Not to line your pocket."

"Every single bakery in Haven sends their leftovers to the Temple. They aren't wanting for anything. These people, my customers, can't afford to pay full price, but they want to pay something. What's the harm in helping them out, too?"

Tressa frowned. "It's stealing."

"No, it's not. Not when Mariah's giving it away. Nothing goes to waste. I swear. Anything I can't sell, I take to the Temple. There's no crime here."

Tressa shook her head. Part of her could almost see where he was coming from. Part of her knew what he'd been doing was against everything they'd been taught.

Soren blinked at her, his eyes growing wet. "I'm

sorry. Don't tell her. My da's sick. I just need to bring home a little extra for the medicine. My family needs the money, but I'll cut you in. We can split what little I get. It's not much."

Tressa retreated farther into the kitchen, horrified. "No."

He hung his head. "I'll stop then. I'll just go back to taking the leftovers to the Temple. I'll stop. I promise. Please don't tell on me. I need this apprenticeship. I'll figure some other way to get the money."

She nodded, not sure what else to do. Watching him walk away, Tressa wondered when his dad had gotten sick and why he hadn't said anything to them. She thought they were better friends than that. She was sure Mariah would help . . . if he just asked.

The next couple of days were awkward and stiff between them, but everything seemed to go back to normal when Inga returned, her mother on the mend. Even so, Mariah made certain to send extra bakery goods home with the girl for a couple of days longer.

Tressa had given Soren significant looks during all such exchanges between Mariah and Inga, but her friend and peer either didn't see them or ignored her. He still did the main job of taking the shop leftovers to the Temple each night, and she'd stopped watching him leave in the evening. But the doubt remained. Though the awkward stiffness lessened between them, Tressa still didn't trust Soren, and that bothered her.

A fortnight after she'd caught him selling the Temple donations, Tressa decided to prove things to herself once and for all. Without thinking too deeply about what she was doing, she followed Soren. When he proved her wrong, she would beg his forgiveness, then convince him to talk to Mariah about his sick father.

Soren walked directly toward the Temple, and Tressa smiled. Then he turned a corner before he got there, and her heart sank. Cutting through another alleyway, she followed him from a distance until he stopped. On the corner of a smaller street, he gestured the basket of bakery goods toward the people passing by. Some stopped. From the easy conversation between them and the exchange of coin for baked goods, this was his new spot for selling the leftovers. He hadn't stopped. He'd lied and hidden his thievery from them all.

Tressa walked away, her heart heavy and her mind confused. If he lied to her about this, did he lie about his dad being sick? Did it matter? Of course it did. Mariah would've helped him just as she'd helped Inga. Would it make any difference if she followed Soren home and discovered his dad ill and Soren too prideful to ask? He had still lied and taken from people who needed the food most.

She sat on a low stone wall and watched people head home from the work day and tried not to feel anything. She didn't know what to do now. Soren had lied, and he was still stealing from Mariah . . . from the poor. From someone. *From someone like me before Mariah took a chance on me.*

Pulling a meat pie from her satchel, she stared at it. She'd made this one today. She'd graduated from just baked goods to filled ones to be sold. It made her proud that Mariah trusted her enough to do so.

As she took a bite, she looked up and saw a snowy white horse wearing a white and blue bridle with a matching saddle blanket. There was no rider astride the beautiful horse. In Haven, that was not unusual. It was a Companion, the symbol of Haven's—of Valdemar's—goodness and a representative of the monarch. She continued to watch until the beautiful horse trotted out of sight on its way to do whatever it was that Companions did.

At one time, she prayed that she'd be Chosen. To become a Herald like those in the legends. In the end, she wasn't Chosen by a Companion but by Mariah. The apprenticeship was nearly at an end. She would have the pain, and the opportunity, to strike out on her own, and to adhere to no one's standards but her own.

Sensing eyes upon her, Tressa turned and saw a small, dirty child watching her. Or, rather, watching her barely touched meat pie. With a smile, she broke the pastry in half and offered the untouched bit to the little boy. As he took it and stuffed the entire thing in his mouth, she made a decision. Breaking off another piece, she handed it to the child before finishing her diminished meal.

She had her own standards to adhere to.

Feeling sick to her stomach, Tressa waited until almost the end of the day to touch Mariah's arm and whisper, "I need to talk to you before you leave. After we close the shop. Alone."

Her mentor and boss tilted her head before nodding. A few minutes later, she sent Inga home early with another basketful of goods for the family—just to make sure all was well. The two of them worked together to close the shop after she sent Soren off with the leftover donations.

When they got to the end of the cleaning and Mariah came back in from throwing out the trash, Tressa didn't know if she could go through with it. She scrubbed the clean floor all the more, trying to find the words.

"Well, then," Mariah asked, "what is it? Are you getting married to our favorite Herald?"

Tressa shook her head. She couldn't find it in her to smile at the jest. "It's . . ." She took a breath and looked Mariah in the face. "It's Soren."

"Yes?"

"He's selling the temple donations. He said he was doing it for money for his family. I caught him a couple weeks ago. He promised to stop."

The older woman crossed her arms, her face a neutral mask. "But?"

"But he didn't." Tressa shrugged. "I . . . couldn't trust his word. I don't know why not. I followed him yesterday. I'm sorry. But I found him doing it again. Just in a different place."

Mariah nodded. "I thought there was something between you two. Why couldn't you trust his word?"

"He said his dad was sick. That's why he needed the money. But we both saw how good you were to Inga and her mom. If he was actually sick . . . Soren could've talked to you. Should've talked to you."

"Would it matter if his da was sick?"

Tressa felt her cheeks flush. "Yes! No. I mean . . . not really. He should've done things the right way. He's taking advantage of you and your generosity. If his dad was sick . . . or is sick, we could help. He should've told us. Told you. As it is, he's stealing from those who have nothing to give. I don't care if every bakery in Haven gave all they had left over to the same temple. You bake enough to donate to them every night . . . and he stole it from them. From you."

Mariah nodded. "Why are you so upset about this?"

"Because it's against everything you've ever taught us. To have integrity in everything we do. To be honest with each other and ourselves." The tears came despite her trying to keep them at bay.

"You did the right thing."

"Then why does it feel so terrible?"

The older woman's face softened, and she sighed. "Because you are friends. Because you want everyone to work to your same level. Because sometimes doing the right thing hurts."

Tressa looked up when Mariah took her by the shoulders. "What's going to happen now?"

"What I had already decided to do when I first discovered what Soren was doing more than a month ago."

"You knew? You were testing me?"

Mariah nodded. "I did. And I was. Now that you have told me, I have several things I need to do. Thank you for not letting me down." She sat at the kitchen table. "But first, we need to talk."

Fury rose and fell in the space of a heartbeat and the blink of an eye. Fear replaced it. Mariah looked old and sad. Tressa sat on the edge of a stool. "About what?"

"Your future, much to my sorrow."

"I don't understand."

"I know. I didn't plan to test you, but when the opportunity presented itself, I had to. For a couple of reasons. The first of which was for my own sake. Soren doing what he was doing made me question everything I'd ever taught you apprentices. Had I not imparted the importance of personal integrity? Had I failed?"

Tressa shook her head. "You didn't fail."

"I know. With you, I didn't. With Soren, I did. But he isn't who we're talking about now. It's you. Are you angry with me?"

Tressa blinked and opened her mouth to say "no" then closed it again. After a moment's thought, she shrugged. "A little. But it also took me weeks to tell you. I'm sorry. You must think the worst of me." She realized how tired Mariah seemed.

"No. Of course not. Even if you hadn't told me. However, if you hadn't, we wouldn't be having this talk." Mariah lifted her chin. "Tomorrow afternoon, you are going to go to the Palace to meet with the head chefs—Jala and Enri—and you will go there with a written recommendation from me. I've known them for years, and they've been looking for a couple of senior apprentices to train to bake for the Palace . . . but every person who works at the Palace must be above reproach. You've proven to me that you are."

"The *Palace*? Me?"

She smiled. "Of course. Why do you think the Heralds stop here so often? They love your baking. The Palace would benefit from someone like you. For both your skill and your integrity. You rose to the occasion, and I am so proud. I knew there was something special about you when you came back and asked for work. Now, I know you'll excel at the Palace—personally and professionally."

Tressa bowed her head. "Thank you. I learned from the best. I am your legacy."

"You are, and I will miss you . . . but not just yet. Tomorrow, you'll help me open the shop."

Tressa smiled. "Yes, ma'am. There are Heralds who can't do without our cheese biscuits, and we don't want to let them down."

A Nursery of Raccoons
Elisabeth Waters

He's really cute.

The words echoed in Maja's head, causing her to turn to glare at Stina, the girl who had been making the most comments about cute boys. Fortunately, before Stina noticed the glare, Maja realized the comment had come not through her ears but through her Gift, which meant an animal had made it. The horses they rode and the crows flying overhead didn't think that way, and the raccoon riding on the front of Maja's saddle was male. *Female raccoon?* she wondered, but she decided not to worry about it now. She had more urgent problems. She was on a horse, in charge of a group of people—several of whom probably wouldn't obey her—in a part of Valdemar she had never seen before, and it was getting dark. Already some of the crows who had been scouting for her had decided to roost for the night. The only bright spot was that she thought they could reach their destination before full dark.

Maja was still wondering just why she was in this mess. She had been perfectly happy living in obscurity in Haven in the Temple of Thenoth, Lord of the Beasts, where her Gift of Animal Mindspeech was both welcome and useful, and her being an introvert who didn't talk to people much didn't bother anyone. She was good with animals, got on with the Brethren and the novices, and obeyed the Prior's orders. She had generally managed to stay out of public view, leaving contact with unfamiliar humans to the more extroverted members of the order. The problem was that now, at age 26, she had become the most senior of the female novices, and the Prior had given her a command that was completely changing her comfortable life.

Lady Magdalena Lindholm, commonly called Lena, had come to live at the Temple when she was ten, and the fact that she had Animal Mindspeech that needed to be trained outweighed her being a highborn heiress. As she got older, however, the balance had shifted, and she had married the previous winter. Being Lena, she had married another highborn novice, and the two of them had left Haven to live on an estate she owned. And, being Lena, she had promptly donated a good-sized chunk of that land to Thenoth's order so that they could set up another temple there. None of that surprised Maja, but the fact that the Prior had put *her* in charge of what he called a daughter house had completely stunned her.

So here she was, riding to their new land adjoining Lena's estate, accompanied by all of the current female novices, several male novices temporarily in the charge of Brother Thomas, who was there to help them get set up before returning to the main Temple at Haven, and—for some reason that nobody had explained to her—a sixteen-year-old boy named Sven-August, who was the son of a wealthy merchant's widow and lived at the Temple as a fosterling. He didn't have Animal Mindspeech, but he was very good with birds, so at least he would probably be useful. Lena had written that the estate had a lot of interesting birds.

Maja had been getting encouraging letters from her friend at frequent intervals, and it was clear that Lena was looking forward to having a temple next door. Apparently she was so eager she couldn't wait for them to arrive.

Maja saw a small party approaching comprised of Lena and several men. The men carried unlit torches, and they didn't even try to keep up with Lena when her horse surged forward to meet Maja's. *Not bodyguards, then.*

"Maja!" Lena's horse pivoted and dropped into a

position right beside Maja's, matching its pace exactly. Lena leaned over to give her a hug that would have dragged anyone not expecting it out of the saddle. Maja dropped the reins she had been holding for appearance's sake and hugged her back.

"It's good to see you, Lena." She looked at the men, who had pulled aside to the verge. "I hope those aren't supposed to be guards; they don't appear able to keep up with you."

Lena laughed. "No, I just brought them along in case you were farther away than I thought, and we needed to light the road for you. I expected you at least a candlemark ago."

"That's because you're impatient. Have you *ever* traveled with your own baggage?"

"Only what I could fit in my saddlebags and on a fast packhorse. Anything else can follow at its own pace." Lena grinned. "As for needing a bodyguard, everyone in this neighborhood knows me, they firmly believe that anyone who tried to harm me would be attacked by every animal in range, and they don't know how far my range is. I'm safer than I was in my mother's arms." She looked around. "It's a good thing we're almost home; I can feel the crows settling for the night." She fell silent for several minutes as their horses walked onward. "I sent a mental picture of the new Temple to all the crows. They can find us in the morning."

"Thank you," Maja said. "Not that the crows aren't perfectly self-sufficient, but I'm not sure I want a trail of them grabbing anything shiny as an introduction to our new neighbors."

"Don't worry. I included the 'crow toys' in the mental picture I sent."

Just then they rounded a bend in the road, and the new Temple came into view. Maja was relieved to find that it looked remarkably like the Temple in Haven. Despite Lena's best efforts, the Temple and Priory of Thenoth was among the poorest of the many temples in Haven. The walls and buildings were sturdy, of course, because they had to contain animals, but the wood to build and repair them came from wherever they could find—or scavenge—it, so the planks were often different colors until they faded to match the older sections. The robes worn by novices and priests alike were simply made from inexpensive cloth, and the inevitable stains were something everyone lived with. Nobody got a new robe until the fabric was so far gone that it couldn't be patched any more. The Prior did have a second robe to be worn when he was not working with animals and needed to impress someone rich or influential enough to donate to the Temple, but donations did not go for jeweled shrines or an impressive altar. The first priority was always food for the animals, followed by food for the people, and then the never-ending repairs.

"I think my people did a good job," Lena was saying happily. "We used the same layout and floor plans for the buildings, so you will all know your way around. Everything is in the same place as in Haven, although the complex is larger. Keven and I thought you might want to bring down some of the bigger animals, given the way the hoof stock is all crowded together in Haven."

"You're not fooling me," Maja teased. "You miss your trip of goats."

Lena made a face. "Only the fact that they belong to the god stopped me from suggesting goat stew for dinner after what they did to Guildmaster Jurgen's courtyard."

"He did send the surviving evergreens to the temple so the goats could finish eating them."

"'Finish' is definitely the right word. You weren't there when they were knocking his servants down in the slush to get at them." Lena grimaced. "The good thing about putting a daughter house here is that Keven and I are the only highborn in the area, and we're not going to get upset by the presence of animals like some of the highborn in Haven do."

"I'm glad of that." Maja sighed. "I still can't understand why the Prior put *me* in charge here. There are so many of the Brethren who are more qualified."

They rode through the open gate, which looked

exactly like a newer, cleaner version of the one in Haven, and everyone dismounted in the dirt courtyard.

Stina looked around. "Where do we sleep?" she asked. "Do we get better rooms than we had in Haven? We should—after all, we volunteered to come here."

Lord Thenoth, I'd so much rather deal with animals. "It's late and almost full dark. Lady Magdalena tells me she duplicated the Temple in Haven, so take the same rooms you had there. For now, dump your packs at the entrance to your dormitories, take the horses to the stables and the other animals to wherever they belong, and make sure they all are comfortable and have food, clean water, and bedding."

"But—" Stina started to protest, and one of the younger male novices moved to her side.

She doesn't need allies. Maja quickly cut her off. "Who's in charge of making supper tonight?"

Brother Magnus lifted a hand. Maja nodded to him and asked, "How long will you need to prepare it?"

"I stocked the pantry," Lena said helpfully. "You should have everything you need."

"About a candlemark, then," he said. He looked at the novice standing next to Stina. "Karl, you're on the roster with me."

"But I have to groom and stable my horse," Karl protested.

"I'll take him," one of the girls said. "I'd rather groom an extra horse and sleep on a full stomach." She smiled, but Karl was still looking at Stina.

"Thank you, Britta," Maja said pointedly. Karl muttered something she hoped was a thank you and followed Brother Magnus to the kitchen.

"That's supper sorted," Maja announced. "Everyone get the animals settled, wash up for supper, and meet in the refectory a candlemark from now."

As most of the group scattered to their tasks in at least a semblance of obedience, Maja noticed that while Britta had two horses to herself, and the other girls were handling their own, two of the boys were vying to help

Stina with her one horse. The shoving and jostling made her realize something.

There was one major difference between the Temple here and the one in Haven.

"Lena, you can feel the Peace of the God in the Temple at Haven, can't you?"

"So can I, and it isn't here," Sven-August interrupted her. He wasn't moving to care for his horse, but at least he wasn't a novice sworn to obey her. "This feels like my mother's house."

"It does not!" Lena said indignantly. "I've been there, and so has Maja. Your mother actually hates animals. This is a newly built temple, and it's up to all of us to bring the Peace of the God to it. And speaking of your mother, Sven-August, why are you here? I wouldn't have expected her to permit it." Sven-August was only sixteen, and his mother still had a legal right to decide what he was allowed to do.

"She was making me crazy, so I told her the Prior was sending a group to your estate, and I wanted to come along and visit you."

Lena looked at him suspiciously. "Doesn't she know I'm married now?"

Sven-August looked sheepish. "Uh, no? It's not as if you had a big wedding with half of Haven invited to it. She's not interested in what goes on at the Temple—and it's been years since Father was part of the Council."

It's also been years since your father was alive, so Mistress Efanya probably doesn't hear the Council gossip either. As Lena and Keven had married very quietly at the Temple the morning after they met, notified the King, and promptly left Haven, Maja realized it was quite possible that most people didn't know Lena was married. *Everyone at the Temple, the King and Queen, and the members of his Council; that's really not a lot of people. I'm sure her rejected suitors are keeping quiet about it—especially Keven's brother and his father.*

"Your mother still hasn't realized that I love you like the little brother I never had?"

"She keeps hoping you'll change your mind as I get

older. The gap between sixteen and eighteen doesn't seem as large as the one between thirteen and fifteen. And once we're both adults . . ."

Lena sighed. "Sven-August, *you* can explain this to Keven. And go stable your horse. Weren't you listening to Maja?"

"Uh, right," Sven-August said. "Sorry, Maja, I'll do it now. And I'll take your horse too." He took both sets of reins and followed the others to the stables.

Lena looked after him and murmured, "Really, Maja?"

Maja shrugged. "The Prior said to bring him, so I brought him."

"Who else did you bring?" Lena asked.

"I think you know most of them," Maja said. "Brother Thomas is on loan and will go back to Haven in three moons, but we have Brother Magnus, so we have a priest. The rest are novices: Britta, Mathilda, Nalini, Stina, Anders, Edvin, Hugo, and Karl."

Lena was obviously running over the list in her mind. "You, Britta, and Nalini—did the Prior send us *everyone* with Animal Mindspeech?"

"Not everyone," Maja said. "He still has Arvid, as well as any of the Brethren who have it—though I don't know if any of the others do have it."

"Does he have *any* girls left there?"

"Not that I know of. He seems to have taken the term "daughter house" literally, and it's not as if girls can take anything more than Perpetual Novice vows—"

"—which don't stop us from marrying." Lena had taken those vows herself.

Maja thought Lena's husband had as well. She was so rattled at the moment that she couldn't remember. She felt movement by her feet and looked down to see something playing with Lena's skirt.

Lena, totally unfazed, reached down and scooped the animal into her arms. "Dexter! How is my favorite raccoon?"

So that's where he got to. Dexter had been instrumental in persuading Lena to move into the temple, so he probably did hold a special place in her heart.

* * *

It was the middle of the night when something like a pain in her right arm woke Maja. As she sat up in bed, she realized she couldn't use her arm. She tried to fight down the panic that was her original reaction and then realized that the panic was (a) still there and (b) not hers. She got out of bed, struggled awkwardly one-handed into her habit, and followed the feeling of panic to the stables.

What she saw there changed *her* panic to rage. One of the horses was not only still saddled and bridled, but the dangling reins were tangled around its right foreleg. Maja, speaking as calmly as she could to the horse, reached up and removed the bridle from its head. Once the whole assembly was on the ground, she could use her left hand to pull it down and hold it so the horse could free its leg. And, thanks be to Thenoth, once the horse could move its leg, she could use her right arm again. It was sore, but Maja told herself that a sore arm was the very least she deserved for not checking *everything* before she went to bed herself.

She unsaddled the horse and got it fresh hay and water, plus a ration of grain as an apology. Then she went to work with the grooming brush and mentally reached out to the horse to see who—aside from her, of course— was responsible for leaving him like that.

Anders had been riding him, and it was Anders who had simply put him in a stall—before being distracted by Stina and forgetting to return and care for his horse. :*Anders is going to care for all of you tomorrow—or today, whichever it is—and I want you to tell me immediately if he doesn't do a good job. All right?:* The horse nodded, and took another mouthful of grain.

Anders started to protest his assignment, but after Maja pointedly explained to him just why she had given him this job, he nodded and went off to the stables. Maja gave out the rest of the morning assignments and was still debating what, if anything, to say to Stina about her part in last night's shameful neglect, when Stina looked across the courtyard and said, "Who's that? He's dreamy!"

Maja looked and realized that her morning had become even worse. "Only if by 'dreamy' you mean nightmare-inducing. The first time I saw him he was throwing knives at Lena's pet finches. Inside, where they couldn't fly away from him."

Stina's eyes widened, and Maja added, "To work, all of you. *Now.*" They scattered, and she turned to face— what was his name? Algott, that was it.

"Good morning," he said smiling pleasantly. "Could I speak to whoever is in charge here, please?"

"That would be me." Maja forced herself not to sigh. *I still can't believe the Prior thought I could do this job.* "I was not aware that the Brotherhood of the Bereaved had a presence in this neighborhood."

"The what?" Algott looked blank, and then actually blushed. "Oh, that. I'd forgotten about it." He frowned at her, obviously searching his memory. "I don't remember meeting you."

"I was the person at the Temple in charge of caring for Aurelia—and Lena. And I have Animal Mindspeech."

He winced at that. Apparently his memory was returning enough for him to guess what she had seen.

"I was also, as far as I know, the last person your order tried to blackmail."

"I'm sorry," Algott said. "I sincerely apologize. It wasn't a real order; we just started it as a joke."

"Given that Lena's brother fell dead at my feet while we were both being questioned about it under Truth Spell, I am well aware of that." Maja was glad that she at least managed to keep her voice calm and level. "So, what brings you to Thenoth's Temple?"

"I'm Lady Magdalena's game warden for this estate—"

"You're *what*?" Maja's voice was not calm and level this time.

"Yes, Lady Magdalena is a gentle soul, and has shown me forgiveness I can only hope to deserve over time. As to why I'm here," he continued, "there is a boy in the village named Johan. He's eight years old, simple, and the son of the milliner. About a year ago he killed some of the godwits for their summer plumage—the feathers are bright orange—and gave the feathers to his mother who made them into hats. She didn't know," he added hastily, "but when Lady Magdalena and her husband came here, they saw the hats at the Spring Faire. I knew the godwits were skittish, but I didn't know why. As soon as I told her, she knew."

"She would," Maja agreed. "What happened to the boy?"

"Standard punishment for poaching around here," Algott said. "Field work. There's generally someone who can use help."

"So has he done it again?" Maja asked.

"Oh, no." Algott looked startled. "Lady Magdalena explained to him that killing birds was wrong, confiscated his slingshot, and arranged for the godwits to leave their feathers in a pile away from their nesting area. That way his mother can still use the feathers."

"That's a typical Lena-style solution," Maja remarked.

"Absolutely," Algott agreed. "But I'm a bit worried now that the Temple is here. Johan has the firm idea that you have all sorts of exotic birds here, and I'm concerned that he might sneak in here and inadvertently do harm."

Unfortunately, he has a point; and our walls are designed more to keep animals in than people out. "Let's go talk to Brother Thomas. He's setting up the mews and the bird loft. Perhaps he would be willing to give the boy a tour."

Brother Thomas was willing. "I'll show the lad what we do here, and either he'll be bored because we don't have anything glamorous like His Majesty's peacocks, or he might decide he wants to help out here. Either way, Sven-August," he raised his voice to attract the boy's attention, "will stick with him and make sure he doesn't hurt anything."

"Absolutely," Sven-August said. "I hate it when people hurt animals."

Maja, remembering Sven-August treating a bird

injured by a hairbrush his mother had thrown at it, nodded.

"Sven-August," Brother Thomas ordered, "walk our guest to the gate and arrange for a time for him to bring the boy. Tomorrow or the day after would be better than today."

"Yes, Brother Thomas." Sven-August and Algott headed for the gate.

"You're doing well, Sister," Brother Thomas said when they were out of earshot. "Don't be afraid to ask for help."

"After what happened to that poor horse last night," Maja admitted, "I'm tempted to do everything. I know I can't, but I think I had better at least do stable rounds before bed."

"No harm in that. I realize that either you or Lena— or Britta or Nalini—could check on all the animals *after* you went to bed, but you'd still have to get up if you found anything wrong."

"Like this morning," Maja sighed. "I feel as if I've been up for a full day, and it's not even noon yet. I can understand why the Prior sent all the girls with me, but having a group of boys the same age is a challenge. I wish we had the Peace of the God here."

Brother Thomas frowned. "I don't know why we don't," he admitted. "The Prior gave me a portion of the altar to use to build the new altar here. Perhaps it needs to be assembled and put into place. I'll do that this afternoon."

"Thank you, Brother," Maja said with feeling.

The altar was in place in the chapel in time for evening prayers, and Maja's rounds before bed showed nothing out of place. But as the days passed, it was apparent that the Peace of the God was still lacking. The animals were twitchy, and the novices were worse.

"I'm not sure whether I'm being punished for the sin of pride," Brother Magnus said one night when he, Brother Thomas, and Maja were meeting in her office after the novices were, she hoped and prayed, in bed. She thought Dexter was watching them—and lately she suspected that he was smarter than most of them. "But when I remember how smug I was when my friends from other orders defined novices as 'creatures who spill lamp oil, break crockery, and giggle,' I want to cringe."

"And those were single-gender orders," Brother Thomas added. "I broke up a shoving match today between Edvin and Hugo over who was going to help Stina in the kennels."

"I hope you sent both of them to work somewhere else," Maja said.

"I sent them both to look after the pigs. Stina is perfectly capable of doing her assigned work without their help, and she's actually fairly good with dogs. Birds, of course, take more skill and a more delicate touch."

Not that you're biased, of course. Maja didn't say that aloud. She didn't feel safe teasing anyone these days, not even the priests, who were grown men and secure in their vocations. *And speaking of vocations—*

"I'm concerned about Stina," she admitted.

"Because she doesn't have Animal Mindspeech?" Brother Magnus asked.

"No, it's not that. Mathilda doesn't have it, and she doesn't worry me the way Stina does. None of the boys have it, including Sven-August, who has more skill with birds than anyone other than Brother Thomas. And if either of you has the Gift, nobody ever told me."

Both men shook their heads.

"What bothers me," Maja continued, "is that she doesn't seem to want to be here."

"As opposed to in Haven?" Brother Thomas asked.

"Doesn't seem to have a vocation?" Brother Magnus said at almost the same time.

"More like acts as if she's serving a prison sentence." Maja sighed. "We get people dumped on us by their families—Keven is an example of that—but generally they've at least chosen the Temple, if not whether to live in one or not."

"She actually did choose our order," Brother Magnus said. "But if you are concerned about her vocation, Sister," he emphasized the title slightly, "you are the one to speak to her about it. It's part of your job as Superior—or as Acting Novice Mistress, whichever applies here."

"Probably both," Maja agreed. "Thank you. I'll talk to her." She stood up. "Time for us to seek our own beds. Is it me, or does morning come earlier every day?"

"It's you," Brother Thomas said. "It's after the Equinox, so morning is actually *later* each day."

"Go to bed, Sister," Brother Magnus said kindly, sketching a blessing over her head. "May Thenoth send you good dreams."

"Amen to that," Maja said fervently. "Thank you, Brothers. I appreciate your company and advice."

What she actually dreamed was that she was in the street in Haven, trying to enter the courtyard of the Temple there, but the stone threshold kept rising up and hitting her knees. She was surprised not to have bruised knees when she woke up.

She was splashing water on her face from the basin in her cell to help her wake up—she didn't bother with a real wash until after the early morning chores—when the shouting started. She swiped a cloth across her face with one hand while reaching for her robe with the other, and ran for the courtyard as soon as she was decent. She remembered as she ran that the Prior had told her that a Superior should be calm and dignified at all times. *I wonder how he manages that—aside from decades of practice.*

She arrived to find Karl and Sven-August rolling in the dirt, fists flying. Sven-August was two years younger than Karl and had been raised by his widowed mother, so Maja wasn't surprised that he was getting the worst of it.

Brothers Thomas and Magnus arrived right behind her, and each of them hauled a boy to his feet. Maja notice that Sven-August still needed to be restrained, despite the blood dripping down one side of his face and what looked like a developing black eye.

"Take it back!" he snarled at Karl.

Karl seemed to be willing to stop the physical fight at least, but he was not in a conciliatory mood. "She doesn't care about *you*," he sneered. "She just likes boys—or men."

"Enough!" Maja said firmly. She didn't need to ask who "she" was. *Time to break this up before they make it worse.* She looked at Karl and didn't see any visible injuries, but it was her job to be certain. "Karl, are you injured?"

It didn't help that Karl looked insulted. "Of course not," he snapped.

"In that case," Maja said, "you are now on silent retreat. Meals will be brought to you in your cell, where you will remain until breakfast tomorrow."

Karl looked outraged. "What about him?" He glared at Sven-August.

"It is my place to deal with him," Maja reminded him. "It is your place to do as I tell you, and I strongly suggest that you consider the state of your own soul and vocation before worrying about his.

"The rest of you, back to your chores," she ordered. "Sven-August, come with me."

She was relieved to see that Brother Magnus had decided to escort Karl to his cell. She headed toward her office with Sven-August limping beside her. As they arrived, Brother Thomas caught up with them. "Sister, before you talk to the lad, perhaps I should patch him up?"

"Thank you, Brother. That would be a kindness." She let them into her office and waited outside. It didn't require her three years of experience with Sven-August to know that he would be mortified to have her patch him up; he was a sixteen-year-old boy. The rumble of voices coming dimly through the door gave her hope that Brother Thomas was talking some sense into the boy, or at least calming him down.

She waited until Brother Thomas came out and said, "He's all yours." She smiled a thank you, and then straightened her face before entering her office. Sven-August stood before her desk, looking thoroughly miserable. She sat down and gestured him to do likewise.

"All right," she said quietly and calmly. "What happened?"

"He called Stina a lightskirt!"

"I do hope he's not stupid enough to actually believe that," Maja said. "Do you think he really does, or was he just trying to provoke you?"

Forced to stop and think about it, Sven-August winced. "He was provoking me. He said she doesn't really like me, that I'm just a spoiled little boy."

"Are you?"

Sven-August looked outraged. "You know I'm not!"

"Well, I certainly didn't think so," Maja said. "So we agree that you are not a spoiled brat and Stina is not a lightskirt."

Sven-August nodded.

"So why do you care what he thinks?"

"He said it in front of Stina," Sven-August explained. "So I couldn't just let it pass."

"I can understand that," Maja agreed. "She's next on my list of people to talk to anyway."

"No!" Sven-August protested. "It not her fault!"

Maja looked at him steadily. "I *have* seen that she seems to notice cute boys—and comment on their looks."

Sven-August now looked truly miserable. "We're trying to keep my mother from finding out."

"Finding out what?" Maja asked cautiously. *Please don't let her be pregnant.*

"That we're in love and want to get married."

I did not see that coming, so I guess they're making a really good job of it. "Are you sure? You're both rather young, and marriage is a lifetime commitment. At your ages, that's how many decades together?"

"We've been seeing each other for two years. Our families lived next door until hers lost their money. They wanted to send her to the Sisters of Ardana, because they could have paid her dowry with books they were going to sell anyway, but she didn't want to go there."

"Why not?" Maja asked. "It's probably a much easier life than this one."

He chewed his lower lip. "It's not my secret to tell," he said at last.

Oh, joy. I can see an interesting interview coming up.

"Are you certain that she still wishes to marry you? With the change in her family's circumstances, your mother is going to be difficult." *Knowing Lady Efanya, very difficult.*

"Once we're married, there's not much my mother can do," Sven-August pointed out. "The law says that we both become adults when we marry."

Maja rubbed her aching forehead. "You know, Sven-August, there is a big difference between legally grown up and *really* grown up. Think about that while you're spending today in your cell."

"That's fair," Sven-August conceded. "And you're right when you say we should think things through. But I'm not going to change my mind. I'll wait if I have to, but Stina *is* the one I want to marry."

"Go," Maja said. "Grab some breakfast and take it to your cell. Stay there."

"Yes, Sister." Sven-August smiled at her and left.

Maja decided to go to breakfast herself before her next interview. It was time anyway, and perhaps it would help her headache. She went to wash up properly before taking her place in the refectory.

They were eating in silence this morning, and Maja found her mind going back and forth between her dream and the prayers she should have said that morning, something about stumbling stones. *Maybe we need some to slow things down here.* In her mind she saw the smooth stones of the threshold of the Temple gate in Haven. *Or maybe not.*

She pulled Stina into her office as soon as the girl finished her morning chores. The first words out of Stina's mouth were, "Is Sven-August all right?"

"Mostly bruised, I think," Maja said. "Is it true that you want to marry him?"

Stina nodded. "Yes. We've been secretly promised for over a year. We were going to talk to our parents when we turned sixteen, but . . ." Her voice trailed off miserably.

"But your family's finances changed," Maja said

sympathetically. "So why not the Sisters of Ardana? Were you afraid they wouldn't let you go?"

Stina stared at her lap and mumbled something.

"I'm sorry, but I didn't hear that."

"I'm stupid, all right?" she said resentfully. "I can't read!"

Maja considered her. "The law says that every child has to learn to read, write, and do sums. Did you not get your certificate then?"

"No, I got it. I can do sums, and write, and I memorized the reading part."

"If you got your certificate without being able to read, that doesn't make you stupid. Quite the opposite, in fact. A good memory is a useful thing to have. I'm guessing you never told anyone."

"Sven-August knows I can't read."

"I thought he must. He told me that why you didn't go to the Sisters of Ardana wasn't his secret to tell."

"Are you going to throw me out?"

"Because you can't read? Of course not. The animals don't care."

"At least Sven-August doesn't think I'm stupid. Or a lightskirt," she added defiantly.

"Nobody with any sense thinks you're a lightskirt."

"Karl said—"

"As I said, nobody with any sense." Maja frowned. "Has Karl been bothering you? Or have any of the boys? Or anyone else?"

Stina kept shaking her head, and Maja relaxed a bit. "So why are you doing the 'what a cute boy' routine?"

"It was Sven-August's idea. Because of his mother. She's, um . . ."

"Back in Haven. And the only way to get her anywhere *near* here would be forcible abduction. I've met her."

"You have?" Stina said in surprise.

"Yes. She mistook me for Lena's maid." Maja grinned. "But she's not here, she's not going to be here, and you can drop the act. And speaking of acting, do you actually *like* animals?"

"Better than books."

"But you're mostly here to wait until you and Sven-August can get married? And to be able to see him?"

"Yes," Stina admitted, "but now I'm here and he's going to be in Haven."

"I'm sure he'll find plenty of reasons to be here as much as he can," Maja assured her. "I'm going to be sending him to Haven on an errand soon, but it's one he'll have to come back from." *I'm pretty sure now that I know what we need for the God's Peace, and it's not an altar.*

She waited two days to give Sven-August time to heal enough so that he could ride easily, and to find the right words for her request to the Prior. Then she sent him off, waited, and prayed.

Sven-August returned with the stone from the threshold of the Temple's gate and a note from the Prior, which said, *"Why did it take you so long to figure out what you needed?"*

I guess I'm not as up to the job as he thought I was. But I will be.

Maja slept that night under the Peace of the God. When she woke, the sun was rising, and there was a lump of fur at the foot of her bed. "Good morning, Dexter," she said contentedly. Then she looked more closely. "Who is your friend?"

:Her name is Alma.:

As Alma stretched, Maja realized that she hadn't been paying much attention to what Dexter was up to since they arrived here. There was going to be another addition to her Temple in a few moons. A nursery of raccoons.

Tables Turned
Kristin Schwengel

"Right now, I'm glad to be bored," Rinton said, staring out from under the overhanging branches at the steady rain. On his right, his Companion stamped a foot and tossed his head in agreement.

They were crowded under what seemed to be the only fir tree for miles, with branches spaced high enough for two horses, but with a full enough canopy to provide some protection from the wintry rain. Even Kiyan, Rinton's giant crow, came gliding down to settle on the Herald's shoulder, shaking water from bedraggled black feathers.

The young woman standing to his left nodded, her pale green Healer Trainee robes splotched darker with raindrops. Her own horse stood on her other side, so that the horse and the Companion framed the two of them beneath the sheltering branches. "Glad I am that the weather did not interrupt our journey until now. It was good to walk the snowy woods again with Grandmother."

It had been Mirideh's first request, after the astonishing alliance with Karse was formalized, that she be permitted to visit her home village. Equally astonishing was that the Healers' Collegium and Queen Selenay had agreed to it, allowing her to travel during the Midwinter break from classes at the Collegium. When he had heard about it, Herald Rinton had volunteered to accompany her, still acting as her protector, as he had been since he had brought her out of Karse.

This time, there was no terror-driven race to the Valdemar border, pursued by a nameless clawing *something* that Rinton dared not look at face-to-face. The Guard kept the South Trade Road clear of snow, and the skies had been calm and fair for most of the days they had been in Karse. Only today, the last day of their travel, had a few slushy flurries turned into a cold rain, slowing them down as they returned to Haven. At first, they had tried to ignore it and press on, since they were barely a half-day's journey from the city, but with no pressing urgency, they had chosen to take temporary refuge under the trees.

"We're so close to Haven that there're no inns nearby, but I think there is a Waystation just a mile or so farther up the road. If the rain doesn't let up, maybe we can make for that and at least get ourselves warm and dry to finish the last few leagues tomorrow. Winter rains make me feel colder than snow."

Miri had opened her mouth to assent when Rinton's Companion stiffened beside them, his legs braced against the ground.

:Hold on.: The words rang between her ears, and she stared, mouth agape, as an inner shock rippled over both Herald and Companion. Rinton's eyes rolled up behind his lids, and only Miri's proximity enabled her to grab his limp body, preventing him from being caught under the weight of his Companion, whose legs buckled as he folded into an unconscious white heap. Kiyan launched himself to a nearby branch, his distressed caws barely denting her awareness as she fought to keep her balance.

Miri braced against the weight of the Herald, and she struggled to control Rinton's slide down her side until he landed in another white heap next to Linx. As soon as the Herald was on the ground, she knelt beside him, one hand reaching under Rinton's collar to find his pulse while her eyes studied the Companion.

As she watched, a tremor passed under the Companion's skin, and she saw the deep barrel of his chest rise and fall, rapid breaths as though he had been galloping. Relieved, she focused on the pulse beneath her fingertips, which skittered and jumped but, thankfully, kept beating. The Herald's breathing was sharp and quick as well, and she took a moment to rearrange his body into a more reclined position, pillowing his head and torso against his Companion's side.

As soon as she had done so, the breathing of both changed, as though the physical contact calmed them. She found Rinton's pulse again—though still rapid, it was now steady and more even.

Miri sat back on her heels and stared at the two of them slumped on the cushion of fallen needles. *What* in Vkandis' name had just happened? There had been no sound other than Linx's warning projected into her head. She had felt nothing, not even a whisper of anything, touching the shields around her mind. Whatever it had been, it apparently was targeted to affect only the Heralds and the Companions, which was a terrifying thought. Fear seized her as she thought of Haven, defenseless without its White Riders.

Not defenseless, silly girl, she told herself. *What of the Guard? The Army? What of Herald Captain Kerowyn's Skybolts?* Even as she calmed her own breathing, Kiyan dropped from the tree to land beside her, and she gently stroked his glimmering blue-black feathers, working her fingertips underneath to scratch at the base of his skull. If a huge crow could ever be said to purr, Rinton's "pet" did so, leaning his head into her fingers with a soft chittering sound.

"Well, now what?" she said to the bird. He cocked his head to one side and eyed her with a corvid's innate curiosity. "Leave them here to go get help I certainly cannot, nor take them anywhere by myself. If—*when* they wake up, who knows what condition they'll be in?"

The crow had no response for her, but even as she finished the words, Linx's ears twitched, and he slowly raised his head, gently turning to look first at Rinton's body leaning against him and then at Miri.

:Ow.: If she didn't know otherwise, she wouldn't have

recognized it as the same "voice" she had heard giving the earlier warning. Faint and faded, the mind-voice reminded her of the carefully quiet way people talked when they were suffering the morning-after effects of a night of excessive drinking.

"What just happened?" Although she whispered, the Companion's eyes flickered in what she could only describe as a wince.

:I'm . . . not sure.: A long silence, as Linx half-closed his eyes in concentration.

"Is it bad?" She assumed he was Mindspeaking with the Companions in Haven, and waited.

:Not . . . bad. Unexpected.:

In her time at the Healers' Collegium, Miri had heard more than one Herald or Trainee complain about the inscrutability of their Companions. "Speaking" directly to Linx, without Rinton as intermediary, she suddenly understood all of their frustration.

:Rolan says not to panic.:

"Who's panicking?" Miri looked pointedly from herself to Kiyan to the still unconscious Rinton.

Linx did not deign to respond but began to move, rearranging his legs underneath him. Miri held onto Rinton's shoulders so that he didn't flop over as the Companion shifted and resettled. She eased the Herald's weight back against Linx's side, pulling one of his legs to a less-awkward bend, then unfastened the stallion's saddle girth, allowing the saddle to slip off behind his back to land in the thin snow at the edge of the sheltered circle.

"If he is unconscious more than a candlemark or two, I will need to look more closely." She hoped the Companion would understand what she meant—he was, after all, the first one to identify her Gift as that of Mindhealing.

Linx only nodded his head a little before his neck drooped in a gentle curve, his nose just touching Rinton's outstretched leg, and he drifted into sleep.

Mirideh blinked. "Not too worried *he* must be, either," she muttered to the crow, who chittered back at her. She stood and set about loosening her mare's saddle girth, pulling out some of her waybread and the last dried berry pocket pie that her grandmother had wrapped up for her. Placing her bedroll against the shaggy tree trunk, she leaned back. "Might as well make myself comfortable, as well."

As soon as she finished the dry waybread and broke off the first flake of the pocket pie, Kiyan sidled up beside her, bobbing his head and half-mantling his wings.

"Here you go, you greedy thing," she murmured with a smile, breaking off a small chunk of fruit and pastry and putting it on the ground. "I know Rinton shared the last of his with you already." The bird snatched up the treat and bolted it down, with a nod of his head by way of a thank you.

Was it her imagination, or had the rain gotten heavier? As if in answer, a few drops snaked their way between the boughs to spatter in the leaf litter around them, and one splashed icy-cold across the top of her head. Miri thought for a moment, then dug in her packs once more to find the small metal dishes she always carried with her, propping them in a low snowbank just outside the tree's sheltering branches to gather the falling rain. Rainwater sometimes seemed more refreshing than the groundwater with which they filled their waterskins, and if Rinton woke with a headache half as bad as she suspected he would, he'd need every bit of refreshing he could get. She put one bundle of soothing herbs handy in her belt pouch—they would steep well enough even in cold water when Rinton woke.

As more drops filtered through to fall upon the four—no, five—of them, she corrected herself, glancing up to the branches where Kiyan had retreated, she once more went to the saddle packs, this time to pull out the heavy oiled cloaks. She draped one as best as she could over the Herald and huddled under the second herself. Kiyan dropped to the ground again and tucked himself up under one edge of her cloak, and she returned to idly stroking his feathers, lost in considering questions she doubted Linx either could or would answer.

All told, it was between two and three candlemarks later when Linx woke, this time much more his usual self and much more concerned for his Herald, who had barely moved in all the time since whatever-it-was had happened.

"Now may I look at him?" Miri had every intention of examining Rinton thoroughly anyway, but the Companion's agreement was immediate. He nodded his head, worry clear in the mind-voice he projected to her.

:*He is there, but not-there.*:

Shifting carefully, keeping her oilskin cloak as close around her as possible, for the soaked boughs were now letting more and more rain through, she knelt beside Rinton. Placing her fingertips against the Herald's temples, she closed her eyes and let her awareness sink into him, becoming aware of surface bruising, the aches of lying on hard ground, the minor complaints that most people would barely notice.

She was strongly aware of the silvery barrier that was his mental shielding, firm and solid, with two "cords" that seemed to spin off from it, one down to the earth, as all Heralds were taught, and one that led to the form of the Companion behind him.

Her eyes flew open and she met Linx's bottomless blue eyes. "Can you help lower his shields, enough that I can see in?" At the Collegium, she had never helped Mindheal anyone who was actively shielded, and she didn't want to risk either damaging Rinton's protection or draining her own energy in pushing through it.

A fractional bob of the white head, although those uncanny eyes took on a slightly wary expression.

"Don't worry, I don't take in anything while I'm there, not like the Mindspeakers who can learn other's thoughts if they're not shielded. It's like—" she cast her mind around for an example, "—like I'm looking at a page in a book to make sure it hasn't been torn or damaged, without reading the words on it."

Linx nodded again, more firmly this time, and she closed her eyes and slipped back into the light trance that allowed her to connect once more with Rinton's mind.

Now, she could sense the silvery barrier had thinned, and she was able to first blend with it, then pass through it.

Miri barely held back a gasp. The unconscious Herald's mind was buried deep below an angry red of pain and injury, as though he had instinctively retreated for protection. Focusing on her own anchor to the supportive earth beneath her, she took several careful breaths. Although she had been working in the House of Healing at the Collegium in Haven, this would be the first time she had attempted any sort of Mindhealing without the direct supervision and aid of one of the full Healers.

"He's so . . . *raw* . . ." she whispered. The sensation in her own mind was as if she were making delicate contact with badly burned skin, as though something had seared into the Herald's mind and left singe marks layered over everything there. With gentle care, she began to allow the white-green of Healing to filter through her and into Rinton.

Sometimes, when she Healed, she could quite literally See a picture in her mind of the effects of the injury and the reaction of the body to the Healing, but this was different. Instead, she felt an awareness in her own mind, as a shadow or an echo of what the Herald suffered resonated within her. She began her work with a subtle, broad soothing, like laying cool cloths on a fevered body. Only when the "raw" feeling had diminished, and she sensed that he was no longer in retreat, did she seek out the strongest signals of damage, guiding a stronger flow of Healing energy into those areas.

She had barely calmed the most injured parts of Rinton's mind when she felt her own focus fading, and slowly she backed out of his mind, one hand dropping to the earth beside her to support her. Her other hand pressed against the bridge of her nose, and she thanked Vkandis that she had thought about the possibility of an overexertion headache.

Half-blindly, Miri shifted to the edge of the overhanging boughs, reached for the now overflowing cups, and poured a few of her herbs into each. She let them sit for a few minutes, until Rinton showed signs of stirring, and brought them with her as she knelt again beside the groggy Herald.

"*Ow,*" he murmured, and Miri was hard-pressed to restrain an ill-timed giggle at how much he sounded like his Companion.

"Drink," she whispered, and pushed one cup into his hands, downing the other herself. He blinked owlishly at her for a moment, then the command seemed to register, and he lifted the mug to his lips. His hands trembled a little, and Miri wrapped hers around his, supporting them and tilting the cup so he could drink without spilling.

When he had finished the entire mugful, he leaned back against Linx and made a slight face, raking his fingers through his short brown hair, the damp strands standing straight up over his brow.

"Not as foul as the usual Healer's stuff," he muttered faintly, and Miri rolled her eyes.

"We don't make things taste bad on purpose!" Even though she kept her voice quiet, her reply surprised even herself with its fierceness.

Rinton blinked at her again, then turned to look past her, to the steady gray rain that half-obscured the road beside them.

"It didn't ease up," he observed.

"No," Miri replied. "And there's nothing *quite* so cold as a winter rain. We'll be soaked before we even make the Waystation."

:*We* have *to get to Haven.*: Linx's voice was firm in both of their minds.

"Of course," Rinton said, but his words were drowned out by Miri's decided "Absolutely not."

Both Herald and Companion turned their heads to stare in astonishment at her. Miri felt something in her quail under their scrutiny, especially the deep blue gaze of the Companion, but she forced herself to sit quietly, without giving in to the childish urge to squirm.

"*You,*" she said, looking straight at Linx, "might have the superb strength and quick recovery of the Companions on your side, but *he* does not." She nodded at Rinton. "I can't say for sure what it is, but his mind has suffered injury, even if he does not notice it or chooses to ignore it. And the *worst* thing in that case is overexertion. Haven is impossible. It's going to be dusk soon, and while *you* can see in the dark even in the rain, my mare cannot. Again, absolutely not." She folded her arms and summoned as best she could the stern aura of Healer Gelsen. No one ever dared countermand Gelsen's directives to his patients.

A long silence, with Rinton and his Companion clearly arguing between themselves over Miri's words.

"But I *feel* all right," Rinton began. "Just a headache . . ."

:The worst headache you've ever felt?: Linx was projecting into Mirideh's mind again, and she buried a smile. It seemed he was on her side already, even though he was the one who first said they had to get to Haven. Perhaps she had scared him with her talk of damage in Rinton's mind. Or perhaps he had learned something from the other Companions in Haven that took the edge off of his urgency. Either way, she knew that what she declared was the absolute truth. Forcing on all the way to Haven was the worst thing possible for someone in Rinton's state.

"You are outnumbered, Herald," she said with a slight smile. "If it weren't for the rain, I wouldn't even want to move you from this place. But the Waystation will be a far better place for recovery. With a night's rest, you *might* be able to manage the rest of the journey tomorrow morning." Her own nascent headache had eased enough, and she stood, shaking the oiled cloak and draping it on a branch to drip out a little bit while she stowed her mugs and tightened the mare's saddle girth.

Rinton sat upright, and Linx gathered his legs beneath him and stood, tossing his head and stamping his silvery hooves, tail twitching as accumulated water droplets flew around them. Mirideh giggled at the sight of a usually dignified Companion behaving like a soaked dog, then leaned over to help Rinton to his own feet. The Herald placed one hand on Linx's withers for balance and support while Mirideh hoisted the saddle back into place and fastened the girth.

"Skinny you may be, but I still couldn't lift you . . ." she began, but Linx forestalled her words by bending his forelegs to go down to his knees, so she only needed to help balance the Herald as he swung one leg over the Companion's back. Once he was in the saddle, Linx carefully rose, and Rinton worked his feet into the stirrups. Mirideh stared in amazement.

"It's something all Heralds and Companions practice," Rinton said when he noticed her reaction. "Far easier with a Companion than a horse. If I can get into the saddle, I can practically sleep here, and Linx can keep me upright." He settled his oiled cloak over his shoulders while Miri eyed the sorrel mare. There was no chance of getting her horse to cooperate in a trick like that.

"She's sweet and biddable enough, but it's a good thing I'm in better shape than you right now." Grasping reins and pommel in one hand, she hooked one foot into the stirrup and hauled herself into the saddle. Securing her own cloak, she gave one last glance around to make sure they had left few traces of their presence under the sheltering tree.

Linx tossed his white head, and the four of them moved back out into the rain, Kiyan flapping along overhead.

As they traveled, Miri hid a smile. Even though Linx had seemed restored, several times she found herself reining in her mare to a slower pace to keep from crowding up behind the Companion. Rinton occasionally swayed in the saddle, but even to her concerned eye seemed in no danger of falling off of Linx's back.

Twilight had settled in by the time they arrived at the Waystation, and Miri leaped from her horse to help Rinton dismount. He stood, leaning most of his weight against his Companion, while she fumigated the tiny shelter with the aromatics all traveling Heralds carried with them. There was only one bedbox, so she put Rinton's bedroll there and guided him to sit while she tended to Linx and the mare. Only when their mounts were settled did she set about lighting a fire, sweeping out the building and gathering what they would need for the night.

Rinton sat staring at the fire, head resting on one hand, slowly sipping another cup of restorative herbs while she moved around him. Unbidden, memories arose of her first night in a Waystation, the second night she had spent on Valdemaran soil. Then, she had sat in anxious confusion, watching while a Herald, whom she had always been told to fear, had tended to all of her needs. This time, it was she who had taken charge of him.

"If some of the folks back in Karse could see me now, taking care of one of the Demon-Riders . . ." She let the words trail off. Some of the villagers she had encountered when visiting her grandmother had been less than enthusiastic about the alliance with Valdemar, and viewed her return with some suspicion. "They wouldn't know what to make of me."

:You are not as you were, and nor is he.:

Mirideh snorted lightly, and Rinton looked up at her in question. "Your Companion is eavesdropping from outside and has chosen to share his opinions with me."

As if I needed proof that I am not who I was. Not only have I spent years among the Demon-Riders, learning to use proscribed Gifts, one of the White Demons has even talked in my head. Thank Vkandis that Grandmother Fidesa never taught her people to hate, like so many of His priests did. I don't think I could have overcome that.

Rinton glanced at the still-open door, out into the deepening darkness where Linx and the mare munched on the grain Miri had given them. His face took on the "listening" expression common among Heralds.

"Linx says that there has been some magical . . . *something* . . . that has happened in Haven, which involved a great deal of magical power. It doesn't make any sense to me. But all the Companions and Heralds were affected, especially those closer to Haven, and those who have Mage Gifts." He glanced downward, seeming embarrassed. "He says I'm one of the ones with Mage Gifts. I don't even know what that really means, other than Linx says I have a lot to learn."

"That makes a bit of sense to me," Miri said. "Your mind felt as though it had been singed, as if a lightning bolt had gone through it. It was far more severe than the usual effects of overuse of Gifts. If there was some sort of strong . . . overflow? . . . in your mind, if you were sensitive to it because of that unknown Gift, everything would be left raw."

Rinton nodded. "Raw is a good word for it." He yawned widely, then glanced around. "Waystations are not known for comfort . . ."

"I've been in them before, remember? This time I'll be the one to sleep on the floor. It's no worse than taking foal watch or staying up all night with a patient in the House of Healing. Better, in fact, because I can really sleep, and Linx can wake me if he senses anything wrong with you." She took the empty cup from him. "Now, sleep. The morning is time enough to think on this more."

The Herald was asleep before she had finished rinsing his cup. Mirideh moved to the doorway, standing and looking out into the darkness. A lighter shape loomed at her side, the firelight from the Waystation drawn to highlight Linx's form.

:Well done, Healer Mirideh.:

Miri gaped at the title.

"How could a Companion determine that? I've barely finished my classes at Healers' Collegium, and there are still more tests, I'm sure." Some days, it seemed that all her time in the Houses of Healing was an examination of some sort or another.

:This Companion believes that the name is right, and earned. I do not think you will be in Trainee Greens after our return.:

She blinked, considering, her thoughts drifting over the day, her decisions and actions related to Rinton's care. In a way, the whole day had been a test of a different type, one that Linx clearly believed she had passed. She slowly nodded, and a subtle warmth and pride spread in her heart.

"Thank you," she murmured to the luminous figure beside her, then closed the Waystation door.

Banking the fire, she curled up on her bedroll, facing the low bedbox where Rinton gently snored. Tomorrow, they would return home, to Haven, and to whatever faced them there.

Expected Consequences
Elizabeth Vaughan

To Lady Cera of Sandbriar, in the Kingdom of Valdemar,

    Greetings,
    Please accept the thanks of the Healers' Collegium and The Crown for the supply of wild kandace. It arrived safely and is deeply appreciated. Once again, Master Jebren has demonstrated his gifts to us.
    The Crown has given leave that the funds we would normally remit to you be instead applied as a credit to Sandbriar's future taxes. Please also be assured that the Collegium is more than willing to enter into this arrangement for the next two years. The Wars sadly depleted our supplies, and our harvest will be some time in recovering.
    On a personal note, I was wondering how Master Xenos is getting along. I understand that the Healing of the injured Herald is proceeding well, but, to be honest, milady, it's just that I've had a request... more like a demand ... to recall him to the Collegium.
    In any event, please accept our grateful thanks for all of your assistance.

Naritha,
Assistant Dean, Healers' Collegium, Haven,
in the Kingdom of Valdemar.

"Mold." Lady Cera of Sandbriar stared at the contents of the pan with dismay. The cold fat with flower blooms pressed into it was dotted with specks of black.

"Mold," confirmed Bella, who'd worked with her on this project.

"Moisture," Master Jebren said firmly.

"Any idiot knows that." Xenos sniffed.

Everyone stared at Healer Xenos, standing in Cera's root cellar in his Green robes, looking down his nose at them. While Cera held him in high regard for his Gift of Healing, his personality left much to be desired.

"Xenos," Jebren said even more firmly. "Perhaps you can aid someone else, somewhere else?"

Xenos huffed and exited dramatically.

Cera and Bella exchanged glances of relief.

"The problem is moisture," Jebren continued. The corners of his eyes crinkled as he gave them an apologetic smile. Master Apothecary Jebren had come to Sandbriar with Healer Xenos and was everything the Healer was not: warm, friendly and willing to share his knowledge.

"But the flowers need to be fresh," Cera protested.

"Fresh, yes, but as dry as they can be," Jebren said. "You need to cloth-dry them and then hang them from the rafters for a day before you press them into the fat. Also, you need a thinner layer of fat in the pan. This is just a bit too thick."

Cera puffed out her exasperation.

Jebren shook his head at her. "None of that now, you have done well, considering you were relying on your memories of your mother's methods." He placed the pan back on the table near her. Cera caught a whiff of spice and flowers, another memory of her mother's stillroom. Jebren continued. "We'll clean this up and start again."

Cera and Bella started to scrape the pans clean. "Once we get the technique down, we can train some others to do this, Bella," Cera said. "I don't want to take you from the kitchens."

Bella rolled her eyes. "I might just stay down here all day if that man keeps getting underfoot. I shoo him away, but how is a body to get any work done when he follows me around like a half-starved cat?"

Jebren choked, coughing. "Sorry. Swallowed wrong."

Cera looked at Bella seriously. "Has he been rude to you?"

"No, milady, not to me, but that tongue of his stings something fierce." Bella frowned. "All in everyone's business and never a kind word."

"He did save Herald Helgara," Cera pointed out.

"Aye, and didn't that poor Herald get her brains all shook." Bella nodded. "Very well. I'll put up with him."

"No," Cera said firmly. "If he is going to hang about the kitchens, put him to work."

Bella and Jebren both stared at her. Cera calmly continued to scrape out a pan. "What about those puffs you make with all the butter and sweets. The ones that take the better part of a day. Weren't you going to make those as a treat?"

"Well, yes, b-but-" Bella sputtered.

"Put him to work with the kneading and folding the dough." Cera looked up with a smile.

"But, milady, he's a Healer and noble born." Bella protested, even as a smile broke out on her face.

"Idle hands make only mischief," Cera shrugged. "If he protests, tell him I said either work or leave the kitchen."

Bella set her shoulders and laughed. "Well, just see if I don't. I'll go get some more of the pure fat for the pans." They could hear her chortle as she climbed the stairs.

Jebren raised an eyebrow at Cera. "I doubt anyone has ever made Xenos work, other than to hone his Gift."

"Maybe they should," Cera said. "If he doesn't like kitchens, maybe I can put him to work in the barns."

"Shearing sheep?" Jebren asked.

"Mucking stalls," Cera said.

Jebren laughed.

Cera smiled at the man. Master Apothecary Jebren was a delight to work with. He'd been hard at work the last few weeks since the Festival, seeing to the shipment of wild kandace for the Healer's Collegium. Between his skill and her people's work, they'd turned a profit for

Sandbriar, and perhaps they had turned a corner on funds for the future.

"I just wanted to thank you—" Cera blurted out at the same time Jebren spoke.

"I can't thank you enough—" he said

They each stuttered to a halt, laughing.

"You first," he said.

"Thank you for teaching this to me." Cera gestured to the pans. "For teaching all of us."

"It's the least I could do for you." Jebren flushed. "For Sandbriar and Valdemar. And let me offer you my thanks for the use of the stillroom and the drying shed and the garden. During the Tedrel War I was kept in Haven, creating medicines. It's good to be back in the garden, amidst growing things."

They both looked at each other for the longest awkward moment. Jebren looked as though he wished to say more, so Cera waited, hesitating, feeling an odd flutter in her chest. She opened her mouth, trying to find words—

Bella clattered down the stairs with a bucket of clean lard. "Here we be—" She drew herself up, looking at both of them with a quizzical expression. "Have I interrupted?"

"No, no," they both exclaimed, busying themselves with the pans.

"Well, then we'd best get this done," Bella said. "The hot's starting to rise outside."

"I wanted to check on the *chirras*," Cera said, starting to press the fat into the clean pans. "But I'll be quick."

"I was going to work in the stillroom this afternoon," Jebren said and then defended himself from Bella's scowl with a shoulder shrug. "It's cool in there."

"Northerners." Bella shook her wooden scraper at him. "You're not used to our heat and our ways. The hot will get worse as the weeks go on, and the afternoon rest is the best way to deal with it. But you'd not be the first out of Haven to work himself sick."

"She's right," Cera said. "Our heat can catch you off guard."

"Then I'll take your advice," Jebren conceded. *Another nice thing about him,* Cera thought.

"See that you do," Bella said. "And I will warn Sir-High-and-Mighty. Now, is this the right thickness for the fat?"

Cera stepped out of the manor house and sucked in a breath as the heat hit her face.

The sun was almost at its zenith, and the morning cool was rapidly fading.

There was a large merchant caravan unloading at the gates, and one of her guards called her over. "Someone to speak to you, Lady."

One of the merchants whipped off his hat. "Lady Cera, I wish you well this day. I've news of the road for you."

"Merchant Hurlbert, my thanks for the well-wishes. The same to you and yours." Cera smiled. "You need to get out of the hot soon."

"Aye, we've a place down by the river that's just right. Perfect with shade and cool water. We'll be there as soon as we unload, Lady. But that's not the news." He swept his hat back up into place. "You've a lordling headed for you, out of Rethwellan. All starched collars and black clothing and a stick far up his . . . attitude, beggin' your pardon."

"Did he give you a name?" Cera asked, putting her own hat on her head.

"Nay, Lady." Hurlbert chortled. "That kind ne'er shared his name with any. We even tried to offer cold water and to sell him lighter clothes, but he'd not deign to hear us. I suspect he stopped at the last town before this and will ignore them as well. Fair sure he's headed your way."

"My thanks, Hurlbert." Cera gave him a nod and a smile. "Safe travels to you."

Hurlbert bowed low and then called to his people to move the wagons out.

Cera started toward the *chirra* barns, waving greetings to the people she saw. For the next handful of weeks, the "hot" would dictate the life of her people. Work would slow as the crops grew under the sun. The worry would be keeping the animals cool, especially her northern-born *chirras.* If they could learn to adapt to Sandbriar, she had high hopes for the soft wool of their undercoats.

Everyone was in the process of withdrawing into the shade. Until now, she hadn't appreciated the way the buildings were built to deal with the brutal heat. Windows placed to catch the breezes and channel them into the depths of the structure. Wide porches to shade the houses and thick trees to block the sun's incessant rays from the roofs.

Who on earth would be traveling to see her in this weather? A suitor, perhaps. That was one of the other benefits of the "hot"; it kept all but the most determined suitors away in this season. She'd made it known that she was a working landowner, with little time other than after the dinner hour to sit and be courted. Since the heat made travel difficult for man and beast, it normally would have afforded her a respite.

Until now.

Cera shrugged. The idea of a suitor arriving no longer caused her to worry. She'd make her own choices—to her benefit and to Sandbriar's.

She passed the building where one of her previous would-be suitors, Emerson the tapestry weaver, had set up his loom, still working on finishing his grandmother's tapestry. No sound of the shuttles being worked, so he was probably preparing to rest for the afternoon as well. Thankfully, Emerson was far more interested in her wool than in herself, and he had made that clear to all and sundry.

She saw Withrin Ashkevron peering out the barn door and hurried her steps, not wanting to keep him waiting. He smiled as she came up to the large barn doors. "Just about to hang the coolers."

Ager, once the old Lord's *chirra* herder, was there as well, and he nodded at Cera as she walked in. Some of the stable boys were tying long strips of linen to rods and filing troughs of water that sat in the doorways where the breeze came in. Men were in the lofts to haul the rods and wet linen up and hang them, letting the strips hang down, cooling the barn.

The *chirras* were all settled in the center of the barn, chewing their cuds, blinking their sleepy eyes at her. Every once in a while, one ear would twitch and then all the ears would twitch, like a wave. Cera smiled at the sight and then gave Ager a hopeful look.

The thin, spare man shrugged. "So far, they are doing well. They've spaced themselves out, see, so that the breeze gets between them."

"No signs of heat stress," Withrin said. "Time will tell if they can truly get accustomed. It is hot," he said ruefully, wiping sweat from his forehead.

"Aye, ya need to adjust too, northerner," Ager said kindly. "Your first time in the 'hot.' Best get ya to a cool place and hunker down. I'll stay with the beasts."

"Emerson's stopped working," Cera said innocently. "At least, I didn't hear him at the loom."

"Oh, er," Withrin grabbed his hat, grinning sheepishly. "Well, I'll just go check on him, shall I?"

Ager and Cera exchanged a glance as he trotted out of the barn. "Think he'll ever work up the nerve?" Ager asked softly.

Cera arched an eyebrow. "Will you?"

She regretted it immediately when Ager's face fell. "Alaina and I seem to be on the outs," he said gruffly. "I need to make sure the boys keep the troughs full. Excuse me, milady."

So much for being the perfect lord of the manor. Cera could have kicked herself.

"Best leave that alone," Old Meron's voice came from one of the stalls.

Cera walked over to him, concerned. Old Meron's brain storm had left him with a limp arm and walking with a cane, but he prided himself on keeping watch over the barns. "You shouldn't be out in the 'hot'," she scolded.

"Just checkin' on guests," he said, nodding into the stall. His three dogs were flopped down on the floor, their tongues hanging out.

Cera peered in.

A Companion lay within, somehow glowing white

against the dark wood of the stall walls. Curled up in the fresh bed of hay next to Stonas was Helgara, the Herald who had been attacked by bandits before the Midsummer Festival.

"Helgara," Cera said softly. "How are you?"

"Lady Cera," Helgara opened drowsy eyes. "Still having trouble with my eyes. Dizziness, too, but much better than dead."

Stonas snorted his agreement.

"Xenos does what he can," Helgara continued. "But some of the healing must be left to time and nature." She smiled. "Not that he admits that."

"Sounds like Xenos," Cera said. "Will you be cool enough here?"

"Yes," Helgara yawned. "I wanted to go out on patrol with Gareth and the Guard that Haven sent. But I was overruled."

Stonas snorted again, his opinion fairly clear.

"Stonas is right," Cera said. "And it was good of Haven to send us support. Those bandits were getting too bold. Sleep well," she added, as Helgara's eyes drifted closed.

Old Meron was waiting when she came out of the stall. "Did you see they caught that old ewe, finally?" He nodded to one of the open pens where one of the biggest sheep Cera had ever seen was penned. The ewe put her head over the pen wall and loudly bleated her displeasure.

"Where did they find her?" Cera asked.

"Down by the river, hiding in the bushes, where I said she'd be. Hates shearing, she does, but mighty fine wool off that old girl." Old Meron limped over as his dogs followed. "Keeping her off feed, so her stomach's empty when we shear her this afternoon. Teach them that wants to learn how to shear and skirt a fleece."

"You best get yourself home," Cera scolded.

"Clacking like an old woman now, are ya?" Old Meron grinned, but he put his hat on. "Come on boys, time for cool water and sleeping off the hot." He mock-glared back at Cera. "You too, milady."

Cera laughed and headed back to the manor. Alaina

would be waiting, with cool cloths, and her bed turned down. But as she strode through the yard, a runner came up, breathing hard. "You're wanted at the gate, milady."

Probably that suitor Hurlbert had warned her of. Cera nodded to him, and started toward the main gate.

She ran into Gareth, coming to find her, a stormy look on his face. "Don't understand a word they say, but I don't like anyone who treats horses that way," he muttered to her.

Cera nodded, looked toward the gate—and lost her breath.

Lord Thelkenpothonar, Sinmonkelrath's father, sat on his fine horse, observing all about him with disdain. When he saw her, an all too familiar scowl crossed his face, one she'd seen on her late husband's face many a time.

Usually just before he raised his fists to her.

Cera froze.

Lord Thelken dismounted and then stumbled, swaying as he grabbed for his horse's mane. The man was flushed, his shirt and coat sweat-stained. His people looked no better, and the sweating horses were breathing heavily and drooling.

Anger flooded through her, that anyone would treat his people and animals that way. Cera breathed, then moved forward. Her people were milling about as Lord Thelken's men tried to assist him.

As she drew close, Lord Thelken glared at her. "I've come for the truth, girl," he spat in Rethwellan.

"I might not speak that tongue, Lady Cera," Gareth spoke in Valdemaran. "But I know rude when I hear it."

"Greetings, Lord Thelkenpothonar," Cera kept her tone polite in the face of his righteous indignation. She gave Gareth a quelling glance, and he stepped back, still scowling at the man.

"Let's see to the comfort of you and your people first." She continued in Rethwellan. "My people will see to you—" she narrowed her eyes, "—*and* your animals. We will talk before the evening meal."

Thelken sputtered, but she ignored him. She repeated her words in Valdemaran for her own people, who moved swiftly. Alaina was in the door of the Great Hall; she could talk to these people.

She gave Lord Thelken a cool glance, turned on her heel, and left him standing in the yard.

Cera's room was ready; Alaina had already turned down the bed. Cera stripped down to her underclothes, wiped down with the cloths, and climbed into bed. She stared up at the ceiling for a moment, half-expecting to start fretting about Thelken, about what she would say, about how he would react. Instead, she found herself musing about the stupidity of the man, dragging his people and animals through this heat without a thought for their welfare. Cera sniffed, relaxed against the cool pillows, and drifted off to sleep.

"The sun's easing, milady," Alaina's voice came softly through Cera's door. "Lord Thelkenpothonar in the biggest guest chamber, and he and all his people are still asleep. I'll be down in the kitchens—"

"Alaina, wait." Cera rose, rubbing her eyes. "I wanted to ask you something."

Alaina walked farther into the room, her eyes down, her face wooden.

"Is something wrong?" Cera pulled on a clean dress. "Between you and Ager?"

The wail that followed caught her off guard. Alaina buried her face in her hands and sank to her knees, sobbing.

"Alaina," Cera rushed over, dropped down beside her and took her in her arms. Alaina was incoherent, crying and moaning. Her handmaiden, who had been with her through all the turmoil of her marriage; all Cera could do was rock her and make comforting sounds.

Marga appeared in the doorway. "What's all this now?"

Cera shook her head, still holding the weeping girl.

"Ah," Marga said. "Wait a bit," and she disappeared.

Cera kept rocking and making soothing murmurs. The sobs grew weaker, but Alaina would only shake her head at Cera's questions.

"Alaina . . ." Ager was in the doorway, then kneeling

on the floor, taking Alaina into his arms. Marga was in the doorway, gesturing for Cera. "We'll leave them for a bit." She pulled Cera from her own bedroom.

"But—" Cera tried to ask, but Marga hushed her as they went down the stairs and ignored her questions until she pushed Cera into the kitchen. "I only asked Alaina about Ager and she burst into tears."

"Probably because she is pregnant," Xenos said airily. He was standing at the table, wearing an apron, his Healer's Greens covered in flour. There was a lump of something on the table in front of him that might have been dough.

"What?" Cera squeaked and dropped on a bench. "Pregnant?"

"Any idiot could see that," Xenos said.

"Xenos," Bella scolded. "You need to be thinking about that dough, not anyone else's business. Take the bowl and towel and go set it in the pantry to rise. And mind yourself."

"Fine," Xenos snapped, and he did so with his usual dramatic flair.

"Pregnant." Cera looked at Marga. "Did you know?"

"I knew something was wrong." Marga sat on one of the benches. "And I knew it was something to do with Ager, but not that."

"Blessed Trine," Cera said, taking a cup of cooled tea from Bella. "Whatever shall we—"

"None of that now," Marga said firmly. "She'd not be the first to get caught up in the Midsummer celebrations, and not the last to find herself in a family way as a result. They'll make their own choices, and we'll support them in whatever they decide."

Cera nodded, but she couldn't help doubting that it would be that simple. Her own experience with marriage had not been a good one. She wouldn't let her handmaiden—her friend—be forced into marriage if there was any chance she would be trapped within it.

As she herself had once been.

The door opened. Alaina and Ager walked in arm-in-arm, both their faces tear-stained but smiling.

Ager advanced and knelt at Cera's feet, still holding Alaina's hand. "Lady Cera, I would ask for your blessing. I have asked Alaina to marry me, and she has said yes."

"Alaina?" Cera looked at her friend.

Alaina came and sat beside her on the bench. "Lady, I am expecting."

A snort came from the pantry.

"I was scared to tell him, to tell anyone, out of shame and fear." Alaina looked at Ager with stars in her eyes. "But all's well, now."

"You don't have to wed—" Cera started, but Alaina shook her head.

"I don't need to, no," she said. "But I want to." Ager was still on his knees, and Alaina reached for his hand.

Ager spoke. "We both know, Lady, that love is a risk." His voice cracked. "A terrifying, wonderful, heart-wrenching, exciting risk. We'd ask your blessing on our journey."

"You have it," Cera said. "But I would ask that you delay the ceremony until the Midwinter celebrations. Give yourselves time to make sure that this is what you truly want."

Ager and Alaina both nodded. Cera leaned forward and gave the couple an awkward hug as Marga and Bella exclaimed their congratulations, coming around for their own embraces.

"Is all the blubbering and dramatics done? Is it safe to come out now?" Xenos called from the pantry.

"Yes, yes!" Bella laughed as she and Marga both hugged the lucky couple.

Once the "hot" broke that afternoon, Cera found reasons to be out and about in the barns and the outbuildings. It wasn't that she was avoiding Thelken. She was letting her temper cool. She did find herself drawn to the shearing shed, where something of a fuss was being raised.

"What in the name of the Trine?" she demanded as she walked inside.

"Teaching the shearing," Old Meron announced over the crowd watching. He'd a stool by the door and a clear view of the action. "The young ones and them that wants to learn." He nodded at the fuss.

Cera blinked. "Jebren?"

Jebren was standing in the center of the crowd, dressed in light work clothes, a fierce look of concentration on his face. Two men were wrestling the ewe up and onto its butt, pressing its back against the apothecary's chest. The ewe was bawling protests, its legs sprawled out in front of it.

Jebren wrapped one arm under the ewe's leg, forcing it up so that he had the ewe's head pulled back against his shoulder.

"Got her?" Young Meron asked.

Jebren grunted, bracing himself as they released the ewe. It struggled a bit, but he gripped the animal firmly.

"Tradition, ya know." Old Meron grinned at Cera. "Teach 'em shearing by first holding the sheep."

Cera gave him a look. "Tradition, yes, with small lambs. That ewe has to weigh as much as Jebren," she said pointedly.

"Oh, aye, aye," Old Meron didn't even try to keep the joy out of his tone. "That old ewe is a tough old bitch, oldest, loudest, crankiest—"

Bleating its unhappiness loudly.

Young Meron had the clippers. "Gonna start on," he warned.

Jebren grunted.

Meron started in. The ewe screamed defiance and started kicking. "Don't let go!" Old Meron shouted, as the others called encouragement.

Jebren struggled with the sheep, holding his own to Cera's surprise. Young Meron was working in long strokes, and the fleece was coming off in one long strip . . . until Jebren made a fatal mistake.

He let the ewe get its front foot free.

The ewe bucked like a stung horse, struggling and kicking out, knocking Jebren to the ground flat on his back, falling back on top of him.

There were hoots and cheering from all around as some of the men moved in to help. To Jebren's credit, he wrapped both arms around its neck and managed to keep a firm hold.

Which was, in point of fact, his second mistake.

The ewe twisted in his grip, and struggled, bringing its rear leg down on Jebren's groin.

Every male sucked in a horrified breath, with a few groans and guilty laughter.

Cera covered her mouth with her hand.

Jebren's eyes bulged out, but bless the man, he hung on, but his legs curled up into the air. Which rather gave the ewe more of a target.

"Let go!" Cera called out.

Jebren gave her a startled look, as if he hadn't known she was there.

"I got her, I got her," Young Meron grabbed the head. "Mind your—"

The ewe stomped Jebren again as Meron dragged her off.

Jebren wheezed painfully as he curled into a ball, his hands covering . . . Cera looked away. "Perhaps . . . I'd best fetch the Healer," she said, her voice quivering as she backed away and fled toward the kitchen.

Bella was scolding Xenos as she entered. "—you didn't let the dough chill long enough, nor fold it enough. What did you expect would happen?"

"All the joy is gone," Xenos announced as he dropped a hard lump of a pastry on to the table.

"Listen to you," Bella scoffed. "One mistake and you give up? You'll get more dough and try again, that's what you do. That's how you learn."

Xenos sighed in resignation. "I'll pitch these—"

"You'll not waste food in *my* kitchen. They'll make teething biscuits for the babes."

Bella rolled her eyes, then caught sight of Cera. She raised a questioning eyebrow.

"One of the ewes kicked Jebren in the, er, crotch," Cera said. "Although why he wanted to learn shearing is beyond me."

"You really are rather dense," Xenos observed.

"Excuse me?" Cera demanded, even as Bella sputtered her indignation.

"Nothing." Xenos started to remove his apron. "I will go heal his bits for the sake of future generations."

Later, Cera sat and waited on one of the upper porches, cooled by the shade and the breeze, watching the sun drift down behind the hills. The *chirras* were out with their shepherds, getting in an evening feed, as were the rest of the livestock, coming out of the shade to graze. She could faintly hear the shuttle of the loom going back and forth, and voices in the kitchen as the staff prepared the evening meal.

Had it really been over a year since her husband's death? Since she'd been given these lands by Queen Selenay? Given a new life and freedom? It felt longer to be honest. So much had changed, herself included.

It wasn't perfect. She still struggled, as did her people. For every battle she faced, for every problem she solved, a new one arose.

Still.

Cera smiled. Perhaps perfection wasn't the goal. Perhaps freedom meant struggle. Perhaps she needed to celebrate every victory, no matter how small, and try again in the face of every failure.

She could call so many people to aid her with this confrontation. Her people, her handmaiden, there was even a Herald close by. She was truly blessed by the Trine with her new family.

She didn't summon them, although she knew they hovered.

She finally had what she needed to face Lord Thelkenpothonar.

One thing was certain; she was done with Rethwellan names. Honestly, all those historical syllables. Cera shook her head, and promised any future children they would not be so burdened. For they would be of Sandbriar and Valdemar.

Cera sat, hands folded in her lap, and waited. She still felt a flutter of fear, or uncertainty. But the only way out was to do.

A sound of steps. Athelnor bowed to Lord Thelken and gave her an anxious look. She smiled at him and shook her head. Athelnor smiled in return, bowed, and left.

"Ceraratha." Thelken stood there, still radiating outrage.

"Thelken." Cera gestured to the bench opposite hers. "Please, sit."

He was still in his sweat-stained black clothing, but he had shed his coat and unbuttoned his high collar. "I want the truth," he demanded, refusing a seat, so righteous and indignant. "Not the half-lies the Rethwellan Royal Court gives me, or the Crown of Valdemar. I want *you* to tell me what happened to my son."

Cera nodded and did just that. She told him of their life in the Rethwellan Court, how Sinmonkelrath had been one of Prince Karathanelan's supporters and sycophants. How they had traveled to Valdemar, and how Sinmon had fallen in with the Prince's plan to seduce, win, and impregnate Queen Selenay.

How the Prince had achieved his goal—and then treacherously plotted to assassinate his own wife in order to become regent.

Thelken sank down to the bench as he listened, growing paler with her every word.

Cera explained how the Prince, Sinmon, and the other supporters had ambushed the Queen. How they had died fighting the Queen and her protectors. "There was no hunting accident," she concluded. "But both Crowns preferred silence instead of the ugly truth."

"My perfect, bright boy . . ." Thelken whispered, shaking his head, the arrogance gone from his face. "Always a dreamer. Always a schemer. Always falling in with others' plans, always looking for the easy path." His proud features spasmed with pain before he lifted his head to glare at Cera. "You could have stopped—"

"No," Cera said. "I could not." She opened her mouth

to go on, to tell of the abuses she had suffered at Sinmon's hands. But no. Might as well try to talk a sheep into shedding its fleece.

"I don't suppose you were pregnant when . . ." Thelken's voice trailed off and he flushed red.

Cera blinked and then narrowed her eyes at the thought that he'd try to claim otherwise. "No, Thelken," she replied. "It's been over a year."

He nodded and looked off in a long, painful silence. "I've lost both my sons . . ." he whispered.

"You are welcome to rest here overnight," Cera said briskly. Perhaps too firmly, but her willingness to be polite was stretching thin. "However, I am sure you will wish to depart early in the morning for your home." She paused. "If you wish to go to Haven and demand more information, you can, of course. I doubt the Crown will offer you much more than I have. Perhaps even less."

"I . . ." Any argument seemed to drain out of him. "Yes . . . perhaps you are right."

Cera softened, a bit. The man was clearly devastated. "You have daughters, Thelken."

"Daughters?" Thelken looked confused. "Well, of course, but they are not capable of—"

He cut his words off and flushed again. "Your pardon, Ceraratha."

"Cera," she said calmly.

Thelken cleared his throat. "Your father told me that as well when I went to see him. He served me jasmine tea and denied knowing any more than I did about Sinmon's death. Does he know the truth?"

"No. It wasn't his story to tell," Cera said. "It was mine." She'd had enough; more than enough. "I will see you again at the evening meal." She gave him a clear nod of dismissal.

He stared for a moment, then got to his feet and jerked a shallow bow in her direction. He blundered toward the door, where she knew someone would guide him back to his chambers.

She rose then, moved over to the balcony and looked out. Over the fields, the stock, and the people.

Her lands, her people, her Sandbriar.

She knew full well the pressure Thelken felt. To have an heir, someone to care for her land and people when she was no longer able. Such a thing promised continuity and stability. The pressure would mount for an heir of her body. But perhaps, just perhaps, there was another way . . .

Jebren was working in the garden below, clipping and pruning. He didn't seem to be suffering any lasting effects of the ewe's ire.

He lifted his head as if sensing her regard and spotted her. For a moment he looked embarrassed, even a bit . . . sheepish. But then he raised his hand in greeting.

Cera lifted her hand in response.

She'd been idle long enough. Cera stepped away from the balcony and headed to the door. There was work to be done, true enough, but first she thought she might go down to Jebren's stillroom and ask if he knew anything about growing jasmine for tea.

To Lady Cera of Sandbriar, in the Kingdom of Valdemar,

> *Hail, Lady Cera,*
> *Please forgive any lingering rudeness I left in my departure. My grief overwhelmed my manners.*
> *My journey home gave me a great deal of time to think and consider your words. I have also sought out your father's wise counsel. I have also consulted my wife in this matter.*
> *May I entreat you to take my eldest daughter as a foster for a year? With her consent, we have delayed seeking a suitor for her hand for that period. I believe that she would learn much from you in that time. Not just about the management of a holding, either.*
> *You would have our grateful thanks for all of your assistance.*

Thelkenpothonar, Lord of Rethwellan

Burrowing Owl, Hidden No More

Dayle A. Dermatis

The Golden Compass Tavern was crowded and noisy, but unlike normal taverns, it was crowded with scholars, and the noise wasn't from increasingly inebriated drinkers arguing with each other but rather from healthy debates between students about engineering principles.

Almost every evening, the Blue-clad Artificer students left their Collegium after their final classes and descended upon the Golden Compass to discuss ideas and plans and concepts.

In the back room, the Master Artificers conducted their own conversations and debates, only emerging when there was an emergency or their presence was otherwise requested, or when they wanted to honor a particularly promising student with a mentorship.

That, Kya coveted most of all.

Except she wasn't a student Artificer.

The Golden Compass was no ordinary tavern, and Kya was no ordinary barmaid.

Kya wove between the tables, carrying plates of spice-rubbed, sizzling skewered meat or toasted cheese, bread, and drinks. As she deposited the orders at various tables, she cast a keen eye over the papers spread across the wooden surfaces.

Here, she was known as Burrow, or Bur, a nickname her father had given her because she reminded him of a burrowing owl, quiet and smart, rumpled and hiding, but aware of her surroundings. Kya had cropped her wispy, white-blond hair short so it was easier to care for—she had more important things to think about and spend her time on, and (she hoped) she'd be less likely to be recognized—and along with her wide brown eyes and slight stature, she did rather look like an owl.

(Unsurprisingly, her mother hated the nickname.)

Here, nobody knew her past, and nobody knew her desires. Here, she was barely noticed as long as she brought the right food and drink to the right people. Nobody noticed her, and she preferred it that way. She assumed nobody cared. Certainly her parents didn't, except when it came to grooming her to be someone she didn't want to be.

Here, she hoped, she could change her future.

She slid a wooden plate of dough-wrapped sausages onto a table, careful to avoid the scatter of papers. All of the food was designed to be eaten with a minimum of a mess, so as to not drip on or smear the paperwork. Someone thanked her without even looking up. She lingered for a moment, perusing the nearest sketch, that of a threshing machine, with measurements and parts identified and notations on how this design would be faster.

Kya had been obsessed with how things worked for as long as she could remember. The eldest, she was expected to take over the estate from her parents, but her interests had always diverted her attention elsewhere. When she was old enough to realize her parents despaired at all the things she took apart to learn how they worked, she had learned how to put them back together after she had examined them. Once she had narrowly escaped being run over by a wagon she was lying underneath, trying to understand how the axles and wheels worked.

Soon after that, her parents—largely her mother—insisted she learned the noble arts, as befitting an heir. But Kya spent more time figuring out how to make the spinning wheels and looms more effective and adjusting them accordingly than she did making thread or cloth.

Spending time weaving and creating wasn't a bad

thing, all told. And her math abilities meant she'd do a spectacular job running the estate's finances—after all, her father said, it was far better to handle the books personally than entrust them to someone else.

But the idea of having to host tea parties, dress up and greet guests, or meet with the estate folk to hear their requests . . . Kya shuddered. She found curtsying and other forms of "noble behavior" to be outdated and dull, but, more importantly, she had no interest in idle chatter with people she didn't know or care about, who didn't share her interests.

Here at the Golden Compass, she ached to be part of a group, adding her voice to the exchange of ideas. *These* were people she wanted to talk to.

Kya lingered at another table, unnoticed, looking over the shoulder of a boy, his cheeks flushed because he kept rubbing them, as he worked on his plans for a pulley system to extract ore from a mine. He was almost there, but Kya saw an error in his calculations, one she thought would've been obvious.

Part of her longed to point out his mistake. But she was just a barmaid, as far as everyone knew, and she couldn't reveal who she really was or what her ultimate goal was.

Although it made her uncomfortable, a twist in her stomach, she knew she could use this information when she applied to be chosen as a mentee to one of the Master Artificers. No, she would never throw someone under a wagon like that. She would bide her time, waiting for the opportunity to show off her own knowledge and skills. What that opportunity would be, unfortunately, she had no way to predict.

But she was going to find some way, *somehow*, to get a mentorship.

And she had to do it before her family found her and dragged her back home.

Her parents hadn't wanted her to come to the Collegium, obviously, so finally she just ran away. She couldn't apply at the Collegium because no doubt that was the first place her parents would look for her. When she learned the Golden Compass was where the Artificer students gathered, she determined to get a job there and learn as much as she could.

She was focused on a singular goal: to invent something so spectacular that it would convince a master to take her on as an apprentice. At that point, surely, her parents couldn't force her to return home.

The fact that she hadn't heard from them or heard a rumor that they were looking for her didn't really surprise her. She had disappointed them, and she wouldn't be surprised if they had washed their hands of her and cast her side in favor of one of her younger siblings.

Her mother would do that. Her father . . . maybe he would understand, after some time.

Unless he forgot about her, too.

Later than evening, the patrons had trickled away, and Kya had cleaned the rectangular wooden tables and smaller square ones, swiped up the coins left for her tips, put the chairs up, and mopped the floor. The last of the fire, mostly coals now, snapped in the hearth, sending the sweet scent of pine and smoke to accompany her work.

She gathered up the papers the students had left behind. If they were abandoned, it meant the student didn't need them anymore. Kya's job was to put them in a box by the back room, and someone would pick them up and scrape them so they could be used again.

And since they were left behind, Kya didn't feel bad borrowing some of them to study. When she found errors, she'd correct them as an exercise for herself, before returning the paper to be scraped clean.

Sometimes she wondered how Anders and Cosa, the proprietors of the Golden Compass, stayed in business. The students tended to nurse a single beer or two throughout the night, if even that. Kya suspected the Master Artificers helped keep the tavern going.

She didn't mind working late. In fact, her willingness to clean up and close down the kitchen at night made her an even more welcome candidate for the job, because it meant Anders and Cosa could have something of an evening together.

She'd arrived without a job history (because she believed in being honest), but she'd assured them she knew how to handle customers, remember orders, and work hard. Cosa had been harder to convince, but when Kya gently pointed out a couple of ways to make their kitchen more efficient, just by reorganizing where things were stored, Cosa had looked at her with fresh eyes.

As part of the deal, she had a tiny room upstairs in which to sleep, access to a privy, and whatever food she desired. No doubt her slight stature had made them think the latter wouldn't cost them much.

They didn't realize how wonderfully the schedule worked for her: it meant her days were free to be spent at the Artificers Guild Library, greedily reading and learning everything she could. Despite her lack of Blues, nobody seemed to care that she was there, as long as she kept quiet and didn't try to take books away or harm them. The librarians probably didn't even notice her.

In the kitchen, she scrubbed dishes and the stove, tidied everything away. Her eyes burned; sleep would be welcome.

Just a few more tasks.

Propping open the back door, she brought out a bucket of scraps and tossed them to the chickens, then came back with food for the poor: ends of bread, rinds of cheese with enough left to gnaw on, bruised fruit, slightly wilted vegetables, untouched skewers of grilled meat. She set these in a wooden box at the side of the tavern.

One more trip, to place empty bottles out for the dairyman along with Cosa's list of cheeses and butter for the next delivery.

That crate deposited along the side wall of the tavern, Kya wiped her hands on her apron, faintly gray no matter how many times it had been washed—which had been many—and headed to the back door. A quick sponge bath to wipe away the sweat and food odors and then blessed sleep.

The estate Weaponsmaster would have been disgusted by her lack of attention.

Two men—or three? Her eyes weren't as accustomed to the dark as she would have preferred. Quiet enough, but not assassin-silent. Just enough to grab her before she realized they were there.

Through her fear, she assessed the situation.

She'd been trained in crossbow and swordplay, as much as befitted someone of her stature, but she had neither weapon at hand. She had a small knife on her belt, which could do some damage, but she couldn't get to it with her arms pinned behind her back and a strong, meaty hand over her mouth.

Anders and Cosa also lived above the tavern, but they'd be asleep by now. A scuffle might rouse them enough to decide the chickens were in a kerfuffle, or something equally trivial.

"Shh now, girl," one of the men muttered, his voice low and rough. "We're not here to hurt ya."

Then what *was* their purpose? The man didn't elaborate, and she couldn't ask for more information, thanks to the hand across her mouth.

Kya forced herself to relax and stop struggling. Sometimes, going limp meant an attacker would ease his grip, and she might be able to wriggle away and run.

Unfortunately, the man holding her was smart enough to keep his hands firmly on her arms, and when a cloth gagged her mouth and ropes bound her hands, she knew she'd have to come up with another plan.

Her heart pounded, no matter how she tried to breathe evenly through her nose as they set her (not gently, but not terribly roughly, either) into the back of a covered wagon. No ambient light leaked through the canvas covering the wagon.

She heard one of the men make a "Hup!" to horses, and then they were in motion.

Why her? What was she worth to anyone? At least, not yet? Not until she proved her worth as an Artificer. She certainly was a terrible heir to her family's estate.

Between her shorn hair and plain clothes and the fact she'd changed her name, there was little reason to believe anyone had noticed her, much less recognized her.

Perhaps they'd made a mistake, abducted the wrong person.

Kya took a deep breath in, filling her lungs, softening her muscles. She had to stay calm and alert, consider structure and weaknesses, pay attention to all details.

She pulled down her gag, but before she even sucked in a breath to scream, she realized the folly of it. It was late enough that few people were on the streets, and the heavy canvas covering the wagon would muffle the sound anyway. The only people who were likely to hear were her abductors. Banging her feet against the sides wouldn't stand out against the rattling wheels against the cobbles.

They'd bound her wrists in front of her, but she hadn't had the foresight to twist her arms so the bindings would be loose when she relaxed them.

She explored them with her mouth, but she couldn't get her teeth to close around the rough rope. Disheartened, she spat out a strand that had caught between her teeth. Kya crawled around the wagon on her elbows and knees until she hit the sides, her fingers scrabbling for anything sharp she might rub or cut the ropes against. She found nothing. When she crawled to the back of the wagon, she twisted onto one side so her bound hands could explore the bindings there.

The ropes that tied the canvas cover down were affixed to hooks or something on the outer side of the wagon. She couldn't reach to untie them even if her hands had been free.

Bruised and bouncing on the unforgiving wooden floor of the wagon, she frantically cast about for another option.

Another breath, then another.

She calculated the weight of the wagon. Not heavy enough for her to knock it over.

There was no obvious way to escape or signal for help. Or . . . was there?

As she'd crawled around, she'd heard the coins she'd picked up jangling in the front pocket of her apron.

She strained, her shoulders pulling painfully, but she managed to scoop some of the money out of the pocket.

Then, it was simple enough to drop a coin out the wagon, onto the road.

Then another.

A little while later, another.

With any luck, they wouldn't be found by a street urchin who could use the money. With any luck, someone would notice the line of coins and realize they were a trail.

All the while, she paid attention to the sounds around her and the feel of the wheels against the road, and she'd counted the number of turns the wagon made, and in which direction.

The road went from small cobbles to rougher ones. They were leaving the heart of Haven, the part with shops and nice houses and respectable taverns, with the wide road that led to the Palace.

Kya jolted and bumped in the back of the wagon, knowing she'd have some fine bruises by the morning.

Rougher cobbles meant another part of the city, a less fine one. She'd done her best to memorize a map of Haven when she arrived. Once they stopped, she'd match up the path of the wagon to the map in her head.

Then a smell tickled her senses, growing stronger, and she struggled not to vomit. She had to breathe the disgusting odors through her nose, and bile rose in her throat, but if she let it rise, there was nowhere for it to go.

Cow dung, rotten hay, and blood. The slaughterhouses.

Then the acrid scent of urine, combined with the sickly-sweet smell of rotting hides. The tanneries.

The slaughterhouses and tanneries, with their noxious smells, were housed well away from the heart of the city. Which meant they were heading toward the Orhan River.

The river was what allowed Haven to flourish: Goods could be easily transported in and out of the docks and stored in warehouses prior to purchase.

The river also meant it would be easy for her abductors to spirit her away without a trace.

Why her?

What was she worth to anyone?

* * *

By the time the wagon stopped, Kya was out of coins, and she had been smelling brackish river water and hearing the occasional cry of a waterfowl. She'd never been to the warehouse district, so she didn't know its layout well, other than from paying attention to the turns of the wagon.

The wagon shook as the ropes holding the canvas cover down were untied. Kya pulled the gag back into her mouth, not wanting to anger her abductors. She also scooted to the very edge, with a vague hope of hopping out and evading the men so she could run.

But when the canvas lifted, she didn't have time for her eyes to adjust—there wasn't much light, but it was more than beneath the canvas—before one of the men pulled a burlap sack over her head. Back into darkness.

One man said, "I'll see to the horse," and another grunted in response.

Suddenly, one of the men swept her up and dropped her on his shoulder. She hated the startled squeak she involuntarily made, her head dizzy with the sudden fright, as well as the fact that she was upside down.

A door opened, then closed behind them, followed by the sound of a lock closing. Based on the tromping, booted feet of the men, there were two in the warehouse with her.

She appreciated the sweet scent of sawdust inside, as it mediated the sour sweat smell of the man carrying her.

Then her abductor's gait shifted, and she realized they were going up stairs. She reached out, her fingers seeking something, anything, to give her clues, but all she got for her efforts was a splinter from touching a rough wall.

Then, just as unceremoniously as she'd been picked up, she was set on her feet. She staggered, the blood rushing from her head making her woozy, and a large hand grabbed her elbow, steadying her.

The sack came off her head, and she blinked in the pale light as her vision tried to adjust. She sucked in cool air through her nose.

She could barely make out the burly figures of the two men. She shrank back, but he still held her elbow.

"No screamin', yeah?" His voice sounded like a grumbling bear. "There's no one t'hear you anyway. But if I hear more'n a peep outta you, I'll gag ya again."

He pulled the gag down out of her mouth.

She tried to ask "Why?" but all that came out was a weak croak, her tongue and throat dry and swollen.

Ignoring her, the men left, and she heard the door lock.

She could see more now. The room was small and sparse, probably some kind of office rather than a storage room. It was almost empty of furniture. The light came from a single candle on the windowsill. In the corner, she spotted a wooden bucket wrapped with metal bands and a pile of rags.

They hadn't freed her wrists, so clearly they didn't understand how a woman could easily use the bucket. She wore a loose tunic and pants because the outfit was easier to work in than a skirt—plus she'd always hated skirts and dresses, their constrictions and limitations.

In another corner, she spied a table bearing a plain brown clay ewer. Could it be? On legs still wobbly from all the emotions she'd gone through, she made it across the room.

Yes! Water. She picked up the ewer with her bound hands and drank. Her throat spasmed, as if it had forgotten how to process liquid, and she sputtered before she was able to get the water down.

It seemed they didn't want her harmed but rather kept in at least reasonably good condition. She wasn't sure whether to be relieved or worried about that.

She went to the candle in the window and held her bound wrists over the flame until the rope fibers parted. She winced; she'd have some painful spots, if not blisters, before long.

She looked out the window, rubbing her wrists. As she'd suspected from the journey up the stairs, she couldn't safely jump, and there was nothing she could see to help her climb down. Farther away, the moon gleamed on the swells and currents of the river.

Because it seemed prudent before she did anything else, she made use of the bucket.

Then, taking the candle with her, she explored the small room, ending at the door. Like many other things, locks had fascinated her from an early age, and she'd figured out how they worked and how to defeat them. But she had nothing with her, not even a hairpin—funny how a frivolous thing could suddenly be useful and important—and she'd found not a scrap of anything in her explorations.

Frustrated, for the first time, she looked up.

And blinked in surprise.

The room had no ceiling. Instead, it opened to the peaked roof above, crossed by heavy beams parallel to the floor.

Of course. The rooms on the upper floor didn't need to be covered. They were just for small storage or offices.

Kya took a deep breath, then another. A plan formed in her mind. It wouldn't be easy, but she had no other choice.

She stilled and listened. Nearby—the next room?—she could hear faint, low voices.

She bit her lip. The simple wooden table was small enough that she could lift it; despite her slight stature, she had a fair amount of strength. If she could move it without making noise . . .

She could. She managed to carry it to the opposite wall.

As much as she'd find the light useful, she didn't bring the candle. It would make her too visible.

Even with the table, the wall was high. She hoisted herself up, pressing the toes of her boots into the wall for leverage. She managed to get herself into the junction of walls between the two rooms, and looked down.

The three men were there. There were three heaps of cloth, indicating their bedrolls for the night, and she felt a little smug that their rest would be so uncomfortable.

The men were sitting around another plain table, playing cards, with mugs of what was likely alcohol at the ready.

She couldn't see their faces, so she'd never be able to identify them. Their voices weren't familiar, either, nor were they unusual. They all had similar burly figures.

"Dunno why her ma just didn't have her da bring her home," one commented. The one who'd cut her gag, with the grumbly voice.

Another other shrugged. "We're makin' the money. Who cares?"

Kya sucked in her breath. She knew why. Her mother thought it would teach her a lesson to be hauled home this way. She probably thought it would make Kya finally be compliant.

She ground her teeth. Her mother was wrong.

Kya calculated her options and considered the way the warehouse seemed to be constructed. Storage at the front, probably extending below the second floor. Upper rooms at the back: one row against the back wall, the other overlooking the warehouse, with the hallway running between. The staircase was at the far end of the hallway from the room they'd put her in.

She could go back into the room they locked her into, move the table toward the front, and climb over the wall into the hallway. But that would likely make enough noise that the men would find her.

Or, she could work her way along the walls to the other end of the hallway and the stairs. If she jumped down there, maybe she wouldn't make as much noise.

The second option seemed safer . . . except for the fact that she'd have to creep along the wall past the room the men were in.

Kya knew how to be silent; she'd spent enough time hiding, trying not to be noticed back at home when she was expected for lessons in etiquette and deportment. And because she was small and short, balancing on the walls didn't seem impossible.

That didn't mean the prospect wasn't terrifying.

She eased down into her room and, as quietly as she

could, moved the table to the front, by the door. She took in deep breaths, silently, the way she'd calmed herself at home when things were stressful. Then she pulled herself up onto the wall, stood, and began her slow, careful journey.

The tops of the walls were about eight inches wide, and the lumber was rough and imperfect. Sturdy enough, though. She wanted to put her arms out for balance, but waving an arm over the room the men were in was too dangerous. She concentrated on putting one foot square in front of the other, slightly angled.

She reached the end of the wall of the room where the men were. Every part of her screamed to go faster now, but she knew that would only end in a mistake. Possibly a fatal one. If she fell, she'd likely hurt herself on top of being discovered.

She was almost at the juncture of the next room when her foot slipped.

She dropped forward, one foot still on the wall, and caught herself on her hands. A moment of fighting for balance, her heart pounding again, biting her lip to keep from making a sound. When she was sure she wasn't going to fall, she still paused, trying to get her internal equilibrium back.

Then, to her horror, one of the men said, "Did you hear something?"

The grumbly voiced man said, "Yer drunk, Davvi."

The third man added, "You tryin' to distract me so you can get a peek o' my cards? Not a chance."

"But—"

"Yer welcome to go check," the third man said.

"And have *you* peek at *my* cards? Not a chance," Davvi retorted, his slightly slurred words proving he'd had more to drink than he probably should have.

Kya waited for a long moment, then another, before slowly, carefully standing up and moving again.

When she got to the far end, she looked down at the door to the stairs across from her. What she saw made her heart drop to her stomach. She bit back a groan of disappointment and panic.

There was a lock on this side of the door.

She had no tools, no way to open it.

She sat back on her haunches and considered her predicament.

Going back to her room and awaiting her fate wasn't an option she cared to consider.

Unable to think of another choice, Kya stood and sidled sideways over the gap over the hallway, her feet on a thin board that had been nailed to the wall, her fingers clutching for any purchase on the rough wood in front of her.

After that, it seemed relatively easy to creep along the top of the corner room's wall until she overlooked the warehouse.

By now, her eyes had adjusted to the dim light, so although the warehouse was bathed in darkness, she could mostly make out the floor and the front wall, the basic structure of the room.

Above her, thick heavy chains dangled from a pulley system on the ceiling down toward the floor, used for hauling hay bales around. Her parents had done their best to show her how the farms under their tenancy operated. Some of it had been quite fascinating, and she'd drawn up some suggestions on how to streamline operations, but her mother had ignored them.

The chains hung too far off the floor for her to shimmy down and then drop; well, she might be able to do it, but the chances of breaking an ankle was too high.

However, there was row of windows along the front wall, with sills that looked reasonably deep. They were higher on the wall than normal windows, for light and ventilation only, too high for a tall man to peer through. Less of a drop than the walls, certainly.

Action stories often told of people grabbing vines or ropes or curtains and using them to swing across or down. But unless the arc length and speed were correct, the adventurer was more likely to slam into a wall than burst through an open window or land gracefully on the ground.

To do it properly, you needed just the right amount of

kinetic energy to reach the far wall, but not so much as to overshoot your target and injure yourself.

And math.

But first she needed to get her hands on one of the thick chains.

Because the warehouse was empty, the pulley system had been cranked back so all the chains were toward the back of the warehouse—and within Kya's reach.

Almost.

She knelt on the top of the wall, gripping it with one hand and reaching out.

She rarely found issue with her slight stature; it helped her disappear in the background. If she had longer arms, however, the chain she needed would be easier to grab.

Kya stretched a little farther . . . and felt her balance shift.

Her stomach lurched, and her gasp resonated inside her head as she threw her weight backward. She almost overbalanced and fell into the room below, but caught herself, wobbling between a loud fall and a bone-breaking one until she finally steadied herself.

She muttered a curse under her breath and looked around.

Inching sideways, she came to a T-juncture where an interior wall dividing two rooms met that outer wall overlooking the warehouse below. She lay on her stomach on the interior wall, gripping it with her knees, and reached out again over the expanse toward the chain.

It took several tries before her fingers brushed against it, and a few more before she could actually get her hand around it. She pulled it toward her. It was heavier than she expected, and she adjusted her stance accordingly.

Finally, she had it. She sat on the wall with her legs dangling over the edge, and slowly, to keep the clanking of links at a minimum, drew the chain all the way up to her.

Kya calculated the arc length of her improvised pendulum, then estimated the difference in height between the top of the wall and the window sill slightly below her. She grasped the end of the chain above her head, slid slightly forward, and used her legs to push off the wall with what she'd calculated was the right amount of force.

Still, she landed harder on the sill than she'd intended, and grabbed on to the side of the frame with one hand. Her shoulder wrenched as she forced her body's forward movement to slow; breaking through the glass would be disastrous. As soon as she could, she eased the thick chain to the side and let it go. It swung back, creaking where it was affixed to the ceiling.

She knew friction wouldn't allow the chain to swing all the way forward again and knock her off her precarious perch. Fortunately, it also didn't allow the chain to noisily slap into the wall, either.

She wanted to stay there longer, catch her breath, but by this point the men had likely heard her hit the sill or the creak of the chain.

So down she jumped. The sill was low enough not to injure herself, but high enough that pain radiated up her shins. She hissed out a breath, but forced herself to clamber down and stagger to the door. That lock was a simple bolt to keep people out; she rammed it open, and then she was outside.

The night was cool and clear, the stars bright, and the three-quarters moon still high enough to show her the street. The smell of the river was stronger now that she was outside, and the only sound was the creaking of the docks.

At first, after a quick glance back at the building, she ran. The more distance she could put between herself and the men, the better.

She was younger and although small, could run. They'd been drinking. She had an advantage, no matter the pounding her shins had taken.

Remembering the path the wagon had taken, she wound her way out of the maze of warehouses and storage buildings, until she stumbled out on the road that led back to the city of Haven.

The road was wide enough for two large wagons to pass comfortably as they carried loads into town or returned to the docks. Although it was dark, save for the moonlight, Kya felt exposed. She could have hidden among the warehouses here, but time was of the essence. The men had probably taken the time to saddle the horses, and she didn't want to be caught out after dawn.

She wanted to get back to the safety of her tiny room at the Golden Compass.

She'd have to leave the Compass, of course. But she wouldn't think about that now, because that was just too heartbreaking. She'd liked Anders and Cosa and, of course, the proximity to the Artificers. She'd have to find another way to be noticed by the Master Artificers.

She'd figure that out later, after she was safe.

As she jogged, she planned. Soon she'd hit the tanneries and slaughterhouses, then finally get to the city itself. She visualized a map of Haven and its surrounding lands, overlaying on it her memorized route the wagon had taken.

Once she got there, she could evade her pursuers.

Fields stretched out on either side of the road: rustling corn, pungent onions, delicate wheat.

Then, in the distance, she heard hoofbeats, coming at a gentle trot.

Kya picked her way down into the ditch between the road and the field, burrowing her way under a hummock of weeds. She breathed carefully through her nose, trying to calm the frantic beating of her heart.

It had to be her kidnappers. They wouldn't run the horses, because they had to keep an eye out for her.

But then, as the clacking of hooves on cobbles came closer, she realized the sound was coming from the direction of the city, not from the docks.

Better than the alternative, but she had no idea if it was someone she could trust. She'd stay put—despite the damp, cold ground seeping through her clothes and the dank odor of the ditch.

A sound came clear with the hoofbeats. Bells, sweetly jingling.

Kya caught her breath. That was the sound of Heralds on their Companions.

What to do? Now that she knew her mother was behind her abduction, everything seemed suspicious. Had she contacted the Heralds as a backup plan?

But, she argued with herself, there was no way the men who'd taken her could have let the Heralds know she'd escaped.

Still, she argued back, she didn't know if she could trust them.

So she stayed in her muddy hiding place, waiting for them to ride by.

They didn't.

The clop of hooves and the jingling of bells ceased when they were alongside her.

"She's close," a woman's voice said. Then, "Burrow? I'm Mieran, one of the Queen's Heralds. We know you're nearby. We mean you no harm—I swear upon my oath to the Queen."

A pause.

"Please don't make me come down and soil my Whites to find you, girl. I will if I must, but you'll make an enemy of the laundry staff at the Collegium."

Kya suppressed a snort. Mieran wasn't wrong. The cleaning staff at the manor had despaired of the messes Kya got into, but they also appreciated the devices she had invented to make their jobs easier, such as the device to affix to the top of buckets to squeeze the water out of mops.

Fact was, she'd lost. They knew where she was—if not the exact hummock, close enough, and they'd find her within minutes.

She could either suffer the ignominy of being dragged out, or . . .

She shrugged backward out of her hidey-hole and stood, aware of her ridiculous state. "Fine, you've found me."

A woman swung down off an impossibly perfect white steed. "The Master Artificers, among others, want your safe return."

Kya gaped at her. *The Master Artificers?*

Mieran was a fox-faced woman with a pointed chin, pale skin, and blue eyes so piercing, Kya could see them in the moon's glow. Her long, straight black hair looped in braids around her head like a crown.

"This is Frind," Mieran continued, gesturing at her Companion. "She agrees to escort you back to Haven."

She held out a hand, and Kya, her mind and body numb with confusion, took it.

She was used to riding horses. Tucked in front of Mieran, she remembered her father taking her on rides before she'd been old enough to go solo.

At first, they rode in silence. Finally, Kya's confusion got the better of her.

"How did anyone know I was gone?"

"The owners of the Golden Compass heard a scuffle outside and then realized you were gone," Mieran said. "They surmised that you'd been taken and came to us for assistance. That was a smart thing, dropping coins to leave a trail." She grinned. "Don't worry, you'll get it all back."

The joke was lost on Kya. Another question was foremost in her mind. She ran one hand through her fine hair, her other hand on the saddle's pommel.

"And . . . and the Master Artificers?"

Mieran took a moment to respond. "Apparently, they want words with you."

Kya didn't know how to respond. After the night she'd had, her brain felt like it was shutting down. Herald Mieran might be crisply official, but Kya still felt safe with her.

She couldn't quite bring herself to believe the Herald *cared*, but still.

She couldn't even begin to comprehend the involvement of the Master Artificers.

Before they continued their journey, the Heralds briefly questioned Kya. She was able to give the name of the warehouse—which she'd taken a brief moment to read painted on the outside before she ran—to the Heralds. She described the men as best she could with the scant information she'd gleaned. Then, two Heralds peeled off to head to the warehouse district.

Mieran took her back to the Golden Compass. Cosa, in an unexpected display of emotion, grabbed her into a hug, and Anders rested a hand on her back, saying, "You gave us quite the fright, girl. We're glad you're safe."

Stunned, Kya blinked back tears. She hadn't thought they'd cared, really, beyond needing an efficient server and appreciating her diligence.

"Now, there are some other people who wish to speak with you," Mieran said.

Kya knew the Heralds and Companions had some sort of silent speech, so she wasn't surprised that word had gone ahead of them.

Mieran led her through the main room of the Golden Compass to the back room.

The Master Artificers' room.

The sacred sanctuary.

She found herself trembling as Mieran opened the door and ushered her through.

At first, she couldn't look at who was in the room, so she turned her attentions to the space itself. Plans and drawings and notes papered the walls. In the center, a sturdy rectangular table with accompanying chairs, as well as a few side tables and chairs. All the same wood and design as the furniture in the main room. There was no pretense here.

"Burrow, isn't it?" a woman said gently. Her pure white hair, still thick, in two braids that poured down her shoulders. She put a comforting hand on the small of Kya's back. "Come, sit down. I'm Master Qualla."

Kya looked around the table as she sat, committing the other four Masters to memory.

A man with wild, untamed, pale red hair; in contrast, his matching beard was closely trimmed. A bald, thin-faced man who would have looked severe except his brown eyes were very kind. A woman with a heart-shaped face, dark curly hair, and curiously bright green eyes. A man with blond hair, receding hairline at the temples, sharp blue eyes that missed nothing.

They were all looking at her.

She wanted to flee. Nobody noticed her; nobody saw her. But they were all *looking at her.*

But this was what she'd wanted, dreamed of, strived towards. Which is why she stayed firmly in her chair. The interminable etiquette lessons kept her from squirming.

Their voices gentle, they first asked about her abduction, which confused her, but she told the truth.

"It seems my mother wanted to humiliate me into going home."

They assured her that the men would be properly dealt with.

More questions. She answered truthfully. She loathed the idea of being a figurehead. She wanted knowledge and math and engineering. She felt herself flush when she said that. But she knew, in this moment, her future hung in the balance.

She was grateful when Cosa brought in a tray of drinks, followed by some of the usual Compass food. Her tongue was dry, and although dawn was just beginning to pinken the sky, she found herself ravenous.

"We've been watching you for some time," the ginger-haired man said, and she nearly dropped her toasted cheese bread.

She wasn't clear on the timeline of things: Anders and Cosa had commented on her. The students noticed she paused over some of their work. And despite what she'd assumed, the librarians at the Artificers Guild Library *had* paid attention to her.

Her whole life she'd tried to be invisible, and she had failed.

Not only failed, but failed in a way that the people she most wanted to be like, the group she wished to be a part of, had taken extreme notice.

Master Ularo, the red-headed man, handed her a sheaf of papers. Curious, she took them. To her astonishment, they were the ones she'd corrected when she found errors. She'd done that just to keep learning—she'd never though anyone would look at discarded work in the box.

"These changes and new drawings, they're your work?" Master Ularo asked. "And no one helped you?"

They continued to quiz her until the sun was well over the horizon, and she was struggling not to droop with exhaustion. She'd been abducted, escaped, found, and now this. No amount of food or drink could sustain her much longer.

Finally, Master Qualla spoke. "Burrow, you have impressed us with your tenacity and knowledge, despite your lack of formal training. Yes, there are gaps in your studies, but those can be easily dealt with. Unless the others disagree, I wish to take you on as my apprentice."

Kya felt as though she'd been shoved against the back of her chair by an unknown force, knocking the breath out of her. She listened dumbly as the other Master Artificers gave their consent.

No. Agreed wholeheartedly.

Through the ringing in her ears, she heard Master Qualla say, "Are you all right, Burrow?"

She sat up straight, and reached a hand out to Master Qualla.

"I would be honored, Master Qualla," she said in a clear, strong voice. "But first I must tell you my real name. I'm Kya, and I thank you for seeing me."

The Dream Seeker
Paige L. Christie

Huddled behind the greeting table, waiting for Hostess
Mero to return from the privy, Teig flinched every time
the inn's door swept open to admit guests and blasts of
frigid air. Even a few months back, the older folks talked
about the unusual amount of snowfall and how the river
ice grew thicker than any time in memory. Then the
weather turned warmer and hard rains came, and parts
of the river broke free while others stayed frozen. The
jammed-up ice forced the water wide from the river-
banks and pushed giant chunks far from the main channel, blocking the roads. Most of the valley sat flooded
and chilled.

In Sweet Springs, things had been tough already, but
now parts of the town sat ankle deep in water. And what
buildings stood just far enough up and away were full of
people. Every person within two days' ride had come
here for shelter. People she had known all her life and
people she had never met filled the inn, every spare
room in town, and even the barn lofts.

Everyone was hungry, and that made them grouchy.
But the worst of it, in Teig's mind, was that not a place
remained for a girl to escape for some peace. Her head
hurt from spending time with so many people packed so
close together.

The only thing that made any of it bearable was having a minstrel trapped here as well. She wasn't a fancy

Bard trained at the Collegium and full of more stories than the sky was full of stars, but she listened to Teig's daydreams and sometimes turned them into simple songs. Her name was Gwenline, and she knew all the songs of Talia, Queen's Own—especially "Travels of Talia," the one that featured Sweet Springs' role in Talia finding her way to her destiny.

The door opened again, and in came a man bundled all in dark gray. Teig rose from her stool as he approached. His name was Hest, and she didn't like him one bit. Every day he slept until midday, then went out to check on his horse. He only came back for dinner. Last winter he'd stopped here for two days. That time a girl named Pekki, a few years younger than Teig, had been with him, and it was Pekki that filled Teig's mind with wariness.

"My key?" he asked, in a strange accent she had yet to place.

She turned, plucked the key from the cubbyhole for room eight, and faced him again. He held out his hand. Even though he wore gloves against the cold, every instinct in her screamed not to even brush the fabric. She dropped the key into his palm. Something of her uncertainty must have shown in her expression, because his eyes narrowed.

She took a step back and bumped into Hostess Mero. "Oh!" She caught Mero's arm to keep from stumbling, and she frowned as she met the older woman's gaze.

"Teig, girl, where's your attention? Did you give this man what he needs?"

"I—yes, but—" Teig looked to the man. He was already walking away. Relief flooded her and she squeezed Mero's wrist. "He's bad," Teig whispered fiercely. She recalled the worn look of the girl who had traveled with Hest, and the stories she told about terrible dreams. "I remember from last time he visited. The girl said he—"

"Oh, Teig, no. No more stories! Last night the merchant from Haven was a 'spy' and the wool dealer was a 'weapons smuggler'! And which one did you decide was an assassin? That poor teacher with the too-big boots on? *Enough.* Thanks for keeping watch, but it's time you got back to your chores."

"But—" Teig protested as she watched the man climb the stairs toward the sleeping rooms.

"What's anyone to do with you? All these tall stories and wary thoughts. Off with you now! Wilhem has a list of things he needs you doing." The woman swept a lean arm toward the common room. "Go!"

With a sigh, Teig headed in the direction Mero pointed. But her imagination was on fire now. Bad dreams. Hadn't everyone in the inn and around town been talking about nightmares? When she was a Herald, everyone would *have* to listen to her! In the meantime, just the thought of the man in gray set her skin crawling.

She tried to shake off the feeling as she crossed the busy common room, with its tightly packed tables and heavy wooden benches and the air heavy with the scent of spiced ale. The space, filled with people and laughter, usually warmed her belly with happiness. But these last days, it seemed gray and sad, no matter how many lamps she lit. The pluck of a string being tuned snapped her from dark thoughts. Teig looked toward the hearth where the minstrel sat close to the fire blazing in the old stone hearth. Just what a fearful day called for!

Ready to make her daily request, Teig headed for Gwenline. Wilhem had warned her that asking for her favorite ballad again was going to earn her a hiding. Even though he'd never struck her since taking her in, the way he said it made her think he actually meant it. But what was a girl to do while she waited for her destiny to arrive—just carry wood and wash dishes? If listening to "Travels" was the only thing that made the endless gray days better, well, what was wrong with hearing it as often as Gwenline was willing to sing it?

One day, this terrible winter confinement would be done, and Wilhem and everyone else would miss having someone to sing about greatness in Sweet Springs. *Especially* once Teig herself was Chosen by a Companion and became a Herald. And that *was* going to happen.

Since the first time she'd heard "Travels of Talia," Teig knew *she* was meant for mighty deeds. She'd planned it all her life, and she was almost thirteen now. Soon her Companion would gallop into town and—

"Teig, mind yourself!"

The shout startled her back into the moment, and she stopped just short of colliding with a knot of travelers huddled around a table watching a card game. Cheeks hot, she stammered an apology and glanced quickly in the direction of the shout. Wilhem stood in the kitchen doorway wiping his hands on a towel. He jerked his head sharply in summons. With a longing look toward the minstrel, Teig bit her lip and wove through the room to stand in front of him.

"Sorry, sorry," she said. "It's just the gray man and Gwenline and the Companion and—"

"Your love of fanciful ideas isn't going to clean the tables or fill the wood box. Anymore wild talk from you today, and I'll have you mucking stalls as far from the bard's tales as I can put you."

"I—"

"I know." Wilhem rubbed at his head as though nursing a deep ache. "This is hard on all of us, and you're used to seeking your own imaginings. But we've all got to get through this until the ice breaks. It's going to get harder before it gets easier."

Teig sighed and nodded. "Do you think a Companion could make it through?"

Wilhem shook his head. "Not a flood and danger like this, young one. And I've told you before, being Chosen isn't for *you* to decide. Enough with your daydreams. Bring me the balum herb from the pantry. Then the wood box needs filling. Get on with you." He lowered his voice. "I'll have a hot bowl of stew ready when you get done."

Coat buttoned tight and hat pulled low, Teig stomped out the back door, pulling an empty sled behind her. The snow, knee deep and ice crusted, pulled at her pant legs as she followed the well-beaten path toward the woodshed. Even though the cold air burned her throat, being out of the crowded inn held more relief than she cared to admit.

She tugged open the shed door, groaning at the weight of it. Every day it seemed heavier. Her stomach growled as though angry at the energy she used.

Frowning, she patted her belly with a gloved hand. The offer of an extra portion of stew was not a bad thing. She pressed her lips together. Not that she'd eat it. One thing she knew from the stories—to be Chosen, she had to be fair. Extra food should go to the children anyway. And *she* was practically grown up.

Children. She paused, staring at the wood pile—now only half as tall as it had been just a week ago—her thoughts shifting to the man staying in room eight. He'd been here before, last winter. Maybe he had stopped in Sweet Springs many times, but she just never paid attention before? She only even remembered him from last time because of the girl he traveled with—a small child, thin and uncertain, probably about ten years old, with no smile in her eyes.

Teig had spent two days trying to get the child to share her name. At last she whispered, "Pekki," in a tiny voice. Glancing around as though afraid the very walls were listening, Pekki huddled in a corner of the common room far from the fire. When not in the room she shared with Hest, she always sat there, lonely and cold. Teig snuck Pekki extra broth whenever she could.

And Pekki had told her of her terrible dreams—full of loss and falling and fear. If Teig had forgotten the details, it was only because she remembered thinking them too terrible to hold in her mind. But she remembered the grief and sorrow in the other girl's voice, and that was enough.

Teig bit her lip again, then shook herself and started picking wood from the pile. Hest. Here again. And where was Pekki? Wherever she was, Teig hoped the girl's dreams were better.

She frowned again as she tossed the wood into the sled. Nightmares. Everyone in town, especially those in

the inn, had them every night. Not surprising, given how
bad everything was, but when had that started?

Musing, she stepped back into the shed and tugged
more wood from the stack. A log dropped from the pile
and landed on her foot. Pain shot through her toes and
she hopped back with a yelp, tears stinging her eyes. She
burst into full tears, cursing her lack of attention. This
always happened when she let her imagination get the
better of her! Dreams were just dreams, and Pekki was
lucky to be home and not on the road with her father
this terrible winter. She sat down to take the weight off
her aching foot.

"That was quite a series of phrases you tossed out,
young miss," said a male voice from the doorway.

Snuffling, Teig looked up at the figure silhouetted
there. "I work in the *inn*."

"Oh, well, that does explain the creative swearing,
but not so much the tears. Are you hurt?" The man
stepped into the shed, and Teig recognized his worn
blue uniform.

Teig's jaw fell open and she sniffed her tears back into
control as she stared in awe. Old Belton, the retired
Road Guard who lived a half morning's walk west of
town. The very Guard from "Travels" who had helped
Talia on her way. Once or twice he'd said hello to her
when he came to town for supplies, but never more than
that. And she'd never spoken to him. After all, he had
actually *met* Talia. Mero said that on the rare occasions
the Queen's Own traveled down to visit the Sensholding,
she sometimes even stopped to greet old Belton. That
hadn't happened since Teig was old enough to remember
but—!

She stared as he chuckled. "I asked if you were hurt."

"What? No—well, just my foot."

He looked at her a moment, then reached down a
hand. "Can you stand on it?"

She stared, then grasped his fingers. "I think so." She
barely finished the sentence before he pulled her upright. She wobbled a moment, more from shock than
pain, then steadied. "Yes."

With a nod, he released her and stepped back. "Now what's got you so upset? The weather's terrible, and firewood's heavy, but I'm guessing that's not all that's wrong."

Teig blinked. What she was thinking was too terrible to say out loud. And even though Belton knew Talia some, he was a Guard, not a Herald. And if she was *right* about Hest, well, that was a Herald-level problem. Since she was going to be Chosen one day, she would find a way to deal with the stranger herself. Some way. She shook her head.

"Hmmm. Well, then, I suppose I'll leave you to your firewood." He stepped out into the gray light and wind and snow. "You know where to find me."

How could she possibly know that? The town was full of people, and his home nowhere close. She watched him walk away. And why would she want to find him? She turned to load more wood.

Teig sat tucked in a tight knot of blankets on her narrow bed and stared out the window. She shivered as she watched the night shift toward gray dawn. Worry crowded next to hunger in her belly. Outside, a few people moved along the packed-snow paths, going about early chores, blowing white breath into the air. Everyone looked tired, and moved stiffly, but something worse happened as they passed the inn—each one shrank in on themselves, ducking their heads and pulling their bright coats tighter around them, as though touched by fear.

No one who wasn't staying in the inn stopped in anymore, not even to hear Gwenline sing and tell stories. And the last four nights had seemed endless, each hungrier and more restless than the last, until Teig dreaded curling up for sleep more than even getting up before dawn. Even more than she dreaded cleaning up the drool from the unlucky refugees forced to sleep with their heads pillowed on the common room tables. Even more than she dreaded seeing Hest.

The man's presence pricked her mind and spirit like a rough-woven blanket. Hiding the flinch that lurked just under her skin whenever she saw him became more difficult with each encounter. His eyes followed her, and it seemed he not only recognized her discomfort, but that it pleased him.

At last, she confessed her fear of the man to Wilhem. Who, while he publicly dismissed the worries as another of her fanciful notions, sighed and decided to humor her. He saw to it that Teig was no longer asked to carry the man's morning tea to his table, or carry fresh basin rags to his door. Those small kindnesses did not bring the ease they might have, as when Mero took over those tasks, she grew leaner and more drawn each day.

The inn, usually a place of comfort and cheer, grew drearier every day. Was it just the continued isolation of the hard winter and the floods? Or were the dreams wearing everyone down a sign of something more ominous, more dangerous? After Wilhem's dismissal of her worries, Teig kept her wondering to herself.

The one bright spot each day was that Gwenline now sang "Travels" every afternoon without Teig even requesting it. And that grace glimmered, a tiny spark of hope in endless gray days. But Gwenline wasn't a Bard, with Gifts. She did what she could to lift the heaviness of each day, but the weight of fear remained, deeper with each waking, as though each night added new doubts and aches beyond the chill and limited food.

With a sigh, Teig uncurled from the bed and got to her feet. Time to get dressed and get to doing what was needed. Why, oh why couldn't she have been Chosen before all this happened? If she was a Herald, she would know what to do.

She crept downstairs, trying not to wake anyone who might have managed to gain some rest in the night. Especially Hest. But the glow from under the door of room eight as she passed told her that he was awake. She slipped past and down to the common room.

Downstairs, few people stirred, but Gwenline raised a hand in greeting from her place by the hearth. Teig slipped into the kitchen, where the stove already burned hot with water boiling in a pot. Teig filled a mug and added tea and a dollop of honey and wound her way across the room, careful not to trip on outstretched feet. Too many belonged to snoring patrons, and it wouldn't do to startle them while she carried the hot beverage.

"Thank you." Gwenline accepted the offering into her nimble hands. True gratitude marked her smile. "Sit a moment. I want to ask you something."

Teig pulled a chair closer to the fire and sat. "Me?"

Gwenline blew on her tea before sipping it, and nodded. "You've been telling me stories since the day I got here. Are they all ones you made up?"

Heat filled Teig's cheeks. Always, someone called her out for telling tale tales and being too whimsical. "Some I learned from travelers." She couldn't keep the defensive tone from her voice.

"Oh, young friend, I don't mean anything by asking. It's just—" She shook her head. "Do you think me singing all these wild tales is doing more harm than good?"

Teig blinked. She wasn't really the person to be asking such things. Her imagination ran so wild she wasn't sure whether to trust what she thought. "I don't know."

Gwenline sighed. "I wish I had the gifts to be a Bard. I might be able to help more around here. Everyone is so sad."

At that, Teig sat up a little. "You think a Mind-Gift would help with this?" She thought back to Pekki. "Do you think . . . a Mind-Gift could cause this?"

With a laugh, Gwenline waved a hand. "Why would a Mind-Gift be so wrongly used? And who would do such a thing?"

"Well there's that man, Hest—"

"Hest? The jewelry merchant?" She shook her head. "He sits right at the front of the crowd every night and requests the most cheerful songs."

Why hadn't Teig noticed that? Maybe because she'd been avoiding Hest anywhere he was in the inn, even if it meant missing Gwenline's evening songs. As much as she tried, she could not dream up a situation where she would find his company entertaining, much less a comfort. "I suppose."

Gwenline smiled. "Your imagination is as limitless as Mero thinks."

"I have to bring in more firewood," Teig said, getting to her feet. If the minstrel didn't believe what Teig was beginning to suspect, who would? She nodded as Gwenline repeated her thanks for the tea, and she went to put on her coat and gloves. The woodshed beckoned.

The woodshed. Belton. Why had he stopped that day to speak to her? Her of all people? Maybe . . . ? He said she'd know where to find him, and suddenly she knew just where to look.

The old Guard hut stood on what had once been the edge of town, before it had expanded. Chilled through, but somehow feeling better than she had in days, Teig knocked a gloved hand against the hut door.

From inside came the sound of shuffling, then the door swung open on angry sounding hinges. "Well young miss," Belton said with a grin. "I was wondering how long it would take you to find me."

"How'd you know I'd come looking?"

"The town's in trouble in a way sometimes only a child can figure out."

"You knew. At the woodshed."

"I was a Guard a long time. I'm not even supposed to be in the blue these days. But it's an old habit. You know, I can tell *something's* wrong, and I feel like it involves the inn. But there are so many people there, I can't tell if the trouble is a *what* or a *who*."

"It's a who named Hest!" Teig said, then bit her lip and dropped her gaze.

"So, you *do* have something to tell me." He stepped back. "Come in. It's warmer than outside, and your story's likely a long one."

Teig glanced back toward the inn, then at the old guard who she'd barely ever had the courage to nod a greeting to. She had to tell *someone* about her worries. She met Belton's gaze, then nodded, and stepped through the doorway.

* * *

Seated on a rickety stool in the mostly abandoned hut, Teig wound down her telling. "And last time he was here, a girl rode with him in his wagon. Her name was Pekki. I thought she was his daughter, but I'm not sure now." She frowned. "She never said it. I just assumed. But she also said that all their travels were full of bad dreams. Hungry dreams. And now that man, Hest, is at the inn and the inn is full of sadness. I hate going to sleep."

She hugged herself a moment, then released the grasp on her arms. If she was going to convince him, she couldn't look afraid. Even if she was. "I tried to tell Mero. And Wilhem. And even Gwenline, the minstrel. But they don't believe me. It's hard enough being trapped here and hungry. They think that's what it is. But it's not. Just not at all."

Belton looked at her, and she looked back. Then he spoke and there was no harshness in his voice, even though his words hit hard. "I've been hearing about you for a while, child. You've had your head in the clouds forever, and now the ground's rushed up to meet you. No one's listening, eh? That's something you brought on yourself, but that's neither here nor elsewhere. I believe you. Now it's time to stop imagining things and *act*."

Teig nodded. "I did act," she said. "I came and found you. You've met Talia. You must know things people don't."

He burst out laughing. "Oh, I know Talia a little, it's true. And a Mind-Gift like hers would be useful right now. But we don't have her. All we have is you and me. And it's been a long time since I was at the Collegium.

"But I'll tell you this—we have some knowledge already. This man is fine with adults but makes children scared. And bad dreams follow him. And hunger."

Teig shook her head. "We're all hungry."

"I'm not. The rest of the town isn't. We're not low on food. Not in just a few weeks. Not even with a few hundred more people packed into town. But at the inn—you

say everyone seems half-starved, except this Hest. What
if he's not hungry because he's getting his fill of everyone else feeling sad and scared? Getting his fill every
night, eating everyone's dreams?"

Eyes wide, Teig hung on his every word, each more un-
believable than the last. Even as he reflected her own
darkest imaginings, she had trouble grasping that something so terrible could possibly be true. Was this what
people felt like when she went on and one with her wild
stories? With her tales of what she would do when she was
Chosen? *Chosen . . . if only . . .* She stopped the thought.

Wishing and wondering for something that wasn't up
to her, that wasn't going to help the people in the inn. It
wasn't going to stop Hest. No Herald was coming, riding
in on a magical Companion. And hoping for more—well
there was no more. No more than just herself and old
Belton from "Travels." That was going to have to be
enough. Maybe she didn't need to be a Herald to make
things better. Maybe she just needed to *decide* to do it.

"I want everyone to sleep well tonight." The determination in her voice surprised her.

"How do we stop him?" Belton leaned toward her.
"Tell me what you know."

She thought and thought, and she told him everything she could remember, both what she'd learned from
Pekki and what she had seen these last few weeks. Then
an idea formed. "Oh! I think I know how to stop him!
But if Wilhem won't agree—oh, it'll be bad."

They waited until Hest left for his daily check on his
horse. When he rounded the building and disappeared
from sight, they headed for the inn.

"Why does he laugh with the minstrel and ask her for
happy stories?" Belton mused as they stomped through
the snow toward the inn.

"Maybe when people feel better, he can make them
feel twice as bad by taking it away," Teig said. "It doesn't
matter. All we have to do is make *him* sleep."

Belton pulled his old blue coat close. They'd considered him carrying his crossbow, just in case, but their

plan required more stealth than aggression. "You're very sure of this."

Teig nodded. Somehow, she was. "There's always a light under his door. And Pekki said—she said he stayed up all night. I remember. Do you think he fed on her dreams? Do you think that's why he had her with him? Do you think . . . she's still alive?"

"I think she was a traveling meal for him, yes." His rough voice went heavy with anger. "As to whether she's alive. Well, once we've got him locked up, we can make sure that's something the Heralds ask him when we hand him over for judgment."

"Yes." Teig nodded fiercely. Once the ice broke, justice would come with spring. "You go in the front."

He stopped and looked down at her. "If Wilhem listens, you won't have to do anything. And it could make things worse if we're wrong."

Teig looked into his lined face. He wasn't so old after all. Or maybe *she* was just feeling older. "I think we're right. And not just because I want us to be." She nodded. "I know what to do."

"All right then," he agreed, and he headed toward the inn's main door.

Teig went around the building and waited for several minutes before entering. She slipped inside in time to hear Wilhem loudly ordering Belton to leave, then complaining just as loudly to Mero about the foolish ideas of washed-up old guards.

Teig's heart sank. The direct approach had failed. Well—on to the plan she'd hoped she wouldn't have to execute.

She darted into the pantry and pulled down jars of dried herbs until she found the one she sought—the blend of lemleaf and hypercum root. As a seasoning mix, it was lovely and subtle, but it could also be used to induce sleep. Though Wilhem said enough to do that also caused a prickly rash around the ankles and three days of terrible bad breath. And that was no fun at all. But if this worked . . . well . . . they'd have the proof they needed to lock Hest away.

Unease twisted her belly as she carried the mix into the kitchen, reading the notes on the paper glued to the jar. She eyed the rich stew bubbling slowly on the stove. If they tried to drug just Hest, he'd likely notice. But everyone eating the same thing . . . She choked a little at the thought. But if no one would listen, how else was she going to stop a man whose Mind-Gift allowed him to feed on people's nightmares?

Still, she hesitated. Then shook her head. No matter what, she couldn't do it, not to people who had done nothing wrong.

"Teig?" Mero's voice came from the doorway. Wilhem stood just behind.

Teig turned, completely caught, and just stared at them.

For a moment, silence held; then Mero crossed the room and took the jar from Teig's hands. She looked at it, then at the stew, then back to Teig. "You really believe this man Hest is doing these things? You and Belton both? Believe it enough to do this?"

Teig met Mero's eyes and nodded. "I know I tell a lot of stories, Mero." But she never disobeyed. Ever caused real trouble. She hoped that would matter now. "But I promise."

Wilhem joined them and stood silent a long time. At last he put a gentle hand on her shoulder. "If you used enough of this mix to knock everyone out, the stew would stink so badly no one would eat it at all."

"But—"

Mero interrupted her. "Hest asks for a Karsian Ale every night with his dinner. Nothing better in which to hide a dose of this. If you're wrong, I'll dump a barrel with him as witness and claim it was contaminated. But if we all sleep well tonight . . . well, then you and Belton can lock Hest up in the old guard hut until a Herald rides through."

Relief and embarrassment warred in Teig's chest. "Thank you," she said. How many times had she dismissed Mero and Wilhem, thought herself destined for better than they? And here they were the ones helping her to save everyone. And old Belton, who used to scare her—well, she never would have sorted it all out without him to talk to.

How much had changed in just a day.

How much would change if they all managed to get a good night's sleep?

Two hours past sunrise, Teig opened her eyes, feeling refreshed and satisfied for the first time in weeks. Outside, the sun blazed, and birdsong filled the air. Birdsong, which could only mean warmer weather was on its way.

From downstairs came Gwenline's voice, lifted in happy song, and joined by a dozen others more joyful than even the birds. Teig dressed with an enthusiasm she hadn't known in days, and headed downstairs.

On the second floor, at the far end of the hallway, Belton nodded to her from where he stood guard outside room eight. He looked confident and strong. She grinned back at him.

Maybe her future was not in a white uniform but in a blue one. Suddenly it seemed a fine choice. Even better than being Chosen.

Shadows and Reflections
Louisa Swann

Petril stared at his reflection in a puddle as a cloud scuttled across the sun's face, casting an icy shadow across the landscape, chasing after clouds piled high in the east over—or perhaps beyond—the Dhorisha Plains. He straightened his shoulders, determined to ignore the nagging at the back of his mind. Nagging that turned to an itch he couldn't scratch.

Something was about to happen. He had no idea where or when or who would be involved. Only this *feeling* that wouldn't let him be.

Overnight rain had left everything sparkling and clean smelling, though that likely wouldn't last long. Midsummer was close, and the days had been growing hotter by the minute. Puddles were rapidly turning to mud. Soon, they would be dust.

Once upon a time, he would have leaped high in the air, coming down in the puddle with both feet, scattering the scant bit of water in all directions with a goodly amount landing on him.

Once upon a time, he'd been a boy with nothing more to worry about than how to beg off fishing with his da—

Homesickness washed over him as violently as a summer storm. Petril ached to stand on the shores of Lake Evendim again, shivering from the spray flung from heaving waves as overhead a screeching gull danced on the wind. He even missed the stink of freshly gutted bluegill.

He could almost hear his little sister singing her favorite song: "Bluegills swimming, one by one, hurrah, hurrah . . ."

Easy peasy, bluegill breezy. Petril snorted and wrinkled his nose at the boy scowling back at him from the shriveling puddle. Lake Evendim was a far piece down the road, almost as distant as the boy he'd been last time he'd hummed that tune. Hard to believe nigh on a year had passed since he'd left home.

He scuffed at the puddle with his boot toe. His reflection, along with the brightly colored reflections of the tents surrounding him—reds and blues, oranges and greens, and some colors he'd never even seen before— blurred and blended in a riotous rainbow before settling back into the cone-shaped merchant tents that made up most of Kata'shin'a'in.

A woman dressed almost as gaudily as the tents *tsk*ed at him as she stepped delicately around the puddle and melded with the crowd.

There were folks everywhere, shoppers and merchants alike, and no one seemed inclined to linger. The air contained a trace of the rain that had fallen overnight, the springlike freshness chased away by the number of folks shopping or plying their various trades.

Closer to the beast market, with its horses and goats and sheep, the ground had been muddied by churning hooves, and the air reeked of animal musk and leather instead of rain. Made sense that the leatherworkers would be near the live animals, though he thought it rather insensitive. No one seemed to care what the animals themselves thought about the arrangement.

Petril cared. He could feel the animals' confusion. Their pain and fear clouded his mind as one drew closer to the beast market. Fortunately, their business had been outside the market, and they hadn't stayed long.

Toward the city center, the beast stench was replaced with the smells of various linens and rugs and the tantalizing aroma of sausages and meat pies as food vendors prepared for the midday rush. Everywhere merchants and vendors strove to outdo each other, voices rising and falling, some in cadence, some not, as they struggled to attract prospective shoppers.

No one paid much attention to a nine-year-old boy.

Which left him time to think.

Da always said Petril thought too much. *Ya spend too much time in yer own head.* And this was one of those times. No matter he'd just turned nine; he didn't feel like a nine-year-old.

He felt . . . *ancient.* Like a flower that stood too long in the sun without rain. Dried up. Ready to blow away.

Tha ain't it, he realized. More like a fisher waiting fer his boat ta sink . . .

"Bryn says it's time to stop wallowing in your own tears." Mira's hand fell on his shoulder.

"Why don't he tell me so hisself?" Petril demanded. He knew he sounded like a frustrated kiddie, but he couldn't stop the words. "Why don't tha 'orse talk ta me anymore? What'd I do ta anger him like?"

"Anger him?" Mira raised an eyebrow. "Boy, he's not mad at you. He just doesn't feel it's his place to Mindspeak anyone but me—unless it's an emergency, of course. Some feel Mindspeaking is an invasion of privacy."

"But he talked ta me afore—" Petril pressed his lips together, refusing to say more. The relationship between Companion and Herald was special; he knew that. So why did he expect to be included in the Companion's conversations?

Why did he expect . . . more?

The answer was as pure as it was simple. Petril was jealous. Bryn had spoken directly to him the first time they'd met. Had made Petril feel . . . special.

And now—now, he was just a kiddie again. Nothing special about him.

Ye ken tha's not right. Ye gotta way with critters.

He'd always had an affinity for animals. Back home, the village goats and dogs, the wild animals of the lake and forest, all were his friends. And then he'd found Bella and her foal—

"Thanks again for bringing Bella home."

Startled, Petril glanced up.

And immediately wished he were someplace else.

The girl in front of him stood nearly as tall as he, though she was a year or two younger (or so he'd been told), with hair the color of raven wings, golden skin, and piercing blue eyes.

Shin'a'in.

He forced a smile and nodded. "Home's where she needed ta be, her 'n the babe."

He blushed at his words—the stable boys in Haven hadn't hesitated to point out how rough and "uncivilized" his speech was; this Shin'a'in girl (*Tari*) had scarcely a hint of an accent.

And (kinda like shoving urchin spines in an open wound) he'd been told the girl could ride like she'd been born on a horse, a skill he longed to possess.

Petril fought the jealous burn in his belly, struggling not to think about how Bella—*his* Bella—had cozied up to the girl the moment the horse had seen her. Sunfish had taken a mite longer, but a few words and a gentle touch, and both colt and mare were acting like Tari was the one who had rescued them from the kidnappers and brought them home.

Of course, Bella had been kidnapped from the herd belonging to Tari's clan, he reminded himself. Sunfish had been born shortly after the kidnapping. Not surprising that Bella was happy to see Tari.

'Tweren't Tari's fault, he reminded himself. Nor was it her fault his mood was fouler than an Evaendim winter storm.

He forced his smile into a grin and pointed at a nearby vendor selling sugar cakes. "Herald Mina here were just 'bout to get us some food, right, Herald?"

"That's right. We were about to grab some sugar cakes," Herald Mira said after a long moment. "Would you care to join us?"

Tari broke into a smile that made the sun fade in comparison. She nodded. "Sharana has the best cakes in Kata'shin'a'in. Come on!"

Mira ruffled his hair as Petril hurried after the Shin'a'in girl, and he gave her a quick grin. He and Mira, along with Bryn, Bella, and Sunfish, had climbed mountains, forded rivers, and somehow found their way through the Pelagiris Forest to Kata'shin'a'in. After all that time together, Mira felt more like a sister than a traveling companion. And just like his eight brothers—and one sister—Mira never passed up a chance to give him grief.

He'd pay for this bit of generosity later. He was sure of it.

Tari wove between tents that erupted from the rolling grassy plains like great fish leaping for bugs, glancing back now and again to make sure they followed.

Petril had been surprised to discover the great city of Kata'shin'a'in was more a forest of merchant tents than actual buildings; what buildings there were seemed older than sand. He and Mira had wound their way between so many different tents that morning, Petril had begun to wonder if he could find his way back to the inn. After the wild bluegill run Tari was leading them on, he was certain to be lost—

The tantalizing aroma of fried cakes—their surfaces coated with sugar—overpowered the other smells, banishing all thought from his head. Tari beckoned to them just before disappearing inside a tent striped with yellows and golds.

Petril followed her inside, struggling not to huff and puff like the overweight beaver he'd once spotted trying to drag a tree back to its dam. He stopped a few steps inside the tent and let his eyes adjust to the dim interior.

A woman wearing a faded blue tunic over her voluminous skirts stood behind a counter laden with what his mum would call "goodies" of all types.

Petril swallowed hard as his mouth began to water at the sight—and smell—of fruit pasties and muffins and buns . . . all dominated by that most enticing of all—the sweet sugar cakes . . .

"Three, please," Tari was saying. "Mother will be in later to pick up supplies. She said to get whatever I wanted, and she'd pay for it when she arrived."

The woman nodded, filled three parchment bags with the sugared cakes, and handed them to Tari with a smile. "Looking forward to seeing your mum. Been too long."

Tari thanked her as she handed Mira and Petril each a bag.

Mira started to frown—an expression Petril was all too familiar with—but faster than he could blink, the frown smoothed into a smile. "Many thanks," she said, accepting her bag with a slight bow. "Bryn also sends his thanks. He loves sugar cakes almost as much as he loves pasties."

Tari immediately turned back to the woman and ordered one more bag "For the Herald's Companion."

Petril couldn't help but notice Bryn's bag was larger—and fuller—than the others.

Without warning, the tents, the clothing, even the sugar cakes—all seemed so *foreign*. He felt like a blue-gill flopping about on dry land, struggling to survive in a land that held little resemblance to what he was used to. He'd learned to sail almost before he could walk, but there were no boats here on the plains. He had no way to fit in with these people, to prove his worth—to the Herald or the Shin'a'in.

Or himself.

Yes, he'd rescued Bella and her babe from Lord Fancy Pants—twice—but he'd only started riding during the journey to Kata'shin'a'in—after Herald Mira asked if he wanted to finish what he'd started and escort the pair back home. Bella had graciously allowed him to ride and he'd made it all the way from Haven without falling off, but he still felt clumsy as a baby squirrel trying to climb its first tree . . .

Mira's face went blank in a manner that indicated she was communicating with Bryn. A moment later, her brow wrinkled.

"It appears we've been 'summoned'," she said, tucking the tops of both bags into her belt. "If you'll excuse us." She bowed her head gracefully toward Tari. "Petril here is rather popular today."

Petril shrugged, trying not to show his confusion.

The Shin'a'in girl bowed her head gracefully and gave him another brilliant smile.

"I know Bella and Sunfish would love to see you again," she said. "You're welcome to stop by the tent whenever you wish. We'll be around for a few more days."

Instead of making him feel better, the invitation sent him deeper into the void he'd been trying to escape. Petril nodded stiffly and followed Mira from the tent.

"We'll stop by the inn first to change," Mira said without looking back. "Put on your best clothes. We are about to meet some Very Important People."

Petril swallowed hard, but didn't ask any questions. He knew Mira would tell him what he needed to know *when* he needed to know it. She rarely offered information just for the sake of chatting. At first, he'd thought it part of her Herald training, but had learned that particular habit was more of a leftover from her childhood than part of her Herald teachings.

The inn they were staying at had to be older than Time—or so he reasoned. The stone was pitted and crumbling, and the beams were pocked with holes. True, the inn was clean enough, and the folks running it were kind. But he got the chills just walking down the hall, and he hadn't been able to sleep a single night since their arrival. He wasn't certain if he expected spirits or demons (likely spirits, demons would scare everyone silly, and the whole place would feel . . . *different*) to pop in at any moment, but *something* was there.

That nagging itch that told him something was about to happen screamed like an osprey diving on its prey as Petril dodged a man dressed in bright orange and green.

Folks 'round 'ere need ta look where they're going, he grumped.

And immediately felt shame wash over him. No reason for him to be in such a sour mood. They'd had a good morning. Herald Mira had a whole list of things to get for folks back in Valdemar, and he'd helped her make plenty of good deals. New saddles had been bought, along with so much tack it made his head spin. Mira had arranged for the lot to be delivered to Haven, so they wouldn't have to worry about hauling it all back with them.

So why had that warning itch become a full-blown infestation? He hadn't felt this squirmy since he'd played in a bed of nettles when he was still in diddies!

They arrived at the inn faster than he expected. "Wash up enough to be presentable, then dress in clean clothes and meet me downstairs," Mira instructed. "No dawdling. Not wise to keep a shaman waiting."

Shaman?

Sweat trickled down Petril's ribs despite the chill that wrapped him in icy arms. He bit his lip, trying to figure out why a shaman would want to see him? Everyone wanted to see the Heralds and their Companions, but he was only a fisherboy. No one wanted to see a fisherboy.

The coppery taste of blood spread through his mouth as he slipped into his room, splashed icy water on his face, and traded his faded tunic for one a little less worn. They'd been on the road so long he didn't have any truly clean clothes left.

He explained as much to Mira when she met him downstairs. Her Herald Whites looked fresh out of the laundry, their very *whiteness* putting his forest green tunic to shame.

"It'll do," Mira said and beckoned for him to follow.

Instead of heading back through the merchant tents, the Herald led the way deeper into the city proper. "Bryn says this is the oldest part of what locals call the Old City."

The area was definitely *old*. Tall, narrow walls rose on either side of them, blocking the view of anything beyond their immediate area. The dirt road was hard as stone, and the air smelled of dust and . . . old stuff. Not the sweet, rotten stench of death, but . . . old. Even though it wasn't long after midday, the shadowy road was dim enough he had to squint at the road so he didn't step in refuse—or worse.

A singsong voice rose off to one side. Petril stopped, drawn to the chanting.

Mira raised an arm. "Keep moving," she whispered. "There's nothing here but a bunch of dried-up religions."

Petril raised an eyebrow, but didn't protest. Mira wasn't much for religion. Every time someone brought it up, the Herald either left the room or changed the subject.

They paused in front of a heavy wooden door set deep into a wall on their left. Mira lifted the iron knocker and let it fall once.

Goose pimples rose on Petril's arms as a deep, gong-like sound echoed behind the door. Less than a heartbeat later, the door swung open, surprisingly silent considering the thick timbers it was made of.

Two figures waited just beyond the opening. The shaman, identified by his headdress, and a woman. Judging by the wrinkles around his eyes, the shaman had seen more summers than Petril's da. He was dressed in a tunic decorated with elaborate stitching and tiny beads and wore a headdress with tiny horns.

The woman had the same raven-black hair, piercing blue eyes, and golden skin as Tari. But this was a full-grown Shin'a'in woman, not a girl. Taller than Mira by at least two hands. She was slim, but Petril got the feeling that slimness was deceiving. She could likely outrun a horse if she so desired.

"Welcome," the shaman said, his voice deep, but not grating. "Please come in."

The room was sparsely furnished. Sitting pillows had been scattered here and there, and tapestries decorated each of the walls. An archway opened to the left, likely leading to the rest of the residence, or whatever the building was used for. Incense—smelling of summer flowers and something that made Petril slightly dizzy—curled and squiggled up the walls from small tables, one against each of the room's four walls, while someone chanted in the distance.

"So, this is the boy who brought Kendira home," the Shin'a'in woman said.

:Mind your manners. You stand before one of the Kal'enedral.:

The voice in Petril's mind—the voice he'd been longing to hear—stunned him for a moment. *:Bryn?:*

:Of course. Pay my words heed. Not only could this woman likely beat me in a race—if she so desired—she could gut you and skin you before you had a chance to blink.:

As Petril was digesting that not-so-tasty bit of information (more like putrid fish than sugar cakes), Mira greeted the shaman and his companion.

"Thank you for inviting us. We came as quickly as we could. If there is an issue—"

The shaman held up his hand. "No issues or problems. D'shayna and I simply wanted to express our gratitude in person."

"Why?" Petril blurted before he could stop himself. That feeling was back, the itching so intense he wanted to strip off his skin and throw it in the fire.

Only there was no fire—

:And you might miss your hide,: Bryn noted. *:Humans look rather silly without their hides.:*

:Da said that kinda thing's a figger of speech. Not meant ta be serious.: Though the feeling wasn't as intense—now that Bryn was talking to him again.

:I do understand—about the figurativeness of speech. Another bit of human silliness. And I'm talking to you so you calm down. You are wound up tighter than a corkscrew still in the pod.:

:I thought ye was mad at me fer something—:

:Nonsense. Mira explained it to you. Now hush, or you'll miss what's coming.:

Miss what's coming? Petril blinked, refocusing on the shaman standing directly before him. Hadn't the man been by the door only a moment ago?

For some reason, the shaman looked amused. Mira cleared her throat. "Aren't you going to answer the shaman's question?"

Face flushed with heat, Petril glanced helplessly at Mira.

"The shaman wants to give you a gift," she said as

though explaining a game to a child. "What is it you would like?"

"This isn't a gift of geegaws and pretties," the Kal'enedral said abruptly. "The true question is—what do you *need*?"

The hair on the back of Petril's neck tightened as the shaman nodded. The old man's blue eyes were cold as ice chips, mirroring the look in the Kal'enedral's eyes.

By the grace of the Old Sturgeon what could they mean? His birthday had already passed. Why should they give him a gift? Something he *needed,* not wanted?

Suddenly the old shaman reached forward and pressed a gnarled finger against Petril's forehead.

:Don't move,: Bryn warned.

Petril couldn't have moved if the room had been set ablaze. His feet were frozen in place while the rest of him . . . the rest of him felt like it was on display for the entire world to see. His deepest, darkest secrets revealed, his jealousies and desires—

The shaman blinked and dropped his hand. He glanced back at the Kal'enedral. "This one is more than he seems."

Petril had "keeled over" just after he'd turned seven—at least, that's what Da called it. Mum said he fainted. All he could remember was things got dark before everything went black . . .

Just like they were doing now—which meant he was about to keel over . . . or someone had turned out a light.

:Breathe,: Bryn ordered.

Petril struggled to pull air past the fear clutching his throat.

D'shayna inclined her head. The room felt icier than Lake Evendim during a winter freeze. "We would speak alone."

Petril's heart squeezed as the pair slipped through the archway into the room beyond. What had the shaman seen? He frantically thought back through everything that had happened since coming to Kata'shin'a'in. Had he broken some law? Offended a high-ranking citizen?

:Peace,: Bryn ordered. The Companion almost

sounded . . . excited. *:Calm yourself. If you had done something wrong, you'd be facing whoever keeps the order around here.:*

Mira put a hand on Petril's shoulder. "Bryn's right. Wait until you learn what's on their minds before letting your mind run wild."

He had time for two deep breaths and one round of "Bluegills swimming, one by one, hurrah, hurrah" before the shaman and the Kal'enedral slipped back into the room. Petril scrubbed sweaty palms against his thighs, forcing himself not to panic.

Likely time ta get meself home after we leave here. All this adventurin's got me guts in a tangle—

"You've got the boy half scared out of his wits," Mira said as the two surrounded Petril. "Mind telling us what's going on?"

Her voice was quiet, but Petril could hear concern in her words. He took heart in knowing that Bryn wouldn't be far off should they need him.

"You have a Gift," the shaman said. He spoke in a way that included them all, though his icy gaze remained on Petril.

Petril swallowed hard. No matter how hard he tried, he couldn't remember saying—or doing—anything that might be offensive. He'd been too overwhelmed. "I kin unnerstand animals. Not talk to 'em, not really. I kin feel what they're feeling. Feel when they're scared, in pain . . ." His head hurt just thinking about the abuse Bella had taken—blows to the head, the poison coursing through her system . . .

"Do you know why the Kal'enedral dress in black?" D'shayna asked. She remained in the shadows beneath the archway.

Petril's heart stuttered, then sank like a poorly thrown stone across water. "Yer on a blood feud."

"Kendira, the mare you call Bella, has been in my family since she was born," D'shayna said. "When she was stolen, my clan sent out a search party. That party was ambushed. The entire group—seven in all—were killed. Their deaths were not . . . honorable."

She paused, and the shaman took up the story. "D'shayna was away at the time. She came home immediately upon finding out what had happened."

"I pledged blood feud," D'shayna continued, "and began hunting down those who murdered my clansmen."

"Only the murderer had already been apprehended and was awaiting trial in Haven?" Mira guessed. She nodded at Petril. "Lord Fancy Pants."

Petril felt his eyes widen. He glanced at the Kal'enedral. "He murdered all your friends?"

D'shayna gave a curt nod. "My blood sister among them."

"I'm sorry," Petril blurted. "I—"

The Kal'enedral held up a hand. "It is no fault of yours. Thanks to you, Kendira is safely home, as is her babe."

"Which brings us to why we are here," the shaman said. "D'shayna wanted to grant you a boon. Something that might possibly help you as you have helped her." He paused. "We have decided to offer you a choice."

The room went still, so still Petril could hear his heart pounding. He *had* done something wrong. He knew he was overreacting, knew they wouldn't possibly *kill* him . . . would they?

He studied the Kal'enedral half hidden in shadow and tried to swallow his fear. "Fear'll send ye ta the deeps quicker than lightnin' if'n ye let it," his da always said. "Set yer mind on somethin' ye *can* do, rather than sweatin' what ye cain't. If'n yer still breathin', set yer mind on that."

Petril focused on his breathing—

"My reading revealed something I had not expected," the shaman said. "Your Gift has only partially manifested. Typically, these Gifts mature on their own, at whatever rate the body/mind/spirit chooses. *Your* Gift, however, has been 'caged,' for lack of a better term. There is a possibility that the entrapment was done by another human—a shaman, perhaps—but I have a strong sense you may have done this to yourself."

Petril's stomach rolled, and he couldn't seem to catch his breath. "What . . . meself . . . why?"

The shaman shrugged. "That is for you to find out. The cage is rather strong. Not too strong to break—if you so choose."

"Think long and hard on this, youngling." D'shayna moved out of the shadows, farther into the room. "If you did indeed cage your own Gift, there must have been a good reason."

It made no sense, Petril realized. Why would he lock away something that could help him . . . *become* . . . what he'd always wanted?

The room spun in crazy circles, and his head started to pound.

Mira put an arm around his shoulders. "Will you give him some time to think? This is a lot for a boy his age to process."

Both the shaman and D'shayna nodded.

"You have until morning. I've been called to perform a . . ." The shaman wrinkled his nose, "*ceremony*. While I would rather remain here, I cannot deny my service to others."

Petril stared at the man . . . and found himself wondering what kind of horns were on the shaman's headdress.

"We'll return in the morning, then," Mira said. She gently turned Petril toward the door. "I think a bit of food and a good night's sleep—"

"Best not make a hasty decision," D'shayna agreed. "I always find a good night's sleep—if it can be had— puts perspective on the problems at hand. Experience has taught me that no gift comes without a price. When I pledged myself to the Star-Eyed, she required sacrifice. Being Kal'enedral is a great privilege and a heavy burden. Your decision will be no less impactful, I believe. Think long and sleep well."

Petril managed to nod as Mira herded him out the door. "Thank you," he called back over his shoulder.

Whatever had just happened?

One day he'd been dreaming of magic and heroes and how he would one day save the world, and now . . .

If'n me Gift was uncaged . . .

If his Gift was uncaged, he could *be* that hero.

Why had his Gift been caged? Who could have done such a thing?

Could I have really done it meself?

He rejected the thought almost as soon as it formed. Such a thing wasn't possible. He didn't even know how to handle—how to *use*—the abilities he had. Putting them in a cage was . . . impossible.

Wasn't it?

Petril stumbled on a loose stone, feeling like the Old Sturgeon himself, carrying the weight of the world on his shoulders, caught somewhere between a boy and a man.

He had a decision to make, a decision that could change his life.

He could either stay the boy he was, doing what little he could to help where help was needed.

Or he could shoulder responsibility. Become the hero he always dreamed he could be.

What 'bout the cage? Wha—

A scream split the air somewhere behind him. Petril's heart leaped like a startled rabbit, and the spit dried in his mouth. He spun, hand going to the knife he'd kept at his hip since leaving home, a man's knife given by his da—

And instantly felt like a full-blown fool.

A handful of urchins scampered past, splashing through puddles and throwing what looked like moldy bread at each other with shrieks and screams. He watched them with a fierce yearning that made his eyes burn.

He missed being home, chasing his sisters, helping his ma. He even missed being teased by his older brothers.

He missed being a boy—

"You can always say no."

Petril shrugged, not wanting to look at the woman behind him. She *always* seemed to know what was going on in his head, no matter she claimed no such Gift.

"The world needs fisherfolk and farmers," Herald Mira continued. "Not everyone is cut out to be a warrior or a shaman, a Healer or a Herald."

His heart skipped a beat. Were it only that simple.

He'd always *imagined* himself doing this fantastic thing or that. He'd spent his days dreaming—fighting off bandits and pirates or becoming a spy for the King's court or maybe even becoming a Herald, as improbable as that had always seemed.

No matter who or what he dreamed of being, he was someone who helped others, who saved lives, who could possibly even save the whole *world* one day.

For as long as he could remember, Petril had wanted to be a hero.

Then Bella and Sunfish had come along and he'd saved them. Twice.

And discovered that being a hero wasn't all light and glory. It was dirty and painful and scary as being caught on the lake during a lightning storm.

He thought about D'shayna, about her clothing, black as the darkest shadow . . .

And found himself staring into another puddle.

The reflection in this puddle was sharper than if he'd been looking in a mirror. Not only could he make out the narrow shape of his face and his hooked nose.

He could see the indecision in his eyes.

See the fear.

Who knew what setting his gift free would do to him? Wasn't it already bad enough he could feel pain that wasn't his? He remembered the rage Bella had felt when she'd been trapped and beaten by Lord Fancy Pants. The anguish and fear for her young foal . . .

Petril gulped. There were times when he wished someone would take it all away so he wouldn't feel what the creatures around him felt.

How could he stand even *more*?

Staring at that puddle, studying his reflection, feeling like a two-year-old deprived of his mum's pasties . . .

The reflection blurred and suddenly—even though she was nowhere nearby—he was looking into Bella's round eyes. Huge, intelligent, knowing.

He had helped Bella when she'd needed it most. Brought her safely home—along with her babe.

And that felt . . . good.

Better'n all his mum's pasties *and* all the sugar cakes in Valdemar.

It hadn't been easy. It hadn't been fun.

It had been *worthwhile*.

A shadow flicked across his puddle, darkening the shimmering water until all reflections were gone.

There was no one to save this time. No boggle to fight, no Lord Fancy Pants to beat.

No one to tell him which path to choose.

When the shadow lifted and the reflection returned, Petril saw only his young eyes looking back over his hooked nose.

Eyes that no longer held indecision.

He knew what he had to do.

He called to Mira, turned around, and led the way back to the shaman's door.

The shaman had insisted they wait until morning. Both D'shayna and Mira (and Bryn) had agreed.

"Too easy to act on a whim," the shaman said.

So Petril waited and waited and waited. He didn't sleep, not much anyway. Morning found him just as determined as the previous evening.

That determination stayed with him all the way through the Old City to the shaman's.

Now he sat on one of the cushions, hands folded in his lap, incense sucking the air from the room. Candles lit the room just enough that he could make out faces but not a lot of detail. Not that he paid much attention to detail—except for one.

Fear. Suffocating, paralyzing fear.

Petril clamped his teeth together so tight his jaws ached. He wanted to ask if the process or ceremony or whatever the shaman did was going to hurt. Did he need to cut himself and share blood with another? Would he get a headache like the one he'd had after cleansing Bella of the poison given her by Lord Fancy Pants?

He wanted Bryn's reassurance, but the Companion had gone silent again. Mira said Petril needed to do this on his own. His eyes burned, his chest felt like a giant sturgeon was sitting on him, and his stomach was a churning cauldron.

He *couldn't* do this. They were asking too much.

He was asking too much.

Of himself . . .

Ye always wanted ta be a hero, he reminded himself. *Saving the world and such. Stop being such a baby 'fore anythin's even happened.*

He opened eyes he hadn't realized were shut, studied the Kal'enedral standing across the room, quiet as a shadow, calm and clear as his reflection had been the evening before. When he'd made his decision.

Shadows and reflections.

D'shayna had told him a little of what it meant to be Swordsworn, what she'd gone through, what she had to give up.

A sacrifice made by a select few. An honor above all others.

Tain't easy bein' a hero, son, Da once said when Petril complained about wanting to be a hero. He knew for a fact Da was right about that. It wasn't easy being a hero, going above and beyond.

Wasn't easy being Swordsworn or a shaman or even a Herald (according to Mira).

Land the fish or sail fer home. Da never demanded his sons do what he told them to do. He did demand they make a decision. *Make yer decision 'fore life makes it for you.*

"I'm ready," Petril said, surprising himself. He could tell by the look on Mira's face he'd caught her off guard.

Everything would change after this, he knew that. But he was ready for that change. He grinned and straightened his shoulders. He wasn't sailing for home, not yet, anyway.

Time ta land tha fish.

All it took was the shaman's touch to uncage his Gift . . .

. . . Leaving Petril feeling as though he'd been caught in a rocky landslide, bruised and battered and wishing everyone would just shut up and leave him alone.

He didn't remember walking back to the inn and falling into bed.

It took a full day of sleep after the uncaging to realize there had been no landslide, and the bruises weren't real. His pounding head kept getting worse, though.

Thousands of voices yammering at him.

Emotions of all kinds pelting him from every direction, emotional hailstones in a never-ending storm.

A storm he'd experienced before.

Flashes of memory surged through the voices, emotion mingling with emotion, voices so mixed he couldn't tell what was here.

And what was *memory*.

Four summers before he'd experienced this storm. Been trying to help his brother with a net and slipped overboard. Panic as the icy water closed over his head. Panic at the sound of voices, both near and far, voices that he *knew* had always been with him. *Voices that weren't human.*

He could taste the fear as an enormous form rose to stop his tiny body as it sank deeper and deeper . . .

:You need to shield yourself,: a familiar voice said.

Petril grabbed hold of that voice and clung tight. "Gonna die, Bryn," he groaned. "Right here 'n now . . . Cain't take no more . . ."

:Nonsense,: Bryn said. *:Give me—:*

:Hold,: said another voice. New, yet strangely familiar. *:I'll take it from here.:*

A shiver ran down Petril's back. Before he could ask who the newcomer was or find out what she (the voice was definitely female) was taking, darkness swept through his mind, smothering the emotions and the yammering voices as if someone had wrapped them in a heavy woolen blanket.

For the first time since leaving home, Petril felt . . . peace.

The same peace he'd felt on that long-ago day—when he hadn't been drowned or eaten.

Da called it a miracle. The sturgeon—large enough to

thrash their boat—had lifted Petril to the surface on the end of its nose.

And vanished.

Had that fear—that experience—caused him to lock his Gift away?

:I've shielded you for now,: the new voice said. *:But Bryn is correct—you need to learn how to shield yourself. You present an interesting challenge, young man. The Gift of Mindspeech coupled with an unusual amount of Empathy with a dab of Healing thrown in. We'll deal with all that later. Right now, you need to come outside.:*

To his great surprise, Petril didn't question the voice. Whoever was in his head meant him no harm, he could *feel* it. He threw back the covers, gave Mira a shaky grin, and headed for the door. It was time to stop hiding in the shadows, gazing at reflections . . .

Staying inside me cage . . .

Taking a firm grip on the handle, Petril flung the door open.

And stepped outside.

At least he tried to.

A bright light blocked the doorway. A light so bright, so white, Petril's eyes watered. He swiped a hand across his eyes, blinked and blinked again.

Not a light—a horse. With vibrant blue eyes—

A Companion.

"Heyla, Bryn," Petril said, wondering at the surge of disappointment flooding through him. Then he froze.

This wasn't Bryn. He'd never seen this Companion before.

Had he?

:We can discuss that later,: the Companion said in a decidedly female voice. She lowered her head and snuffled at his tunic.

And drew back with a snort. *:Smells like you missed a bath or two, but that can wait. First things first, young-ling. You are mine and I am yours. Look into my eyes. Time to banish your shadows for good.:*

His imagination had finally taken over, Petril decided.

According to Mira, a Companion never asked anyone to look into their eyes . . .

He had to be imagining . . .

His hand moved as if possessed, reaching up and touching the Companion's warm nose. Soft as velvet but solid and . . . *real*.

Petril's knees threatened to buckle, and once again, the world dimmed . . .

And then the world brightened, the light growing with such intensity he thought he'd go blind. Joy bubbled inside him, growing and growing, till he thought he'd burst into hundreds of pieces too small to feed the tiniest fish.

It *was* real. He'd been *Chosen*.

He'd imagined this moment, imagined so hard it hurt. Known that if a Companion was to come looking for him, Petril would go with him—or her—faster 'n a fish snagged a bug.

But no Companion had come knockin' on his door, as his mum like to say.

Until now.

And all those imaginings were nothing more than watered-down milk.

Chosen.

Now he could make a difference. Now he could help in ways he'd only dreamed of before.

Now he could be the hero who just might . . . someday . . . save the world.

Petril laid a hand on either side of the Companion's nose, drew in her grass-scented breath . . .

And looked into her vibrant blue eyes. Eyes so alive, so . . . knowing.

A thought swept through his mind as he found himself drawn into the Companion's gaze, an icy splash of reality like the foam off a winter wave.

No more easy peasy blue gill breezy.

From now on, life would be a *real* adventure.

Flying the Nest
Michele Lang

K'Valdemar Vale blazed in all its tropical glory as Sparrow packed her bags yet again, for what seemed like the millionth time. Life pulsated all around her as she fussed around in her *ekele*, putting things to rights as best she could. She had taken so many trips on Herald business over the years, said so many little goodbyes to this place.

But this time was different. This time felt like a forever goodbye, to what was gone and could never be called back again. She swept the floor one last time, a huge lump in her throat. Took a moment to glance up, and there was her best friend in the world.

Roark.

Hertasi don't cry, she had it from Roark's own authority. But mothers like Sparrow sure did.

Roark's mouth widened in his toothy grimace of a smile. "When little birds fly the nest, the grown birds fly too," he said, his scratchy voice and his unblinking amber eyes betraying no emotion.

But Sparrow had learned over the years the signs of grief in her dearest, homebody friend. The way his dewlap fluttered, the restless clicking of his sharply clawed fingers, all betrayed the same twisting wrench of approaching separation that Sparrow felt.

Sparrow swallowed past the lump in her throat, cleared it. "I know *hertasi* don't tend to go on long trips," she said. "Any chance you would like to come with us anyway?"

Roark's low, bubbling laugh rose out of his spindly, iridescently scaled chest. "No, dear one. I will stay here, in the warm and the flowering, and will leave it to you and your Herald kin to venture out to where it is cold, and dirty, and . . . out of sorts. Such a mess as Haven is not the place for me."

His gaze met hers, clear and unwavering as always, and Sparrow wanted to protest that she, too, was not meant for mess and trouble. Her heartmate, Cloudbrother, had been Chosen by a Companion, but Sparrow had been chosen by a *hertasi*, her personal wizard of domesticity, Roark himself. She had some skills in the healing arts, but no Gift meriting formal Greens. Sparrow's real magic resided within these walls, in her kitchen, in her weaving. In her love of family.

And once again—and now for good, she feared— Sparrow had to leave her place of magic behind.

"They're waiting for me outside," she managed to force out, her voice choked with the tears that stayed locked in her throat. "Goodbye, my beloved friend."

Sparrow had broken their long, unspoken pact to never say goodbye when she left on Herald business. But they both knew why she had decided to say goodbye now.

Roark held out his clawed hands. Sparrow first clasped them in her own fingers, then pulled the *hertasi* close for a brief but fierce last hug goodbye. "Bless you, and may the Mother keep you," she whispered into the top of his scaled head.

:Goodbye, little Sparrow: he whispered in her mind as she untangled herself from his cool, bony, reptilian embrace.

She closed her eyes, took a deep breath . . . and let her home go.

And when she opened them again, she realized Roark had silently slipped away.

Without looking back, she stumbled from inside the *ekele* out to the brilliant, blinding effusion of sunny glory in the clearing. The air was alive with the buzz of singing insects and the triumphant songs of Bondbirds perched high in the flowering branches above their heads, calling her to life.

Time to face forward. Time to ride.

As always, there waited Abilard, Cloudbrother's magnificent Companion. Cloudbrother sat astride him, resplendent in his Herald whites, tall and slim as ever in the saddle.

But this time, a second Companion stood in the clearing, her nostrils flaring, her jeweled eyes taking in the sight of Sparrow with a gentle, knowing gaze.

Milini had Chosen Sparrow's son, Thistle, just the night before. And she had brought with her not only the Choice, but an urgent summons to Haven for Thistle's father, Cloudbrother.

So, for the first time, Tis no longer sat in front of his father as they departed the Vale, his child's fingers tangled in Abilard's mane. Now, he sat astride Milini, looking as though he had always been with her. His serious, tense little face was relaxed now. It was as if he had been waiting for Milini to come for him from the moment he had been born.

And she had finally arrived.

Deep down, Sparrow had always known Tis was destined for the life of a Herald. But just as deeply, she had always hoped she would have a little more time with him. The boy was scarcely ten.

:We could not ever leave without you, Sparrow,: Abilard said to her, and he sent a wave of gentle, loving warmth along with his words, an affirming embrace that despite her lack of Gift, Sparrow was part of this tiny Herald tribe. *:You are the heart of us.:*

Sparrow could not Mindspeak in reply, so she stepped forward and caressed his strong, rippling flank with trembling fingers. Abilard had always treated her with especial tenderness and respect.

Her heartmate sensed her standing alongside his left leg. "I hope you're ready to ride hard, sweetling," he said, his voice quiet, his eyes, as always, permanently closed, unseeing. "Milini made it clear that we needed to get to Haven as soon as we can."

Sparrow forced her voice to be cheerful. "Hah, hurry up and wait, that's the Herald way. Or this time, wait and hurry up. No worry, we will go nice and early now, and be well on our way."

Cloudbrother had been blind since almost succumbing to a terrible illness as a young child, but Sparrow knew he could sense her misery. Her heartmate was so strong he could afford to be gentle. He reached down, knowing how to find her cheek, caressed her gently and ruffled her hair.

"I'm sorry," he said, his voice low. "You have all of the scut of the Herald's life and none of the glory. But without you . . ."

She knew everything that he didn't say aloud. Cloudbrother had proven his mettle as a Herald over and over again, battling demons to the death, saving the Vale itself from attack, bringing rain to the thirsty land of Iftel.

But his ordinary eyes could not see, and in the realm of the ordinary, the earthbound, the practical, he needed Sparrow to extend his reach in the everyday world.

And she was so happy to do it, to help her sweetheart in the mundane so that he could leap into the realm of the mind and give his Gift. As he was quick to tell everyone, from his time of training in Haven, "Sparrow and I come in a pair."

At times like this, it meant everything to know that her heartmate understood the sacrifices she had made, too. They were not so obvious and grand as his own, or as the sacrifices that every Herald made, but they were no less real to her for being ordinary.

Sparrow climbed up on the mossy stone they all used as a mounting block in everyday life. She was ready now. She settled in behind her heartmate, wrapped her arms around his muscular waist, and relaxed against his strong, supple back.

Time to find adventure once again. Thistle was in the place he belonged now, astride his Companion, and in her heart of hearts, Sparrow knew she, too, belonged on this journey of danger and opportunity.

* * *

Despite the urgency of the summons, they traveled as slowly as they could, as much to give Tis time to bond with Milini as to enjoy the late spring weather. Even after they left the Vale, northern Valdemar bloomed with joy, and birds—sparrows, jays, and songbirds— rustled in great profusion through the branches in the leaves above their heads.

The Forest of Sorrows had mellowed in the years since Cloudbrother had vanquished the demon Zeth, who had sought to force his way through the Forest and through Cloudbrother himself in order to destroy and control. Though they rode through wilderness, and all wild lands contained danger, the mordant sickness was out of the forest now.

But Cloudbrother had paid a steep price for his victory.

The ancient trees along their journey through the Forest grew so thickly their branches intertwined and tangled into a canopy above their heads as they trotted along. Even in midday, they rode in cool, dappled shadows.

:Mama?: Tis spoke into Sparrow's mind.

With a start, Sparrow skittered out of her reverie. She shot Tis a glance to where he rode, looking absurdly small astride Milini. He knew she could not reply to him; he called her to let her know he was thinking of her.

He met her gaze, his eyes sharp and intense as always. And then his face broke into a luminous smile, one of pure wonder and delight.

Oh, her intense, driven child. He had been waiting for this day since the day he was born. And now he was on his way. She didn't need to tell Tis all about the challenges, the sacrifices. He had seen the choices his father made, the hard decisions.

Tis wanted all of it.

How could she begrudge him his destiny? She couldn't. In that moment, riding alongside, she was grateful for the chance to see him off. And Sparrow had no idea that it would be her—the little bird, the little mother—who would face the greatest challenge once they arrived.

*   *   *

That night, they stopped to rest at a Waystation outside the village of Brach. They could have stayed at an inn in the village itself, but without ever discussing the matter, all the members of the party knew they would prefer to take their own company, apart from other travelers.

It was a clear and cloudless night, and before they turned in, the five formed a circle under the swirling stars, around a small fire to keep them warm after their evening meal. They spoke in low voices and looked at the stars more than at each other.

"Get ready to work hard, son," Cloudbrother said, the note of sadness in his voice so faint that only Sparrow could discern it. "Once you get to the Collegium, the time will flash by like a single candlemark. You'll see."

"Do you think I can do it?" Tis asked, uncertainty trembling in his words. "The other kids are going to be so much bigger than me."

:*You are Chosen now for good reason*,: Milini whispered reassuringly. Her voice was cool and clear, a bell's chime in the spring darkness. :*I have no doubt you will find your way in Haven, and your joy as well.*:

She was the perfect Companion for Thistle, her calm coolness a needed contrast to his dark intensity. Sparrow was often intimidated by the Companions she had met in her years of service at Cloudbrother's side. But Milini, tranquil and steady, always sent ripples of peace and serenity through Sparrow's mind and heart every time she spoke.

The fire guttered low, down to the cinders. It was time to sleep . . . they planned to rise with dawn's light and ride for Haven. They made their simple preparations for bed, and in their shelter, Sparrow and Cloudbrother curled up together next to Abilard, while Thistle rested his head on Milini's flank.

Quiet and darkness settled over them all like a warm, soft blanket.

And yet, most uncharacteristically indeed, Sparrow could not sleep. Because she knew that she and Cloudbrother could no longer fly in their dreams.

They had been grounded ever since his battle with the demon had stolen his Gifts away. Before this, from the time they had been children far smaller than Thistle, Sparrow and Cloudbrother had met on the plane of dreams, held hands, and flown the clouds together.

It was their special place of connection, the place where Sparrow had first fallen in love with him. But they could no longer go there. That elemental home, they had lost without the chance to say goodbye.

Instead, Sparrow whispered into Cloudbrother's ear, a tiny puff of sound too quiet to wake the others. "Are you still up?"

Cloudbrother stirred. "I am now, love."

Sparrow grinned into the darkness. She knew he'd said the words with a smile on his beautiful, scarred face. "It's so dark in here, I can't see the hand in front of my face."

"When a body is trying to sleep, that's usually a good thing."

Sparrow sighed. "Yes, but . . ."

"But . . . a mother bird is restless, guarding her fledgling."

She snorted, as delicately as she could. "Well, I guess. I just . . ." She hesitated, not sure if she should go on with her thoughts. Not sure if it was fair to destroy his sleep because hers eluded her.

"No, go ahead, say it."

"What's going to happen to me? To us?"

Silence greeted her words, urging her to continue. "Once Tis is gone, it's just you and me again. Is Abilard . . . going to go back to the Grove now?"

Cloudbrother knew what she was after. His Gift was gone, away with the demon, and his life in the Vale had been anticlimactic indeed after such a battle. Did Heralds retire? After all that Cloudbrother had gone through, maybe the Council was going to suggest a rest of some kind, for both Cloudbrother and his Companion.

His voice remained steady. "My love, this pairing is for life, just like with you and me. Boredom is a greater sacrifice sometimes than death. But I'm sure that Abilard would never leave me, and there is a reason we are all together. And I'm thinking that tomorrow, at the Council meeting, we are going to find out why."

Sparrow thought about it for a bit, matching her breathing to his, trying to relax. "But what's going to happen to us? Once Tis is off to the Collegium, what are we going to do with ourselves?"

Cloudbrother hesitated for a long time before replying, so long that she wondered if he had fallen back asleep. But then he turned, pulled her closer, tucked the crown of her head under his strong chin.

"I am still a Herald, still and forever," he said, his voice serene and sure. "But I have a sense, sweetheart, that you have a new path to follow, the way I do. We are in a turning of the seasons. And no matter what happens next, we are going to travel that new path together."

She considered his words, savored how they settled, like a balm over her heart. "You always know just the right thing to say," she whispered gratefully. "Whatever happens, as long as we face it together, we will be all right in the end."

Sparrow dropped off at some point and only awakened the next morning after the others had already begun their preparations to leave. Bleary-eyed, she stretched out on the floor, stiff muscles protesting, then creaked to her feet.

She got ready to go in a few minutes. "No breakfast?" she asked. Hoping deep down they would pause a little longer. Because the thought of dropping Tis off and riding away filled her with a wild and irrational grief. She wanted him to go, but she also couldn't bear it.

"No breakfast!" Tis said, brooking no opposition. "Let's go, Mama. We can have something when we get to Haven."

Sparrow restrained a smile. He was reciting Sparrow's usual "time to go" speech, using her own words against her now. That's what kids were supposed to do.

It was an easy ride now to Haven, through a well-populated and prosperous countryside. *:The Council* *meets at midday,:* Abilard said, his Mindspeech clear in Sparrow's mind, oddly formal. *:They are expecting us there then.:*

A frisson of worry worked down Sparrow's spine. The Council! She had never appeared before it, and imagined an imposing spectacle. Not for the first time, she was relieved not to stand in the center of scrutiny, instead staying in a supporting role.

It was not until they reached the outer limits of the great city that Sparrow learned the truth.

:Mama,: Thistle said again. This time his words in her mind thrummed with a hint of anxiety layered over his excitement. Of course, he would be nervous as they got closer to the Collegium.

The Companions moved at a steady trot now, and Sparrow had to concentrate on maintaining her seat behind Cloudbrother. Even so, she looked over at her son and nodded reassuringly once again. She wanted to tell him that he was equal to the challenge, that all endings lead to new beginnings, that love was greater than fear and would sustain him through his times alone.

But to be a parent was to be continually surprised, and challenged, and sometimes gobsmacked. Because Tis wasn't looking for her approval.

:The Council wants to talk to you—especially you,: Tis continued, his words sharper this time, so clear and crisp she could all but see them rising in her mind like long slashing shadows. *:You are summoned too, not just Papa.:*

Sparrow had to grab Cloudbrother hard to keep from tumbling off the back of Abilard's muscled rump. "Me?" she managed to splutter, not just at Tis, but at all of them.

Cloudbrother half-chuckled, half-groaned. "Well, remember what I said last night about traveling a new road together? That road is starting in the Council, sure thing. They want to see the both of us, but there's no need to worry. You won't be on the spot all alone, promise," he said in his ordinary, warm, encouraging voice. He spoke to her as one villager to another, instead of in the language of Heralds and power-infused creatures.

Sparrow had ridden with Abilard and Cloudbrother from the Vale to Haven any number of times before this, and Cloudbrother himself had appeared before the Council, for reasons ranging from mundane to shocking.

But this time, it was Sparrow who was called.

"Have I done something wrong?" she asked, her voice shaking. She couldn't even pretend to take the news calmly. "Why else would they want to see me? I'm not a Healer. I'm not a Herald. I'm—"

She cut herself off from saying it—she was a nobody. But she didn't need the power of Mindspeech to convey what she believed to their small party.

Sparrow felt a gentle caress of kindness emanating from Abilard, refuting her nonspoken words with pure emotion.

"Don't say it, or not-say it, my love," Cloudbrother replied. "You are the heart of us, Abilard is right. Without you, I would be dead many times over, Tis would not exist, the Forest itself would be blasted to ruin by now. You don't go about with airs, all fancy. No, you just make everything happen. There can be nothing to fear from the Council. Only good is going to come from this, I'm sure of it."

Cloudbrother's words shocked her. After so much adventuring, she had thought that her days of adventure were done.

But now . . . the thought of a new adventure, a new challenge, one that she couldn't even imagine . . . part of her wanted to hide away at home in her role as the "little mother." Her father's nickname for her as a girl.

But those days were long over. She was no girl. Sparrow was the heartmate of a Herald, the mother of a Herald to be. On the Council's orders, she had traveled many times to far off, dangerous lands on desperate missions, fought off terrible threats to Valdemar in the heart of her home.

But until now, she had always hidden under the protection of Cloudbrother's wings. With a not-unpleasant shock, Sparrow realized that she had so much more to offer the Council than her role as a helpmeet.

Playing small was a false humility.

If the Council needed her to serve, she would do so gladly. Mixed in with her growing amazement was a lingering fear of the unknown and a wistful longing for her home, her nest.

But Roark was right. Time to fly.

:Mama, you always tell me to let things unfold in their good time,: Tis said. *:Soon enough, we will know what's what. Until then, we are still together.:*

Sparrow couldn't bring herself to answer. Instead, she buried her face in Cloudbrother's clean, snowy Whites, inhaling the clean smell of the linen mixed with his ineffable sandalwood scent.

Tis was right. But between losing him to the Collegium and now knowing the summons to Haven was about her, Sparrow was hard-pressed to follow Tis's sage advice.

Haven overwhelmed Sparrow the way it did every time she entered the magnificent city. This time, she didn't have time to visit her big brother Keeth, now advanced to a Captain of the Guards and living in his sprawling house filled with a mob of kids down the Hill, outside the gates.

Instead, they rode straight for the city center, for the Collegium. They passed through the final set of gates, waved through by the guards, and there it was.

The Collegium. And the Palace.

The sight of the dormitories and the broad green stretching between them instantly called Sparrow back to Cloudbrother's time here as a Trainee. Her eyes blurred with tears as she made out the tiny corner window of the room where they had stayed together, as a special dispensation.

Sparrow was not a Trainee, but she was embedded with Cloudbrother's group of them, and she had experienced the making of a Herald at a single remove.

Milini and Abilard halted in the middle of the green, and they all took in the sight of the crisscrossing pathways, the graceful trees swaying in a light, fragrant breeze, the flags flying at the tops of the buildings, Heralds, Healers, Bards.

It took Sparrow's breath away, and the years too.

The spell was broken by Tis's voice. "It's huge," he said, his eyes goggling as he stared at the campus all around them. "It's enormous! It's a city within itself."

Tis had not been in Haven since he was a toddler, and apparently he did not remember his babyhood visit. It didn't matter—Sparrow was as awestruck by the sight of the Collegium as Tis was.

"Let's report," Cloudbrother said, his voice soft. "You will find your guide and a late breakfast too, I suspect."

:We will take it from here, Herald,: Milini whispered. *:A quick farewell, now.:*

Cloudbrother twisted in the saddle as if he could see the Companion and his son, the newly Chosen. He opened his mouth as if to speak, then sighed and nodded, a lock of silver hair falling in front of his sightless eyes.

"Yes, that is the right way," he said, his voice gentle. "Farewell, Thistle. You will do us proud, I am sure."

And all at once, the separation was complete. Sparrow and Thistle exchanged one more long glance. She willed herself still, absolutely still except for one hand raised in farewell, and she smiled at him, one last smile.

He smiled back, bent his head in thanks, and then he and Milini turned to head toward the main Herald dormitory.

Sparrow watched them go in silence.

"He'll be fine, Sparrow," Cloudbrother said. "He is going to have the time of his life."

"I know," she replied. "He is meant for this. But I miss him already."

As Abilard wheeled and cantered for the Palace, Sparrow settled into a static calm. She no longer worried about the Council, because she was in that liminal place between an end and a beginning. She was sure the Council would have a pivotal role to play in what would come next, but at this moment, she was still focused on the most recent goodbye.

The Palace was stunning in its magnificence. Sparrow had expected it to have altered from her memory, but if anything the edifice was even more exquisite than she remembered.

Abilard took them through a massive courtyard covered in fine white gravel, the little stones crunching satisfyingly under his silvery hooves. They passed beneath an ornate marble arch, intricately carved with the royal arms of Valdemar, and into a second, smaller courtyard, this one paved in serpentine swirls of colored bricks.

The door at the end of the pathway was shaped from a gigantic chunk of stout wood, looming far above Sparrow's head. Abilard drew close to a mounting block that had been set up for a graceful dismount at the great entrance. First she, then Cloudbrother, slipped from the saddle, their legs sore and stiff from the long, unbroken ride. Sparrow surreptitiously stretched her legs under her long skirts, wiggled her toes to get the feeling back.

"Here we go, then," Cloudbrother said under his breath as the gigantic double doors swung open, revealing the two ceremonial Guards, one at each door, guarding the way.

The one directly opposite looked the trio up and down.

Burst into a huge smile of recognition.

Keeth!

It was Sparrow's brother . . . that big, loveable dunderhead had made his way up in the world, indeed.

"What are you doing here, little mother!" he exclaimed with a booming, disbelieving laugh. "Last I heard, you was doing your witchy ways up in the great northland. Don't tell me *you* are the one what got summoned to the Council for afternoon session! Will wonders not cease."

"Hello, my big brother!" Sparrow entirely forgot herself, she was so happy to see him again. "My little one was Chosen just the other day, and he is down in the Collegium right now, getting settled. Lucky for me we could combine trips, all on the spur like this."

Keeth beamed. Bless the man, he was comfortable in his own big, loud life, and he was happy for her in her Herald-driven one. "I am not surprised, my bells and whiskers no! That little fella was Herald born, sure as I'm alive. Good for him. I will watch out for him, don't you worry, Spark. I will do it, all the time, I'm right here after all."

The childhood nickname warmed her heart all the way through. "I better go," she said. "I don't want to keep the Council gentlefolk waiting on us."

He nodded, then playfully slapped the other guard's shoulder with one enormous, meaty hand. "That's my little sis, if you can believe it. We grew up in a goat pasture of a village up north near the border, and look at us! One in the Palace Guard, t'other rides with the Heralds."

Keeth took a step closer, bowed awkwardly at Abilard and Cloudbrother. "Good to see you again, bond brother mine." He glanced at his fellow Guard, more serious now. "My little sister Spark's heartmate, this Cloudbrother, I bet you heard wind of him as the Cloud Born, the Herald that brought the rains to Iftel some years back, in the bad drought time."

The other Guard's face lit up in recognition, then he bowed deeply and motioned for them to pass. "My honor, fine folks, kindly head straight on until you reach the Council Chamber. A new built one, you'll see, fine and grand."

"Thank you, so much," Sparrow murmured. "Couldn't have a better omen than your smiling face, big brother."

"Oh, now. An honor to see you both, and Mr. Abilard too, of course. An honor. If you can, stop by the house on your way back north, and we can put up some vittles for you and make you at home. If you can't, I know, a Herald's life, I understand. If you can't, ride in peace and light, little Spark."

She reached to him from where she stood between Herald and Companion, and their fingers touched, just for a moment.

:*This is where I leave you two, for now,*: Abilard whispered into her mind.

And before she could turn away from her brother to wish Abilard goodbye, he wheeled and clattered away, his magnificent head held high, his silvery-white tail flowing gaily behind him. The sight of him warmed her to the core . . . clearly Abilard wasn't worried in the slightest.

Sparrow smiled her farewell to Keeth, and then she and Cloudbrother paced together down the enormous stone hallway to the Council room, where Sparrow was the central order of business. By now it was after lunch, but she could not imagine taking the tiniest bite.

By the time they were admitted to the Council, the meeting was well underway. Liveried pages hurried to and fro in the cavernous hallway outside the Chambers, enormous parchment rolls wedged under their arms or in coarse canvas bags, quills stuck behind their ears.

The entire room was taken up by an enormous semicircle of a table, deep mahogany and polished to a mirror-like shine. High windows rose behind, sunlight shining through like a sunset through primeval forest branches. The personages collected along the semicircle were all backlit in shadows.

Sparrow searched the faces of the Heralds she saw scattered through the room, but she recognized none of them. Cold fingers of worry slipped around her heart and gently squeezed.

It was fully as scary as she had imagined, and the silence that greeted them was both unearthly and unnerving. After a moment's hesitation, she made a small curtsy—it never hurt to be polite.

A woman dressed in an intricate gown of russet silk with yellow peeking through slashed sleeves and glittering stones all along her bodice, with blonde hair piled high on her head, regally bowed in acknowledgement of Sparrow's polite curtsy.

"I will introduce myself," the fine lady said. "I am Lady Darandell. I build hospitals, and supply them with tools of the healing arts. I suppose I am something of an artificer and something of a benefactress. We have been asked to convene to consider you, and your heartmate both."

Sparrow swallowed hard and resisted the urge to curtsy again. "We are here to serve," she replied, and though there was a little tremor in her voice, Sparrow stood proudly next to Cloudbrother. "Though," she admitted, "I'm not sure what you should do with the both of us."

Lady Darandell smiled, and her glamour dazzled Sparrow and spooked her in equal measure. "There are those here who believe that your heartmate should be allowed a retirement. Do you not think he should have some rest?"

The silence weighed heavily in the room, with only a creak of a chair or tap of a foot to break it. Sparrow shot a glance to Cloudbrother as he stood tall and waited.

"Ask Abilard, I'd say . . . he and Cloudbrother can answer that question for you the best," Sparrow finally replied. "I don't understand. Why do you wish to ask me about Herald business at all?"

The Lady leaned forward, her expression brightening. "Because, Sparrow, regardless of your heartmate's future, we are here to consider your own mission."

"*My* mission? I've been serving my mission all this time. Helping Cloudbrother."

"But I do believe that mission is complete. If I do not mistake, your heartmate's mission is now to help you. And I am sure your Herald will gladly serve, as always."

Her heart pounding, Sparrow whirled to face her heartmate. "I don't understand, love . . . help me to understand what the Council is getting at."

But it was not Cloudbrother who answered, but Abilard, whispering again into her mind, and her heartmate's too. :*I believe that it is your turn now to take the lead,*: Abilard said, with a caress as gentle and strength-giving as he had ever given her. :*And I say we three have only just begun.*:

It was only in this moment that Sparrow understood that in actuality, Abilard *had* Chosen her, as surely as he had Chosen her heartmate when he was a young man and near death from the fever that had blinded him. Without her, Cloudbrother could not have become a Herald. And while Sparrow herself was not a Herald, one could certainly serve the Crown and Valdemar in other ways.

"We are a pair," Cloudbrother said aloud to the Council, and he reached for her hand. Gratefully, Sparrow slipped her fingers into his, and he squeezed gently. "I will support my heartmate and help her in her mission, as she has helped me in mine."

The Lady nodded, and all at once the tension in the room dissipated like a morning mist. "Yes, this is what I was hoping," she said. "We need help, a Healing of sorts. All across Valdemar, mothers, fathers, sisters and brothers, say goodbye to those they love who are Chosen, and who ascend to their destinies as Heralds. The best and the brightest leave their homes, and often they leave huge holes behind."

Sparrow had never considered it from that vantage point, but it made sense to her. Longfall could have used Cloudbrother's wit, his strength, his insight, and his courage. His home village was poorer for his having left.

"You don't need to be Chosen to have a mission in life," Sparrow said.

"We think so too, but those who are left behind sometimes do not see it. We want you to ride Circuit, Sparrow. To help people like you, people who sometimes may lose their way when their beloveds become Heralds. You have known both sides. We need you to be a bridge."

Sparrow considered the offer. She had been Chosen, but it was up to her to accept this mission. And it was her so-called "ordinariness" that made her perfect for it.

It was time for them to fly the nest, all together.

Her heart soared, now.

"I will do it," Sparrow said. "But on one condition."

"Name it."

"My heartmate and I have never had a honeymoon. Let us go to the vineyards on the road to Iftel for a week or maybe two. And then we'll come back to work."

A low murmur rose and fell in the room, like the crash of the winter waves on Lake Evendim.

"You ask but little," the Lady replied. "Your wish is granted, with our blessing. Return here in two weeks, and we will send you on your way."

For the rest of her life, Sparrow would remember this moment.

It was the end of everything.

And the beginning.

Snowbound
Brigid Collins

Herald Marli tilted her head and sniffed the cold air as her Companion, Taren, carried her along the road toward Shaded Vale, a village nestled deep in the hills north of the Karse border.

"Blizzard's definitely coming in," Marli said, scanning the slate-gray sky between the boughs of pines already bearing a sprinkle of white. "Way the air's tasting now, it'll be here soon."

:*Oh, no you don't,*: said Taren in his haughtiest tone. The bells on his harness jingled in time with his steady steps. :*I'm not moving one bit faster than I already am. Or do you really want a tumble down the hillside into some ravine we'll be unable to clamber out of?*:

To accentuate his point, he deliberately—but carefully—stepped closer to the edge of the road he had been walking along for the past quarter-candlemark. *Road* was a generous term for what amounted to a bare dirt track at the top of a ravine. Little dribbles of snow went tumbling down the slope to their right.

Years of trained reflex had Marli tightening her core muscles to help Taren keep his balance. "All right, I get it. In fact, I already got it. I don't know where you get this idea that I've got a reckless streak. All I want is for us to arrive in time to help the villagers prepare for this storm."

Taren's mental voice rang with exasperated affection. :*That is* precisely *where I get the idea. Always willing to*

171

go haring off into a dangerous situation if it means you can help someone.:

"I'm a Herald," Marli grumbled. "That's what I'm supposed to do."

:But you'll be no help to anyone if you're trapped and injured at the bottom of a ravine. We'll continue at my pace, and we'll get there in time. Don't worry, dearest.:

Marli stroked the white curve of his neck and tried to follow his suggestion. But worry was in her nature, and always had been. From her younger years before Taren Chose her, when she was a simple farm girl betrothed to the miller's son and doing what she could to settle disputes in her small hometown, through her training at the Collegium when she'd helped fellow students suffering the ache of homesickness, to her internship with the mute Herald Selte, who'd taught Marli how to read the weather by being observant and open, but who'd also radiated loneliness like a fire radiates light.

She'd worried a lot during that internship. They'd been riding Circuit during the worst summer drought in recent history, teaching people how to reduce and fight the inevitable fires. A fight against the flames at Selte's home village had proven to be the very thing Selte needed to open herself back up to other people. These days, Marli couldn't be prouder of her friend's progress.

But Havens, she could do with a warm fire to fight right now! Something about winter, and the onset of winter storms, made it harder for Marli to shut out her own loneliness. The cold and snow had always had that effect on her. Back before Taren had Chosen her, she'd had the promise of a future husband and, later, children to get her through her winters.

That obviously hadn't happened, and now it never would. Such a fundamental set of life events, which most people took for granted. She certainly had. She'd come to terms with her loss, if only because she had to. People counted on her to be at her best, which meant burying those melancholy thoughts down where they couldn't distract her.

It wasn't so bad, after all. She had friends, she had Taren, and she had a constant sense of purpose.

But purpose didn't buffer her against the cold. Though she was bundled up in a set of fur-lined, down-stuffed Whites, the wind still cut through. Her nose buzzed with numbness. Her fingers were stiff within her wool-lined sheepskin gloves.

Marli bit her tongue against the urge to wheedle Taren to go faster. Instead, she looked back up through the trees.

The clouds flew overhead, dark gray and low enough she felt she might touch them if she stretched. The sharp taste of snow colored the air.

The storm would break in the next half-candlemark at best.

Taren went taut with sudden alertness. *:Someone's out in the trees.:*

That startled Marli out of her fretting. Her mind flashed on, and quickly abandoned, the idea of a representative from Shaded Vale come to escort them the rest of the way. These hills attracted droves of bandits from a variety of places. Holderkin who'd lost their place at home for one reason or another, deserters from the conflict at the border, both Valdemaran soldiers and Karsite refugees, other folk too hardened against their fellow man to belong in any law-abiding community.

All types who hated Heralds. People who would have no qualms about attacking someone riding in Whites on the brink of a blizzard.

Marli had plenty of experience with their sort. Much as even the thought of killing left her mouth sour with bile, she wouldn't hesitate to defend herself.

Tightening her grip on the saddle pommel, she ranged out with her Farsight to scan their surroundings. Her right arm moved subtly toward the sword sheathed at her side.

She was too slow.

A figure dressed in wintery forest camouflage leaped out from the brush covering the hillside to their left. The evergreen foliage hissed with the force of the figure's launch. A thin woven scarf covered the attacker's entire head, ensuring only their silver-gray eyes peered out.

Those eyes flashed like lightning.

A peculiar sensation trickled over Marli as she drew her sword. Everything slowed as if encased in snow. The attacker was at Marli's leg and grasping for Taren's harness as if to snatch a bell from it before she could properly position her blade in defense.

The eyes roiled like storm clouds.

Marli felt as if she might be swept away and battered to pieces.

Taren reared and struck out with his hooves, but the attacker moved nimbly aside only to return and slice at Marli with a knife before reaching again for Taren's ringing harness.

A thin line like fire lanced along her calf, and she gritted her teeth against a groan.

The pain broke whatever strangeness had come over her, though. With a clearer head, she fell back on her training.

Her sword met the next jab with a jarring metallic ring.

Her attacker had to be a bandit, the way he held that knife, the way his clothing obscured his features, the way hunger burned in those eyes. A ne'er-do-well like this who would attack a Herald on Circuit could have no other profession.

Removing such threats to Valdemar's peace and safety was a Herald's duty. Marli wouldn't kill if she could help it, but she couldn't let this one go unrestrained, either. Bandits could be rehabilitated, with patience and kindness.

Surprise, then disarm, echoed her weaponsmaster's voice from her memory.

Even one who understood a Herald's Mind-magic would still be caught off guard by something suddenly flying at their head.

With her Fetching Gift, Marli tore a naked branch off an aspen behind the bandit, deliberately making the shivery crack ring in the frigid air.

Those storm-churned eyes widened, and the bandit dove for the road barely in time. The branch snagged the bandit's headwrap as it whooshed overhead, revealing a sharp, coarsely stubbled jaw and rough-cut, dirty black hair.

Marli swung the branch back over the bandit and extended her Gift to her sword. She could control two objects at once, even more if she exerted herself.

She maneuvered both branch and sword through the air, intending to pin her adversary in place long enough to restrain him more effectively. She moved as well, leaping easily from Taren's back despite his agitated snorts and stamps.

:*I could step on him,:* Taren offered.

:*You step too hard.:*

Marli's breath clouded, and warmth raced through her body. Strenuous use of her Gifts had that effect. But it wouldn't last long. During the fight, the storm clouds had finally begun dumping their snow, and the small piles by the roadside were growing rapidly. There would be no arriving at Shaded Vale in time now.

Anger flooded her. How dare this selfish man hinder her journey? Didn't he realize he'd have nobody to steal *from* if the nearby village succumbed to the inclement weather?

"Idiot," she muttered.

"Ain't the one prancin' 'round all 'lone," growled her captive. A slight shift was all the warning Marli got before the man's knife hurtled toward her face.

Damn it! Automatically, she batted the projectile aside with her Fetching. The distraction cost her her hold on her weapons. The branch fell to the snowy ground with a thump.

The sword clattered as it bounced against every rock in its tumble down into the ravine.

The bandit was on his feet again, his head lowered in preparation to charge Marli.

Taren reared, front legs flailing for the man's face, the Companion's scream strangely muffled in the whirling snow.

Marli's heart seized. "Taren, no!"

In her mind, the ravine yawned wider in anticipation.

Marli threw her Fetching with no attempt to finesse it and grappled with the steep hillside itself. *I need a wall,* she thought. *A safety net to catch him.*

But she was either too late or too forceful, as Taren's hooves connected at the same moment the hillside crumbled under the bandit's feet.

The peculiar slowing effect from earlier returned. The snow fell so violently it enshrouded the hills like a fog. The bandit tipped backward into this snow-fog, his body disappearing as the whiteness enveloped him. His thunderstorm-gray eyes alone pierced this veil.

Don't let me fall! he seemed to call out to her.

She jumped.

:Marli!: Taren shouted.

Marli made some soothing reply. She hardly knew what she said.

She'd never used her Fetching to hold another person, but she reached to catch the falling bandit now. He flailed against her, panic driving his arm into her stomach and his heel against her already injured calf. Marli only grunted and redoubled her efforts so his limbs wouldn't strike the stones.

With her Farsight, she looked to the ravine floor and angled her body to shield her enemy-turned-ward from the impact.

The last thing she saw before the whiteness overwhelmed her was the blue of Taren's eyes widened in terror, peering over the edge of the cliff.

Kimfer's head rang with every curse he knew, most of them aimed at himself.

This "trial" was supposed to be simple, a mere formality. Track the solitary rider on the fancy horse. Slip down to the ribbon of road before the snow made such passage impossible. Cut a single silver bell from the ridiculous harness. Get back to show off the prize and earn his place with the hill bandits for the winter, because there was no way Kimfer would spend another winter fending for himself. He did this sort of maneuver—and for more hefty loot—all the time in the warmer months without picking up a scratch.

How had he gotten so out of his depth?

Oh, right—because he'd forgotten the Heralds were all witchfolk.

Had two years on his own in the wild truly caused him to forget the lessons his holderkin family had instilled in him through fear and blood? *Never trust a Herald, Kimfer! Not even to be a proper mark!* His own stupidity had allowed his quarry to turn things around on him.

His stomach had wanted to climb out his throat when he met her chestnut eyes in his first assault. Felt like they looked deep inside him, saw secret, dirty things he never even showed himself.

Why had she jumped after him?

Large flakes of snow were falling. The cold wetness seeped through his too-thin clothes, and the wind cut right to the bone. Storm was rolling in for sure now. Would've been nice if the hill boys had lent him one of their superior coats for this "trial" of theirs.

The Herald woman lay under him, not moving beyond the tempest the wind made of her short waves of brown hair. Whatever witch power she'd used to hold him during their fall had dropped away the moment they hit the ground, but Kimfer couldn't bring himself to move away just yet. She'd protected him from the worst of the impact—*why?*—but he still felt rattled.

Carefully, he rolled off his mark-turned-rescuer. The snow had piled so high around them he couldn't roll any farther away from her. He lay shivering beside her, his heavy limbs wrapped around her as if they were lovers.

The shivers became shudders at that thought.

But she looked so pale. Neck looked like it was angled bad, too, at least from his vantage point. Had she really broken herself to keep him from falling to his death?

A faint flutter at his fingertips dispelled that thought.

Working himself up onto his elbow, he got a better look at her. Her neck wasn't at so bad an angle after all, though it couldn't be comfortable draped over an icy rock like that. With a light touch, he arranged her head so it lay straighter.

Now, why had he done *that*?

Her eyelids fluttered. Kimfer thought he heard her moan, but it might have been the wind. She was clearly stirring, however, and he didn't fancy being around when she regained awareness. No telling what someone with witch powers like hers might do in her situation.

Now that he was sitting up, he could take better stock of himself. Moving his joints revealed no pain he couldn't handle. Turning his head didn't throw spots in his vision.

He was good to hoof it out of this place, and he'd better make tracks before the blizzard got any worse.

The new plan came together as fast as the snow fell. Find the rocky slope of the ravine. Climb to the level of the road. Grab the fancy horse. Break it to his command. Ride it into camp. Earn his place as many times over as there were bells on that ridiculous harness, plus the worth of the horse itself.

Kimfer didn't *like* the idea of taking up with bandits. Not that stealing bothered him in the slightest. He did it himself all the time. But society was a resource like any other, and it could be overtaxed just as easily as deer could be overhunted. Kimfer couldn't enjoy the company of people who weren't smart enough to figure that out.

But the season's first blizzard was here, and the time to put aside his scruples had definitely arrived. Thoughts of hot food, ready shelter, and a warm—if lonely—bedroll fueled him as he struggled to break a path through the snow. Funny, back when he still had his hold to welcome him, he'd thought his tastes wide enough to allow anyone into his bed, whatever gender, whatever profession.

The things you learn about yourself after everything goes up in smoke and the only option is to struggle for survival alone.

The snow had piled so high here at the bottom of the ravine that it came to midthigh. Despite the cold, he was sweating by the time he'd managed a single horse length.

Even that meager progress had wiped him so completely he had to stop and pant. The pain in his chest from that damned horse's kick had grown, too.

Hunching against the buffeting snow, he couldn't help glancing back over his shoulder at the Herald woman.

The snow was building up on top of her, and the white outfit she wore made it seem as if she were already buried alive. Only her face and a few wisps of brown hair were visible.

Her eyes were open, and she was staring at him.

At the sight, misery and fear and something else he couldn't identify twisted in his guts.

Can't trust a Herald, his memory argued. *Never know how they'll use those witch powers.*

But how could he leave her to freeze to death after she'd specifically used those powers to save him?

Why, *why* had she saved him?

While he stood paralyzed with indecision, the Herald woman stirred. Clumps of snow rolled off her, and those big chestnut eyes drifted closed and open again.

"Bar . . . ret?" she said. "You're . . . here?"

Her voice sounded like the exact mixture of misery and fear that currently roiled in Kimfer, including that other thing he hadn't been able to name.

Loneliness.

It decided him. Nobody—witch-powers or no— deserved to die alone in a winter storm.

He was back at her side in an instant, kneeling in the snow and checking her more thoroughly for injuries.

"I'm here," he said. She started to cry out, to reach for him, and he reassured her. "I won't leave you."

Not until he'd learned why *her* innards churned the same way *his* did, anyway. Not until he understood why she'd jumped after him.

Consciousness came in spurts. An uncomfortable floaty sensation left Marli confused and reaching for something she couldn't quite make out.

Where was Taren? Who was pulling her through the snow? She opened her eyes once to find herself propped in a depression of rocks while her once-betrothed, Barret, moved about piling snow into gaps in the little shelter. The sight made her sigh, even as she told herself it couldn't possibly be him.

Her head hurt worse than it ever had, even during her Collegium days. She remembered using her Gifts quite a lot earlier, but not enough to have caused this pounding. Maybe she should ask not-Barret to take her to Healers?

He was beside her again, his eyes like storm clouds ready to pelt her with hail. Barret's eyes weren't like storms. They were like wheat—boring, unripened wheat. Wheat never talked to her the way storms did.

"Keep still," said her companion, his storm eyes flickering like lightning.

Her Companion! Where was Taren?

But her head hurt so bad, and what concentration she had kept drifting back to not-Barret. She couldn't form a single thought to send to Taren.

"Barret?"

"You're not alone," said not-Barret.

Marli fell back into unconsciousness.

When she woke again, she was stiff with cold. A tiny fire crackled and danced near her feet, and the *drip-drip* of water echoed off the rocks she lay against. Otherwise, all was silent.

The dripping came from the wall of snow that blocked nearly the entire opening of the little shelter. A channel had been dug leading to the open air to allow the smoke from the fire to escape. Though continued snowfall had tried to block it, the fire's heat helped keep it open.

A heavy weight had wrapped itself around her, pressing against ribs that throbbed. Moving her head carefully so as not to spark more pain, she discovered the weight to be a person, arms and legs pressed close, sharing heat.

The bandit who'd attacked her.

The one she'd leaped after when he fell from the road down into the ravine.

Relief flooded her. She'd managed to save him, after

all. He must have done all this work, finding and preparing their shelter, building the fire, making sure she didn't freeze to death.

. . . Why? Shouldn't a bandit have cut free the moment he could?

Then again, all the signs Marli had read of this storm had indicated a heavy snow and furious winds. Maybe her attacker-turned-caretaker had tried to leave her but had simply been unable to make any progress alone.

As if her thought roused him, the bandit awoke. He came awake all at once, like any Herald who'd spent time on the Karse border would. Or, she supposed, like someone who lived his life outside of society.

He saw she was awake and tensed as if he intended to reach for a weapon.

Marli knew she ought to work out how to defend herself, wonder where her own weapon was, or reach with one or both of her Gifts for something to use. But she was too hurt, too tired, and too busy staring at the bandit's face to do any of the things her training had drilled into her.

Now that she got a good look at the bandit, she realized he looked nothing like the boy she'd once been promised to. His dark hair hung lank and dirty over his face like he had something to hide, and stubble grew coarse over his chin and cheeks. He was lean, nothing but muscle and bone, a body made of hardship and survival rather than a good day's work and plenty to eat after. His very expression conveyed how closed-up he was, how little he had to say to the rest of the world, and how little he cared for anyone else's well-being.

But his eyes remained as stormy as ever and, to Marli's training, held no secrets from her.

He was worried about her, both scared she was hurt badly and nervous she wasn't hurt badly enough. He was uncomfortable—not physically, he was too used to the wilderness to care about sleeping in a tumble of rocks, but emotionally. Something was moving in his heart, and he didn't understand it, but he thought it had something to do with her.

Well, Marli knew what it was. It felt like when Taren had Chosen her, but sadder. It felt like when she'd first placed her hand in Barret's, but with fingers meshed more tightly. She'd loved Barret with all her heart, and she'd cried her eyes to dust when she had to leave him. Though she had friends around her in her new life, though she put on a mask of happiness for their sakes, her heart had remained dry and crumbling.

This bandit was a raincloud drifting over her, heavy with strange water.

"It's a Lifebond," she said.

She read slow relaxation through his eyes before she sensed it in his body, still stretched against hers. He didn't want to trust her, but he couldn't help himself.

"Somethin' you witchfolk Heralds do to keep honest men entangled?" he asked.

"Honest men don't attack lone women before a snow-storm."

"Lone women don't travel afore storms, 'less they're stupid."

"A Herald is never alone. Or do you think my Companion nothing more than a high-bred saddle horse?"

The bandit colored. "So, you *don't* know what it's like, then."

Silence descended, interrupted only by the continued crackle of fire and drip of melting snow.

Marli shuddered in the cold. Her ribs ached, probably one or two of them broken in the fall. "There's different kinds of alone."

Another long silence stretched. Then: "You ever been so alone you tried to rob a fancy lady of a bauble just to buy your way into a group of bandits for the winter?"

"No. *You* ever been so alone you threw yourself into everyone else's problems just to forget how alone you are?"

"No. 'M pretty good at thinkin' 'bout me."

Marli sighed. Her entire body hurt too much for the cold to numb her, and she didn't know whether to feel grateful or bitter about the scant warmth her bandit was sharing with her. Their physical closeness held no awkwardness, at least. There simply wasn't the energy to be embarrassed.

Gingerly, she tucked her aching head under his chin. The stubble scratched at her scalp as he swallowed.

"My hold didn't trust Heralds none. Hard to picture havin' a whatever-bond with one," he said. His chest rumbled against Marli's forehead.

"Hard for a Herald to imagine being Lifebonded to a bandit," she said, then frowned. "Didn't? What changed?"

"There was . . . you know a couple summers past, when the heat got so bad you felt like breathin' would scorch your lungs? Didn't have enough water for the crops nor the animals, let alone . . . There was a fire."

"I'm sorry. I'm so sorry."

"Anyway. Do fine 'nough on my own the rest of the year. But I won't spend another winter without someone around me. Can't handle it. Bandits'r the only ones'll take a vagrant like me in, provided I prove I can bring somethin' to the table."

"Winter is," Marli said, struggling to get the words through her dry throat, "the *worst* time to not have a family anymore."

The bandit pushed himself to his feet and moved to the wall of melting snow. Cold air swirled against Marli's newly exposed side. She tried not to shiver harder.

"Here," said the bandit, holding a handful of snow to her lips. "Eat some. Need water if you're gonna get better. Think your horse is fancy 'nough to have gone for help?"

Marli let the snow melt on her tongue. "Taren isn't a horse. He's definitely gone on to Shaded Vale, where we were headed. They ought to have a Healer there, at least. And . . . thank you."

"My fault in the first. Shoulda known not to take a Herald woman for a mark."

"Marli."

"Marli, then. Kimfer."

"The blizzard is over, Kimfer. If you can, you should knock down our snow wall. Once my head stops pounding so much, I can use Farsight to help Taren and the Healer find us here."

Kimfer sat like a block of ice beside her. "And after that? What happens to . . . us?" He pronounced the word like it had a taste he'd never encountered before.

The storm outside had subsided, but the one in Kimfer's eyes still boiled on. He looked as though he wanted Marli to soothe that storm, to do something to quiet it for him.

"I can't change how the weather behaves," she said. "All I can do is to read the signs and prepare accordingly."

Kimfer looked at her for another beat of silence. Then he gave a curt nod and turned to open their shelter.

:I should have kicked him harder.:

:You shouldn't have kicked him at all. I'm fine.: Marli winced as the Healer Taren had brought from Shaded Vale touched her injured ribs. *:Or, I will be soon enough.:*

Taren lashed his tail in disagreement and continued staring through narrowed eyes at Kimfer.

The bandit tended the larger fire he'd built in the middle of the ravine. The wind had blown the snow into piles high along the walls but had scoured the center clean. While he'd built, she'd shouted in Mindspeech until she finally found Taren and led him to her, finding the safest path through the fresh snow with her Farsight.

:You wouldn't have fallen if it weren't for him.:

:If you hadn't kicked him, I wouldn't have had to go after him!:

Taren's tail switched harder. *:You're certain it's a Lifebond? Maybe you're just feeling grateful he didn't leave you to freeze.:*

:I'm certain, dearest.:

:Hmph. Well, we can fix him, then.:

Marli laughed, then winced again. *:We can offer him help. Only he can fix himself.:*

"I've done all I can here," said the Healer, stepping away and wiping his brow. He'd worked himself to a sweat using his Gift on her. "There's a bed at home with your name on it, Herald. Let's get you up in the saddle."

Kimfer turned from the fire and scowled. "She's got broken ribs. Shouldn't ride a horse with broken ribs, any fool knows that."

Before Marli could calm Kimfer, Taren stomped through the snow until his nose was an inch from the bandit's.

Whatever the Companion said to Kimfer, he kept private, even from Marli. But Kimfer's face went slack with surprise, then red with discomfort, and finally turned ashen. He swayed as if he were about to lose his balance.

Finally, Taren came trotting back to Marli's side, nose in the air and smug attitude pouring off him.

:Had your say, then?: Marli asked. Taren knelt beside her, and the Healer helped her get herself astride.

:Just giving him some incentive to fix himself, like you said he had to.:

Marli's head still hurt too much for her to roll her eyes.

Taren rose, moving carefully to keep from jostling her. The Healer mounted behind her.

But before Taren could take off, Kimfer was at his flank, knife out. With a slice like a flash of lightning, one bell was separated from Taren's harness.

" 'M no bandit, *horse*. I work alone. But this is for me."

Taren curved his head around to snort in Kimfer's face.

Kimfer ignored it and sheathed his knife. He cast one final look at Marli, his eyes as stormy as the first moment she'd looked into them. But around the edges, light was showing through, like the distant horizon from the midst of torrential rainfall.

Then he clenched his fingers around the bell and turned away.

Marli still didn't know how the future would play out for her, but the heartache of her past seemed more distant now. Maybe she'd never get to experience those milestones so common to everyone else: marriage, children, a family of her own. But she at least knew her future wasn't quite as empty as she'd previously thought.

She'd read the signs. Now it was time to prepare.

She had a new storm to set her worrying nature to

studying, but her heart whispered that her winters were going to be easier to weather from now on.

Kimfer stood at the foot of a path up and out of the ravine.

He could go to the hill bandits. He had the prize they'd asked for digging into his ungloved palm, after all. They'd have hot food. They'd have tents.

They'd hold the same beliefs about Herald women his holderkin had held. That alone would help ease his mind from its spinning. It would be *comforting*.

His chest still hurt, but he wasn't at all certain it was from the witchhorse's kick anymore.

But as he opened his fingers and looked at the tiny bell, a thread of warmth worked through him, and he knew the words he'd thrown out as a parting shot had been true: He would never return to the hill bandits. Let someone else try their stupid "trial."

He worked alone. He *survived* alone.

Alone, and yet . . .

He tucked the bell away in his belt, right beside his knife. It was a little piece of her, something she'd recognize anywhere.

And with that witchsight of hers, she'd be able to find *him* anywhere.

A few moments passed before Kimfer realized he was smiling.

He would continue to work alone, but he would never *be* alone ever again.

Hunching against the cold, he started up the path.

The More Things Change, the More They Change More

Fiona Patton

Haven in late summer was a city at its finest: warm days giving over to cool nights, tree-lined streets in the upper quarters filling the air with bird songs, and markets and one-day fairs in the lower quarters filling the air with the sounds of bustling commerce.

As another beautiful morning dawned, casting an almost magical pink and orange glow across Valdemar's capital, Padriec Dann stood on the roof of the tenement house where generations of his family had made their home and stared down the ten long blocks to the Iron Street Watch House, where generations of his family had made their living. Along both sides of the street, all manner of wooden signs, both painted and plain, swung gently in the breeze, proclaiming the industry of blacksmiths, tinsmiths, locksmiths, bell makers, braziers, kettle-smiths, ironmongers, and the dozen other trades that worked in or with metal. As the first of the shops began to open for the day, Paddy frowned.

He knew every one of their neighbors, from masters to apprentices, shop owners to servants, families and friends, rivals and enemies. He knew how long they'd been there, how prosperous, diligent, or honest they were.

Or weren't. He'd prided himself on this knowledge from the first day his ma had allowed him to climb down the tenement steps by himself and stand, staring out at the huge, brick and cobblestone world stretching out before him. A world protected by the Danns—his da, granther, brothers, cousins, and uncles, every one of them Watchmen. All he'd ever wanted was to stand beside them in the pale blue and gray uniform of the Haven City Watch.

He'd had it all planned out, too: sweeper at age seven, runner at eleven, Chief Runner at thirteen. He'd make lance constable, then constable, corporal, sergeant, and maybe even captain. He would live with his parents until he and Rosie, his first and only love since the age of six, started their own family. They would move across the hall or down a floor and raise a new generation of Watchmen to protect the street.

His street.

Then two years ago, everything had changed. His da had died in a fire in the Iron Market grounds, then his granther had passed away a year later. His brother Aiden and his family had moved to their own flat, taking their brothers Jakon and Raik with them, and his brother Hektor had married and moved into Aiden's old room, leaving Paddy to sleep alone for the first time in his life.

He'd thought it would make him happy, and it had at first—then all he'd felt was lonely.

Which was silly, he admitted, because Hektor and Ismy had two babies in the flat to liven things up, and his sister, Kassie, now a messenger bird apprentice at the Watch House, was still home. And their ma . . .

Turning abruptly, he left the roof, pounding down the stairs without caring how much noise he made. A moment later he was out on the street and running, not toward the Watch House but away from it.

Several blocks later he rocked to a halt, leaning against a pinmaker's shop, breathing hard.

Everything had changed.

Everything.

He glanced around with a scowl, daring anyone to comment on his red face and disheveled appearance,

but the only people out this early were four littles playing gameball in a nearby close.

His mood sank even farther.

He'd been the gameball champion of Iron Street until
his growing number of responsibilities had allowed him
less and less time to play. Last week, he'd given his
prized possession, the pig's bladder ball his granther
had gifted him at age six, to his cousin Trebor. He'd
thought he'd been all right with it at the time, but now
he guessed he wasn't. Not really.

And now the street itself had changed.

Strangely quiet for the last few days, people stopped
their conversations when he went by, looking anywhere
but directly at him. Everyone seemed too busy to stop and
chat, nobody had time to even exchange a few words, and
nobody would tell him what was wrong. This stung. Paddy
knew everything, sometimes even before the people involved knew. He was trusted, confided in, but now . . .

He touched the black and purple bruise on his left
cheek.

It had all come to a head yesterday.

*"We're not good enough for the Danns anymore now,
huh? You gotta get all cozy with outsiders!"*

Camden Wright, one of Paddy's senior runners who'd
been avoiding him for days, had finally cracked the silence.

Paddy had stared at him in confusion. *"What're you
talkin' about?"*

"Your ma . . ."

It hadn't taken much more. When Lance Constable
Farane had finally pulled them apart, both youths had
torn uniforms, bleeding knuckles, and a broken friend-
ship. Hektor'd yelled at them, Aiden'd yelled at them.
Neither he nor Camden would say what had sparked the
fight, but everyone else knew.

And, at least now, he knew.

"Your ma . . ."

Of all the changes, he'd never thought she'd be one of
them.

The city bells began to toll the hour, and he straight-

ened up with a growl. It would soon be time for his shift
at the Watch House, and for the first time in his life, he
didn't want to go.

He started down the street, walking slowly and mo-
rosely, then abruptly headed up a narrow close and onto
Harp Way, which paralleled Iron Street to the north.
The shops here were a bit larger, a bit fancier, their
wares a bit more exotic: musical instruments and surgi-
cal tools and the like. The lanes and closes which inter-
sected the Way were also larger and more exotic, and
they were named for a more expensive style of goods
and trades: Stave Court, Lower and Upper Ink Streets,
and Tapestry Row.

Paddy walked past Glazier's Terrace as fast as he
could. He would not look up that street. He would not
look for a certain glassmaker's shop, or a certain glassmaker; a certain fancy, exotic, artisan glassmaking, inter-
fering, not-a-Watchman outsider with a real glass-paned
front window on his shop displaying goods Paddy's family
wouldn't even think of buying even if they could spare the
money. Which they could, because they weren't that poorly
off, but still, there was little left at the end of the day for
extras, and certainly not for extras made of glass. They
drank from ceramic cups, had wooden shutters on their
windows, and the occasional tincture from the herbalist
came in a pot and went back once it was emptied. Even
Kassie's prize possession—a small bird-shaped music box
ordered for her by their granther just before he'd died—
was made of wood and metal. Clearly this man's family
catered to a wealthier class of people than their own.

He scowled, trying to stretch out his shoulders in a tunic that had been too small for a month now, and kicked
at a loose cobblestone. His tunic was too small and so was
his shirt, the sleeves riding up past his wrists. And his
boots were too tight. He'd soon need new ones, and he
didn't think he'd saved up enough money yet. Maybe he
could make do with a cast-off pair of Jakon's or Raik's
until he could afford them, but his ma wouldn't like it.
The Danns might wear hand-me-down uniforms, but

they didn't wear hand-me-down boots. His ma would insist on buying him a new pair, and he didn't want her to. He brought home his own wage. He would buy his own boots. And if he couldn't afford them yet, he'd wait.

Growling low in his throat, he carried on along Harp Way for another three blocks, then turned down another narrow close. He was five steps in when he heard the scream.

"Stop that boy!"

Paddy acted at instinctively, spinning about and heading back up the close at a dead run. The youth racing past collided with him, and they went down in a tangle of arms and legs. Paddy took an elbow in the face and a foot in the stomach before he managed to overbear the other youth, but a burst of laughter pulled him up short.

"Codi?!"

Flat on his back, Paddy's knee in his chest, Codi Vinney continued to laugh. "Hiya, Pazers!" he said gleefully. "What brings you to this neck of the streets?"

"Get up!"

"Duck!"

The woman who'd screamed had caught up to them by now and she aimed a blow at Codi's head that hit Paddy on the shoulder as he dragged the other youth to his feet.

"I want him arrested!" she shrieked, swinging at him again as Codi continued to laugh.

"I've got him, Mistress Auklet," Paddy gasped, "You can stop now."

"I'll stop when he's rotting in a cell!" she shot back, her face turning a dangerous purple. "Look what he's done to my frock!"

She waved a brown-stained pleat in Paddy's face.

"Honest, Pazers, I tripped and bumped into her," Codi protested, still laughing. "Besides, she has plenty more where that came from."

"I'll show you plenty more, you little turd rag!" She managed to box his ears, which just sent him into another peal of laughter.

"He's smeared rotten fruit onto my clothes for the last time, Padriec Dann!" she shouted. "You lot do something about him, or my husband will!"

"I will, we will. Codi, come on!" More to get them both away from the enraged woman's fists, Paddy hustled Codi down the close as fast as he could drag him, only slowing when they turned onto Iron Street.

"You can let go of my collar now, Chief Runner Dann," Codi said with an overly dramatic wheeze to indicate that Paddy had a hold of his neck a little too tightly. "I'm not going anywhere. You know me; caught is as caught can."

"Yeah, I do know you," Paddy snapped back, but he released the other youth and rubbed at his shoulder where Mistress Auklet's blow still stung. "I've known you our whole lives, and I know her too. What's wrong with you? She'll skin you alive one day!"

Codi shrugged. "No, she won't, Pazers. You'd stop her."

"Don't be sure."

Codi started laughing again.

"Look, seriously," Paddy said. "This has gotta stop. I know you don't like her, but you can't keep smearin' her clothes and dropping bugs into her pockets! You're not eight years old anymore!"

"No." Codi's expression changed from genial to enraged with frightening speed. "Neither was my little sister when that woman accused her of being a thief! She was six! I don't forget and I won't forget!"

Paddy sighed. "Maybe not," he said more quietly, "but one day soon you'll be an adult, and the Watch'll have to do somethin' more about this. So, I'm tellin' you—I'm *askin'* you—as a friend, please stop."

"Fair enough. Consider it done."

Paddy rocked to a halt. "What? Jus' like that?"

Codi thumped the dirt from his tunic absently. "Sure, jus' like that. All you hadda do was ask."

"I've been *askin'* for six months!"

Codi folded his arms across his chest and grinned. "No, you've been tellin' and yellin' and scoldin' for six months. This is the first time you've actually *asked*."

Paddy gave him a deeply suspicious look. "An' that's all it took, huh? Askin' one time?"

"That's all it took."

"Bollocks. You're up to somethin'."

"Am I?"

"Codi . . ." Paddy warned.

"What? Can't me helpin' a friend out be enough?"

"No. Not with you."

Codi burst out laughing again. "Honestly, Pazers, you kill me." He mimed wiping a tear from his eye. "Besides, maybe I don't have to do anythin' anymore. Maybe I've found somethin' out so perfect, so ripe, that all I gotta do is sit back an' wait."

"What?"

"Hm?"

Paddy took a deep breath. "What have you found out, Codi?"

His friend waggled a finger at him. "Now that'd be doin' your job for you, wouldn't it? But maybe . . ." he added as Paddy's eyes narrowed, "if you're really good, I'll give you a hint."

Paddy waited. "Well?"

"Well, what?"

Paddy just crossed his arms, and Codi snickered. "All right, all right. Don't ya think they dress a bit posh for their livin'? Why d'ya think that might be?"

"He's a stationer an' she's a pattern drawer," Paddy replied, refusing to be drawn into useless speculation. "That's a pretty posh livin'."

"For all that finery? I don't think so. She's got a different frock for every day of the week, an' he drinks the good stuff. Lots of the good stuff."

"Your point?"

Codi just shrugged. "All I'm sayin' is that I hear rumors from time to time; rumors that might be worth lookin' into. An' not just about the Auklets neither," he continued. "Some pretty strange rumors like how one of my all-too-serious-rules-followin' old friends was fightin' in the street like a common brawler." He indicated the bruise on Paddy's cheek. "An' the reasons for it."

"Codi—" Paddy warned again.

"I'm just sayin' I hear a rumor, an' then what do I see but Padriec Dann standin' at the foot of Glazier's Terrace, all ready to mix it up again."

"I was not ready to mix up anythin'," Paddy protested hotly.

"So, what were you doin' there?"

"I was goin' to work."

"Really? Your work's in Iron Street, an' you live in Iron Street."

"So? Maybe I was just . . ." Paddy trailed off.

"What? Checkin' him out?"

Paddy glanced away. "Maybe."

"Makes sense. I would have too if he were courtin' my ma."

"He's not courtin' her! He's jus' . . . he's . . ." Paddy clamped his mouth shut.

Codi tipped his head to one side. "Jus' what?"

"I dunno."

"Want me to find out for ya?"

"No!"

"You sure, 'cause I could just amble over there, all innocent like and . . ."

"*No!* Seriously, Codi. Leave him alone. He's . . . they're . . . they're . . ."

"What?"

"Good folk. I guess," Paddy said grudgingly.

"Yeah. They are. Big family, two of 'em our age, Robyn an' Orlenda. Honest, hard workin', Haven born an' bred, though not directly in Iron Street, so I suppose that does kinda make him an outsider. Now Ren—" he continued before Paddy could answer, "—that's his name by the way, Master glassmaker Ren Jessan, lost his wife five years ago. He used to run with the Danns an' the Brownes when they were all littles together, so I hear. Good friends with yer da, by all accounts, till he apprenticed on Glazier's Terrace an yer da disappeared into the Watch House."

"Sounds like you ambled over there already," Paddy groused.

"Yeah, well, I like to keep an eye out for my friends,

an' I'm friends with Robyn an' Orlenda too. Want me to introduce you?"

"No. Not right now," Paddy amended when Codi raised an eyebrow at him.

"Well, when 'right now' comes along, you just let me know. 'Course," Codi added with a wink. "Right now might come sooner rather than later, 'cause they just might know what I know about the Auklets."

When Paddy made to press him, he shook his head. "No time for that now," he said as the city bells began to toll. "Aren't you gonna be late for work? Better take me in, Chief Runner Dann, or someone might accuse you of favoritism, an' then I'd have to smear somethin' nasty on their clothes to defend your honor."

He laughed as Paddy gave him a dark look. "I hate you sometimes."

"No you don't. You love me like a brother."

"Yeah, well, I hate them too sometimes."

Corporal Hydd Thacker, the Day Officer in Charge, shook his head wearily when they arrived at the Watch House a few moments later.

"Aren't you getting a bit old for this kind of nonsense?" he demanded when Paddy explained the reason for Codi's arrest.

"Funny, that's just what Chief Runner Dann said."

"No doubt. And why aren't you at work? Doesn't your da's brewery require all of its apprentices?"

Codi nodded pleasantly. "As it happens, I was on an errand for that very business when *Mistress* Aucklet stumbled into me. I think she must have been drunk," he noted in a conspiratorial whisper. "She was weavin' back and forth like a sailor in a high wind."

"Uh-huh." Corporal Thacker jerked his head toward the stairs leading to the cells. "Get him squared away, then send someone to his da," he said wearily.

Paddy nodded.

One of Codi's cousins arrived a few hours later, paid his fine, and took charge of him. Codi waved cheerfully at

Corporal Thacker as they left, then winked at Paddy, just returning from a run.

"Yer uniform seems to be gettin' a bit tight these days," he noted. "Specially around the pockets."

Paddy glared at him. "You didn't."

His friend gave him a wide-eyed look. "Didn't what?"

Paddy crossed his arms, refusing to check his pockets as Cody laughed. "You will," he said as his cousin pulled him through the door. "You always do."

Paddy waited until he was home that evening before finally giving in to temptation. Reaching into his pocket, he pulled out the tiny round stone the color of a game-ball. With a sigh, he opened the lid of a small wooden box by his bedside and added it to the others inside.

He'd known Codi Vinny his entire life, had been pulling him out and been embroiled in one scrape or another for as long. With a smiling countenance and an absurd sense of ethics that exasperated his family and his neighbors alike, Codi might have become an accomplished pickpocket, but that had, fortunately, never appealed to him. If pressed, he would have said it was no challenge, but Paddy knew differently. Codi was honest whether he liked to admit it or not, he was just . . . Codi.

If he liked you, you found all kinds of things hidden in your pockets, from sweetmeats to tiny toys, even flowers. He and Paddy had played gameball together for years, until more adult responsibilities had pulled them both away. But Codi still hid the ball-shaped stones in Paddy's clothes whenever they got together, and even though he knew he would do it, Paddy'd never been able to catch him in the act.

However, if Codi *didn't* like you, for whatever reason, the *gifts* were a lot nastier, ranging from rotten fruit to bugs to clods of manure, not always dried. And he really hated the Auklets.

Paddy frowned, wondering what the other youth had found out about them to make him so gleeful. In the old days Paddy would have learned it before Codi, but that had been the old days before . . .

"Want me to introduce you?"
"Yes. No. I dunno know. Maybe."
"No."

The town bells had just finished ringing three when he was awakened by the sound of pebbles hitting his bedroom shutters. He sighed. For years, Codi hadn't bothered to remember that Paddy shared a room with his older brother. Not that it really mattered; Hektor could sleep through anything, but still.

Paddy pulled the blanket over his head, determined to ignore the other youth, but when the sound of pebbles became the sound of rocks, he rose with a curse.

Crossing to the window, he threw open the shutters and glared down at the moonlit street.

Below, Codi waved at him with a cheerful disregard for anything but their soon-to-be-recent- adventure. He gestured. Paddy shook his head. Codi raised the rock in his fist, and Paddy closed the shutters with as quiet a slam as he could manage. He would just keep at it.

It took a few minutes for him to find a shirt and a pair of breeches, then he let himself out of the flat and padded down the stairs in his bare feet.

He met Codi at the door to the tenement.

"What?" he hissed.

His friend drew back with an air of mock injury. "I thought you wanted to know what was goin' on with the Auklets?" he asked innocently.

"Sure, in the daytime," Paddy shot back, pulling on his boots.

"Daytime's not the time anythin' happens, Chief Runner Dann. You know that. C'mon."

Codi led the way down Iron Street, through the close they'd used that morning, and along Harp Way. But instead of making for the Auklets' shop on the corner of Inglenook Lane, Codi carried on, turning up Glazier's Terrace. Paddy stopped, and his friend gave him a quizzical look.

"What? I tol' you, Robyn an' Orlenda know what's goin' on, so they're comin' too."

"Why?"

Codi just gave him a grin. "Chicken?"

"No!"

"Shh, dummy, you'll wake up the whole street."

"No. I'm not chicken," Paddy repeated through gritted teeth.

"Then c'mon. Or do you wanna wait till the wedding' to meet them?"

"What wedding!? Never mind. Whatever, just go, jerk."

They crept toward the Jessans' shop, freezing as two figures materialized from around the back. They stared at each other for a long time, then, as if reaching a wordless consensus, the two figures headed over, eyes narrowed, legs as stiff as two cats approaching an unfamiliar tom. They fetched up a careful distance away, close enough to talk without waking the neighborhood, but far enough to avoid coming into contact with each other.

The smaller of the two crossed her arms.

"Whose your friend, Vinny?" she demanded.

"I'm Padriec Dann," Paddy answered for him.

She turned an angry look on Codi who just chuckled. "What? You figured I bring Captain Travin?"

"No, but there's plenty of other Watchmen who *aren't* Danns," she shot back.

"None as good. Look," Codi continued before she could answer, "We've got more important things to do tonight than sortin' out whether you lot can stand each other, so sort it out now; then we can go catch the Auklets in the act." He leaned against the shop wall, arms crossed, with every sign of waiting all night. Paddy and Orlenda gave him equally dark looks, which he happily ignored.

"Fine," she growled. "I'm Orlenda, that's Robyn, an' there's six more of us, plus cousins. We protect our own. We don't go looking for trouble, but we don't run from it either, even if that trouble comes from the Watch. And we're only out here as a favor to Codi."

Paddy gave a harsh snort. "If I'd known what Codi was up to, I wouldn't be out here at all," he stated, "but

since I am here, we're a big family too, an' we're not
used to . . . outsiders showin' an interest in any of us."

"We're not either," Robyn agreed mildly.

They fell into an awkward silence. Finally, Paddy
shifted. "So . . . your da . . ."

"What about him?" Orlenda demanded.

*. . . Why's he after my ma? Why's he hangin' around
a Watchman's widow? Aren't there any widows around
his own street that he can go after? Whys he messin' with
our family after we only just got over our da's death an'
then our granther's. Why does everythin' have to change?
Jus' why?*

Robyn seemed to understand the conflict going on
inside Paddy's head. "Seems like they met at the Rose
Fair last month and just got to talking," he offered.
"They're both a bit lonely, I guess."

"He's got us," Orlenda interrupted.

"You know it's not the same thing, Orlie," Robyn
said gently.

"I don't see why not," she muttered.

"We've been talking about it for a while," Robyn said
to Paddy. "So that when our father finally does tell us
about it, we'll know what to say."

"He hasn't?"

Robyn shook his head.

"Ma hasn't either."

"Maybe that's because there's nothing to talk about,"
Orlenda added.

"Maybe," Paddy allowed, then gave a frustrated
grunt. "But everyone in the street thinks there is, an' I
can't fight 'em all."

Orlenda scowled at him, then allowed herself a sour
smile. "Me neither."

"So, since everyone thinks they know how it stands
with our parents except us," Robyn said, "we should at
least figure out how it stands with us."

"So, how does it stand with us?" Paddy asked.

Robyn shrugged. "Well, I guess we can agree that we
love our father and you love your mother, right?"

"Yeah . . ." Paddy answered suspiciously.

"And we want them both to be happy, right?"

". . . Yeah . . ."

"But . . . ?"

Paddy made to answer then shrugged. "No buts, I guess."

"Great." Codi straightened. "You can all talk to your folks tomorrow an' tell 'em you're all fine with becoming one big happy family. Now, c'mon." He turned to go.

"Wait, what?" Paddy and Orlenda demanded together.

Codi raised both hands. "We've sorted out one piece of business tonight. You three aren't gonna start fightin' in the street. Now it's time to see to the next piece of business, so let's get goin' before the Auklets finish up what you two told me they're gettin' up to every bright, moonlit night. All right?"

Paddy, Robyn, and Orlenda glanced at each other, then, as one, they shrugged. "All right."

Robyn pointed. "The fastest way is to cut through the Clock and Crow's back court. It tucks up against the Auklets' place. We can hide behind their privy."

"Lead the way."

The four youths crept along the street, then slipped down a narrow alleyway beside the local tavern. Weaving through stacks of empty ale barrels, they reached a low stone wall a few moments later. One by one, they swarmed over it, then crowded behind the small wooden privy at the back of the Auklets' garden.

Paddy peered out. He could just see several figures, carrying bundles and hooded lanterns, coming and going through the cellar door, and he whistled silently as he saw the glint of fine metal in the moonlight.

Codi elbowed him in the ribs. "Tol' you they dressed too posh for their livin, didn't I?"

"Yeah."

"Wanna arrest 'em now?"

Paddy gave his friend an exasperated look. "There's at least four of 'em," he hissed back.

"So, there's four of us."

"No." Paddy turned to Robyn and Olenda. "You figure they'll be at it tomorrow night, too?" he whispered.

She nodded. "They usually do, as long as the moon gives enough light."

"All right, then. I'll talk to Hektor in the mornin', an' he'll sort it out."

"Can I be there?" Codi asked, a martial gleam in his eye.

Paddy shook his head but gave his friend a brief smile. "Sure. Why not, it was your tip."

"Great. No poop in your pocket tomorrow."

Paddy scowled. "The day you put poop in my pocket is the day you die, Vinny."

It took all three of them with their hands over his mouth to keep Codi from giving away their position.

The next day, Paddy finished his shift and left the Watch House feeling, if not better, then at least not worse. The Auklets had been caught red-handed receiving stolen goods and had gone more or less quietly—at least until Codi had burst out laughing at them. But Hektor and the five other Watchmen he'd brought with him had subdued them easily enough. They'd given up their contacts immediately, and half a dozen other thieves and fences now sat in the Iron Street cells. Paddy had received a commendation, and Codi had received the satisfaction of seeing his enemies brought low. All in all, it had been a reasonably good day.

Kassie met him at the door to their flat, jerking her head silently at the staircase that led to the roof. He took the steps two at a time and found his ma sitting in the shade of Kassie's pigeon coops. He joined her, glancing down at the two mugs on the small box beside her.

"I saw you coming all the way up the street," she explained. "Stiff as an angry rooster." She shook her head. "Nothin' grows like gossip in a town garden."

"An no one drives it to market like a Watchman," Paddy agreed. " 'Cept this time it was more like draggin' a dead horse up a flight of stairs to get a word outta anyone." He glanced shyly at his mother. "Codi says I gotta ask you about it, 'cause everyone else thinks they know what's what, so we should maybe actually know."

She nodded. "I've been trying to figure out how to talk to you about it for a while now," she admitted, then smiled. "I remember when you first showed an interest in Rosie. It was all I could do to keep your da from teasin' you about it."

"I remember." Paddy stared out at the city for a moment. "So, uh . . ." he began. "He's uh . . . a glassmaker, huh?" He tried to keep his voice neutral, and he thought he'd managed it until his mother laughed.

"Of all the things that you might have had trouble accepting, I should have known that would be it."

He frowned, embarrassed. "Well." He stared out at the city again. "So . . . uh . . . do you . . . uh . . . you know . . . like him?"

"I do."

"You gonna marry him?"

She sputtered in her tea. "Padriec Dann, what makes you ask such a question?"

Codi, he thought sourly. *An' here he is gettin' me into trouble again.*

"Well, isn't that what happens when you like someone?" he asked instead.

"Sometimes, yes. Not always. Sometimes people just become friends again because it's nice to have a good friend to talk to."

"But you do like him?"

She sighed. "Yes, Paddy, I do."

"So, you might marry him, someday."

She sighed again. "I might. I don't know." She looked at him. "How do you feel about that?"

He frowned. "I dunno," he answered. "Better than I did before I talked to Robyn and Orlenda."

"Oh?" Her expression wasn't angry, but it wasn't too happy either. "And what have the three of you decided?" Her voice had picked up a tinge of mother-warning, which he couldn't help but smile at.

"That we all want you both to be happy," he said.

"Even if it means we gotta get along like a . . . you know . . . family like, sort of."

Her expression softened. "Well, I'm relieved to hear that."

He leaned against her, and she put her arm over his shoulder and drew him close.

"Your hair's gettin' long," she noted, tickling his ear with a lock of her own.

"Maaa . . . I'm not five!"

She chuckled. "No, you're not. Still . . ." She brushed his bangs out of his eyes. "It needs cutting. I'll grab the scissors later. An' it looks like I need to find you another shirt, that one's getting tight across the shoulders."

"Yeah, an' my boots are too small," he admitted.

"You're growing up so fast."

"Yeah, lucky stupid me," he groused, and she tweaked his ear.

"Language."

They fell into a comfortable silence, then Paddy glanced over at her. "Ma?"

"Hm?"

"How come things gotta change so much?"

She smiled softly. "Because that's the way of the world, lovey," she answered. "Good and bad. All we can do is enjoy the good and hold on to each other through the bad. But not everything changes."

"Like what?"

"Like my love for my youngest baby boy," she said, squeezing him tight. "You were so adorable when you were born, all pink and round, and sweet-smellin' like a little sticky bun! I couldn't get enough of your little tiny toes and your little button nose." She tickled him, and he twisted out of reach.

"Ma!"

"What? Still mad that you're growing up too fast?"

"I . . . guess not."

"Well, all right, then." She pulled him close again. "I'll make you a promise right now," she said. "Whatever happens, whether you grow up to marry Rosie one day or I decide to marry Ren Jessen, we can always come up here and talk it through. No matter what changes we face along the way, the more things change, the more that never will. Deal?"

He leaned his head against her shoulder. "Deal."

He squirmed, and she glanced over at him. "What?"

"Nothin'. Jus' a stone in my pocket that's diggin' into my hip."

She laughed. "See, not everything changes, does it?"

"No, I guess it doesn't."

They sat and watched the sun set, turning the streets of Haven a magical pink, then orange, then purple, before heading back downstairs together.

The Choice Makes the Chosen

Stephanie Shaver

Herald Wil loved being back in Haven, back in *his* quarters in the Herald's Wing. He'd gotten so used to singing his daughter Ivy to sleep in a Waystation that a real bed felt like a luxury.

But no matter how safe or comfortable he felt, the unease always came back. He could not escape the sense that this was all on borrowed time.

Just enjoy it, he told himself as he crouched by her bedside. *Enjoy this moment.*

"What do you want to sing?" he asked.

"Mm." She rolled over and yawned. "The goat song?"

"Haven't done that one in a long time, *liebshahl*," he said, using his father's word for *beloved daughter.* "Remind me how it goes."

"Goat goat goat, *go-o-o-oat.*"

"*No-o-o.*" He tickled her until she giggled.

And then she obliged, in her sweet, high child's voice.

Oh, pure white blooms
The perfume of hope!
Pray you aren't
Eaten by goats!

It had been a favorite of her mother, too. Wil hadn't failed to notice that Ivy had inherited Lelia's perfect pitch and quite possibly the beginnings of her vocal range. Hearing in his daughter the ghost of the Bard he'd loved made him smile—but his heart twinged.

He sang along, the words rumbling in his off-key baritone. Then he gave her a kiss, a last sip of water, and stood to leave.

He heard her whisper, "Are you going back to find the lady who made the bad stuff?"

Wil turned to look back at her, the light framing his ghost-white hair. "I am."

"Be safe," she said, rolling over.

"I will."

In the outer room, the Bard Amelie—Lelia's last protégé—sprawled on a couch, reading.

She glanced up from her book with a smirk. "Nice Whites."

He looked down at his grubby clothes. All the joints had patches, and the whole ensemble looked as though it had been handed down multiple generations. She'd found him the set of rags, he knew not where. He was afraid to ask.

"They've seen better days," he said.

"I wish you'd let me come," she said, a little more serious.

"But you're watching Ivy," he said, innocently.

She shot him a sour look. "Arrangements could be made. You know Maresa always has an open invitation. Or we could put her in the stables. Aubryn would gladly watch her."

Wil smiled. The unpaired Companion Aubryn had been a good nanny to Ivy while he rode Circuit, and sometimes he still watched her during the day; but now that they'd all returned to Haven, she'd been under pressure by the Groveborn Stallion to Choose again. She had resisted so far, but he no longer had much faith in Aubryn remaining a reliable part of his entourage.

"Maybe someday. Not tonight," he said. "Don't wait up."

His Companion waited for him outside the entrance to the Herald's Wing, already saddled by some unknown Trainee. As soon as he got within reach, Wil Mindspoke and Vehs answered.

:Chosen.:

Hearing him again sent a crash of relief through Wil that threatened to bring him to his knees, even now. That one-word greeting seemed to say: *I can still hear you, you're still my Chosen, it's going to be okay,* all at once.

The sun hadn't set yet. Down in the city, workers would be starting dinner. By the time Vehs got him to where they were headed, meals would be complete, and the time would be right for Wil to start asking around.

:Are we heading back to the Lane?: Vehs asked as Wil swung into the saddle.

:Yes,: Wil said.

Back to Little Pudding Lane.

Back to looking for the poison that had stripped Wil of his Gifts, and the hunt for the woman who had made it.

He'd returned to Haven looking like he'd stepped out of legend: white-haired, stormy-eyed, rumored to be haunted. The last wasn't true, though he *had* survived two poisonings and put down an insurrection. He'd done it all while riding Circuit with his very young daughter at his side. The only thing he'd failed at was catching the woman behind the uprising: Lady Androa Baireschild, who went by the *nomme de guerre* of Madra and who commanded a monstrous construct she called *Lord Dark*.

But Madra had succeeded in her own ways; she'd stripped him of his Gifts of Foresight and Mindspeech. And while he could still speak with his Companion, it was only when they were in physical contact—paltry crumbs compared to the rich feast of conversation he had once enjoyed with his best friend.

To his surprise, Talia, the Queen's Own, had come to talk to him about his missing Gifts just days after his return.

"A similar thing happened to me once," she'd said as Ivy played in Companion's Field with Talia's son and Aubryn. "Temporary, not permanent like yours."

"I remember from Myste's report. Some mushroom Ancar's agents slipped into your food?"

"Yes, goatsfoot." She shuddered a little. "Afterward, Selenay and I talked, and we asked the Healing Circle to investigate whether there were other substances like that. . . ." Her brow had furrowed. "They assigned a very talented botanist named Yelyza to research it. Unfortunately, her genius came with . . . complications."

"What kind?"

"Dipping into her cupboard a little too often. Pickling her brain with her own tinctures. They say the dose makes the poison, and she knew exactly how much to take." Talia looked sad. "She'd sunk deep into debt, eventually moving into a tenement somewhere—she kept apart from the Circle. She said because she preferred living in the Lane, but . . . we talked a few times, and I knew she felt shame for how low she'd sunk. She just couldn't escape the gravity of her own flaws."

"Do we have her research?"

Talia shook her head. "It's been three years. No one's heard from her. It wasn't wholly unexpected when she disappeared. I don't get the sense anyone looked too hard for her. But now I have reason to believe foul play may have been involved."

"Why didn't the Circle try to help her?"

Talia took a deep breath. "That's the problem. They did. They assigned a Mindhealer, in fact. Can you guess who?"

Wil grimaced. "It was Madra, wasn't it?"

"I'm afraid so. Of course at the time, no one knew she was a traitor to the Crown. Tell me, do you remember Carris?"

"Of course." Wil had caught a couple of Madra's conspirators, Carris being one of them.

"Her capture has proved useful. We put her under Truth Spell, and she's verified some of what I suspected. Madra exploited Yelyza, and rather than curing her, encouraged her depravity. But Carris had two things to say about Yelyza. First, she wasn't part of Madra's conspiracies."

"No?"

"No. And second, Madra *never got Yelyza's research notes*. She got the end product but not the method of manufacture. And it vexed her."

"So what happened to Yelyza?"

"I still don't know," Talia said. "Neither did Carris. I mean—she could be somewhere in Haven? With her research."

"Hm." Wil rubbed his chin. "But if Madra knows even a little bit about how to make this poison, she might be impatient and desperate enough to try to recreate it, research or no."

"There's that, too," Talia said. "If it's anything like goatsfoot, it uses ingredients so rare they only grow in one part of the country." She shrugged. "If you find Yelyza's research, it could help you triangulate Madra's location."

Wil exhaled. "Well, I worked back from something of Madra's before with the weapons cache. I can do it again now. And I think you're right. Without an army, she's going to seek the path of least resistance."

"Of course she is," Talia said, archly. "She's highborn, after all."

The publican of the Rusty Nail took a look at Wil in his guise and said, "You're either a fool or a whiteshirt." He raised a brow. "Which is it?"

Wil tried to maintain his bland demeanor. He'd visited nearly every dive in Pudding Lane—this was the first to call his bluff. Subterfuge had never been his interest; that had always been Lelia's forte.

Or maybe it was his shockingly white hair. That didn't help, either.

"Honestly?" he said. "I've been accused of both."

The publican snorted. He had a pair of hulking brutes lurking off in a corner. The man made a gesture to them that seemed to mean "stand down."

"Whiteshirts don' come down t'th'Lane," the man said, taking out a rag and slapping it on his bar.

We do, actually. They're just better than me at hiding

it, Wil thought. "I'm looking for a woman named Yelyza. She—"

"Yelyza." The publican's brows furrowed. "Oof. Ain't heard that name in a while."

"But you have *heard* it." His heart beat quicker.

"Aye." The man shook his head. "Crazy lady. She came in wit' 'er notes an' scribbles—bits an' bobs all in 'er pockets. Like t'do li'l tricks of makin' things disappear up 'er sleeves. Clever. But crazy."

"Have you seen her recently?"

"Nah. Not fer years."

Dammit. "Any chance you know where she lived?"

"I tryn't t'know these things," the man said, very serious. "But she drank 'ere ev'ry other night with her landlady. An' betimes the Twins—" He pointed across the bar to the two brutes. "—do some, ah, *repairs* fer her. If ye ask'm nice, they ken take ye to the flat she rents out. Fer a price." He gave Wil a meaningful look.

Wil tapped the purse on his belt.

The publican whistled. "Theng! Tharg! One o' ye escort this gentleman to Letti's, if y'be so kind."

"Ahl do eht," said one.

"I wanna," said the other, starting to rise.

"No!" the first one said, glaring at her. "Y'got t'gravy last time, Tharg. *My* turn."

She growled at Theng, who growled back. For a moment, Wil feared the two would come to blows.

Then—

"Fine," Tharg muttered, sitting down in a huff. "Go."

"C'mon, milord," Theng said, lumbering across the room.

Wil departed with him, his sister sulking and watching them intently as they walked out the door.

"That's it," Theng said, pointing.

That was a three-story house on Little Pudding Lane. Too dark to really make out, but it seemed to be in order.

"Did you know Yelyza?" Wil asked.

"Not much, neh. One day, she jest stopped showin'."

"Didn't anyone think that odd?"

"Neh." Theng shrugged. "Sometimes people jest stop showin'."

Theng scratched his butt and made hoarking noises in the back of his throat as Wil mulled over the scene.

"Which floor did she live on?" he asked.

"I *think* the top," Theng said, sniffing his fingers. He started to say more, then very deliberately stopped, giving Wil a sly glance.

Wil sighed and took two coins out of his pouch, holding them up to sparkle in the starlight. Theng put his palm out, and Wil very *carefully*—he did *not* want to touch those fingers—dropped them.

"Thankee." Theng grinned, then got a mock look of surprise on his face. "Och! I *jest* remembered. Letti ha'n't rented Yelyza's room since she went missing."

Wil blinked. "I'm sorry, what?"

Theng pointed. "That dark part there?"

Wil nodded. He could see now, by the late evening's gloom. All of the rooms had a bit of a glow—lantern light, candlelight, stove light.

All but one.

"That's th'room she don' rent."

Wil's mind raced. He badly wanted to talk to Vehs. The instant back-and-forth communication they used to share would have been invaluable right now.

"Do you know why?" he said at last.

Theng shrugged. "Letti's house, Letti's bidness."

"Right. Last question. Where do I find Letti?"

"Rusty Nail, betimes." Theng shrugged. "She drinks, like all o'us."

Wil studied the building. *What's in there?*

And on top of his Mindspeech, he longed for his Sight and a chance to catch a shadow of the past.

Lord Grier always seemed to have a glass of wine near him, but sometimes he had reason to drink many more.

Today, that number was six—along with complementing bottles.

Wil sat patiently in his seat in the highborn lord's study as the Healer swirled, sniffed, and finally tasted the first glass full of red liquid. Then he wrote a note in a leatherbound journal, set the glass down, and moved on to the next one in the row.

"Tastes like raspberry jam," he said. "Pleasing. Pleasant. *Very* pleasurable."

"Are you pleased?" Wil asked, deadpan.

Grier "hmphed," smirking at Wil over the rim of the next glass, a lighter garnet-colored draught. "This one will be . . . mushroomy."

"Sounds *great*," Wil said. "So. Why would someone *not* rent an apartment for three years?"

Grier sipped his wine. His face abruptly twisted with revulsion, and he spat into a waiting bowl.

"Are you all right?" Wil asked, alarmed.

"Me? Yes. This vintage? *No*." Grier put the glass far away on the big oak study table, then downed the previous glass in several gulps.

"Poison?" Wil asked.

"What? *No!* Why would you—oh, right." Grier grimaced. "No, sometimes—wine goes bad like that. We'll have to dump it and burn the barrel." He made a note in his book. "Usually I can tell *before* I drink it. That one snuck up on me." He picked up another glass, regarding it as if it harbored an asp inside before taking the tiniest of sips. His expression smoothed into relief, and he took a longer, larger gulp. "Better. Now, what were you saying? Apartment. Hm." Grier set down the glass and wrote a note. "Something's inside there?"

"Or some*one*."

"Hmm. Are you going to break in?"

"Honestly, I'm hoping she just lets me in." Wil stared off into the fire. "I don't have a lot of hope she will."

"Probably not." Grier continued his tasting and note taking.

"Shouldn't hurt to ask."

"It might."

"What if I ask as a Herald?"

"Hah. What do *you* think?"

"I mean, I'm really only half a Herald anymore, so—"

Grier gave him a stern look. "Wil."

"I jest." Grier looked unconvinced, but Wil drove on anyway. "I've already decided to get someone else to ask anyway."

"That's good," the Healer said. "It'll make all of us who worry about you going off alone feel better."

"Who's worrying about me?" Wil asked, confused.

"*Us*," Grier said, finishing the final glass of wine. "Maresa, Amelie, Lyle, me—you nearly died. *Twice*."

"I'm aware of how close Ivy came to being an orphan, thank you." Wil glanced across the room, where a thick candle burned down the marks. "Which reminds me. Your courier. Did they. . . ."

"En route," Grier said, sprinkling sand on his notes and blowing lightly on the ink.

"Good." But his heart sank a little. "Thank you."

Grier looked up at him. "Have you told Ivy yet?"

Wil shook his head.

"Are you waiting until *he* gets here?"

I don't want to talk about this. "So which wine gets to go to the ball?" Wil asked.

Grier went along with it, pointing at the first, fourth, and sixth glasses. "It will be a fine going-away party before we head back to the Manor. And that, sadly, will be the *only* thing I have to look forward in of this entire affair."

"If you hate it so much," Wil said, "why do you do it?"

"Because politics," Grier said. "And tradition. We always hold a fête before we leave Haven. Also, Drusillia would divorce me and dump me in a ditch with a broken spine if we didn't." He picked up one of the half-full wineglasses and swirled it, holding it up to the light. "Androa always handled the parties, you know. Saved me from it."

"That's not something I'd have imagined Madra being good at." That one of Wil's staunchest allies happened to be the brother of one of his greatest enemies served as a reminder of how complicated his life had become since the days of hunting rabbits in the foothills around the Ferryman's House in Cortsberth.

"Oh, you didn't notice her penchant for elaborate

plans?" Grier grinned. "She always picked the wines,
though she thought the Baireschild vintages were better
for *preserving* things than drinking. She preferred Or-
thallen's vineyards. . . ." His face darkened. "Because of
course she did."

Someone knocked on the study door. "Come," Grier
said.

A young page in riding leathers entered. "Milord,"
she said. "Urgent summons from the Queen."

Out in the street, Wil watched as Grier rode on a
hastily saddled mount toward the Palace. A query toward Vehs yielded no answers, and together Herald and
Companion rode off on their own mission—with one
important stop first.

Wil closed the book and pulled the covers—unfamiliar,
but scented with lavender and cedar—up around Ivy.

"But how did the kitty get into the closet in the first
place?" she asked.

"Because he was very naughty," Wil replied. "And
went off alone from his family when he shouldn't have."

"Silly."

He kissed her forehead as she yawned. She'd adapted to
sleeping in strange places. Tonight, that place was "Aun-
tie" Maresa's, because tonight he'd finally caved into pressure and opted to bring Amelie along on his adventures.

She looked happy in the big bed. No, not just happy.
Content, clean, well-fed—

Stop torturing yourself. You did your best.

"Stay safe, Dada," she said, dreamily. "Don't let the
bad lady get you."

He stroked a stray lock of dark hair—Lelia's color,
not his—away from her forehead. "I'm doing my best to
keep her away from me, sweetie."

From both of us.

Letti sat at her table in the Rusty Nail, pouring herself
another cup of ale. She'd nearly finished the books for
the month, and every tenant in her five-flat building had
paid up on time.

Five flats, five tenants. And each one knew if they didn't pay, they got a visit from the Thug Twins, who'd make them pay one way or the other. She vetted her tenants well. She rarely had a vacancy, and didn't have one now.

So when the gel approached her, asking to rent out her sixth flat, it came as a surprise.

"Wut in hell you talkin' 'bout?" she asked.

"Yer Letti o'the Lane, right?" the young woman said. "Ye've got a sixth flat? Been empty a'while. C'mon." She swung a full pouch in front of her, its contents jingling. "M'money's good."

Letti squinted at the young woman. Bright-eyed, with dark red hair, she didn't look a fool, but she talked like one.

"Ahm Letti," she said, "but *yer* daft, cuz I ain't got no sixth flat."

"C'mon, Letti," the gel said. "Ah know ye got one."

"Yer touched," Letti said. "G'awn. Get."

The woman closed her hand on the bag and withdrew ever so slightly. Then, softly, she said, "Yelyza."

Letti blinked. She felt as though someone had stabbed her eyeball with an icepick—and then just as suddenly, the sensation passed. "What?" she said.

"Yelyza," she repeated. "Y'ken that name?"

Letti wrinkled her nose and scowled. "Ne'er heard it."

"Hunh. Y'sure y'ne'er shared a drink'r two wit'er?"

Letti leaned forward. "Now lissen 'ere. Yer tellin' me 'bout flats I don' 'ave, and drinkin' partners I ne'er knew, has it mebbe occurred t'ye ye've got the wrong person? Leave me be!"

The young woman retreated, and while it pained Letti to see her money go, she didn't miss her questions.

Wil knew within moments that they were being followed.

"Wil?" Amelie said, trying to catch up with him. He took her arm and tugged her alongside him, putting a finger to his lip and shaking his head slightly.

He caught sight of the figure out of the corner of his eye—no face, just a silhouette. Big enough to be a challenge. He started frantically Mindcalling.

:Vehs! Vehs!:

They ducked down a side street, then up a lane, down another alley, and over to a wider road lit by streetlamps. The quick movement seemed to lose their pursuer.

Even so, he couldn't stop the panic clawing at his chest.

:VEHS!:

And miraculously, the Companion appeared.

He boosted Amelie up in the pillion seat and scrambled into the saddle a moment later—Vehs taking off before he had fully settled in. If their pursuer still followed, they'd quickly lose him now.

:I'm glad you heard,: Wil thought.

:Not immediately,: Vehs replied. *:But your fear, I think, boosted the Call enough that I heard and found you.:*

The wind felt good on Wil's face, and once he'd calmed down a bit, he could think more clearly about the exchange between Letti and Amelie. He queried Vehs, who replied with surprise, then affirmation.

:We need to talk to Grier,: he said. *:Can you get us to the Old Palace? And tell my heart to go back into my chest?:*

:Yes on the first. You're on your own for the second.:

Amelie stood in confusion before the door to the Baireschild quarters in the Old Palace. "What are we doing here? Isn't Grier back at his manor?"

"He should be," Wil said, knocking, "but he's not."

It took a few minutes (and several insistent knocks), but Grier answered, his robe mostly around his body and his hair absolutely everywhere. He sashed the robe a little tighter when he noticed Amelie.

"How," he said, blearily. "How'd you know I was here?"

"To quote a great woman, you're highborn," Wil said, dryly. "And I figured as soon as the emergency session ended, you would head to the closest bed—which is here, in your family's quarters in the Old Palace."

"Are you sure your Gift is gone?" Grier asked.

"Very."

"Hmph." He gathered his hair over one shoulder. "I was asleep, you know."

"And I was dealing with your sister's collateral damage," Wil said, walking past him into the room beyond and helping himself to a glass of Evendim smokewine from Grier's private reserve.

"What now?" Grier said.

"Your sister meddled with Letti's head."

The magnitude of his allegation floored Amelie. "That explains it!" she said, excited.

Wil took a large swallow from his glass. "Yes."

"Explains—what?" Grier said. "Who's Letti again?"

Amelie relayed her conversation with Letti with eidetic perfection, right down to the accents. At first Grier listened with confusion, but realization dawned rapidly.

"Hellfires," he muttered. "Yes. Androa was a strong enough MindHealer that this was within her power."

"So it's reasonable to believe she made Letti forget about the sixth room *and* Yelyza."

"It's reasonable," Grier said, walking over and pouring his *own* glass of smokewine. "But I've been thinking about this, and something's bugging me—how does an empty room *stay empty* for three years?"

Wil frowned. "What?"

"Squatters. A property in the Lane isn't just going to sit idle." Grier sipped his drink. "Something doesn't add up."

"Also, why not just kill her?" Amelie asked.

The men both looked at her.

Amelie spread her hands. "What does this gain Madra? Why bother with all this?"

"Something's in that room," Wil said, softly.

No one spoke. Then Wil tossed back the glass and said, "That's it, I'm getting in there. Now."

"Hold on," Grier said. "The *right* thing to do is to get Letti to the House of Healing."

"Sure," Wil said. "*After* I've been in that room."

Grier pinched the bridge of his nose. "Wil."

"Grier." Wil clapped his hands together. "You *wanted* me to break in before. For all we know, we open her mind back up, and she decides to go in, steal whatever's useful there, and throw it in a fire or the Terilee or sell to the highest bidder. Then I'm back to square one. My best opportunity is now, while she's oblivious to all this."

"And is it really breaking and entering if she doesn't know it exists?" Amelie said.

Grier rolled his eyes. "For the record," he said, "this is insane. But give me a moment."

He went off to his bedroom and returned fully dressed.

Amelie stood and stretched. "Thank goodness—neither of you offered me smokewine and frankly, I was getting bored."

"You two don't need to come along," Wil said.

Amelie and Grier exchanged a look.

"One of us needs to," he said.

She shrugged. "Why not both?"

Letti's tenement had an inside staircase with landings on each floor for the individual flats. No locks on the entry—the three of them entered unchallenged, navigating the creaky steps to the top. The lack of good egress made Wil's skin crawl. One overturned candle, and frantic tenants piling down the narrow stairwell through the equally narrow door would turn the cramped enclosure into a death trap.

Like the stairwell, the landing didn't provide room for more than two of them. Grier held up a lantern while Wil examined the door.

The first thing he noticed was the lack of dust or dirt on the lock and handle—in fact, someone had oiled them recently. Wil touched the handle, and it turned.

It can't be this easy, he thought, opening the door on the darkened room.

Wil caught a glint of metal from the glow of Grier's lantern just a moment before Tharg, the sister thug, appeared not eight feet away with something in her hand.

The Herald didn't think—he dropped his shoulder and threw himself at her.

They landed in a heap—Tharg swearing and yelling, "Get off me, dammit! I ain't fightin' no Herald!"

Grier had stepped in, and now Wil could see that the

metallic glint came from a ring of keys in Tharg's hands, not a weapon. He rolled off her.

The woman stood up, glowering. The four of them crowded into the flat. Wil could see shelving and rows and rows of bottles along one wall. The air smelled musty and a little floral.

"Yer a Herald, yeah?" Tharg said.

"I. . . . am," Wil said.

"Wish ye hadn't run off," she said, rubbing the back of her head. "Been tryin' to talk to ye since that first night."

"What?" Wil said.

"Ye heard me," she said. "E'er since the rich lady's money ran out, this ain't been worth m'time, and I'm tired of scarin' off the squatters."

"Hah!" Grier said, and stamped his foot. "*Knew* it."

Wil ignored him. "What rich lady?"

"The one 'at killt Yelyza," Tharg said.

They came back with more lanterns to light the room fully. Along the way, Tharg spilled everything she knew.

She'd been paid by Madra to watch the flat and make sure no one disturbed it. The handsome advance had come with a promise of bonuses for good work.

Except *those* never materialized. Madra had vanished nearly as soon as she'd given Tharg the money—after spending a few nights in the room, rifling around for something. Tharg knew this because she had been the one asked to keep watch.

There was more.

"Yelyza and 'er drank toge'er," she said. "The fancy lady'd come 'ere wit' a bottler two, they'd have a time o'it, whoopin' and talkin'. I'd keep watch then, too." She looked uncomfortable. "Don' like what she did t'Letti. Jest glad she didn' do nuttin to me."

That you know of, Wil thought.

He moved around the small apartment, trying to find—what? Something. He quickly deduced why Madra had left it intact and guarded—the room was practically an apothecary, complete with Yelyza's notes. The dusty bottles had held up well. Yelyza had capped them and sealed them in such a way that the contents hadn't dried out. All had labels glued to them, with tidy script indicating the contents, and then painted over with a wash of clear resin so they wouldn't run if they got wet. A complementary label on the back even listed the ingredients and what they were dissolved in. What Grier knew, he described. Most of them seemed to be soporifics and hallucinogens, a smattering of deadly poisons.

The only items out of order were a few bottles that had been smashed against a wall. Stains still marked the wood, and glass glittered on the floor.

He couldn't imagine Yelyza doing that. The tidy room, the neat handwriting, the resin that kept the labels from bleeding—all this indicated a woman who loved details and order.

As she'd done with her labels, so Yelyza had done with her notes, painting them with a thin resin to prevent smearing. It made them stiff, but Yelyza's tiny handwriting fit neatly on pages the size of his palm, and all fit into a single leather-bound folio.

But after a candlemark of cursory examination, they came to a realization: All her research, while interesting, was for well-known cures and curiosities. None of it fit the bill for "Gift-stripping poison."

When it became clear this wasn't leading anywhere, Wil inspected the floors and walls, looking for hidden caches, tapping for false or loose boards. He imagined Madra doing the same thing three years ago, growing more and more frustrated until she took her rage out on a few helpless bottles.

Didn't find what you were looking for? he thought. *Neither can I. And we still don't know what you did with Yelyza.*

Defeated, he slumped on a rickety chair. A series of pegs hung by the front door. The motheaten remains of a cloak clung to one, its lining cleverly sewn with empty pockets. Then an empty peg. Then another disintegrating cloak. And caked, dried mud below them where boots should be.

You put your cloak and boots on. You went out the door one last time. Where?

It would have been spring or late fall, judging by the mud.

Talia said she was last seen three years ago . . .

"Tharg," he said, "why do you think the fancy lady killed Yelyza?"

"Cuz one night they went off drinkin' tog'e'er," she said. "An' Yelyza di'n't come back."

Wil stood and approached Yelyza's wall of tinctures and potions. The containers weren't uniform, but then, he imagined Yelyza probably used whatever bottle she could find—and saved her coin for the contents. "Did the fancy lady ever bring over bottles like these?"

Tharg shrugged. "Mebbe?"

The bottles were all shapes and sizes, but some of them Wil knew. He'd poured smokewine out of one tonight, and Grier had done his tasting out of some that could have been twins to these.

Where would you take someone to guarantee they weren't found again?

An odd thought occurred to him. It didn't seem likely, but then—this was Madra. What slices he'd seen of her indicated she had a perverse sense of humor.

"Grier," he said. "I need to see your basement."

"Why?" And then, in a low moan, Grier whispered, "N-o-o-o. . . ."

Wil walked past the barrels in Grier's wine cellar, pretending he wasn't a ferrymaster's son and that he knew what to look for.

"The mansion is empty during late spring and summer, right?" he asked.

"Usually," Grier said. "The family only occupies it in fall and winter."

Wil studied the line of wine barrels. "Which of these has been here for at least three years?"

Grier gestured to a number branded into the side. "That's the year it was barreled. So, anything from this section—" he pointed, "—on."

"And which tasted off when you did your sampling the other night?"

Grier pursed his lips in thought, then walked over and tapped one.

"I see a plug in the top. Can you open it for me?"

Grier pushed a step stool up against the barrel and pulled the plug out. Wil peered inside, but he saw nothing but darkness. He looked around and saw what looked like a glass stick; he grabbed it and lowered it into the hole, rotating it around until he felt it bump against something . . . soft.

When he pulled the stick out, a small scrap of half-disintegrated fabric clung to it.

"What the hells is that?" Grier asked.

Wil stepped down. "Did your sister have access to the mansion three years ago?"

Grier nodded, all color draining from his face.

"I think you should open up that barrel," Wil said.

It took some effort. Wil stood by as Grier and his people conducted the task.

And when they did, they found Yelyza.

Wil sat with his daughter on a freshly made bed. Sunlight streamed in through the window, and bits of dust danced through the sunbeams.

The morning he'd been dreading for weeks had finally come. He had worried less over his words than how Ivy would react.

It all came down to this: He had to choose between being a Herald and a father.

And he had made his choice.

"But *why* can't I go with you anymore?" she asked, clinging to him.

"Because the bad lady is . . . very bad. Badder than I realized when we started. If she hurt you, it would break my heart into a thousand pieces."

She started to cry.

Vehs. It hurts so much. I wish you could hear me right now.

Someone knocked on the door to his quarters, right on cue.

"Let's go see who that is," he said, gently.

She snuffled and wiped tears away as they went to answer it. Then she opened the door, and in the entry stood Langfirch, her grandfather.

"Ho, little," he said to her. He nodded to Wil. "Son."

"Grampa!" she exclaimed, and embraced him.

"Papa," Wil said.

"Glad to see you're not dead," Langfirch said to him, scooping up his granddaughter.

"Doing my best, Papa," Wil replied. To Ivy he said, "*Liebshahl*, what if you stayed with your grandfather for a while?"

"Well, if my sister was trying to get me to swear off wine, she accomplished it," Grier said.

"Do you think that's what she meant to do?" Wil asked.

"Who knows? It probably made her laugh silly to stuff Yelyza in a wine barrel that she knew I'd eventually sample, or at the very least discover the contents of. *Anyway*—" Grier held up a stiff slip of paper. "*This* was in the barrel."

He handed it to Wil. The botanist's notes. A little grimy, but legible, thanks to the thin wash of resin.

"'Take,'" Wil read.

"The opposite of 'Gift'," Grier said.

"Thanks, I hate it." Wil turned the page in the light. "So, Madra meets the botanist Selenay's tasked with finding Gift-blocking poisons . . ."

"Yelyza shows her 'Take,' Madra gets the one bottle she has—"

"Which has the ingredients written on it," Wil said, remembering Yelyza's labeling system.

"Mm-hm. But *Yelyza* has the *notes* for *making it* on her. Madra brings her over for a drink, kills her to keep the research out of the Queen's hands, but inadvertently stuffs her into the barrel *with* her research. Then Madra goes back to the apartment, thinking she'll find the notes there, and runs out of time looking for them, so she just . . . seals off the room, intending to come back for them eventually." He shook his head. "If she'd taken just a few moments to search Yelyza's pockets . . ."

"Maybe she did? Yelyza's sleight-of-hand may have been as much for fun and games as it was to protect her research from being filched." Wil mulled this. "Then again, maybe Madra didn't. I don't mean this as a slight against your house, Grier, but criminals aren't always the smartest lot."

Grier snorted. "I'd drink to that, but—well."

Wil studied the ingredient list—ridiculously, three items long. Two of them he knew—spirits, angelica root—and one he'd never heard of.

"What's cauldroncap?" he asked.

"Seems that mushrooms are not our friends," Grier said. "Like goatsfoot, it's a fungus. And it grows in exactly one part of the Pelagirs." He pointed to a map on his wall. "Here."

Wil let out a long, slow breath. "There it is." He nodded to himself. "Right. I'll talk to Cyril tomorrow. There's going to be signs of her and that construct of hers if they're there. This feels right."

"You don't have your Gift anymore."

"It still feels right."

Grier abruptly brightened. "So . . . we're leaving soon, right?"

"*We?*"

"Well, as you like to remind me, this is my *sister's* collateral damage. Also, you keep needing my help." Grier rubbed his hands together. "And this way, I get out of having to run the Baireschild Estates for a little while. My wife's better at it than me, anyway."

Wil started to answer when the door opened and Amelie bounded through.

"Did you tell him?" she asked, excited.

"We were just getting to it," Grier said.

"Wait, you told *her* before *me*—" Wil said.

"I'm all packed," she said.

"You—what are—"

"You need me," she said. "You're *really* bad at false-face, Wil."

Wil put his head in his hands.

"We want to go soon anyway, before Haven goes full riot," Grier said. "The Heir just showed back up in Forst Reach out of thin air, no one knows how, and rumor has it there are gryphons flying around."

Wil lifted his head again. "What?"

"That's what the emergency Council was about." Grier raised a brow. "Strange things are afoot, Herald. I have a feeling we need to find Madra now more than ever. We should go. Preferably tomorrow."

Wil narrowed his eyes. "Before your wife's party."

"That's just serendipity, that," Grier said.

Out in Companion's Field, Wil stood silently with one hand on Vehs' shoulder and watched the sunset.

His Gifts wouldn't be coming back. His daughter had started a long journey to Cortsberth. And tomorrow morning, he'd start in the opposite direction, toward the Pelagirs.

Cyril had been in touch with a Herald who had reported some odd goings-on in the parts of the Pelagirs where cauldroncap spoored. Dead livestock found half-eaten or bloodless, and something large moving about that fit the description of Lord Dark. It wasn't ironclad because, well, *the Pelagirs*, but it was still better than anything else Wil had to go on.

:*Congratulations on finding the botanist,*: Vehs said.

:*What's left of her,*: Wil replied.

:*You still did better than any of her friends. No one thought to check the madwoman's wine cellar.*:

:*Guess I'm still a Herald after all, even without—*:

:*Wil.*: The thought hit him so fiercely it rolled him back on his heels. :*Gifts don't make you a Herald. Your heart does. The Choice makes the Chosen. Sight and Mindspeech do not.*:

Wil bowed his head, too overwhelmed to reply.

Aubryn approached and came to flank him, so that

he stood between the Companions. He reached out and touched her as well.

:*Is Vehs giving you a hard time?*: she said. She had the power to project into minds, and he could still hear her, too, if they touched.

:*Not without just cause,*: Vehs replied.

:*Hmph. I should come along with you too, then,*: she said. :*Keep you in check, old man. Also, I have a feeling my new Chosen is where you're headed. At least,*: she added, slyly, :*that's what I'm telling Rolan.*:

Vehs touched Wil's forehead with his muzzle. :*Wil. No matter what, you* are *my Chosen,*: he said. :*You will always* be *my Chosen.*:

Wil nodded, silent, not sure why he needed to hear it but grateful for it anyway.

:*Now let's go save the realm,*: Vehs said.

"Together," Wil said.

:*Together.*:

Trial by Reflection
Terry O'Brien

Shasta sighed when she looked up from her reading chair across her small workroom at the calendar chalked on the slate on the wall over her desk and at the circle around tomorrow's date. She knew that tomorrow, at breakfast, her tutor, Timiyon, would ask if she was prepared to take her Journeyman's Trial that day, and she would just shake her head. She knew he would nod and offer her chalk and a cloth to change the date to when she felt comfortable. After all, that is what he did after the last time she put off her Trial, and the time before that and . . . She pictured counting the number of times on her fingers in her head, stopping when she ran out of fingers to count.

She just didn't feel ready. She couldn't quite understand the difference between an Apprentice Mage and a Journeyman, or what happened during a Journeyman Trial, only that she desperately wanted it, and needed it to help her understand how to use the magic that surrounded her. Timiyon was the smartest man she ever met, but he once told her that what little he knew about learning magic was drawn from his frequent interactions with military and Court Mages as a member of the General Staff of Lord Martial Daren, now Prince Consort. The two Mages who came to examine her didn't even get beyond introducing themselves: one refused to work with her until she was "cured" of her deafness, and the other blasted her with incomprehensible chaos in her head that only gave her a raging headache. She loathed the idea of facing other Mages, and Timiyon agreed; fortunately, the general Royal offer that all Mages come to Haven for training was not yet a specific Royal command.

Her musing was interrupted when the door opened and Timiyon stepped into the room, followed by a familiar yet unfamiliar figure; Shasta stood and nodded politely to him. He wore the familiar dark blue uniform of the Guard, but she didn't recognize him. Timiyon smiled and pointed at him, then commenced finger-talking to her. *(Shasta, this is my friend Jayan. He just got promoted and assigned here.)* Timiyon finger-spelled his name for Shasta, and she repeated it, watching herself to fix it in her memory. *(He arrived yesterday and is already working: he wants my help with a problem in town.)*

Of course he would: Timiyon wasn't too forthcoming about his past, modestly claiming he was just a supply officer, but from what hints she gleaned from his stories, she was sure his job included solving problems.

(And by that, he means us.)

(Yes!) Shasta nodded fiercely. Of course she would help. Anything to avoid thinking of her Trial.

Shasta noted how Jayan glanced between Timiyon's nimble fingers and Shasta's energetic reply. As he did many times before, Timiyon then explained Shasta's situation: how her mother had contracted spotted fever when she was pregnant, and with no Healers around to ensure the health of her and her yet-to-be-born daughter because of the Storms. How she learned the alphabet on her fingers so her family could talk with her. How he became her tutor when the Herald who examined her said she had the Mage Gift instead of the Fetching Gift as everyone believed after her Mother's spools of thread began to fly around her when she was upset, and how he taught her to focus her Gift as best he could.

While Timiyon explained her situation to Jayan, she examined him as he shifted awkwardly from one foot to the other. He had tousled brown hair that would never accept a comb, eyes that showed his every emotion, a mouth that seemed to like smiling except that it was frowning right now, and a neat uniform with an officer's gold braid. She liked him.

Jayan mouthed some words, and Timiyon translated them. *(Jayan says Thayler, the gold merchant, was found unconscious in his counting room just after dawn this morning. The Healer says she doesn't know what happened to him but that it wasn't natural. Jayan suspects magic.)*

Shasta hid her smile behind a cough and her closed fist, remembering what Timiyon told her when he first started tutoring her: *A Rethwellan Royal investigator once said that magic was always the answer when there was no seeming answer. Not that he was always right, but magic always made his job more difficult.* Of course, only a nonMage would ever make such a statement: even *she* knew that magic was rarely the answer to anything.

Shasta's family moved to Sunrise Crossings, the Valdemaran trade town next to the improved road across the Valdemaran and Karsite border, when it was first built less than a decade ago. It was a convenient place for merchants from Rethwellan and Hardorn to join Valdemaran and Karsite caravans traveling between Haven and Sunhame. Shasta appreciated that the town was on one side of the road and the stables and cartwrights and other businesses and buildings to support the caravans were downwind on the other.

Jayan escorted Shasta and Timiyon into the tallest building along the main street, up to the third floor, and into Thayler's office.

(This is where his housekeeper found Thayler this morning. He was lying on the floor beside the counting desk.)

Leaving Jayan to observe from the doorway, Timiyon motioned her into the room with his head, and Shasta nodded. There was only one door, an iron-banded oaken door, and only one window, a broad, barred stained-glass window of the Sun-in-Glory that was certainly illuminated by the first rays of the Sun, which, in turn,

illuminated the large wooden desk before it. Two Karsite
style padded benches instead of chairs were placed before the desk, and another bench was sure to be behind
the desk. Shasta also noted the many lamps on each wall.

Timiyon pointed toward the window. *(Weaponsmaster Alberich has something similar in his quarters in
Haven. Very similar, indeed.)*

Shasta raised a querying eyebrow in response. Of
course he would know that: he probably even saw it.

Timiyon tapped Shasta's hand. *(Magic?)*

Shasta focused herself. There was magic here, the
feather-fall tingling sensation along her fingers that
magic always had, but there were fraying tag ends of
magic that felt like a spell was present. The closer she
moved to the counting desk, the more present that feeling seemed to be, but she didn't know enough about
magic to tell what spell or how long ago, and she signed
that to Timiyon.

Timiyon sighed. *(Gold is notorious for holding on to
bits and pieces of magic. Thayler holds monies for foreign
merchants. Rethwellan strongboxes have strong protection spells on them, mine certainly did; it could have come
from them.)*

Jayan's querying raised eyebrow was met with a
shake of Timiyon's head. Jayan hung his head slightly at
the news, then shrugged his shoulders.

Moments later, Shasta and Timiyon were back on the
street. There was a caravan mustering for departure, and
Timiyon helped with the logistics, an interesting diver-
sion in his semiretirement. Shasta, however, noted his
distracted stare and was convinced he was thinking more
about Thayler than loading caravan wagons. *(If what
happened to Thayler is not natural, then who? Why?)*

Timiyon smiled. *(First we find the how. Find the how,
find the who. Find the who, find the why.)*

Timiyon and Shasta walked into the mustering yard at
the cartwright's, and immediately into chaos. Several
men in comfortable Valdemaran garb, severely plain
Hardornan clothing, ostentatious Rethwellan finery, or

richly embroidered Karsite tunics were either arguing among themselves or arguing with an exasperated man in a leather apron. A young student in shabby clothing leaned against a post and alternated burying his nose in a book in one hand and drinking from a flask in his other hand. A bald, blunt-faced man wearing gray velvet finery and a prominent Sun-in-Glory pendant sat on a bench nearby eating with birdlike precision, neatly slicing an apple and stabbing pieces to eat. A narrow-faced, slender-boned man in a severe gray uniform sat next to him, guarding a heavy iron chest and watching everyone through narrowed eyes as if he suspected each and every person there a potential thief, especially the Karsite family of two harried adults and four very active young children. Shasta wouldn't trust any of them.

When one of the merchants happened to look away and notice Timiyon, everyone clustered around him, demanding his attention, much to the relief of the leather-aproned farrier. Timiyon quickly learned that Basidi hadn't opened the business that morning and couldn't be found; Merrow, Basidi's partner, left for Karse yesterday noon to help with her cousin's first childbirth. That left Timiyon as the only person in some measure of authority.

Timiyon convinced the merchants and travelers to follow him into his office, where he could sit and rest his ailing knees, then spent the rest of the morning and most of the afternoon answering questions, scheduling tasks, offering recommendations, and generally soothing frayed tempers. Shasta stayed by his side the entire time. It was no different from the interminable town council meetings Timiyon was forced to endure. Shasta sat meekly on his left, paying close attention to the participants, all of whom ignored her completely. When he wanted her advice on what their faces were saying, Timiyon would rest his hand on his leg, under the table, and Shasta would reach over and tap the lengths of his fingers in the precise location and order to finger-spell her comments. He would sometimes reply in the same manner.

By dinner time, the merchants and travelers were

mollified, the cartwrights, blacksmiths, and farriers were finished for the day, and the caravan just might leave as scheduled in the morning once Timiyon sorted out all the paperwork tonight and *if* Basidi returned tomorrow to make the final approvals.

Timiyon walked up the double set of stairs to Basidi's office, sat down behind the very messy desk, and went to work. Shasta followed him into the room and looked at the couch opposite the desk. The cushions were in disarray, one leaning against another and a third laying on the floor. She knew from Timiyon that Basidi sometimes worked late and slept there when the caravans mustered.

A vague feeling prompted Shasta to step closer and reach out her hand; the same fraying bits and pieces of magic she had felt in Thayler's office were near the couch, but here, the only gold she saw was a golden Sun-in-Glory token on the floor next to the couch.

Shasta snapped her fingers, and Timiyon got up and walked over to look where she pointed. He picked up the token and lifted his lenses to peer at it more closely. *(This is a journey token, usually worn by followers of Vkandis who have made the journey to the Great Temple in Sunhame. There was one like it on Thayler's desk.)* Timiyon's eyes held that same intense glitter he got when translating a difficult passage. *(Two of the three richest people in town acting strangely, two of the three most prominent Vkandis worshipers, two of three involving something at their office, and two of the three . . .)*

Timiyon closed his fist, then smiled. That left Merrow, the trade factor, Basidi's partner, who matched the caravan merchants with goods and took orders from distant merchants. *(Rules of three: Something unusual happens to two of the three, I suspect something will happen to the third, as well.)*

Shasta could believe that—she had never trusted Basidi or Merrow. She also knew there was one slight problem: *(Merrow is in Karse.)*

(We can still check her office, just to be sure.) She followed Timiyon into the next room over. Unlike the messiness of Basidi's office, Merrow's was very neat and

orderly; the only thing out of place was a small golden Sun-in-Glory token on the desk. Timiyon leaned over to peer at the token. *(It is the same as the others. What do you think?)*

Shasta didn't reply; she didn't need to reach out, she felt the magic tremble across her skin as soon as she came within arm's reach. She stood next to Timiyon and reached out, slowly, with one hand. She felt a knot of magic there, pulsing, with a string playing out somewhere in the distance from the center. She reached closer and felt the knot quiver, then a tag-end of it lashed out at her. There was sudden implosion of air rushing inward, surrounding herself and Timiyon with darkness.

Shasta fought the urge to brush her hand across her eyes to make sure they were open. Even in the darkest of rooms, there was always some faint light her keen eyes could see. Now, there was only thick darkness. Then she noticed the pain of her left arm awkwardly pinned against Timiyon's side and her legs and feet tangled underneath her. She twisted herself to free them, only to slide down, coming to rest on her back against Timiyon's legs with her arms and legs above her like an overturned, pitiable beetle.

She felt Timiyon crouch beside her, taking her arms and lifting her to her feet; then his hand traveled up her arm to her hand. He cupped her hand and gently finger-spelled his question, then finished by drawing the questioning glyph on the back of her hand: *(Where?)*

She reversed their hands and replied. *(Inside something. Like egg.)*

(Trap spell.)

Even Shasta recognized that.

(Light?)

Light, she could do. It was the first and simplest magic she ever figured out for herself. She reached into the magic within her, concentrated, and wove spiderwebs into a wan ball of amber light that appeared over her open hand. In a brief moment, she could see herself and Timiyon reflected in the curved surface around them

before the light flared so blindingly and brightly white
that she closed her fist and canceled the spell. She
blinked several times to clear the sunspots and tears
from her eyes.

Timiyon dropped her hand, and she suspected he was
knuckling his eyes to dry them. It was a long moment
before he took her hand in his hands again.

*(Recognize spell. Trap for Mage. Daren's grandfather
took throne from oathbreaker brother. Mage ally made
spell to trap royal Mages.)*

Shasta smiled. He might not know magic, but royal
history he knew very well.

Timiyon continued. *(Spell famous. Court Mages copy.)*

(This happened to Thayler?)

She could feel him nodding through the shaking of
his hands. *(Think so. Followed Vkandis. Always had
light. Then darkness. No light. No sound. Vkandis Hell.
Shock anyone.)*

(No sound?)

(No sound. Trap silenced. Like you now.)

(How get out?)

(Unlock outside. Needs Mage.)

Shasta nodded; that was understandable, the spell
was a jail, and that meant a jailer, and keys. *(Master?)*

(Journeyman locks, unlock. Simple spell, was told.)

Shasta made a silent vow to herself and to whichever
gods listened to *never* learn or cast the trap spell, ever, *if*
she ever completed her Journeyman Trial. *(Only way?)*

(Break spell from inside. Dangerous.)

(How?)

(Reflects spell like mirror.)

Shasta thought a moment. *(Does more. Makes bigger.)* She had felt the magic of the trap amplify as well as
reflect the magic of the light.

Timiyon was still and silent for a long moment. *(Very
dangerous.)*

(Now what?)

(What can we do?)

(We escape!?) Shasta couldn't help her hands shaking, but she couldn't tell whether it was from anger or

fear. If there wasn't another Mage to unlock them, then she had to do it herself.

(Why?) Shasta was certain Timiyon agreed, but he was testing her again.

(Mage escape. Jail still locked. We stay.) After all, jails were not meant to unlock themselves. *(We escape, catch Mage.)*

(Mage careful. Knows trap sprung. Not panic.)

Shasta pondered that point for a long moment. *(Mage planned escape?)*

(Mage smart. Retreat planned.) Timiyon was back to using military analogies, expecting the worst of his opponents. *(Candlemark across border, disguise, Sunsguard bribes, safety.)*

Shasta pondered that point for a long moment. *(Wait candlemark, then release?)*

(Maybe not from distance. Mage safe, why bother? Bigger problem. Not made for two people. Air gets stale. We fade, we die.)

Shasta gulped and clapped her other hand across her mouth. *(How long?)* And how did he know that? Timiyon was constantly bringing up odd bits of information like this. The one time she questioned him about it, his silent sad smile and slow shaking head told her it was a question best left unanswered.

(Can't tell. Small space, two of us, think not long. Candlemark, maybe two.)

(We escape.) This was now more than just a matter of justice in Shasta's mind, it was a matter of survival.

(We escape, chase Mage, maybe catch Mage, we live. Not escape, Mage escapes, maybe we die. Agree. Escape.)

(How?)

Timiyon was very still for several long breaths. *(Don't know.)*

(Scared.)

(Scared, too.)

Not right! The thought tore through Shasta's mind, and she lashed her fist out against the mirror wall. Her fist bounced back forcefully, causing her to ram the point of her elbow into the opposite wall. It was only by

jerking her arm around herself, and almost striking
Timiyon, that she avoided striking the near wall again.
She bit her lip as tears flowed from her eyes.

(What?)

She was so distracted by the pain that she barely felt
Timiyon's question until he repeated it, again. She finally
spelled out her response through the pain. *(Hit mirror.
Mirror hit back. Hit elbow. About hit mirror again.)*

Timiyon's fingers trembled on her own for a long
pause. *(Spell hit mirror. Mirror send spell back. Hits
mirror, not you. Repeats.)*

(So?)

(Spell break mirror, or spell drain magic. Trap breaks.)

Shasta thought about the idea, and she also thought
about being trapped here with a spell bouncing around
like an angry wasp. *(Can't control direction.)*

(Make pipe. Direct spell.)

Shasta pondered the idea of a pipe, just big enough to
guide a spark of a spell down its center, back and forth.
She reached for the magic inside her and around her and
wove a pipe out of spiderwebs between the closest, flat-
test sides of the mirror, taking special care to keep the
pipe from touching the sides. She had to pause more
than once, reaching for more magic, melding the rifts in
the pipe, making sure to leave a seam to insert the critical spell. But when she reached for the magic around
her to create the spell, all she found were tattered ends
that sparkled into nothingness at her touch.

Shasta sagged back against the mirror. *(No more
magic.)*

Timiyon took her fingers gently. *(Always magic. Find
magic.)*

She gripped his hand so hard that it hurt her fingers,
too. *(Can't!)*

Timiyon gently pried her fingers apart. *(Magic is.
Trust self. Imagine what is.)*

Water. Timiyon had told her that Mages said magic
was like water, how it moved and flowed, how it carved
channels and made streams and rivers. Magic didn't feel
like that to her; it wasn't water, something poured out of

a cup. Magic was pieces, a start and an end, of different lengths, of different colors. Then she remembered her mother's sewing room and the skeins of thread hanging on the walls, so many colors, so many thicknesses, so *many* of them. *(Thread! Magic is thread!)*

(Imagine magic threads. Color? Shape? Size?)

Shasta gulped several deep, calming breaths. She was very good at imagining things. *What would a stream of magic threads look like?* She imagined a stream of threads, thin threads, thick threads, like the varied warp and weft of her mother's rag-rug loom, flowing in many directions at once, and found it around her. *(Yes.)*

(See it. Touch it. Feel it.)

She imagined dipping her hand into the slow-running streams. They flowed around her fingers; some of the streams stung like nettles, some tickled. She reached for a thin, passive thread, plucking one color from a twisted skein that slithered along like a serpent. The thread was straw-amber in color, smooth and slippery as the finest silk, about the length of her outstretched hand, and no thicker than a strand of her hair. She imagined, no, she *felt* the thread pulse in time with her heartbeat.

(Take it. Hold it. Use it.)

She imagined twisting the thread around her fingers, pulling it out of the stream and knotting it into the spell she wanted before sliding it through the slot in the pipe. The pipe sealed itself as she removed her hand. The spell waited, trembling slightly as if in anticipation. With a mental touch, she set the spell in motion. She felt it slowly slither forward, and she felt the feather-light shock when it struck the mirrored wall and was reflected back. It was only just a little faster when it struck the opposite side of the mirrored wall, and the shock was just a little stronger. Each time afterward, it was just a little faster and just a little stronger.

Soon, it was beyond her power to control. Soon, the shock of it striking was thundering in her very bones faster than her own thundering heartbeat. Soon, Shasta was wiping the sweat from her face.

The pipe was glowing a dull, sullen red. She pulled

away from the heat of it as far as the trap spell allowed. Timiyon's hand in hers was limp and dry. At this rate, air was the lesser of their worries. Something had to break, soon, and Shasta worried that it might be her or, worse, Timiyon.

The last thing Shasta remembered was being so hot that the sweat dried on her forehead before she could wipe it away. She opened her eyes and then winced and wished she hadn't. The familiar wooden ceiling of Timiyon's house spun and danced, and she hurriedly slammed her eyelids shut. The skin on her face and arms felt tight and tingly cool, and she smelled mint and grease. Heat sickness. The new workers at her father's farm from farther north were warned about too much sun and heat, and she often helped the local Healer deal with the few who ignored those warnings. Now she knew how they felt.

Then came the gentle hand on her shoulders and the cool spout to her lips and the cool, cool water filling her mouth. She drank two full cups of water and another of broth before she was laid back down. She tried to rest, she knew she needed to rest, but she had to look and find Timiyon.

Timiyon was lying in the next bed. Dmiri, the town's Healer, was holding a sick feeder to his lips, just as she had for Shasta moments ago. Dmiri pointed her out to Timiyon, and he turned and smiled and waved weakly at her.

Shasta laid back against the pillows and closed her eyes.

When Shasta next opened her eyes, the early morning sunlight through the windows was brightening into day. Timiyon was propped up on pillows, resting but not sleeping, since he twitched nervously during his afternoon naps. She reached across and brushed his arm with her outstretched fingers, and he turned his head toward her and opened his eyes. *(Sorry.)* Her fingers were clumsy through the bandages, but the message was plain.

He smiled in honest relief. *(Not your fault. I didn't*

expect the spell to generate heat. An experienced Mage would have known that.) His hands were similarly bandaged, but he seemed to manipulate through them much better than she did, as if he had done this before.

(We escaped.)

(Yes, we did. Thanks to you.)

Shasta felt the heat rising to her cheeks. *(What happened?)*

(You remember the merchant with the guard and the strongbox? He was the goldsmith who made the tokens. His guard was the Mage who set the trap.)

That got a double-raised-eyebrow look in reply; she might have suspected them of many things, but she didn't expect this. *(How did they find them?)*

(They were eating dinner in the common room when you triggered the trap spell unexpectedly, so they decided to flee. Mage complained about his stomach and said he had a potion, so both returned to their room. They packed their gear and snuck down the back stairs; when he stepped into the sunlight, about when the spell broke, he collapsed. Goldsmith screamed, brought innkeeper, innkeeper called Guard, and Guard brought Jayan. Goldsmith was in shock, babbling about Vkandis' punishment.)

(Punishment?)

(Mage was Karsite black-robe.)

Shasta waved her hands to interrupt him. *(Black-robe?)* She remembered hearing whispered tales about them.

Timiyon nodded. *(Black-robe. Vkandis priest. Demon-summoner. Corrupt. Fled to Rethwellan when Solaris became Son of the Sun.)*

(So what happened?)

Timiyon sighed. *(They already had plan to escape across border, meet allies, then release us. They didn't know it was the two of us, the delay could have killed us. When you started your spell, the trap spell drew magic from the Mage. Spell went out of his control, like runaway team of horses. Very clumsy. When the spell broke, he collapsed. Healer says shock. He is in Guard custody, still unconscious.)*

(Was it Vkandis' punishment?)

Timiyon shrugged his shoulders and then winced. *(Who can say? My little knowledge of godly intervention is that it is usually more dramatic, or more direct.)*

Shasta smiled, showing lots of white teeth. She was more certain than Timiyon: the Mage was now in the same state as they had been, lost in the dark. Vkandis' punishment, certainly.

(The Heralds will deal with her.)

(Goldsmith?)

(Talked all night. Jayan is very happy.)

Shasta leaned back on her pillows, then suddenly sat up again and looked toward Timiyon. *(Thayler?)*

(Awake, nervous. Can't sleep, nightmares. Terrified of the dark. He needs a Mindhealer.)

(Guilty?)

(Was, not now. After Solaris, he confessed, paid fines, accused several prominent nobles of crimes, all in secret, then moved here to escape them.)

Shasta cocked her head and raised just one inquiring eyebrow: *And you knew this how?*

Timiyon sighed. *(I have a confession to make, myself. I didn't retire here at random. The Crown suspected people like Basidi would use their positions here for criminal purposes, and I have experience in these situations. I was more than just a supply officer, I was a special investigator for Lord Martial Daren himself, and that took me to some very bad places and I learned some very bad things that I didn't want to burden you with. I am sorry that you were involved with that.)*

Shasta dismissed his apology with a slight smile and a slow wave of her hand. After all, he was the one who taught her that her Gift included a responsibility. *(Basidi?)*

Timiyon grinned, showing his own less-than-white teeth. *(Quite guilty. He spent all day confessing to Vkandis. He returned after sundown and confessed to the Guard. Jayan said it was a long list of crimes. Smuggling, helping nobles escape Sunsguard, bribes, extortion, no slaves, though.)*

(Merrow?)

(Just as guilty. Still in Karse. Sunsguard alerted.)

So that was the *why* and the *who*. Shasta was still curious about the *how*.

(Goldsmith made gifts for them. Mage put trap spell on trinkets, trigger spell at night. Trap left them in darkness and silence for a candlemark, then release. Vkandis follower sees Vkandis punishment.)

(Why do this?)

(Why? Arrogance. Revenge. Thayler named names, his was one. Basidi and Merrow promised help to escape, took money, reneged.)

(But why did the spell trap us?)

(Spell originally created to trap Mages.) He pointed directly at her. *(Are you a Mage?)*

Shasta pictured the magic around her, not just random bits and pieces of magic, but the warp and weft of magic threads. She could touch them, she knew which ones to touch and which ones to avoid, and she could use them. She stretched out her hand and plucked a single thread of magic from a nearby ribbon and twisted it into the desired shape; a mote of bright white light hovered above her palm for several seconds until she released it. *(Yes. Mage.)*

(Then spell worked. You have Mage Sight?)

Shasta nodded, hesitantly. Not exactly. It wasn't Mage Sight as the Mages described, it was something else. *(Not Mage Sight. Mage . . . Touch?)*

(Mage Touch, interesting. Something new.) Timiyon sighed and smiled. *(Dmiri says we should well enough to get up and move about by tomorrow. I am looking forward to it; there is a bottle of fine wine I would be pleased to share with you. After all, it is, or it should be, customary to celebrate the completion of one's Journeyman Trial.)*

Theory and Practice
Angela Penrose

Bruny missed her fingering again, and the slow, mellow ripple of harpsong she'd been working on turned into a twanging wad of sound that jabbed her ears and made her jerk her hand away from the strings with a grimace.

She glanced across the room to where her roommate, Seladine, reclined on the bed with a book of history in her lap.

"I be that sorry," Bruny said. She rubbed her forehead, where a headache was growing, and glared down at the harp. "This one line do be fighting me something terrible."

Seladine gave her a rueful smile and closed her book with one finger marking her page. "You've been working hard," she said. "Maybe do something else for a while, let it rest a bit, and then try again later?"

Bruny shifted on her stool and leaned back against the wall of their room. The stone was so cool it felt like leaning on a mountain—the walls of the Bardic Collegium were as thick as her arm was long, at least to the wrist, so the students didn't drive each other to murder when they were all practicing at once. Generations of students had roughed up the walls of the dormitory rooms, chipping and carving a bit here and a bit there, to make them echo a little less.

Practice rooms were lined with tapestries to absorb sound, but sleeping rooms were bare stone boxes unless the students themselves brought in soft goods to hang. Bruny had come a little over a year ago with two changes of clothes, her toothbrush, her comb, and nothing else. Seladine's landed family was wealthy by comparison to Bruny's, who were sheep tenders in the Tolm Valley far to the north, but even Seladine hadn't come to Haven with a wagonload of tapestries.

And this time of year, with auditions for the Midyear Recitals looming over all of Bardic, the practice rooms were always full.

"I do have that rhetoric piece I should be doing," Bruny said while staring up at the much-gouged white plaster ceiling. A stack of worn, cloth-covered books teetered on the low table next to her narrow bed, the sight of them—ignored all day since classes ended—sending thorns of guilt through her. "And music theory be glaring all up at me, with Bard Breeanne may'p thinking like a nice sleep wi'book neath pillow be enough to memorize all!" She groaned and got a smirking nod in return from Seladine. "But the trials for Midyear be one week acome, and I be *not* ready!"

She paused, then said, "I *am* not ready," with a scowl at the grammar book half-hidden under her bed. She knew she needed to learn to speak the way people in the capitol did—the way everyone else outside the Tolm Valley did, it seemed. Bards were known as great orators as well as great musicians and singers. Seladine had pointed out—gently, carefully—that by the time she graduated, Bruny needed to be able to speak like a lady, or she'd never find a place in a great house.

That did be one more thing—*was* one more thing—to fret on, but right then she didn't have space in her head for those worries. Graduation for her was at least four more years away, as late as she'd started. The coming trials loomed so huge, she couldn't see anything else beyond them.

"If you work yourself into a muddle, you'll stumble at the trials even if you do master your piece," Seladine pointed out. "You work so hard, and that's wonderful— you're determined to catch up as much as you can, and

I admire that, honestly. But there are limits, and I think
you've reached them. You can only stuff so much into
your brain at once before your head explodes!"

Seladine slipped a feather into her history book and
laid it on her bedside table. "Come on, it's nearly dinner
time. Let's go see what there is to eat, and after we'll
take a turn around the garden. After you've had some
food and fresh air, you can come back and torture your
fingers some more."

Bruny scowled, but she set her harp carefully in its case.
It was borrowed from the Collegium, and she'd be that
mortified to let it come to damage. Although sometimes
she was sore tempted to bash it against the stone wall.

She followed Seladine out of the room and up the
hallway, watching how the older girl walked and trying
to copy her.

Seladine was a lady—not a titled lady, but still, her
landowning family was gentry, and she'd been raised to
all the ladylike manners and ways Bruny lacked. She
walked smoothly and gracefully, her head high but not
stiff, her shoulders straight—not slumped forward, nor
pulled so far back she looked like a child trying to impress a bully. She made the rust-brown trousers and tunic
all Bardic students wore look like something a lady would
wear to work her embroidery and drink wine in a salon,
while Bruny's always seemed wrinkled or stiff. Her tunic
was always either puffed too high over her belt or pulled
down so far she looked like a corn cob ready to shuck.

Seladine had helped her so much in the last year,
showing her how to braid her hair to keep it neat all
day—which had felt odd at first, because in the Tolm,
only men braided their hair.

She'd shown Bruny where everything was, helping her
organize her studies for the classes that always seemed
likely to bury her. Bruny had learned to read and figure
as a child, and a bit of the history of her people, and in
the Tolm that was enough. When she'd come to Haven,
she'd imagined she'd learn more songs to sing and may'p
learn an instrument. There was that, to be sure, but so
much more—language and history and mathematics and

rhetoric, religions and law and politics and mythology, composition and music theory and ensemble and music history, plus Gift training, and with so much more to come that thinking too hard about having to learn *all* of it gave her the cheebies.

They cut through a courtyard, a checkerboard of brown-speckled flagstones and gaps where sweet herbs grew. Two groups were taking advantage of the early evening shade to practice outside—one a trio of horns, and the other a group of seven who were playing different kinds of pipes while taking turns singing.

She knew the students in the larger group; she'd performed with them the previous year. Making music with a group was a joy she'd not had back home, and the pipers had welcomed her among them—a particularly generous act, since she'd only been playing her vertical pipes for a couple of months at the time and could barely play "Silly Sheep."

Delvan, who played the double clarinet, had worked out a simple part for her that required only three notes and proper timekeeping. With some determined practice, she'd mastered it well enough that she could relax while she played and let her Gift float free. She'd been the only Gifted member of the group, and the others had seemed happy to have her, even with her baby-level playing.

She caught Delvan's eye and waved as she followed Seladine across the courtyard. He raised an eyebrow at her and kept playing, but just as she stepped through the doorway back into the building, she heard the pipe music slide to a stop. Dinner called to everyone, even determined music students.

After dinner, Seladine went off with her own friends, a group of older students who were all looking forward to graduating and going out into the world. Seladine pointed a finger at Bruny and said, "Garden! At least twice round!" before vanishing into the milling after-dinner crowd.

Bruny took the two loops around the garden, walking between the low, clipped hedges and beneath the spreading trees. She was sure Seladine had meant for her to take a ladylike stroll, but she set out at a rather fast stride. It *was* good to get some late sun and feel the breeze, though, and she slowed down some to listen to other students, singly and in groups, playing and singing here and there.

Soon enough she turned back to their room, finding it empty. Good—Seladine wouldn't have to pretend to ignore Bruny's sausage-fingered jangling on the cursed harp.

She played for an hour, practicing the one tricky place over and over. Thought of the trials next week sent panic bubbling up in her gut.

She set down the harp and spent a dutiful hour with music theory, one eye on the striped candle, determined to give her most difficult music class a proper go before returning to her harp, determined to master the song. She continued until Seladine finally returned and scolded her into bed.

At lunch the next day, Delvan slid onto the bench across the table and said, "Ho, Bruny! We hardly see you anymore—what have you been doing?"

Tessy, who played a bone flute so sweetly Bruny fancied she could call birds out of the trees, sat down next to Delvan and smiled and waved at her. Students flowed into the big, timbered hall, surging between the long tables, calling to friends. The squeak and thump of shifting furniture and the clank and clunk of cups and plates merged into a raucus song, like a thousand geese gossiping.

"Practicing, what more?" said Bruny with a tight smile. "Trials just a few days acome, and my song do be fighting me hard."

"I've seen you practicing with your harp," said Tessy. "It's wonderful that you've gotten so good in such a short time. I remember you were so worried about catching up, and see, you have!"

"Oh, nay! I still be struggling like a lamb in the spring mud! The harp be that difficult, but I do be determined to master it!"

Tessy and Delvan exchanged a quick glance, and Delvan said, "I see. Well, you've clearly been working hard. Best of luck!"

"Thankee! I did hear you all at your practicing yester-eve, and it sounded that grand."

"Thanks!" said Tessy. "There are seven of us this year, and we're doing 'Firby at the Fair.' It has seven verses, so we're all playing, and we each sing one of the verses."

"That be a fine idea," said Bruny. "You have the fun of playing together, and each has their bit to shine in, too."

"Exactly," said Tessy with a nod. She paused, then added, "I'm sorry we didn't ask you to play with us this year, but you were so focused on your harp piece, it seemed you'd made your plans, so we left you to it."

"Oh, yay, it be exactly that way. I done be practicing this song forever it seems. It be a good performance piece. I just have to keep working at it."

The girl sitting next to Bruny nudged her with an elbow and held out a platter of roasted, sliced meat, pig from the scent, and Bruny turned her attention to serving herself. Trays and bowls flowed down the long tables, and by the time everyone had served themselves and settled in to eating, the conversation had turned to who someone named Zaden was snogging with this week, and Bruny let herself forget about her yet-unmastered harp song for a while.

That evening, just as the late sun was setting, Seladine put aside her book and said, "If I help you with that for an hour, will you go to bed right after? If you lose any more sleep you're going to fall unconscious right in the middle of your performance trial."

Bruny stopped right where she was and huffed out a sigh. "Yay, and I'd be that grateful."

"Excellent," said Seladine. "Give me a play through, then. Show me where you are."

Bruny turned back to the first page of her music, sat up straight and began again. The first bit went well enough, but when she got to the tricky bit at the end of the verse, she jangled it again and stopped with a groan. "It tangles my fingers every time! If I do play at quarter time, I can get through it, two out of three times, may'p. But if I do play it properly, my fingers do turn into clumsy sausages."

Seladine nodded, waited a moment, then said, "Well, keep going. Let's see how the rest of it sounds."

"That's all I do have," said Bruny, ducking her head. She felt embarrassment burning her face, and the panic began to bubble up in her belly once more.

There was another moment of silence, then Seladine said, "That's all you have? You haven't worked on anything past there?"

"I did doodle with it a time or two, but I done be working on the first bit. If I be not able to get past that, what do the rest matter?"

"Oh, Bruny! You know better than that! You practice the whole song! I should have—" Seladine stopped and squinched her eyes closed for a full breath, then another. "All right, then. Start over. Quarter time. And whether you flub it or not, keep playing, all the way to the end."

"But—"

"Start! You have four days, Bruny! It won't help you to learn the tricky bit and then flub the rest of it! Go!"

Bruny shut up and played, quarter time. It sounded like a tinkly dirge, and she slowed down even more—just a little—toward the end of the verse, but she made it through with her fingers untangled. She gave herself a silent cheer, just a tiny one, and kept going. There were three verses and a bridge, plus the chorus. Next to the tricky bit at the end of each verse, the rest was . . . not easy, but not straining-difficult, either. She was sure she could get it easy enough if she could just master that one part.

She had the vocals down perfectly; singing wasn't a problem, and she was happy enough not to have to fret over it.

Going along at quarter time, she plodded and plunked her way through the song, with only a couple of flubs, which annoyed her all the more after having got through the tricky bit.

"All right," said Seladine. "Good. Now, once more, quarter speed again. Keep going no matter what. You tend to pause when you make a mistake—don't do that. Keep playing, pretend you were perfect. It wasn't your playing that made a mistake, it was the audience's ears."

"What? None will be believing that!"

"It's not about them, it's about you." Seladine cocked her head at Bruny and gave her a sly grin. "If you believe you're perfect, it shows in your playing, in your face, in your posture, everywhere."

"That be not fooling the Bards, I do wager."

Seladine laughed and shook her head. "No. That is, it won't fool them into thinking you were perfect if you made a mistake. But they do judge you on your whole performance, and confidence and stage presence are part of that."

"But—"

"Even if it won't fool your instructors, it's a good skill to practice. By the time you're playing for patrons, you will be perfect most of the time, so far as they can tell, and projecting confidence will make perfect sound even better. Work on it now and you'll have it later."

"I do suppose . . ." Bruny still wasn't sure if there was a point to it, but she did see how *not* stopping and wincing whenever she made a mistake would help—better not to tie a bow around the neck of a flub.

She played it again, flubbed the tricky bit at the end of the verse twice, but kept going both times, and made two new mistakes—but not the same ones she'd made the first time—in other places.

Seladine, who by then was looking back and forth between Bruny and a history text, said, "Good. Again."

Bruny played through the song four more times before they pinched the candles and went to bed.

Late the next evening, Seladine let her play the song at half speed. She flubbed the end of the verse the first time, but got it the other two times, and made three other mistakes.

"Again."

She played it again.

"Again."

*   *   *

Three days later, when it was her turn to sit on a stool in front of the panel of instructors and play her trial, she'd played the song at full speed, with the vocals, fourteen times. The last two in a row had gone clean from beginning to end, and Bruny was nursing a tiny bubble of hope down in her gut.

She heard Seladine in her head saying, *"Good, play it again,"* and began.

She made it all the way through without any mistakes.

Two days later, every student in Bardic was milling about the dining hall, waiting for Bard Cambrie, who was organizing the Midyear Recitals, to come in with the playlist. Bruny knew a lot of the Trainees to recognize, a few to say hello to, but she wasn't close with all that many.

She saw Seladine huddled with a cluster of girls her own age, chatting and laughing and casting glances over their shoulder toward the main doors every few moments. Bruny knew their names but that was all, and she didn't feel comfortable intruding on them.

The pipe group entered in a herd, talking and shoving and poking each other. Tessy spotted Bruny across the room and waved, then beckoned. Bruny smiled and slipped through the mob to say hello.

"Bruny!" called Tessy as soon as she was within a few strides. "Any word?"

"Nay," said Bruny. "I done be here a good quarter hour agone, and there be nothing."

"A couple of years ago they were over an hour late with the list," said Kindal, young man a year older than Bruny, who played the oboe. He shrugged when everyone in earshot groaned. "It'll come when it comes."

"Whenever it comes, we'll make it," said Delvan. "We did fine, and they always favor ensembles."

"It's no guarantee, though," said Tessy. "They refuse groups now and again."

"But hardly ever," said Delvan. "A group has to make a right muck of it to get sent down."

"Truly?" asked Bruny. "Why?"

"There are only so many spots in the program," explained Delvan. "Soloists really have to earn their place. There's no guarantee of a performance spot—not like the seasonal festivals, where everyone gets to perform at least once—but they do want to give as many Trainees as possible a spot. Solos are much more competitive because they're . . . they're taking five times as much cake, as it were. They have to deserve it."

"Oh," said Bruny. It made sense, of course it did. She just hadn't thought on it that way before.

And if everyone was hoping to be a famous soloist someday, then it was practice for how competitive *that* would be. There were only so many great houses, after all.

"Well, ye did be that wonderful," said Bruny. "Ye did play that fine, and the song did make me laugh! I'm sure ye will be getting a spot, nay matter."

She got seven smiles and a babble of thanks. Tessy said, "You were very good too. You're so much better on your harp, I could hardly believe it."

"I done be practicing," said Bruny. "Seladine did help me. She did make me go slow and slow and slow and slow until I did be about to scream! But it did work, and I did play the whole thing with no flubbing."

"It was kind of her to spend time coaching when she had her own piece to work on," said Delvin.

"Oh, yay, it did be," said Bruny with a nod. "She be the kindest person I ever did be meeting, truly."

Just then, Bard Cambrie came sweeping in through the doors, holding a parchment scroll. The noise fizzed up with excitement, then died down to nothing while Cambrie strode across the hall, her Bardic Scarlet cape billowing behind her. She didn't usually wear it around the Collegium, and Bruny thought she was deliberately putting on a grand show.

Deliberate or not, it worked. She was the focus of every gaze in the room as she unrolled the scroll and held it up against the wide plank where announcements were posted. Her left hand must already have held tacks, because she unhooked a tiny hammer from her belt with the right and tapped the tacks into the corners of the scroll, *tap-tap, tap-tap, tap-tap, tap-tap*, then turned and gave a regal nod to the gathered students before striding off just as grandly as she'd arrived.

As soon as she was out of harm's way, the Trainees surged in a mass toward the scroll.

It took some time before Bruny got a look. She scanned down the two columns on the playlist.

Her name wasn't on it.

Bruny sat in a corner of the garden and watched the shadows creep across the neatly scythed lawn, one grass blade at a time.

All that work, for nothing.

She'd been fooling herself anyway, just a prideful little girl, thinking she could take a solo spot on a program after barely a year of study on one of the hardest instruments.

What had she been thinking?

All her life, back in the Tolm, she'd been the best singer in the valley. It was just so, like having gray eyes or brown hair.

But here, she wasn't the best at music anymore. She wasn't even the best singer. Others had finer voices, with more training. Others had the Bardic Gift. She wasn't special, was just an ordinary girl from a valley nobody'd heard of, who thought she could be the best again if she just got the trick of it.

Even working as hard as she could wasn't enough. She was below and behind everyone else, and however hard she ran to catch up, they were running too, and they'd always be ahead of her.

She wondered whether she should just go back home. She was nearly seventeen, old enough to marry. She knew sheep, and hard work. Surely she could find a man who'd consider her for a wife?

The sun had just vanished behind the garden wall when she heard, "There she is!" and two sets of feet crunching along the graveled path. She looked up to see Tessy and Delvan approaching.

"Ho, Bruny!" called Delvan. "You're hard to track!"

"I do be sorry," said Bruny. "I just did want to be quiet for a bit."

"Yes, well." Delvan stopped and looked at Tessy, who stepped up and sat next to Bruny on the cooling stone bench.

"We discussed it, everyone, and we all agreed. That is, if you'd like to play with us at the Recital, we'd like to have you."

"That—? What?"

"Since you don't have a place," said Tessy, her voice low and earnest, "you can play with us. I know you don't care for the pipes much, but you play them quite well in class, and you could join our group, if you wanted to."

Bruny's thoughts were twisting all about in her head, and she did her best to chase them down. "I'd be that grateful if—but I do care for the pipes! That is, I do think the playing of the pipes is great fun. They be just, I can't sing while I do play them, so I do need to work on the harp. But could I be joining you? Will they be letting me? Since I did not play with you at the trial?"

"There's more leeway with groups," said Delvan. "We'll have to get permission, but it shouldn't be too difficult."

"That—it'd be that fine to play with you! Do be thanking all the others! I'll be thanking them myself, when we do get together for practice!" Bruny's head felt light and swoopy, like it was flying into the sky on feathery wings. It wasn't a solo place, but not getting to perform in the recital at all had been that horrible, and playing with the pipe group had been that fun the year before.

"There's just one thing," said Tessy, her face still earnest. "The song we chose, it only has seven verses. That's why we chose it, because it fit us. If you join us, you'll just be playing. There won't be a verse for you to sing. I'm really sorry, but it's too late to choose something else and start practicing all over."

"Nay, nay, it do be fine!" Bruny was a bit disappointed, but not enough to send her all the way back into the glums.

"Excellent." Tessy gave her a smile, then stood and held out her hand to pull Bruny up. "Come on, we'll get you a copy of the music, and we can start practicing."

Bruny let Tessy tug her to her feet, then followed them back to the Collegium, her feet nearly dancing.

Seladine was waiting when she finally made it back to their room that night.

"Bruny! Are you all right? I saw you didn't make the program—I'm so sorry!"

Bruny found herself pulled into a tight hug, and she squeezed Seladine around the waist in return.

"It do be fine, truly," she said. "Tessy's pipe group—the folk I did play with last year?—asked me to play with them this year too, and I said I will be doing that. I will be playing my pipes with them, so the practicing will not be so hard."

"Oh!" Seladine straightened up, her hands on Bruny's shoulders, and studied her face. "Well, that's good. It's lovely that you'll be performing after all. That was very kind of them. And you can try for a solo again next year. With twelve months to practice, surely you'll make it then!"

"I do be supposing," said Bruny, although to herself she wasn't sure she'd be ready by then. It was a year away, though, and not something she needed to think about.

Bruny practiced the Recital song with the pipe group for a few days before they all trooped over to Bard Cambrie's office to get permission for her to play with them. Cambrie asked to hear her play the song, as they'd been sure she would. Bruny did fine, and Cambrie added her to the program with a firm nod.

Bruny spent the next two weeks immersed in the pipe group, playing and bickering and filing off rough edges. The music they made together was so much richer than any one instrument alone, it buoyed her up until she felt as though she were floating along a wide, gentle river on a raft of song.

She had more time for her other studies, too, and once, four days before the Recital, she got a nod from Bard Breeanne in theory class. It wasn't a smile, much less a word of praise, but it was something.

When the day came, Bruny dressed in her best uniform, took up her pipes and met the rest of the group in the courtyard before heading out to the big lawn near Companion's Field where the Recital would be held, the day being fine.

Anyone from any of the Collegia or the Court who wanted to come and listen was welcome. Although the Midyear Recital wasn't as much of an event as the seasonal festivals, it still drew a huge crowd—more people than lived in all the Tolm Valley.

Bruny reminded herself of how much fun she'd had at the same event last year and how much she enjoyed playing the song. Not being able to sing was a shame, but she loved to play, and that was enough. When they took their places on the stage, Bruny watched Delvan count the time, then began.

The song was about a sheep named Firby whose family took him to the fall fair. He escaped and dashed off to enjoy the fair on his own; he managed to dance, taste the cakes, race, throw hoops, get a kiss from a girl, judge the ale competition, and get back to his pen in time to win the badge for best sheep. It was great rollicking fun, and the whole audience was laughing by the second verse.

Delvan gave Bruny a nod, and she nodded back, then let out her Gift.

Her joy in the music and feeling of fun in the song wafted out to the other pipers and then through the listeners.

This was what she wanted to do, she realized. Playing music with other musicians—something she'd never done before arriving in Haven—was what she wanted to do for the rest of her life. She loved singing, true, but making music with others, sharing the pleasure of it, creating music together that no one of them could ever have created alone, *that* was what she wanted to do, needed to do.

Seladine was determined to be a lauded Bard in a great house, and Bruny was sure she'd achieve that. But Bruny wanted to be part of an ensemble, part of something larger than herself.

They played all of Firby's adventures, then stood and bowed into the audiences applause and cheering and laughter. They'd all done wonderfully, and Bruny knew she belonged with them.

Tools of the Trade
Phaedra Weldon

"Mother!"

Imra didn't acknowledge her son's call as he burst into her chambers. She simply continued packing, discarding the things she felt she would no longer need and artfully rolling the things she did need to fit comfortably into her saddle.

Her son moved to her side and put a hand on her shoulder. "Please . . ."

She didn't look at him. Not now. Tarron had the ability to sway her decisions with a simple look, and she would not give him that chance today. "You should not be here."

"The Queen calls in the Heralds," Tarron said, moving to place himself to be in her line of sight. "I am but a Bard in training."

And there his eyes caught hers. His blue to her hazel. He looked so much like his father. He had been a handsome man, a master at his Bardic Gift, and yet a faithful and loving husband and father. She had lost him too soon, and Tarron had lost his father too early.

"Please don't do this."

She put a hand on his cheek, and he placed his own warm palm over it. "I have to. I can't stay here any longer."

"That's nonsense. The Collegium has offered to make you a teacher. Your Empathic gift and your skill at mediation could be useful."

"P'sshh . . ." She said and moved around him to finish putting things into her bags. "I just . . . can't."

She knew what he was going to say, so she braced herself for it. "You're only running because tomorrow is the anniversary of Saelihn's death."

Imra closed her eyes. There it was. There are moments in every Valdemaran's life that sing of despair and loss. She could see the loss in others' eyes when they talked about their loved ones. But there was nothing—not even the death of her husband—that could compare to the loss of a Companion.

Her Companion.

Sweet Saelihn.

"I'm sorry," Tarron said in a soft voice. He put his hand on her shoulder again, and Imra hadn't realized she'd lowered them as well as her head. "I have no Companion. I wasn't Chosen as you and Father were. I only have you."

She turned then and pulled him into her arms, amazed at how tall and strong he'd become at the age of fourteen. "Tarron, I'm not dying. I'm just going to travel. I need to . . . I have to . . ."

"You have to leave before the Fields are full of Companions again."

Imra was shocked at how well he knew her. Just as his father had. She pulled back and kept her hands on his arms. "It's not jealousy. It's . . . sadness. Even after a year, I feel I am only half-living. And sometimes . . . I fear the best part of me died with her."

"I sometimes wish for a Companion, but seeing your sadness and despair, hearing you cry in your sleep for her, perhaps that is something I should rally against."

"Oh, no, no, no." Imra shook her head. "There is no greater bond, no greater joy than being Chosen. I wouldn't trade anything for the time I had with her. Do you understand? If you were to be so blessed, take it, and hold onto it as long as you can."

"But things are getting dangerous out there."

Imra patted his cheek and turned back to her bags. "I will be careful. I have been on more Circuits than you can count on your fingers and toes, Tarron. I am not old and feeble. So, now you go." She looked at the last thing left on the bed.

Folded with precision and starched to perfection were her Herald Whites. She hesitated as she reached for them, and then picked them up slowly and stared at them.

"Take them with you," Tarron said. "They were and are still a part of you."

Perhaps. She hurriedly stashed them into her last bag and buckled everything together. "Now," she turned and patted him. "You need to get going."

"I can walk you to the stables—"

"No, I can call in some students who have nothing better to do than gawk at all the Heralds." She pulled him to her and hugged him tight. "I will be fine, as will you. I will let you know when I find a place to settle down."

He gave her a wary look but returned her hug, wiped his face, and raced out of the room.

:*He'll write a ballad about this one day.*:

That's what Sae would have said.

Imra took in a deep breath and went to call for help.

The road north took Imra through several of the old familiar villages and towns she'd visited while on Circuit. As she came into Restinn, she passed more Heralds on their way back to Haven. Many knew her and waved, but she also saw the sadness in their faces.

Sadness because they knew Saelihn was gone.

She caught up with old friends, made new ones, and worked on a few projects here and there. Through it all, no one asked where her Companion was. Imra assumed they all knew and were respecting her privacy.

By the time she'd moved past the anniversary of Saelihn's death, Imra had traveled through Endercott. It was several miles outside of town, but not close enough to Polsim, that her pack horse threw a shoe. Imra guided him to a large wide tree flush with new summer growth and examined the hoof. She'd had the shoe looked at while in Briarley, but apparently the blacksmith had done a poor job, or was entirely untrained. Either way, she wasn't close enough to either town, and her horse couldn't move much farther without the shoe being tended to.

"Heyla!" came a small voice from above.

Imra kept her calm and looked up into the tree. She spied a gangly young boy spying back at her. "Heyla. And whom do I have the pleasure of speaking with? A child of Valdemar, or a tree spirit come to drop upon unwary travelers?"

The child laughed and jumped down from a distance Imra would have thought twice about attempting. He was nearly her height, thin and awkward. She guessed him to be close to her son's age. His hair was long and pulled back in a leather tie. His face was smudged with dirt, as were his hands and feet. He grinned at her, and the smile was infectious. "I'm no tree spirit. My name's Izli."

It was then Imra realized she'd made a terrible error. This was no boy, but a girl! "How do you do Izli? I am Imra."

"Oh, wow," the girl immediately got on her hands and knees and looked at the hoof.

Imra started to tell her to be wary in case Telidji decided to kick. But the beast of a horse seemed very content to let the child examine him.

:I would never kick a child . . . unless they deserved it.:

Imra dismissed Sae's memory and watched Izli as she examined the hoof. She realized the girl had some experience with horses. "Do you know of a blacksmith?"

"There's one in our village."

"Polsim?"

"Oh, no. That's a good day and a half ride. I live over there." She pointed to the forest in the distance. "In Carnei."

She pronounced the name as "Car-knee." It wasn't a village Imra had heard of before. So she said as much.

"Yeah." Izli stood up and rubbed the backside of the horse. "We're bigger than you think and smaller than we should be." She laughed. "Or that's what my mother says. She owns the inn in town."

"So you do get travelers."

"On occasion." She pursed her lips. "I got some tools close by, so I can reshoe him. But it won't be permanent. You'll need Riduil to fix it."

Imra assumed Riduil was the town's blacksmith. "All right, Izli, then I put myself in your capable hands."

The grin that spread across that dirty face was priceless. "I'll be right back."

Imra retrieved a few treats from her bags as she pulled them off of Telidji's saddle. Then she removed the saddle as Izli reappeared. She carried a bag of tools and proceeded to use a nearby stump to help her reshoe the horse while Imra settled him.

Once finished, Imra reset the saddle on Telidji but repacked her bags on Mouse, her riding mare. She took Mouse's reins and Izli took Telidji's as the two headed across the field to a dirt path hidden by tall grass and disappeared into the tree line.

"How could this place exist and yet I've never heard of it?" Imra said as she walked beside Mouse, half-expecting the horse to answer her.

Carnei was indeed a charming place. Small in size, closer to a village than a town. And it was nicely groomed! Izli led them through a stone arch between several copses of trees. Flowers, shrubs, all manner of decorative plants lined the stone walk. The first buildings were well-constructed utility stores, ready for travelers in need of supplies for their journey to either Polsum or Endercott. All Imra could think about was how great this place would be for a Waystation. It was a bit out of the way, but that would be a good thing for any Herald needing protected shelter.

In her mind, she could hear Sae agree.

The village appeared to be built in an octagon, the town "square" around a hub with a well in its center. The town blacksmith, jeweler, apothecary, general store, and even an inn were all visible from the well. The stone-paved ground was well worn and didn't hurt Mouse's hoof too much, but it was still obvious she was in pain.

To the left of the well, in front of the inn's entrance,

a man spoke atop a platform. A group of thirty or more villagers stood around him, listening. Some were incensed and loudly voicing their own agreement, while others watched with crossed arms, a position Imra noticed as signaling skepticism.

As they maneuvered the horses around the crowd, many people gave Izli a warm greeting, and most gave Imra one as well. Without her Whites, Imra had most often met with suspicious stares and hesitant good mornings. This village was in and of itself, an enigma.

Izli took Telidji directly to the blacksmith. Imra stood nearby, her attention torn between the care of her horse and the man on the platform. He was her age, of that she was sure. Mid-thirties, with a head full of well-trimmed hair, a thin beard that edged his strong jaw, and dressed in well-kept working clothes. Imra took in the smell of the flowers planted in pots and planters around the octagon, and she reveled in the fall of cherry petals from the trees that gave the whole scene a splash of color.

"—around us. Do you see the beauty of this place? The village feeds from Crown Lake. That system of surface irrigation is a system *we* built," he thumped his chest. "Us. As a village. With our sweat and muscle. Yet our crops wither because we can no longer draw from what our forefathers bore."

"What exactly are we supposed to do about it, Reyis?" one of the listeners called out. "What exactly do you expect us to do about it? Connak owns the land. He swears he has to tax the use so the town doesn't shut down."

Imra frowned at that statement.

"And I call that nonsense," another villager called out, though Imra couldn't see him among the people gathered. "We've used that lake since the Herald set up the agreement between the people and the Errel family. Connak can't just decide one day that we have to pay for the water, especially now when we're sowing seeds and need it."

"I say the bugger's filling his own pockets," a young woman close to Imra yelled out, and there were cheers from the crowd. "The Errels are the wealthiest family this side of Polsim. They own everything, 'cept the fields north of Reyis's farm. This isn't what the Herald planned."

"Careful, Merelyn," the man on the platform, Reyis, called out, and some people nodded. "Or those loyal to the Errels will seek revenge on your cooking."

Someone laughed. "Seems more to me Merelyn will take revenge *through* her cook'n regardless."

There was a bout of laughter, and the woman who called out, Merelyn, waved at them all and then disappeared into the door of the inn.

"Imra." Izli appeared at her side. "Come."

She joined the girl at the blacksmith's as the argument in the octagon continued and met the owner, Riduil Araric. He was heavyset, but not from lack of movement. His girth was that of muscle, hard-bound and sturdy. He was bald save for the sprout of hair from his chin, which he kept in a very short braid and a blue bead.

He greeted Imra with a smile. "Nice to meet you, lass. Don't you worry about yer horse. I can get him shoe'd in no time. Have him ready for travel tomorrow."

"That would be wonderful," Imra returned his smile. "Would you recommend the inn for my stay?"

"I would," he said and then he leaned forward, and with a conspiratorial glance to his left and then his right, whispered, "But I wouldn't eat the food. There's a nice tavern at the end of the road out of town, toward Polsim."

Izli pushed at Riduil's side, but the man didn't move. "You stop that. My mom's cooking isn't that bad."

Imra looked at Izli. "Merelyn is your mother?"

"Yeah," Izli said and moved past them to take Mouse's reins. "Come on and I'll show you in. We've got rooms."

With a nod of goodbye to Riduil, they stabled Mouse, and Izli helped carry Imra's bags into the inn. The interior was just as impressive as the exterior. Soft white plaster walls were accented by thick wood beams that ran along the ceiling. Lamps flickered high above and flames on sconces illuminated each of the tables. The floor was well-kept, a detail Imra hadn't seen often in all of her travels on Circuit.

The crowning glory of the main room was a grand hearth in the back, made of the same stone as the town's entrance. Atop the mantel sat a collection of lanterns, a few of which Imra knew were antique. The place smelled a bit odd—as if someone had dumped a lot of cinnamon and oregano into a fire.

Merelyn greeted them, coming out of the kitchen and moving around the bar where a single customer drank from a large mug. "Well, hello. I seen you in the crowd."

"Mother, this is Imra. Her horse threw a shoe, so Riduil's taking care of her."

"Well, good. Izli, put her things up in the largest suite—"

"Oh, please. No. Just something small," Imra interjected.

But Merelyn put her hand on Imra's shoulder. "As you can see, we're not crowded. I get a few travelers from time to time, but only because they take the wrong path from Endercott to Polsim. Izli, the bags."

Izli rolled her eyes at her mother and took the bags up a set of stairs to the right of the bar.

"Now, can I get you something to eat? It know it's just before noon, so you've got to be hungry. First meal's on the house."

Imra looked around at the empty tables and said, "Do you usually get busier after noon?"

The man at the bar gave a snort.

"You be quiet, Simon Dod," and she flicked a towel at him. "Pay him no mind. He's in his cups."

"The ale's the only thing good around here," Simon said. He turned on his stool and smiled. He was older than Imra, with graying hair and a full beard. But his clothing was nice and clean, and he wore good shoes. "If you want to eat—"

"Not here," Merelyn held up her finger.

"I noticed a rather odd smell . . ." Imra began as she moved around the bar and into the kitchen—and stopped at the entrance. The place was an unmitigated disaster. Flour decorated just about every surface, as did sprinkles of spices. Meat sat out on the center table, half cut and without covering! There were vegetables and fruit mixed in bowls and in a bin close by where it was obvious whatever was on the bottom was rotting.

No . . . she would never eat anything that came out of this kitchen. Imra pivoted and looked at Merelyn behind her.

Merelyn shrugged. "I'm not a cook. I do better at building things than making things taste good."

Imra sighed and removed her shawl. She set it on the only stool not covered in something and rolled up her sleeves. "Well, then, given I have plenty of time before my horse is ready, and you're not expecting a crowd for lunch, I'd say we start by cleaning this place up and sorting out what you have." She held her finger up when Merelyn opened her mouth. "I'm hungry. And there's enough here to make a nice stew, an apple pie, and I believe some bread, though I can see flour replaced dust in this room, I'm more interested in where the bag itself is."

Four hours later, in a very clean, and very organized kitchen, Imra and Merelyn stood at the center table. Stew simmered in a pot over a fire, an apple pie cooled on the window sill, and three loaves of bread rested on a rack nearby. Before them were twelve glass containers filled with what Imra insisted were the most essential spices to good cooking. "I'm going to point and you tell me what's inside."

Merelyn nodded.

"And remember—think of this as your tool belt. Or your tool case. These are your hammer, saw, lathe—"

"I got it. Just point."

So Imra did.

"That's . . . cardamon . . . no, carda*mom*. Ginger . . . cumin . . . tumor—no, turmeric. Coriander, rosemary—that's an easy one—mustard, oregano, black peppercorn, bay leaves, basil—oh, and cinnamon."

"Very good!" Imra now pointed at one of the containers. "What is it and what is it good for?"

"That's basil. You can eat the leaves fresh or cooked. It's taste is more subtle than the peppercorns. Enhances chicken, fish or lamb. It's really good in tomato dishes—I'm not a fan of tomatoes—"

"So you've said several times."

"—but it's very good at enhancing the flavor of potatoes, cabbage, squash, and we used it in the stew."

Imra patted her shoulder.

Merelyn put her hands on her hips. "You were right. As long as I think of them as—"

"What is that smell?" Izli demanded as she came into the kitchen. Behind her was Simon, and behind him came the man from the platform, Reyis. Up close he was nice to look at. His eyes were dark brown and very expressive.

"Merelyn," Reyis said. "Who is your new cook?"

"She's not a cook! She's staying here while her horse is reshod. This is Imra. Imra, this is Reyis Loraqen."

"Nice to meet you." Reyis' hand was warm and calloused. "Is it possible to get some of that stew I see in that pot. Oh, and some of that bread."

"And apple pie!" Izli gushed over the still steaming treat. "Mother! Did you cook all of this?"

"She did," Imra said.

"With instruction from Imra. And, yes. Simon, would you like some too? You know you never—" She turned to the stew to find Simon bent over the pot with a big wooden spoon. "Simon Dod!"

And he dropped the spoon in the stew.

Merelyn laughed as Imra and Izli helped dish out bowls, broke bread, and poured cups of weak ale.

No one spoke until the pie was cut and shared, and a man wondered into the kitchen. He asked about a room and a plate of whatever that wonderful smell was. Izli and Merelyn jumped up to immediately accommodate their new guest, leaving Imra and Reyis alone.

Suddenly nervous and hearing Sae's voice in her head, urging her to make conversation, not awkward silence, Imra grabbed two mugs from the sink, filled two tea strainers and poured hot water into both. Reyis stirred his own tea, dunking the strainer into the steaming water a few times.

"This smells as wonderful as everything else. Is this new? Merelyn rarely makes tea."

"I brought this with me. I used to make it at—" She stopped herself, before she said "the Collegium."

"At?"

Imra shrugged it off. "So, the speech."

"Oh, that." Reyis sighed and hung his head. "I'd held in my frustration as long as I could at Connak's declaration. And when I found out he's been out of town since having his lackeys hammer that notice up—"

"Who is this Connak?" Imra interrupted, and then felt her face grown warm. "I'm sorry. I didn't even know this place existed until today, so I don't know much about it. I don't know what kind of government you have, who the leader is, or how this place came to be."

"You say that as if it was a failing."

"I—" she hesitated. "I used to travel a lot. To think this place was here—"

"Oh, we're not hiding ourselves," Reyis stirred his tea and set the spoon to the side. "Or we're not trying to. We have things to sell and need a tourist trade. The way the we do things now is we ship to Polsim and sell there. But it would be easier if they came here."

"So why don't you advertise? Have the name of the town placed on road signs. Word of mouth—or word of Bard?"

Reyis held up his tea in front of his lips, the steam curling into his bangs that stuck out from his forehead. "Because Connak insists we're better off keeping the village secretive and closed." He laughed. "He would hate to know you're here."

Imra sat up. "Why?"

"Because you're an outside influence. Like I said, we've had the occasional traveler, but they're ushered out of town quickly. The only difference with you, the only reason I even stuck my neck out and got on that podium, was because the son of a donkey isn't here."

"Where is he?"

"His henchmen said he went to Haven to beg the Queen for a Herald. The surface irrigation has become an issue, and he believes a Herald can assure the villagers he's right that we need to tax its use so that we can keep the town thriving. It was a Herald that originally set up the system several years ago, back when we had that bad drought. And those same conditions are coming up again. Only thing is, no one was prepared for him to actually shut off the water."

"He shut it off?"

"Yeah." Reyis sipped his tea, smacked his lips and sipped more. "This is good."

"Keep going. This is getting to my original question. Who is this Connak? How did he shut it off?"

"I'll answer that in reverse order. He shut it off by secretly building stopgaps on the channels. And he keeps them shut off by hiring muscle to prevent anyone from removing them. As for who he is—" Reyis shrugged. "He's one of the remaining descendants from the Hold that built this village. The original family had the name Carnei, but Connak doesn't. The family's always been in charge of governing the village even after the Hold lost its fortune and those inside moved to seek new lives here. The Hold's still there, and the other relative is there. They're a recluse, and no one ever sees them. Merelyn still sends supplies to them because she's also a relative, but it's a distant one."

"Is there no actual governing body? Like a council or eldership?"

"Oh, yes, there is a council of seven, with Connak being that seventh member. He breaks the ties, and pretty much controls the votes. He has the most wealth in the village, and in truth he has done a lot for us, including brokering the deal that allows us to sell our wares in Polsim."

Imra rubbed at her chin. "That sounds a bit . . . fishy."

"Don't it?" Reyis grinned. "But what are you gonna do? He has the majority."

"So why don't the people, if they feel that strongly, just vote in a real mayor or leader? Someone not connected to the family or wealth? Someone that would more easily unite the village instead of divide it?"

"Because," Merelyn said as she and Izli came into the kitchen. Izli moved to the stew and started putting together a tray for the guest. "The town hasn't carried a vote since Connak took over."

"So only the council makes decisions?" Imra looked from Merelyn to Reyis.

"Yes," Reyis sipped more tea.

"And who votes in the council?"

Merelyn broke a loaf into fourths and placed a piece on the tray. "Connak. The council changed when he came in and announced his place. He displaced the ones the Herald set up with his own loyalists."

So he went to get a Herald to back up his demands? The man would have a rude awakening. Any Herald would insist on seeing the original agreements the previous Herald set out as voice of the Queen and would see the events of the past years had become a power grab. There was no reason for Connak to bring in a Herald, because they could actually unseat him.

She said as much. Izili delivered the meal and came back to listen.

"The Queen has called in as many Heralds as she can," Imra said. "There's no way that even if he sent in a request, one would get here in time to sow the seeds."

"You know a lot about the court," Reyis said. "Are you from Haven?"

"I—" Imra swallowed. She shrugged. "I listen. It's just about all I'm good for these days."

"I'd say that's a big fat lie," Merelyn said, making Imra look at her sharply. "Look what you did for me and this room." She gestured around. "In one day, you showed me this kitchen is not my enemy, but it's a room where I can *build* wonderful food. Yes . . . it's still going to take time for me to learn and understand spices and baking chemistry, but I'm not afraid of it anymore."

Reyis lifted his tea. "Here, here. There has never been a better meal come out of this kitchen. And if she can repeat it tomorrow, and the day after, this inn's food will overtake the popularity of the tavern."

Izli laughed. "I hope so. Connak owns that place."

Imra pursed her lips. "You said there was still someone at the original Hold? Do they see visitors?"

Izli answered first. "She does."

"And how do you know that, young lady?" Merelyn asked sharply.

"Because I visit her all the time. Oh, don't be like that, Mother. She's nice, and I do things around the place. It's just her and a single servant." She looked at Imra. "If you're ready for a bit of a walk, I can introduce you."

"Lead on," Imra said, winking at Merelyn before she followed the girl out of the kitchen.

They were met at the door of the old Hold by a stooped man Izli called Goat. Imra thought at first she was being rude, until he said it was indeed his name—and that the lady of the Hold was expecting them.

The place had definitely seen better days, Imra was sure. Izli explained that parts of the place were closed off. Only those Aerus and Goat lived in were open.

Aerus. Why was that name so familiar?

Aerus Carnei was a small, frail-looking woman. Her shoulders were rounded with age, and her white hair was neatly groomed into a braid that draped over her left shoulder. But strong determination twinkled in her eyes. She greeted them with a warm smile and insisted they sit with her by the fire while Goat fetched them tea. She commented on how nice Izli looked today, then turned her attention to Imra. "You look very familiar to me."

"Your name rings a bell for me as well," Imra replied. It might be that she had met Aerus in Polsim or Endercott during her many travels.

Aerus dismissed the familiarity with a wave. "So, have you finally come to ask for my help?"

Imra glanced at Izli. "I beg your pardon?"

"Well, it was only a matter of time before that scoundrel decided to make a profit off the channels. And I must say, that Herald's idea was quite the talk for a while, though the original plan was for the irrigation to be used on *my* lake and not his."

Imra frowned. "*You* have a lake?"

Izli nodded. "It's actually larger than Connak's."

"And it was that lake the original documents agreed

upon. But after the Herald continued on his way, Connak seized the opportunity to cement his claim to being the town leader. He volunteered his own water supply and became a hero to the villagers. But you see, that wasn't going to last because the rat's got one very big problem."

Imra smiled. "He's a gambler."

Aerus opened her mouth, then closed it. "Yes. Seems you know my grandson better than I thought."

"Grandson?" Imra's jaw dropped.

"I don't claim him most days. Please, tell me how you knew?"

"Because he said he was going to Haven to ask the Queen's assistance. But he didn't go that way, or I would have seen him on my way here. The only travelers heading to Haven now are Heralds. He's gone to Polsim."

"Or Devin. Either has areas of ill repute. He'll come back with even more debt and some sob story about the Queen refusing him, or maybe even putting him in charge."

"That would be a lie." Izli stomped her foot.

"Since when did that stop Connak? And the bad thing is, everyone in that village seems to think it's somehow preordained, since he's a descendant."

"But you carry the name," Imra said.

"Only by marriage. My dear sweet Vincent died a few years ago, not long after the Herald left our little village. As long as he lived, he was the leader. And when he died . . ." she looked past them into the fire. "A part of me died too. But by the time I awoke from my sadness, my grandson had bullied his way into taking my husband's place. I know about his people on the council. They were not voted in, but bought in. And as long as they allow their fear of him to rule over them, he always will."

She rose and walked to a chest in the corner, opened it, and took out a roll of parchment. The act seemed ceremonial to Imra as Aerus turned and offered it to her. It was still sealed by wax, pressed with the icon of a tree.

"What . . ." Imra began.

"This is the original document signed by the families of the town, and by my husband, willing that lake to the village and her people. All the preparations were made to start construction on the irrigation channels—the lake is a high enough elevation to permit fast travel and an ease for valves. The only thing it needs is someone to lead them to the lake and guide them to complete the work."

"Oh . . . I can't—" Imra tried to hand the scroll back.

"Take it. Give it to Reyis, if he's still around. He was the only one with the balls to stand up to Connak. If you can't lead them, then use what you have to support him."

Izli pulled on Imra's arm. "Let's go and find Reyis. Connak'll be back soon. There's not much time."

"I don't think I can—" Imra said.

"When people invest in something that is theirs—and that piece of parchment says the lake is the town's— you'd be surprised how hard they'll fight for it." Aerus patted Imra's hand and yelled, "Goat! Get them a horse. We have no time to spare!"

"Yes ma'am," came the reply.

Izli ran through the door. But Imra hung back and stared at Aerus, feeling a hidden strength there. Something she no longer had. It surprised her when Aerus wrapped her hands over Imra's. "I lost myself for several years, little one. While the world around me lived and changed and went on without me. She would not want you to give up on life, not when you still have the gifts those Chosen have."

It took Imra a minute to understand that Aerus *knew*, somehow, that she had been a Herald. Maybe she finally recognized her from some visit to a neighboring city. Regardless, the acknowledgement was enough for her to pull Aerus to her and hold her tight beside the fire.

"Fight," Aerus said. "Fight for what is right, fight to bring people together. The Queen gathers her Heralds because there is danger coming, and all of us will have to move as one."

Imra brushed back tears as she turned to hurry from

the great room of the Hold. Goat brought them a horse of darkest brown, and together she and Izli made their way back to the village.

Once Reyis had the document in his hand, had the town notary witness him open it and read it out loud, it took him no time to call a town meeting that night, much to the protests of most of the council—the ones on Connak's payroll.

The meeting was held in the inn. The place was packed, not just because the village seemed to have grown excited at the prospect of solving their own irrigation without having to pay to use the water, but also because a few who tasted the stew and pie earlier couldn't stop speaking about it. It seemed Merelyn had magically learned to cook!

It became obvious to Imra that her dreams of a nice bath and a good night's sleep were far away. Not only was Merelyn going to need help in the kitchen, but Reyis was going to need a bit of guidance navigating the fine print of the agreement. She gave assignments to Merelyn and Izli, drafted a young woman nicking a piece of bread into serving with the promise of free food, rolled her sleeves up and dove into the meeting among the heads of the families who crowded around. She took turns in both places and by the end of the evening, well after midnight, the family heads had drawn up plans for a work schedule to begin digging new channels.

One of the men involved suggested they save time and join the irrigation channels already in place from Crown lake below where they travel out of Connak's border. Reyis agreed it was a nice idea, but it would be something they'd need to include Connak in. He wasn't going to be too happy about the village working around his tax idea. Imra had to agree—though what they planned was legal and fair, Connak struck her as someone who would not be too pleased about losing control.

Reyis and a group of five would head up to Aerus' Hold early in the morning to talk with her and see the lake and discuss the preparations that had been previously started, then they would report back to everyone else. Imra and a few others helped clean up the main room as well as the kitchen, and once finished, Imra gave Merelyn and Izli a hug before she went upstairs.

With it looking as if the town had found its footing again, Imra decided she would leave the next day once Telidji was reshod and continue her journey to Devin. She hadn't thought that in less than twenty-four hours she would have become so attached to a place and its people. She hoped they would find success in their choices and wished them luck.

Imra was surprised to find Izli in her room when she returned from the privy the next morning. The girl was still in her sleeping gown and seated on the bed, her hands in her lap, staring at the floor. "You're going to leave. Mother guessed it."

"Yes." Imra moved close to her. "It's time I moved on."

Izli looked up at her. "Is it because you're secretly a Herald? If you are, can you show me your Companion? Please? I've always wanted to see one up close. I hear they can talk to you—Imra? Why do you look like that?"

Imra hadn't realized she'd backed away from the child until she stood against the wall. Her heart thundered in her chest, and sadness and anguish pushed their way up her spine and settled once again on her shoulders. "How—" Was this possible? She'd said nothing about the Collegium, or even mentioned having once been a Herald at all. How did Izli even know? Why would she suspect?

But then the child stood, her expression one of worry and fright as she went to one of Imra's bags and slowly retrieved the set of Whites. Izli held them with reverence as she placed them on the bed. "I—when mother told me to take your bags up to this room—I was going to sort your clothing. And then I saw these, and I knew. You were sent here by the Queen in secret to end Connak and his wicked ways."

"Izli—"

"And I waited to see your horse, but it never came,

and then it happened. You made Mother's cooking good
and the town has a purpose again. I heard stories about
the Herald that saved us. And now you're here." She
came close to Imra. "Please, show me your horse. I want
to see it."

The look of longing in the child's eyes touched Imra.
She saw Heralds and their Companions as magical be-
ings. Perhaps, in some sense, their Companions were.
Imra's only gift outside of being a Herald had been a
slight ability to influence people. She had used it to teach,
to help students see the solutions, whereas before they
blocked their minds from opening. Just as Merelyn had
blocked her ability to cook. Just as Reyis had blocked his
ability to see a simple way through a problem.

Izli turned and put her hand on the Whites. "Do you
have to wear them to make the horse come?"

"No," Imra said, and she realized she said the word
too loud, too sharp. That single word carried so much of
her pain that it held power, and Izli moved away from
her, away from that power. It was dark and consuming
and threatened to eat at her, take her down with it the
moment she remembered what she had lost.

Imra stumbled a step as she moved to the Whites and
placed a shaking hand on them. She let tears fall and
heard the pat as they made dark spots on the pristine
cloth. A swirling, howling abyss of despair filled the room.

Until . . .

*:I lost myself for several years, dear one. While the
world around me lived, and changed, and went on without me. She would not want you to give up on life, not
when you still have the gifts all of those Chosen have.:*

It was Sae's voice, but it wasn't. The words weren't
hers. They were Aerus' from earlier. It would be so like
Sae to remind her of important things. A mental tap to
the forehead, as if to say *wake up*.

She had no idea how long she stood there, her hand
on the Whites, her mind's eye focused on Saelihn. Aerus
was right. She'd known somehow, about Imra's loss, because sadness finds kith and kin, and in that shared dev-
astation there can be comfort.

"Imra?"

Imra slowly sat on the bed. She pulled the Whites to her and hugged them to her chest, her eyes closed. "Her name was Saelihn. I was Chosen when I was your age. I'd raced across a field to find my brother and tripped, but he'd fallen into a well. She found me and showed me where. She spoke to me in my mind, a voice so full of love—" Imra felt tears welling up, and she let them fall. "I felt as if I were whole, and the world opened up for me."

Izli didn't say anything as she moved to sit on the bed beside Imra.

"We were together for eighteen years." Imra sniffed. "We were on our way back from Circuit. Coming from the south. I was tired and wanted to be in my own bed by nightfall, though Saelihn insisted we should find a Waystation and rest there. But I wasn't listening and insisted on a path around the mountain. It was a narrow, bending, treacherous path. A stupid decision. But Saelihn took me anyway, because she knew I'd try it on my own if she didn't."

There was silence in the morning, an escalating tension.

Imra took a deep breath. "I didn't see the rocks. But I could hear them above us. She . . . tried to run, to get us out of the way. But I was hit and knocked off her back."

Izli had her hands on her face, her eyes wide.

"I don't remember anything after that. Just darkness and a consuming loss. When I finally woke in Collegium, I was . . . Saelihn was . . ." Imra sobbed. "She saved me, stood over me, took the pounding of the rocks to protect . . . me. They found her—"

"No!" Izli was on her feet and wrapping her arms around Imra, holding her tight. "No, please. You don't have to tell me anything else. I can't even . . . I don't want to know."

Imra wrapped her own arms around Izli and sobbed. She cried the tears she'd held back for nearly a year, held in the arms of a child she barely knew.

Minutes passed before the tears stopped and Imra felt spent. Hollow. But she felt, in a sense, renewed. She had not told anyone or spoken about Sae's death to anyone.

Until now.

Izli wiped at her face, took the Whites and carefully placed them back in the bag. "I'm sorry. I didn't know they could—"

Imra nodded. "They can. And it's hard to be without her voice in my mind. I am no longer a Herald. I haven't been for nearly a year. I left Collegium to find a family again, a place to belong in a different paradigm. They live in Devin, or they did before I was Chosen. My brother should still be there . . ." Her voice trailed off when she heard a commotion downstairs.

"What is that?" Izli said and pulled back from Imra as the sound became loud.

Seconds later the door burst open and two men Imra recognized from the square the morning before moved in, followed by a large man with shaggy salt and pepper hair. He shoved Izli out of the way and rounded on Imra. "That's her! Arrest her and lock her up!"

"What?" Izli shouted. "Connak, what are you doing? She hasn't done anything wrong!"

"She's incited the village against its leader. She's a troublemaker, and I was warned by the Queen to be wary of such interlopers who would take advantage of the unrest in the world. She'll stand trial as soon as we find Reyis and arrest him, too."

The two men grabbed Imra by her arms and unceremoniously led her out of the inn. People stared as she was manhandled and shoved against the center well. Imra half-expected the townspeople to run away, so as not to become a target of Connak's anger.

To her surprise, they didn't. In fact, several of the women stepped forward and shoved the two men out of the way and stood between them and Imra. She looked around in alarm. What were they doing? Why were they putting themselves in the path of what was obvious danger?

"Knock it off, Connak," Merelyn said as she stepped out of the inn with Izli behind her. "Imra's done nothing wrong."

"Like hell she hasn't." He whirled on Merelyn and

stepped up into her space, but Merelyn didn't move. No one did. "I've been to Haven, to ask the Queen for her help." He turned and addressed the growing circle around them. "And she has assured me I am right in taxing the use of the lake on my land because it is mine. A Herald will be dispatched as soon as one is available and will back up my claims. There will be no more disputes." He glared around as if to challenge anyone from speaking out.

Imra had seen this situation many, many times in her travels. She had also settled arguments with less of a claim than Connak's. She knew he was lying. She knew in her heart he had not been to Haven because the Queen would never have agreed with him, nor would she have put up with his bull-headedness. And he hadn't been gone long enough to get to Haven and back. But she wasn't a Herald anymore.

"You are such a liar, grandson," said a familiar voice to the group's right.

Reyis, accompanied by Riduil and Simon, led the large chocolate mare she'd ridden home on last night. And seated atop the mare was Aerus herself. A dark cloak covered her shoulders and the horse.

Connak stepped forward as if to challenge Reyis and his grandmother. "You think dragging this ancient remnant of a long-gone Hold changes things? *I* am the leader in this village."

"By what vote?" Aerus said. She did not dismount, and Imra smiled. Her seat put her above everyone, even Connak. "Where is your legal tenure? What voice made you king, Connak? Surely not the people assembled here."

"The council made me leader, and you cannot challenge it. Only a Herald can."

"But we have a Herald here," Izli burst out. "And you would have put her in jail!"

Imra cringed inwardly. *No, no, dear child.*

:Let her speak, my dear one.:

Voices, murmurs. The people glanced around as if to see a Herald and their Companion appear from the air.

Izli pushed her way through, Imra's Whites in her hands. She stood in front of Imra and held them out. "I can't believe—I won't believe—that you are only a Herald if you have a Companion. A Herald is the voice of the Queen. They fight for justice. They take care of Valdemar."

Reyis handed the reins over to Riduil and walked through the crowd to stand beside Imra. "Aerus told me you were once a Herald, not long ago. One she met in Polsim many years ago. And from what I've seen—what I now know—you have dedicated your life to aiding us in our time of need. You have listened to this village's bickering and its successes. In just the short amount of time you have been with us," his voice rose just a bit as he looked around, "Imra has taught Merelyn to cook—"

"Ah, bugger off, Reyis!" Merelyn commented.

Others laughed.

"—and she helped us organize as a village should. Just this morning, the original council met with Aerus Carnei, and we created a new contract." He reached into his jerkin and held up a folded document. "To restart and build the surface irrigation from the lake *we* the people of the town of Carnai own, as set up by the original agreement negotiated by another Herald." He held up the document Aerus had given to Imra the evening before.

"Lies!" Connak stomped forward. "*I* am the leader. This woman isn't a Herald! She has no say here!"

"And you never traveled to Haven," Imra finally yelled out. Bolstered by Reyis's words, she straightened her shoulders and took a step toward Connak. He was so much taller than she was, and he had bullies on his side. But Izli's words carried her along. "I no longer have my Companion, but I still have the Queen's sense of what is right and what is wrong. Wrong is paying lackeys to bully others into getting your way. Wrong is taxing the village to use a body of water that was never included in the original document." She pointed to the document in Reyis's hand. "*That* document. Sealed until witnessed yesterday upon its opening." She moved her finger and pointed it at Connak. "You were *never* in

Haven because I came from Haven, down a road you have never traveled."

"You lie!"

"I'm afraid not," Aerus said. "I have friends in Polsim, and I'm sure they will testify that you have spent the past week in Polsim, gambling." She smiled sweetly at him. "If you protest, I am more than sure those same friends will call in your debts?"

Reyis lowered the document and raised his other hand to command attention. "I raise the vote of the people of Carnei to dissolve the council set up by Connak Errel, and reestablish the former council."

A resounding cheer went up around them. Imra felt her heart soar and clutched her Whites to her chest. So much had happened in such a short time. Her head was spinning.

"Vote seconded," Riduil shouted out. "All in favor?"

Another cheer went up.

"Passed!" Aerus held up her hand. "And now, if you don't mind, I'd like to visit this inn and have some of that stew Simon Dod raved about in the middle of our meeting this morning."

Riduil helped the matron down from her horse as Izli ran up to her and led her to the inn. Villagers patted each other on their backs as the new council—the former council—formed a circle around Connak.

"Imra."

She nearly jumped out of her skin to see Reyis was still beside her. His expression was warm in the mid-morning sun, and he tucked the papers back into his jerkin. He then placed his hand on the Whites against her chest. "I can't even imagine what kind of loss you've suffered. When I was a child, my sister was Chosen, and I resented the Heralds for a very long time, because they took her away from me and my family. She was killed by Karse soldiers, and I blamed the Heralds and the Queen. But, to know you, and to know your grace and your fairness, tells me that I misjudged them and their purpose. Reading the words laid out in those documents told me my sister had labored hard to set out the rules of Carnei."

Imra blinked a few times. "It was your sister who originally solved the irrigation issue?"

He nodded. "Not many really remember. Not many know she and Islian passed from this place a year after. Like I said—I blamed the Heralds. But not anymore."

Reyis moved his hand from her Whites to her upper arm. "You may not wear them anymore, Imra. But you live them, as you were born to do." He laughed when he heard Merelyn's voice calling for Imra. "And as you were born to keep helping Merelyn navigate that kitchen."

Imra laughed as they made their way to the inn. She tucked the Whites under her arm as they entered and smiled at the villagers inside, many talking and laughing, and making plans to work tirelessly until the new irrigation channels were in place. Once in the kitchen, she placed her Whites in a cupboard away from the mess of cooking, rolled up her sleeves, and gave instructions to those volunteering to help.

"Hey, Imra," Simon Dod said from the bar. "I nominate *you* as new village leader!"

"Seconded," Reyis called out.

Imra put her hands to her face as those gathered threw up a cheer for her. Silence entered the square as everyone present waited for her answer.

:*I think you've finally come home,*: the ghost of *Saelihn* said to her, and Imra felt the memory of her Companion's love and pride.

"Well?" Simon said, his hand out. "Will you stay and lead us, Imra?"

Looking at their faces, Imra wiped away tears and nodded. "Yes . . ." She fanned at her face with her hands. "I would be honored."

The Border Within

Brenda Cooper

The chill of a damp spring breeze bit Marjom's cheeks as she and Herald Graylan rode in the center of a wide road shadowed by tall trees. Her arm hurt where she'd wrenched it in a fight that morning, and she was so tired it was hard to keep her head up and watch the sides of the road for wild animals or bandits.

Marjom's Companion, Hannra, Mindspoke, *:We're almost there.:*

As if he'd heard Hannra, Graylan echoed her. "The inn is close."

She answered them both back at once as she straightened her spine and stretched. "I could ride for another hour if I had to."

Neither of them called her on the possible lie.

The Forest Sow Inn needed a new coat of paint and a carpenter's touch. Nevertheless, light spilled through the windows and promised heat, meat, and wine. The stable girl, Lisette, jogged up happily, a wide smile on her face. She curtsied to the two Companions, Hannra and Yinna, her eyes shining with adoration for the graceful, silver-white horses that she clearly knew were much more. Astride Hannra, Herald Marjom noted with wry amusement that Heralds evidently didn't rate as highly in the child's view.

As the girl bent low, Hannra said to Marjom, *:Maybe you should greet me that way.:*

:Unlikely, old friend,: Marjom retorted. *:You'd get a fat head.:*

Hannra stopped, lifting her head so her Herald could dismount. Marjom clutched a hank of Hannra's mane for balance as she slid off her saddle. The ground slapped her feet as she took her full weight onto them. Damned old bones.

Herald Graylan slid easily off Yinna, but he looked over at Marjom with concern, making the older Herald grimace. She must have let out some audible note of pain. *Well, damn Graylan, too.* Someday he'd understand the difference between young bones and old ones.

Lisette almost danced toward the stables as the Companions walked amiably behind her.

Marjom used a wide smile to put a good face on her bad feet but lost it again as she started toward the inn door. Graylan came up beside her and offered his hand, but she shooed him away. "I'm fine." By the time they got through the door, she could walk more or less normally. The first few steps after riding all day hurt, but she'd only fallen from the pain once, and that had been after an ice storm three weeks ago. She was fine. Just fine.

She straightened her uniform, the movement wrenching her sore arm. The bloodstains from this morning's fight with three teenaged bandits had faded to dull red-brown, and light brown dust from the cold wind that had harried them through the afternoon coated the fabric. Graylan might look worse. The same fight with the teens had resulted in a rip in his pants. As if to underscore how ragged they looked, an older couple stood up to give them a table near the fire. She glanced down to verify they were leaving empty bowls before sliding into the offered seat with thanks.

A familiar serving girl filled glasses with both winter red wine and water. Before she could take the first sip of wine, the innkeeper, Hans, brought them bowls of vegetable stew, orange with fat winter carrots and too much pepper. She managed one bite before the door flew open to admit Herald Kenso. He was round for a Herald, with an easy gait and broad smile. She raised her glass, happy to see him. His Whites were still quite white and didn't show any sign of scuffs, mending, or even laundering.

She scooted over as he neared their table. "Well met," she said as he sat down. "What brings you out here to the very edge of Valdemar?"

"It's time I took my turn watching Hardorn."

"We can use the help." Marjom shook her head, mentally abbreviating the day's events. "We had to sort two refugee trains today. A big one with three families—twenty-two people!—was clean. They're farmers Valdemar will have a use for. There was one of Ancar's plants in a group of four deserting soldiers, though. Problem was, he had made himself well-liked. It took all afternoon to prove him a danger."

Kenso took the water glass that had appeared in front of him and drank it down in one long pull. "How'd you prove it?"

She sighed. "We *knew* he was bad. You develop an instinct after decades out here. But we had to dig up facts to convince his three new best friends."

Graylan leaned forward. "We interviewed each of them separately and picked apart their stories. Luckily, that also exonerated the other three, who plan to fight for us. Every sword helps."

Kenso had already finished half his wine. "You'll have to teach me the best tricks." He turned to Marjom. The look on his face made her stiffen. A brief flash of . . . sympathy? "You've been called to Haven. They're expecting you in a week."

She almost dropped her water. Haven? "I'm needed here! We don't have nearly enough Heralds to manage the Border and do any kind of normal Circuit. We could use twenty more, and two fistfuls of Healers!"

Kenso's hand stopped with his flask halfway to his mouth. He had gone quiet, maybe talking to his Companion, or perhaps trying to remember the exact words he was supposed to say. He was a kind, affable Herald, with good instincts and a heart that was twice as big as his rounded belly. He hadn't been Chosen based on his memory or lightning-quick wit. She had ridden a full

Circuit with him once, and they'd had to return to towns twice to find things he'd left behind and once to finish a conversation he'd left hanging.

Now he closed his mouth and shook his head. "It's orders. You have to go."

Her heart sank. She asked Hannra. :*Do you know what they want?*:

:*I'm sure it's something good, Chosen,*: Hannra replied. :*They must need you. And maybe we can rest a bit.*:

:*There's no time for resting!*:

:*Isn't there?*:

Marjom frowned. :*What's changed? Last week you suggested I start planning for the summer, even though it's barely spring. You mentioned we needed to get some lighter Whites. Besides, you dislike Haven as much as I do!*:

Whenever they'd been called back for any reason, both she and Hannra looked forward to getting back here, where smallholders struggled against nature and looked out for each other against common enemies like wild animals, raiders from Hardorn, and the weather. Simple enemies. Better that than the politics of Haven any day.

:*It will be fine. I'm sure of it.*: Hannra was holding something back. Which meant Marjom wasn't going to like it.

She dipped back into her stew, trying to look calm, and then asked Kenso, "Is everything in Haven all right?"

"Yes. As far as all right goes when you're expecting a Border war any day. You'll find it a little chaotic. But they were clear that I was to send you back. Five days!"

He'd already told her *that*. She glanced at Graylan, and it was easy to see she'd have no help there. He'd been fine to ride Circuit with, but she'd often felt he'd prefer someone he could talk to more easily. Someone *younger*.

If she started out at first light, she could get back in four days. She didn't want to leave, and if she had to leave, there were better places to go than Haven. But Heralds served Valdemar, not themselves. Still, the stew had turned to sand in her mouth. She choked it down with the bad wine, then pushed herself up, her feet throbbing again. "I'll go pack." She glanced at Graylan. "Is there anything you want me to leave you?"

Kenso spoke. "You're to travel light. So just leave anything I'll need."

She took a deep breath to force calm. "Anything else you forgot to tell me?"

His eyes widened, and again she felt sure he was hiding something. Not that she could do anything about it. She could Mindspeak with Hannra, but not with other Heralds. So she nodded stiffly at him, also bobbing her head toward Graylan. "Very well, gentlemen. I'm tired." She turned toward the stairs to hide the unexpected tear streaking down her cheek. No matter how badly she wanted to run up the stairs and shut the door behind her, age forced a sedate pace. She kept her head up and tried like hell to keep her shoulders back, too.

There was no reason for her to be upset. Except the memory of that sympathetic look on Kenso's face burned like a slap.

Haven practically glittered as Marjom and Hannra neared it. Houses and shops spilled outward from tall walls. Travelers jostled her as a steady stream of people headed into the city. The golden light of a late spring afternoon filtered through the bright yellow-green of new leaves and the pinks of early tree-blossoms.

Each day, the journey had been slightly easier, the roads wider and safer, and the houses and fields they passed in better condition. Well, Haven was richer than the Border and could afford to put on a nice show and fill its gardens with bulbs. But it still bothered her. Queen Selenay poured resources into the Border's defense, but nothing Valdemar had been able to do made the Border feel so safe as this.

Still, Haven was even more full of chaos than usual. Students in Grays bustled here and there, and Healers walked quickly, sometimes burdened with herbs. What had Kenso said? The rumored Border war was coming soon? The last two weeks where she had been were, if anything, slightly quieter than most.

No one seemed to be waiting for her as she rode into the stables. That meant no one saw her wince as she slid down. She stripped her own tack and turned Hannra loose to find her dinner without anyone to see how her hands shook as she undid the girth. But now what was she to do?

She sighed in relief when a young girl came around the corner of the barn, saw her, and helped her rack and store her tack. "Thank you," Marjom told her, smiling.

"My pleasure. You came from the Border?" The girl was blonde, with merry brown eyes and a round face over a sturdy frame. She looked too young to be Chosen, but she wouldn't be wearing Grays without a Companion. "What's it like there? I heard it's terribly hard." She picked up Marjom's saddlebags and slung them over her shoulder as if they were feathers. "I'm Candry. We were told to watch for . . . returning Heralds, but tomorrow."

"My name's Marjom."

"Hi, Marjom." Candry's smile spread across her face like light. "I'll take you to your quarters and bring you dinner."

"No need. I don't have regular quarters in Haven. I'll just take one of the rooms for Circuit Heralds."

"Oh, no, ma'am. I know where to take you."

Ma'am? And how did the girl know where she was supposed to go? Marjom frowned but followed as the girl headed through the wide barn doors.

Candry stopped and let Marjom catch up. "When did you get your Whites?"

What a thing to be asked! Marjom had to do the math twice before she believed the answer. "Forty-six years ago." She stepped carefully around a stray dog. "I was twenty-two. I wasn't chosen until I was eighteen."

Candry smiled. "I was fourteen. There's one boy here who was chosen at twelve."

So young. Was that due to the coming war? "How old are you now?"

Candry led Marjom down a street lined with newly planted purple snapping dragon flowers. "Seventeen. I'm to ride my first Circuit soon."

Marjom wrinkled her nose at the strong smell of fresh compost rising from the planting beds. "That's exciting." She remembered how she'd felt the same year. Apprehensive. Certain that she'd fail. "Are you worried?"

"No." Candry turned her head toward Marjom. "I think it will be grand. I was born in a small town. Shedsville. Perhaps you've heard of it?"

"I've been through there. It's nice." It was, and small was a good description. There was a single inn with six beds, but enough tables to feed fifteen families. Maybe no more than about thirty families total in the farms around it. Shedsville was far enough away from the Border that it felt safe, if poor. "I liked it."

"Good." Candry stopped, waiting for Marjom to catch up again. "It's not much farther."

Marjom gave in and asked, "Where are we going?"

"The new wing. Just around the corner."

Marjom stopped. She hadn't known they were building a new wing. "I haven't been here for years."

Candry stopped again, the saddlebags swinging easily over her strong shoulders. "Would you like a hand?"

As in, *Could she walk faster if someone held her hand?* "I'm fine." Marjom straightened and managed to make her stride a little longer.

They rounded a corner, and their likely destination loomed in front of them. Even though the last of the day's light softened the edges, the housing looked fresh and new, just whitewashed, and somewhat hastily assembled. Two stories tall, a little imposing, but pleasant. The planters near the big, welcoming doorway hadn't yet been planted, although fresh dirt sat in piles beside them, also smelling of compost.

Candry was already forging ahead and through the open door.

Marjom recognized an older Herald, Chalena, who had once taught her how to fix saddlery. Chalena leaned against the doorframe. Her hair had thinned and whitened, and her hands bore the distinctive dark spots and bruising of very old age. She had seemed old when she was teaching Marjom how to use a hammer and a spike to open holes in leather on a bridle or saddle that needed to be field-fit. So she was, what—twenty years older than Marjom? At least. Chalena's cheeks looked like they were trying to hide from her eyes, and her lips looked smaller and thinner than Marjom remembered. In spite of her body's obvious betrayal, her eyes had the same warm and slightly worried look, and her voice still spit steel. "Welcome home."

"Home?"

"Yes. We're almost roommates. You've been assigned a room just down the hall from me."

Marjom's reaction was unbidden and immediate. "I'll be leaving again in a few days."

A look of pained sympathy crossed Chalena's face and then disappeared. Kind of like the look Kenso had given her.

Marjom's voice trailed off as she continued, "Back to the Border. I've . . ."

"Let me make tea."

"I don't want tea."

Chalena shrugged. "We have stronger medicines. But wine is no good for your bad feet."

"Who told you about my feet? I'll take the wine."

Chalena smiled. "The kitchen is this way. We just opened a week ago. We're calling the place Heritage Hall. Do you like it?"

"I . . . I can't possibly . . ." The pale blue walls of the entry transitioned to a soft yellow, and toward the ovens and fire, a beautiful orange. Tapestries on the far wall by the head and foot of a long dining table softened the look further. A window ran the length of the table, displaying what would clearly become a garden, although now it was mostly mounded soils and empty raised beds. Red clay pots underneath the window held young oregano, marjoram, and other herbs healers carried with them. A prettier place by far than the tents and poor inns she'd been frequenting for the last twenty years. Prettier than the usual Circuit rider's housing in Haven. "It is beautiful. Maybe I will want to be here one day. But I'm needed at the Border."

Chalena hesitated briefly. "You need to sleep. You've had a long day. Can I pour you that wine now?"

Maybe she should have asked for tea. "Yes, wine would be great."

The wine was far better than the fare they got at taverns and inns. Just like everything else about Haven. Softer and nicer, and a reminder of the differences in wealth between Valdemar's capital and the Border towns. She grimaced, but she drank it. Wasting wine because it was too good made zero sense. "So, who called me here?"

"Selenay."

"Surely not." Marjom would have known that. A command from Selenay would have come with her seal, and besides, Marjom had never met the queen. She'd seen her riding inspection on troops and speaking at a multitude of events, but Selenay wouldn't know Marjom from an ant.

"There are two more Heralds coming in tomorrow. You arrived a day earlier than we expected."

Marjom laughed as the wine began stealing her unease. "Border Heralds don't have time for grass to grow under their Companion's hooves. We move all the time, sleep little, almost never in the same place. I can't imagine sleeping in the same bed for a week!" She took another sip of wine. "We're expected to be everywhere at once."

"You'll like it here," Chalena said in a tone Marjom remembered from when the older Herald needed her to finish her homework years ago. Part promise, part threat. "Your room is the last one on the right." It sounded like a dismissal, but Marjom sat still, unmoving, staring ahead.

Chalena got up without another word and hobbled slowly down the hallway.

It was a retirement home. She could smell it, see it. Only in Haven. No place like this existed in Border towns. The old died plowing fields or failing to outrun bandits. And they lived—*lived*—until the moment they died. Heralds did *not* retire. Not field Heralds. Not often. She looked around. This was not where she wanted to die. Maybe, *maybe*, she would die faster in the field. Being slow could hurt her there. But here? She'd have years of doing what? *Gardening?*

Marjom stared at the window and the potted herbs and the sunny paint until she couldn't keep her eyes open, and when she stood up, her feet screamed at her.

She ignored them and walked as quickly as she could to find her room.

The next morning, she slept late. The bustle of the city drew her outside to walk the streets. Haven still smelled of flowers and compost, but also of leather and fear. A page bumped into her with his arms full of boiled leather armor, and not five minutes later she dodged a stable boy carrying simple tack, the type she used at the Border rather than the flouncy stuff the rich merchants used. The attempts to get decorative spring planting done were halfhearted, as if Haven didn't quite have the heart to acknowledge the season.

An exhausted messenger galloped past her on a tired horse that could barely keep its head up. A group of armed men and women gathered by a gate, looking ready to head out to fight. Even though it was too early in the year for the day to be truly hot, it was bright and tiring. She found a bench in a small park and reached out to Hannra. *:Are you well?:*

:Worried. There have been serious attacks against the Border in the last few days. Closer to Haven than we were, too. So it's good to be here.:

Marjom recalled the messenger. *:We'll leave soon.:*

Hannra didn't answer.

Marjom waited awhile, and then said, *:I don't intend to stay here and wait out the war. We are still useful.:*

:Of course we are.:

If she hadn't promised to be back for lunch, she'd go find Hannra in Companion's Field and demand a more in-depth conversation. But she had, and Hannra had enough of a stubborn streak that it took work to pry secrets from her.

Another messenger passed her, this one going the opposite way. Carrying a reply back to the Border, and thus to the front of the war with Ancar?

Her stomach complained that she had been ignoring

it, so she headed back. The Heritage Hall kitchen looked almost full. Three more Heralds milled about, waiting, while Candry and a male student who looked a few years younger carried plates of soft breads and bowls of dried bean and apple soup to the long table. Like her, the newcomers all had gray hair. Herald Jolsten, whom she had ridden two Circuits with, walked with a decided limp that was new to her. Herald Debda's head hunched a little forward, and her hair had thinned considerably, but she was otherwise just as pretty as Marjom remembered her, with a tall, rangy form and a wide smile. She introduced herself to Herald Witman, a small, slight man who looked half the size of Debda but who had a strong handshake and brilliant blue eyes.

To her surprise, Chalena didn't invite them to sit, even though the table seemed to be set and the soup must be getting cold. Instead, she waited by the front door, fidgeting, watchful.

Finally, the old Herald stepped back, and a small, redheaded woman with freckles spilling across her nose came in. Chelena looked like a cat who had just killed a bird as she turned. "I presume Herald Talia doesn't need an introduction?"

She didn't. This was The Queen's Own Herald, and seeing her was almost as surprising as seeing Selenay herself would have been.

Talia smiled brightly, although she looked drawn and tired. But then, her job was to advise the Queen and keep her safe in the midst of one of the most dangerous times in Valdemar's history. Of course she was tired.

Talia sat at the head of the table, and Candry rushed to bring her water and a bowl of soup. Talia sipped the water and ignored the soup, gesturing for everyone else to sit. After the room was quiet, she cleared her throat. "I am very sorry that we didn't tell you much. But Ancar has spies in many places. We were afraid that word would get out that we have called you home. That might have made you targets."

A bunch of old Heralds? Targets? That made no sense.

Talia continued. "We are taking almost every Herald who is capable of fighting with us. That includes many of our teachers. We're even taking some of the oldest students. Yet we cannot afford for the remaining students to sit untrained; Valdemar will have need of them as soon as they are ready." Talia leaned forward, catching the gaze of each of the people sitting around the table. "We need to supplement the teaching staff who are being left behind."

Marjom couldn't help herself. "But I *can* fight. I was fighting five days ago."

Talia's face softened. "And we thank you. We value all of the service each of you has offered Valdemar. Most of all, we value the tricks and ideas and experience you have learned in your long service. All of you have spent your life helping to keep Valdemar safe, and all of you have done it outside of Haven. That is of great value. We've called you back to create a corps of older Heralds who will work from here, collecting, writing down, passing on, and teaching what you alone know."

Marjom sat back in her chair. The words sounded good, but what they really said was she would never go back out to her beloved forests and smallfolk but would die here, inside the walls of Haven.

She caught Talia's eye, raising her hand a little, conscious that she was the only one questioning the Queen's Own and that it probably wasn't seemly. But she didn't care. When Talia nodded, Marjom said, "What if we'd rather die at the Border? What if there are people out there who are counting on us?"

Talia's face stayed soft, but her words fell like stone. "Then you and they will both be thanked for your sacrifice. You are needed here."

Hannra wouldn't take her out of Haven against orders from Talia. No way.

Marjom was well and truly trapped. Heralds served where needed, and a real battle was coming. And now she had ended up on the sidelines.

She'd have to find peace with this. But how?

Talia nodded and hurried out. The others started in on their now cold soup. Marjom didn't touch hers.

By the next morning, no one had arrived with any specific orders. But Marjom was a field Herald. She didn't sit still. Before the sun had been up a full candlemark, she found herself back out in the city. But today, she wasn't going to just wander the streets. She started at the stables. She passed Candry forking hay into a stall full of milk goats. She waved, wondering how the girl had drawn stable chores when she was clearly close to being a graduate. Candry waved back but didn't stop to talk.

Marjom Mindtouched Hannra lightly, just enough to make sure she was comfortable in Companion's Field, before she started looking for cleaning supplies. Even if she wasn't going to need it for a while, she never left her tack to sit long without being oiled and checked for spots that needed repairs.

She sat in a stiff-backed wooden chair in the tack room, a rag in one hand and her reins in the other. Reins were mostly decorative for Companions, particularly in Haven, but Heralds used them outside, if just to make the Companions appear a bit more like horses. They could also be handy to hang onto, or to signal a Companion in full gallop if you didn't have the attention for Mindspeaking. A twitch of leather reins took a second, and words took three or four seconds. That could matter.

"Good morning."

Marjom startled. She looked up to find Candry standing in the wide doorway. "Hello. How did you end up feeding the goats?"

"I was looking for you, and I offered to help with animals. Our holding was a goat farm, and I had expected to grow up raising and milking goats. I often do the morning feeding. Lessons won't start for an hour."

"Are you homesick?" Marjom asked.

Candry blushed. "It's lovely to be here, and I wouldn't trade away Blackie for anything."

"Someone named a Companion *Blackie*?"

"She has a black spot on her nose. Or had. It's faded to gray, and I'm told it will be invisible soon. She told me it was a birthmark." She smiled. "Besides, I didn't name her. We never do."

"True enough." The Companions' choices often implied a sense of humor. "When do you leave?"

"It was going to be in three months. But now I'm to ride out next week. They sent me to look for you. There are three of us going out early from my class, and we're to spend three days with you and another of the Heralds who came back."

The reins slid through Marjom's fingers, slightly slippery with saddle oil. What should she say? Of course, she would go, but what did she know to teach youngsters this green? "Tomorrow?"

"Today. Can I help you finish your tack? Are you doing your saddle, too?"

Before she could answer, Candry pulled a saddle horse over, dusted it off, threw a used blanket over it, and started for Marjom's saddle.

Marjom hung the bridle over its wooden peg and poured a thin stream of fresh oil across her cloth. She supposed someone would have eventually done this for her, at least here in Haven. "So, when you're in the field, you'll have one other Herald with you, maybe a few others sometimes. Once I did a whole Circuit with just me and three Healers. That must have been twenty years ago, a summer when a sickness came through, and we could only save three out of four even with the Healers." She started rubbing the mud off her stirrups. "But they knew nothing of tack. I had to take care of theirs as well as mine. If I remember, they'd always been in town before. The whole trip was hard for them." She was getting lost in memory, so she forced herself to refocus. "If you forget anything . . . cleaning or mending or food or first aid materials—it can hurt you, or even kill you." She checked to make sure that Candry was paying attention and grunted in satisfaction when she saw the girl's eyes were wide, even though surely she'd had this lesson somewhere before. "Here's what goes into the most basic of field packs . . ."

Half an hour later, the saddle was put away, and Marjom was doing her best to keep up with Candry in spite of her aching feet. They arrived at a small classroom with a cheerful fire and a tray of hot tea. Herald Witman was already there, and he scooted over to make room for her. Sitting down felt good.

Besides the three students, all of whom looked like mere children, there was one other person in the room, a small woman of middle years in street clothes with bland features. As soon as Marjom arrived she nodded and said, "You all may begin. We'll bring lunch in three hours. For today, the students have prepared questions."

Left unsaid, the implication that the Heralds were expected to develop a lesson for the next day.

Candry directed a question at Marjom. "What scared you the most the first time you were on Circuit?"

That was easy. "We were in the woods one night when three bandits surprised us. They wore bearskin coats and came from upwind, and somehow even the Companions . . . ."

She and Witman told three stories each about fear before lunch arrived. As the students started to set out the food, Witman took her outside. "We should change the topic," he told her.

"To what?"

He smiled "What do you think?"

"Failure. They have to learn to fail."

"All right. Then after the break I want to work on courage."

"That's broad," she said. "What kind of courage?"

He paused. "The courage to do what you have to, even when you don't like it."

He had that right. She smiled at him as they started back in. Apparently, she wasn't the only one chafing at this assignment.

By the time they finished, she felt as tired as she did at the end of a full day of protecting the Border. The students hurried off to somewhere, chattering, leaving her and Witman to walk back together. He moved as slowly as she did. She didn't mind. It was easier than keeping up with Candry. They were silent, so she spoke to Hannra. *:How was your day?:*

:Excellent.:

She did sound happy. *:What did you do?:*

:I spent the day testing Blackie's reflexes.:

Whatever that meant. *:Was that fun?:*

:Yes, and now I'm tired. You feel tired, too.:

:I am. Sleep well.:

When they were halfway to Heritage House, Witman broke the long, companionable silence. "That was better than I thought it would be."

She pursed her lips. "I miss the Border. Already. Where were you?"

"In the north. Not as much fighting there. But there have been some wicked storms, even for this time of year. We lost a few barns to twisters. We had to spend three days dragging livestock out of flooding pastures. The storms seem like a bad omen."

"I hope not."

"Me, too. I'll be glad of a bed tonight."

It was her turn to say, "Me, too." Her feet didn't have any sharp pains like after a day of riding, but all of her joints ached. The cooling night wasn't doing anything to help her move more easily. "I'm ready to just sit still and not talk to anyone until tomorrow."

As if his voice felt as worn as hers, he merely nodded.

They rounded the corner and Heritage Hall came into view. "I really hate that name," she said.

"Me, too."

Still, the windows spilled light cheerily into the street, and the planter boxes had been finished sometime today while they were gone, making the place look a little bit more settled.

Chalena opened the door for them, and the surprising chatter of students and some older voices as well spilled into the street. "Welcome home."

"Who's here?" Witman asked.

"Some of the Heralds who get to leave because you came back, and the students you helped today. And a few others. The party is to celebrate your sacrifice, and welcome you to your new role."

As a retiree. She swallowed, and she felt her eyes flash with tears that she breathed away. Today hadn't gone too badly. And she'd get better at teaching with practice. She looked around at the food and the many people, and she heard both celebration and apprehension in the undertones of the conversation.

Chalena stepped past them to greet someone else.

From the corner, Candry raised a glass.

Witman leaned in and said, "Is it that bad?"

Had he seen the tears, or did he understand because he felt the same? "No. No, it's not too bad." She glanced at Candry, who had turned back to her circle of friends. "No. We can still be useful."

The table overflowed with food and drink. Bright candles and oil lamps illuminated almost every corner of the big kitchen and dining room. The smell of fresh baked bread and fresh meat helped her perk up. Maybe she wasn't, actually, too tired for a glass of wine and some conversation. She smiled at Witman. "Wine?"

He smiled back. "Yes. And I like chocolate. I think I see some."

Maybe they'd let her go back at the end of the war. Maybe she could find a student Healer to work on her feet.

She reached out to Hannra, showing her a quick taste of her day, the students. *:What do you think? Bandits tomorrow? Or something about small-town diplomacy?:*

Hannra's reply washed through her, warm with amusement and pleasure. *:I think that whatever it is, you should enjoy it as much as you did today.:*

Marjom reflected on that for a bit before replying. *:I did enjoy it.:*

She followed Witman after the chocolate.

Temper
Mercedes Lackey

Lerryn Twoblades did not look like much of a fighter. He wore the same scuffed brown leathers as any of his company, and his woolen cape had seen better days. His boots were good, but a merc needed to take care of his feet. He didn't even wear his savings—which had to be considerable, for a captain of such a well-reputed merc company— in the form of chains or bracelets. In fact, his only concession to rank was a round Guild Captain pin of enameled copper showing two crossed swords bisected by a lightning bolt, used as a cloak-clasp. Thin and not particularly tall, and just now at rest, he wasn't very imposing, either.

But when he had walked alongside Kerowyn, it was immediately apparent that he was whipcord and steel over bone, and moved with a lazy grace that spoke volumes to anyone who had studied hand-to-hand combat. Those limpid brown eyes missed nothing; those foppish curls covered a skull with frightening intelligence inside it.

Kerowyn had sent Lerryn her letter of introduction this morning, as soon as she had arrived in the tiny village of Bolthaven, where the Skybolts had their winter quarters. And now, at his request, she was meeting Lerryn not in those winter quarters but in the largest building in the village—the tavern. The village was so small there was only one tavern, but anyplace a merc company wintered, there would always be at least one tavern.

Bored mercs needed a place to go, a place that wasn't their quarters.

Tarma had said you could tell a lot about a company by the tavern in their winter quarters. This one was clean, with an enforcer in the corner who looked like he knew what he was doing and was big enough to be a match even for Hellsbane's strength, and the servers were a mix of the sexes. They looked like they knew what they were doing too, or at least that was what Kero had judged in the brief time she'd had to survey the common room before Lerryn appeared.

Instead of discussing her joining his company, he had asked her to take him to the stable, where he took stock of her Shin'a'in warsteed, Hellsbane. According to rumor, there wasn't a single horse in his entire mercenary company he couldn't handle, and it seemed to be true; his abilities included Hellsbane, which had surprised the hell out of both Kero and her horse.

Then they went back to a private room, which was scarcely big enough to be a closet. Since it had a desk and two chairs, it appeared that Lerryn had commandeered the tavern's office. Once he began to speak at length, it was no secret why the Skybolts were fanatically devoted to their Captain.

"So," Lerryn said, once they had both settled into the two chairs in the tiny room. "According to this—" He tapped the folded paper from her mentor, Tarma shena Tale'sedrin, that Kero had sent to him when she first arrived in Bolthaven. "You're *that* Kerowyn. I'd sent to your teacher to see if she had any protégées she'd send my way, or any former students she could recommend, but I didn't expect to be facing Kerowyn of 'The Ride.'"

"The Kerowyn of 'The Ride' wasn't that impressive, Captain," Kero said dryly. "I assume you know about my grandmother's sword?" She patted the hilt of Need gingerly. This was neither the time nor the place to be waking the damned thing up. At Lerryn's nod, she continued. "I barely knew the hilt from the edge. I was basically the sword's puppet. It did everything, because the only skill I had with a blade was at the dinner table, and the only skill I had as a Mage was the same I have now— none. That song should have been called 'Need Takes Control.'"

Lerryn just raised an eyebrow, perhaps surprised at her modesty. "Well, you of all people ought to know about the liberties musicians take," he said instead. "So, since your mentor sent you here, I assume that you no longer depend on the sword?"

"Only for protection from magic, and the fact this hunk of tin is an expertly forged weapon no one has ever been able to break." She didn't add anything about the ongoing war of wills—if you could call what the sword had a "will"—that she and the blade had. Need had run her grandmother around half a dozen countries righting the wrongs of women and getting paid little or nothing for her pains. Kero did not intend to allow a piece of metal to interfere with her making a living. "But about that business of me being *that* Kerowyn," she continued. "I'm going by Kay Taldress for now."

Lerryn allowed himself a thin little smile. "Not trading on your fame, then?"

"No, Captain," she said firmly. "There are three things that *fame* will get me. Challenges from people who want to say they could take me, contempt from people who think I'm trading on it, and groveling from people I'd rather not have anything to do with. I'll make it past my recruitment stage in the Skybolts on my own skills."

"You're smart for someone as young as you look," Lerryn said.

"Observant," Kero corrected. "It was a long road to get here. I had plenty of examples of all three of those sorts of people on the way."

And in fact, it hadn't taken her long to adopt the name of Kay Taldress. Naively, she'd assumed that once she was far enough away from home, no one would have heard the song about her rescue of her brother's newly-gotten bride. But no; it was a catchy tune and a good story, and she'd generally hear it two out of every three stops at inns and taverns. It no longer made her wince to hear it, but with familiarity had come a good bit of retrospection on the road. What, exactly would her life had been like if she *hadn't* made that ride intending to track the raiders down herself and looking for help to do so?

I suppose Grandmother and Tarma would have gone after them. That might even have been why Tarma intercepted me in the first place; she might already have been on the way to take stock of the situation. Still . . . how much could they have accomplished?

Probably more than I am giving them credit for.

And then what would have happened to her? Once brought home, Dierna had quickly put her own stamp on the household—an accomplishment made easier by the fact that there had been no one there to oppose her will, since the Old Lord had gone down fighting, and Kero's brother didn't care what went on inside the walls of the keep as long as meals were on time and the household was well-run. *So unless I'd been willing to play obedient handmaiden . . .* Well, there were a lot of ways to get rid of an inconvenient female relation. Packing her off to a religious order was one. Marrying her off to someone old enough to not be too picky about a second or third wife was another.

Or Grandmother could have asked for me herself. In which case I'd be right where I am now. But would she have? Or would she have assumed that the blood I got from her was too thin in my veins for her to pass Need to?

"Well," Lerryn said, breaking into her thoughts. "If that's how you want to play it, present yourself and your horse at the garrison tomorrow and ask to see the recruiting sergeant. But coming in this way means you'll be in for the hazing every new recruit gets."

"Would you want me otherwise?" she countered.

"As a student of Tarma shena Tale'sedrin? Absolutely. And you can still present yourself as such—you don't have to claim your name, but you can claim your teaching. You're not the first of Tarma's students to take to the road." He tilted his head to the side, offering this as a sort of tasty bait.

Which she wasn't taking. "And plenty of people know

Kerowyn was Godmother's last student." That was thanks to Prince Daren, who'd been her fellow-student, and hadn't been shy about telling tales of his experience. "No, I'll take the hard road."

"As you wish." Captain Lerryn rose and offered her his hand to shake. "I don't usually look at the new recruits until they've been with the Skybolts for a week, so don't expect to see me before then. Good luck—Kay Taldress."

She shook his hand firmly. "Thank you, Captain."

They left the little office room without anyone taking much notice of them. Evidently he did business in there often enough that it was commonplace.

She went up to the bar and ordered pea soup, bread, and beer, then found herself a seat at one of the smaller tables. All three came quickly, delivered by a male server who, with humor and discretion, made certain that food and drink were *all* she wanted before heading back to the kitchen. The beer was smooth, the bread was brown and came with a spread made of bacon drippings, and the pea soup had plenty of bacon in it. The common room was quiet at the moment; when she'd arrived it had been full of locals getting fed their dinner before going back to work. This wasn't unusual; plenty of people in a village didn't have kitchens, only hearths, and they depended on the inn or tavern for their substantial midday meal. Travelers just passing through should start arriving about now. The Skybolts wouldn't turn up until after their evening meal in their garrison. How many of them—well, now that was the question. If Lerryn was as good a Captain as Kero thought, there would be no strong drink allowed in the garrison itself. So anyone that wanted to drink anything stronger than mild beer would have to come here. Some people might turn up for entertainment—the tavern appeared to have a resident musician, judging by the gittern tucked into a corner of the hearth. Some small tables for two at the back of the room had game-boards carved into their surface, so there could be those looking for a game or gambling with travelers. So it looked as if the tavern got quite a bit of regular custom.

But what was most notable about this place was the

quiet aura of order. There was some smoke—that couldn't be helped at this season, the wind would come from uncertain directions, and not all the smoke from the fireplace would go *up* the chimney. But spills got mopped up immediately, orders taken and delivered quickly, and there was a general feeling that while high spirits were expected, excess would be dealt with by means of expulsion—and there would be no appeal to the Captain afterward.

That, combined with her impression of Lerryn, left her with a favorable feeling about the Skybolts.

She finished her meal and headed for the door that led into a double row of—well, they couldn't be called *rooms,* they were more like enclosed bunks with wool mattresses, one up, one down, with wooden shutters that could be pulled down and latched, and room at your feet for your belongings. There were sixteen of these things, eight on each side of the narrow corridor. Right now, she was the only one availing herself of this luxury of relative privacy. In most places like this, everyone staying overnight bedded down in the common room after the tavernkeeper closed down and went to bed himself. On the way, she retrieved her packs from behind the bar where the barman was keeping an eye on them for her, tipped him by way of thanks, and sought her upper bunk, carefully selected as the warmest of the lot. It was quite comfortably warm—so warm, in fact, that she suspected the tavern's ovens were on the other side of that stone wall.

Her bedroll was already laid out, ready for her to get some sleep. She climbed in, latched the shutter down, kicked off her boots, and rolled herself up in her blankets. It had been a long, hard day of riding, and if what Tarma had told her was anything to go by, things were about to get . . . interesting.

Kero was glad of her thick woolen coat with its overlapping fronts; it was cut in the Shin'a'in style, though she didn't expect anyone here to recognize that. Although there wasn't any snow on the ground, the grass in front of the Skybolts' gate was dead and yellow and furry with a hard frost.

The recruiting sergeant eyed her and Hellsbane with a bored expression. As instructed, Kero had presented herself at the gate of the Skybolts' winter quarters and asked for him. This had been a reasonable amount of time after the trumpet had sounded for reveille and she could be certain he'd eaten his breakfast. It was never a good idea to get between the man who could decide whether or not to hire you and his breakfast.

Sun shone down out of a cloudless sky but didn't impart anything in the way of warmth. "So, ye think ye've got the makings of a Skybolt, do ye?" he asked rhetorically. "Got any combat experience?"

"A little, Sergeant, sir," she said. "Bandits." *True, that.*

"Training?"

"Grandmam rode with Idra's Sunhawks. She trained me." *Also true.*

The sergeant cocked an eyebrow at her. "No good in th' kitchen then?" he asked, with just a hint of mockery. *If I didn't already know a third of the Skybolts are women, I might take offense at that.*

She didn't rise to the taunt. "Burned the oatmeal, Sergeant. Every time."

He guffawed. "Ye wouldn't be the first t' trade a frying pan for a sword, gir-rul," he said. "Well, I can see ye got yer own horse an' kit. Let's see how well ye handle 'em."

He signaled for the gates to be fully opened, and Kero led Hellsbane through.

The winter quarters for the Skybolts was surrounded by a wooden palisade—not unusual for a merc company that could actually afford its own dedicated winter quarters. This was as much to keep gawkers out as anything else—and was mostly for the safety of the gawkers, since they never seemed to know not to wander in the path of charging horses or pairs of fighters. Most of the enclosed area was devoted to practice grounds; the barracks, kitchen, warehouse, and stables were all lined up on the side to Kero's left, and there were lookouts stationed on a walkway just below the top of the palisade on that side.

Besides those watchers, each of the four corners of the palisade had a watchtower above it, with a lookout stationed in it. It was good practice to keep a standing watch at all times, and if anyone was stupid enough to attack Bolthaven, the watchers could sound a warning, and everyone in the village could get inside that palisade before damage could be done. A good percentage of the villagers would be retired mercs and their families living on their savings and people who worked for the Skybolts when they were in quarters. There might even be a few spouses and partners of the mercs living in the village, since Lerryn didn't have quarters for families.

"I'm gonna figger anything ye can do a-horse, ye can do afoot, so get aboard that ugly mule ye brung with ye," the sergeant said. "And give me four passes on the archery targets. Make it at thirty paces. Walk, trot, canter, an' gallop."

Kero swung herself up into the saddle, retrieved her short horsebow from the sheath and strung it, and slung her quiver of arrows over the pommel of her saddle, securing the reins there as well. With a touch of her heels, she sent Hellsbane off on the first pass at the targets. Reins were more of a suggestion for Hellsbane; she responded to leg pressure and touches on her neck. Kero didn't bother with a bit and doubted if Hellsbane could have been persuaded to tolerate one. Shin'a'in warsteeds never used one and certainly didn't need one.

Walking—that was no problem. She managed to center all four arrows in their respective targets. Trotting, however—that was another question altogether. Hellsbane was a superbly trained Shin'a'in warsteed, but that did *not* mean she had a smooth trot. Kero considered herself lucky she got arrows in the target circles at all. The canter was a relief after that. The gallop had its own challenge of getting four arrows off in such rapid succession that she had no time between them.

At least they all hit. She rode Hellsbane up to the targets and collected her arrows, then gathered up the reins and returned to the recruiting sergeant, whose face was utterly unreadable.

By this time she had an audience, which was to be expected. While mercs in winter quarters would be expected to keep in training, that did not mean they spent all day training. Mercs were no different from anyone else, really; they'd train just as much as they had to, and laze about as much as they thought they could get away with. Watching a potential new recruit get put through her paces was as good an excuse as any to slough off.

"Do the same with them javelins I see ye got," was all he said. So Kero repeated the exercise, with the only difference being that since she only had eight of the javelins, she had to pause between the trot and the canter to retrieve her weapons. She took the opportunity to examine her watchers out of the corner of her eye.

They didn't appear impressed, but they didn't appear *un*impressed either. Good. Not that she was doing any less than her best! These were supposed to be some of the best fighters in the Mercenary Guild, and if *she* could impress them—that would not be a good omen for the quality of Lerryn's people. Tarma hadn't just sent her out to earn her living. Tarma had sent her out to keep learning. If the reactions of the Skybolts lounging behind the recruiting sergeant were anything to go on, skillwise, she'd probably be just about their average. Which should be good enough to get her in and still give her plenty of people she could learn from.

When she finished retrieving her javelins the second time, the sergeant directed her to go up against the training dummy for mounted fighting. "I'll call the shot, you take it," he told her. This was a comfortable drill, familiar, enlivened only by the fact that this dummy was on a pivot, and when you hit the arm or shield, the thing would spin, potentially cracking you in the head with one of its arms as it did so. This wasn't the sort of dummy she'd trained on, so it took a couple awkward ducks out of the way before she figured out that an un-called block was expected of you.

This was probably as much of a test of Hellsbane as it was of her; a recruit could, potentially, turn up with a green horse that would be no damn good in the field without a lot of extra work between now and spring. A warhorse had to endure a lot, and do so as calmly as her rider.

Most fighting horses were mares or geldings. Bardic songs about heroes on "their mighty stallions" were full of crap. No one with sense was going to go into battle on something that would turn unreliable at the first whiff of a mare in season.

Her guess was affirmed when the next thing the sergeant asked for was to "put your mare through her paces."

So she had Hellsbane wheel on her heels sunwise and widdershins, rear and lash out with her fore hooves, kick back low, kick back higher, gallop in tight circles, then in tight eights, rear and pivot at the same time, and finally jump nearly vertically from a standing start and lash out with her hind hooves at the top of the jump.

All the while she was sticking to Hellsbane's back like a burr.

Now the sergeant was impressed. *As well he should be. I'll bet there isn't a horse in the Skybolts that can match Hellsbane.*

When she was done, Hellsbane had barely broken a light sweat. The sergeant came up to her stirrup and looked up at her.

"Any experience fightin' with a unit?" he asked.

"No, Sergeant, sir," she said, shaking her head. He *tsk*'d, but with a faint smile. "Well, that's easily remedied with drillin'. Yer in, gur-ril." He looked over at the spectators and beckoned to a dark-skinned, black-haired woman with shoulders many men would envy. Kero couldn't tell if there were muscles to match those shoulders under all the layers of wrappings she wore, but there probably were. "Lidreth! I'm assignin' Kay Taldress to you! Get her squared away."

The woman snapped to attention—not a crisp sort of "attention," like you'd find in, say, the Rethwellan army, but brisk and efficient. "Aye, Sarge," she said, and crooked a finger at Kero. "With me, recruit."

Kero dismounted and followed her, leading Hellsbane across the barren practice grounds toward the stable. Lidreth was not the talkative sort, it seemed, and was disinclined to point out the obvious—like which buildings were which.

Kero approved of the stables as soon as she entered the door. There weren't a lot of windows open, but the predominant smell was straw, not dung or urine. The horses all had loose-boxes, and all the beasts that she could see were warmly blanketed against the cold. Lidreth took her to an empty stall about the middle of the back row and indicated with a nod that this was where Hellsbane should go. It was already furnished with a water bucket and a thick layer of straw. Under Lidreth's gimlet eye, Kero rid Hellsbane of her tack and the saddlepacks, brushed her down, blanketed her, and got her food and water from the common stores.

She was just finishing the job when someone—had he been one of the lurkers?—came nosing up to the stall. He was almost exactly Kero's height, knotty and balding and missing a couple of teeth, which was scarcely unusual in a merc. He surveyed Hellsbane with the air of someone who thought he knew everything about horseflesh and guffawed. Kero stepped outside the stall to put herself between him and the gate at the entrance.

"What kinda mule did ye come in here with, gir-rul?" he chortled, reaching over the wall of the stall toward Hellsbane, who flattened her ears with a warning snort.

"Don't touch my horse," Kero replied, shortly.

The man paid no attention and reached for Hellsbane's halter.

Faster than anyone other than Kero would have believed, Hellsbane snaked her head around, extended her neck, and snapped—not at the man's outstretched hand but at his face peering over the wall of the stall. Her teeth clicked together an inch from his startled eyes.

With a muffled curse, he pulled his hand back in a

fist, clearly prepared to clip her across the nose. Kero's temper flared.

But he wasn't watching Kero, who grabbed his wrist just as he swung, redirected the motion and pulled, sending him tumbling over his own hand and landing on his back on the floor of the stable.

Breath driven out of him, he could only stare up at her.

"I *said,* don't touch my horse," Kero repeated, fighting down anger. "She's war-trained. And I just saved you from losing your hand. If you'd hit her, that would have been the last time you ever hit anything with that fist."

"You heard the recruit, Hadrick," Lidreth drawled, but in a way that made it an order. "Don't touch her horse. *I* don't care if you get mustered out as an amputee, but your squad leader might." She stared at him as he picked himself up out of the straw. "And a war-trained horse is worth more than you are. If anyone interferes with this beast, I'll know who to look for."

"Yessir," Hadrick replied, and not in a tone that made Kero concerned that he might try to meddle with Hellsbane once she was out of sight. In fact, Hadrick sounded downright contrite.

"Follow me, recruit," was all Lidreth said, dismissing Hadrick by the simple means of ignoring him. "Bring your kit."

Kero quickly loaded herself up with everything that didn't belong with Hellsbane and followed as Lidreth led the way out of the stable, into the barracks, and up a set of stairs to the right.

"Women's quarters," she said, opening the door into a room full of cots with chests at the feet and heads, and pegs on the walls that sported a variety of heavy garments. "We catch a man in here, he leaves singing soprano. If you've got canoodling to do, do it in the village, or get permission to use one of the two rooms off the commons for it. The rest of us need our sleep."

"Yessir," Kero said, as she was directed to an empty cot, one already made up with a couple of thick blankets and a pillow.

"Weapons in the chest at the head of your cot. We

have practice weapons to use for drilling. One knife no longer than your hand on your belt. Draw it on a fellow merc, and you'd better have a good reason. Everything else in the chest at the foot of your cot. There's a lock with a key in it. If you need more bedding, say so; you won't be impressing any of us if you're keeping us awake at night with your teeth chattering. Jakes are through *that* door," she pointed to the far left corner. "We take it in turns to clean 'em twice a day. I'll put your name on the rotation. There's a steam bath next to the kitchen. Take one not less than once a week, and we'd all take it kindly if you did it more often than that, preferably after drill or just before lights out. It holds ten, and it's generally full from noon to lights out, and under no circumstances should you *ever* use it to get frisky. We take it in rotation with the men to clean it every morning. The men have it for the next month, so don't worry about that for now."

As she spoke, Kero was stowing her things: weapons in the designated chest (and she thought she sensed a faint grumble from Need as the lid closed down over the sword), everything else in the other chest, key on the leather thong around her neck that held a Shin'a'in talisman, and her bedroll added to the bed.

"Meals at the bugle call. We have a kitchen staff, so there's not much kitchen-patrol duty. Strongest drink allowed in quarters is mild ale. You want anything different, you go to the tavern."

Kero took up a semirelaxed stance—not at attention but not "casual" either. Lidreth gave her a once-over, probably assessing her from her clothing, now that her coat was hung up on the wall.

Kero was pretty sure she was going to fit in just fine; her boots were good but not too good, her woolen trews, leather tunic, and thick, knitted shirt were neither too old and mended nor too new and unworn. The trews had the proper leather patches inside the thighs that anyone who spent a long time in the saddle would have, and those patches showed the right amount of wear. The only thing about her that was "odd" would be the Shin'a'in talisman that marked her as a member (or at least an ally) of Tale'sedrin Clan, which, technically, she was, since White Winds Mage Kethry was her blood grandmother and Tarma shena Tale'sedrin her grandmother by adoption. And she very much doubted anyone here would recognize that little token, with its stylized vorcel-hawk.

The point was, Lidreth was not going to see someone who didn't fit the mold of "capable fighter looking to go up in the world by joining a merc company." And Lidreth's next statement, or rather question, matched that. "Got your Guild membership?"

Membership in the Mercenary Guild took a one-time fee and a cursory sort of background check. That is, they'd hold you for a couple of days in the Guild Hall to make sure you weren't a habitual drunk or a drug addict, and they'd make sure you didn't have any debts chasing you. The fee alone usually was enough to sort most of the wheat from the chaff.

What that fee got you was the right to get hired through the Guild—which meant better jobs—and a chance that the better merc companies would take you.

Kero nodded and showed the little tattoo on the back of her wrist. Oh, you could have that faked, of course, but if it was found out (and it would be) the pain of getting it removed with prejudice and without painkillers wasn't worth it.

Lidreth nodded. "Got any questions?"

Kero shook her head.

"Not even about the food?" Lidreth grinned.

"You've got a cook *and* staff," Kero pointed out. "They can get fired if they mess up too often. Not a lot of other jobs out here, so that's incentive not to burn the food."

Lidreth clapped her on the back. Hard. "I like you," the merc proclaimed. "So I'm gonna warn you. You're the only new recruit, so you're gonna get the scut work, like cleaning the common room. If one of us says you're to do something, as long as you don't have other orders, you do it. That's just how it is. You dropped Hadrick, so you can bet he'll pile his share on you. That's how it is too. It'll keep up till Captain or Training Sergeant Drall says *stop*."

Great. Kero resigned herself to days of drudgery until her fellow Skybolts got tired of teasing the new recruit. *Look at it as exercise,* she told herself. *It can't keep up forever.*

A fortnight later, she was reconsidering that thought. And, indeed, reconsidering the idea of staying with the Skybolts at all. She found herself in a constant battle with her temper except when she was in the women's barrack room or on the drill field; as a consequence, she was spending as much time as she could in drilling.

Not that most of them were *bad*—most of them weren't; they'd send her off on random errands for no good reason, and often for no purpose, but it was good-natured and not all that frequent. Certainly no more than once or twice every couple of days.

But Hadrick! The man seemed determined to make her life a pure misery. And the worst of it was, he was so clever about it that none of the others ever caught him at it. Say she'd been set to sweep the common room; whoever's turn it was to do it would remind her that for now, she was the Skybolts' dogsbody and would set her to it. And that was all well and good, but the moment she'd put the broom away, she'd come back to a right mess, and no one around except Hadrick, lounging in a corner and smirking. And it was all to do over again, and not just once, mind, but as many times as it took before someone else came in and put a stop to his fun. He'd "accidentally" bump into her at meals with the intent of spilling her food or putting her face into it. She'd go to saddle up Hellsbane for a drill or exercise to discover the reins had been tied into intricate knots; she'd taken to going out to the stable early just to have the time to get whatever mischief had been done undone before there was an inspection or drill.

Then there were the pranks she was sure were him but couldn't catch him at—like finding her ale had been salted or her tea had been interfered with. Fortunately her grandmother had taught her how to tell by taste when things were in her food or drinks that had no right to be there, so whatever the latter had been intended to accomplish had been thwarted. But her temper, never all that certain, was fraying fast.

Tonight that temper was close to breaking after finding her ale salted *again,* and although it was nowhere near as warm and comfortable as the common room, she retreated to the women's barracks to oil her leathers and brood.

This nonsense was exhausting. She'd never worked so hard in her life. She'd never had to control her temper so much; fighting in barracks was forbidden, and much as she wanted to beat the goddess-loving crap out of Hadrick and wipe that smug smirk off his face with the floor, she knew what that would get her. A stay in the brig—

—which might be a relief at this point.

But the rest of the punishment for an altercation would be to have her pay docked and *paid to Hadrick.*

No. Absolutely not.

She wasn't the only one having second thoughts about staying.

Every time she laid her head down at night, Need would grumble distantly at her, and she knew why. *Why are you allowing yourself to be treated this way?* And why was she? It made no sense. What would Tarma have done in this situation?

Wiped the floor with him—

Maybe.

It wasn't as if he had hurt her in any way. No, it was just harassment. Constant harassment. Harassment that wasn't doing her any actual harm but was definitely rubbing her temper raw.

Not that my temper is all that good, she admitted, and even though the temptation was great to just walk away and find some solo jobs or even another company—well there was no guarantee that she wouldn't encounter someone else just like Hadrick in the next place, now, was there?

I . . . have no idea. She'd never had much to do with

fighters, or fighting, until she'd been forced into riding to the rescue of her brand-new sister-in-law because there was no one in the keep left standing. *Had everyone else here been sure they wanted to be warriors all their lives?* Or had they just fallen into it—not exactly the way she had, but because parents had been fighters, or because it was the only way for someone born poor to get out of being a farmhand all their life?

Gah, I'm thinking too much. She decided that for once she'd go down to the tavern for a couple of drinks of good strong beer to get the taste of that salted ale out of the back of her throat.

She unlocked her chest, got a few coins, and bundled herself up in her coat. She thought about taking Need, and decided against it. There was always the chance the sword would decide to have another mental wrestling match with her if she put it on, and she definitely was not in the mood.

The tavern was surprisingly full—full enough so that she spotted Hadrick before he spotted her, and she was able to get her beer and maneuver around the place to keep his back to her while she found a seat, a lone stool no one else seemed to want, against the wall and behind the table he was at, half-sheltered behind a support pillar for the roof.

Hadrick was gambling with three men who weren't Skybolts. They didn't look like freelance mercs either, which meant they were either travelers or locals. She sipped her beer and watched, for once finding herself in the position of seeing without being seen. Lidreth and two other Skybolts were watching the game, standing behind two of the strangers.

And it wasn't long before Kero realized he was cheating.

It was a complicated game involving dice and moving pegs on a board. There were two dice, and every time it was his turn to throw, he palmed a die of his own in and out again, restoring the original before passing it on to the next man. The advantage was slight, but it was just enough for him to keep winning.

Her temper, already fraying, came within a hair of snapping. Well, that certainly explained how he was salting her drinks and pulling all those other tricks and getting away with it—he had first-class levels of sleight of hand, and if she hadn't been looking at him from the angle she was, she'd never have seen it.

And she was just about to rise up and scream out her accusation, giving vent to all her frustration and anger, when with one last supreme effort, she throttled it all back down. First, she'd have to catch him when the loaded die was on the table, because someone as good as he was could make the damned thing disappear, and there'd be no proof. *Keep your temper,* she told herself. And she kept it throttled down—but it might have been the hardest thing she'd ever done since she'd gone to study with her grandmother and Tarma.

And the next several passes gave her no opportunity. For some reason, he didn't bring the die out. Maybe because he was far enough ahead he didn't feel he needed the edge.

But she kept her eyes on the dice so closely that on the third pass she realized something else.

The man next to Hadrick was cheating too.

He wasn't quite as good as Hadrick, and unlike Hadrick, he always returned what was probably a loaded die into the same pocket. And in the same moment that she realized that, Hadrick slammed the man's hand down on his crooked die before he could switch it out again.

"Bleeding cheat!" Hadrick roared. "Gotchu!"

And as he jumped to his feet, he dropped *his* loaded die into his belt-pouch.

His opponent leaped to *his* feet, but before either of them could do anything more, Kero jumped in between them and pinned both their hands to the table.

"He might be cheating," she shouted, *"but so are you, Hadrick!"* She caught Lidreth's eye. "Check his belt-pouch—he just dropped the loaded die in there that he's been using all night."

The two men froze, perhaps because they were surrounded by a room full of people, as Lidreth came around to Kero's side of the table and fished in Hadrick's pouch, coming up with the telltale die, which she held up, then rolled. "Six," she proclaimed, then rolled it twice more, just to verify it would come up six each time.

Two Skybolts pinned Hadrick's arms behind him; two locals did the same with the stranger. Lidreth scooped the stranger's die off the table and rolled it to confirm that it, too, was loaded. Then she looked at Kero.

"Well?" she said. "What do we do with 'em? Throw 'em both to the dogs?" And she nodded at the crowd, who looked perfectly prepared to beat both of the cheaters to a pulp.

"Don't look to us to back you, either," said one of the Skybolts holding Hadrick's arms. "You brought this on yourself."

Hadrick said nothing. And Kero thought about the last fortnight, and all the grief he'd heaped on her, and her anger flared—but then it died.

"Take Hadrick to Twoblades," she growled. "And turn this one over to the keeper." And she'd have said something more, but the silence in the tavern was broken by someone clapping, slowly.

The crowd divided to let Lerryn Twoblades himself through, still applauding. Kero gaped at him, as the people holding Hadrick and the stranger dropped the captives' arms and let them go.

"Well done, recruit," the leader of the Skybolts said. "Good answer. And good job of keeping your anger under control while Hadrick plagued you. I thought for certain you'd have snapped long before this. Most people do."

"This—was all a test?" Kero shook her head numbly. "Do you do this to *everyone*?"

"Everyone—well, not the little show of cheating. We save that for people who pass the temper test," Lidreth admitted. "Those, we give a chance for revenge. The whole village was in on this part."

"But—" she was going to ask *why*, but then she realized what the answer was. Because Twoblades required that his people be able to work together no matter what

was going on off the battlefield. People who couldn't
control their tempers couldn't do that. Neither could
people who plotted revenge over grievances. Hadrick
watched her face closely and rubbed the back of his
head ruefully.

"I dunno if you'll—" he began

"Apology accepted," she said. "Provided *you* sweep
the common room and clean the steam bath the next
four times my name comes up on the roster."

"Hey!" he began to object. "But—"

"You salted my ale, you put bitters in my tea, and you
dropped greenwort into my stew, which would have
given me enough wind to drive everyone out of the barracks if I'd eaten it," she said steadily.

"I'd've thrashed you for that, Hadrick," Lidreth said,
with a scowl. "I might anyway, just because you tried."

Hadrick sagged. "Agreed," he replied, head hanging.
"Guess I'm getting off easy. Anything else?"

"Aye," she said. "Don't touch my horse."

Somewhere in the back of her mind, she sensed Need
sighing with resignation, and smirked.

The Hawkbrothers' Ways

Death and the Vales

Larry Dixon

The Tayledras know for a fact that some of them will become spirit-beings in the service of the Star-Eyed after their death. History has shown that such a transformation is most likely if they have been a strong, stable mix of heroic, loving, resourceful, and wise in their life. They also know that these transformations occur in a timeframe they have no control over; a spirit-being could manifest the moment after someone's death, or a generation hence, but the most important takeaway is this: A Hawkbrother who is driven to be effective in improving the world while alive wants to keep doing so after their mortal death.

It is also understood by every worshiper that a prayer to the Star-Eyed is not actually meant to go directly to the Star-Eyed but rather to those who act in Her interest. This is encouraging to those who wish to be in Her service after death—just because you're dead, that doesn't mean the action stops. There have also been instances of servants of entirely different deities responding to a plea, a number that has sharply increased in recent years, concurrent with the first stirrings of the Mage Storms.

Along with this is the simple acceptance that once someone is gone from the material world, who and what they become will be altered in ways beyond a native Velgarthian's capacity to fully understand, akin to a small cup being expected to hold a lake. So the Hawkbrothers embrace what they know of a person in the material world and make the most of that.

Hawkbrothers understand that matter, and life itself, exists at many sizes relative to themselves. They understand germ theory in a particular way. Life forms can be found living on or in other life forms, from such examples as primary predators consuming their prey, to parasites that thrive on the skin and in bowels. Feather mites are the tiniest things visible to the naked eye, but they certainly have recognizable effects. The concept that life forms exist that are far smaller and far larger than the senses can detect is only logical. Being in the Pelagirs, they also know that such life can manifest in unpredictable ways due to chaotic magic mutations, so the Tayledras have a policy of cremation over burial. Consigned to heat intense enough to vaporize a body, there is no risk of a Pelagirs-altered life form creating havoc from a buried body.

Additionally, the Hawkbrothers' spiritual connection to the air is incorporated into this. Hawkbrothers know that the wind carries particles, so by cremating a body, a person's physical substance is released to the wind, and it will surely be breathed in someday by those who remember them. Indeed, all the Tayledras ancestors are thought to be breathed in as motes in the air, carried aloft on breezes forever until they find a home as part of another Hawkbrother's breath. This contributes to their society's long-term cohesion—everyone's ancestors become a part of everyone.

Death is still greeted with shock, regret, sadness, and mourning. Every species in the society feels it differently, according to their biochemical and emotional makeup, but the need for comfort is universal. It is not unusual to see occurrences such as a *dyheli* embraced by a human scout while their Bondbird preens sympathetically at their hair, or a few *hertasi* appearing long enough to leave blankets and refreshments, squeeze the scout's hand, and then vanish again.

Beneath the ground level of a Vale, where the Heartstone, gardens, and workspaces are, the immense complexity of the Vale's support systems and *hertasi* civilization is centered around the colossal heat-sink structure in which the Heartstone's flares are grounded. Each shell around it serves multiple purposes, from glassmaking furnaces and baking ovens to forges, hot water sources, and thermal-based ventilation blowers. Under a Vale, the passages and rooms are large enough for even a gryphon or Companion to walk, and every Vale has at least one beautifully ornate, brightly lit funereal chamber.

Funeral proceedings occur every three days. When recovering a physical body is possible, it is considered respectful to do so, unless it would result in great harm to attempt it. All bodies, from beloved animals to friends, from *dyheli*, *tervardi*, *kyree*, gryphon species and more, are prepared in adjacent rooms. *Hertasi* and, occasionally, human ascetics engage in thorough and respectful removal of all artifacts and any body parts that are desired by others, such as a gryphon wanting their fallen friend's crest-feathers or, more practically, primary feathers being harvested for reuse to replace others' broken ones. The bodies are wrapped in rough blankets made by students. This practice not only gives students practice in weaving but also helps them feel connected to the cycle of life and death and the continuum of their craft, knowing that their own bodies will be wrapped by blankets made by future students. Perfumed, wide leaves are then tied with twine atop these shrouds in a decorative pattern.

A funereal chamber can hold many people, but it is not considered rude if a person is unable to attend in person. The tasks of a Hawkbrother are many, and death seldom occurs at a convenient time, so this is reconciled. Beaded ropes representing those who could not be present are hung on stands bearing long wind chimes.

The shrouded bodies are arranged on simple wooden rafts, which are hoisted by staged counterweights onto large carts. All of the machinery of the funeral chamber is beautifully ornate, silent-smooth, and perfectly maintained. *Hertasi* clad in the layered garb of priests operate the devices in a dance of graceful progression, not a crude throwing of levers. The carts, bearing their burdens, are drawn slowly to the multiple doors of the ovens.

The hertasi engage in a final test of the doors that lead into the ultimate cremation oven, the heat chamber below the Heartstone itself. An unmistakable deep vibration, akin to a huge drum being struck, is the indication that the last door has tested as operational. This is the cue for these traditional words to be spoken by all the attendees on either side of the bodies' path to the first door. It is begun by a *hertasi* priest on the eastern side and spoken in a call/reply between both sides, to form the complete chant.

"This is the heaviest weight,
    But I am strong, and I bear it.
This is the most solemn part of their story,
    But while we live, their story will be known.
This is the emptiest I feel,
    But that feeling is not for myself.
They are a traveler beyond us,
    In the vastness of all realms.
Their absence gives me the challenge,
    That I can create in their memory.
As their body goes,
    What they were transmutes into what we will be.
What they were,
    Taught us.
What they gave,
    Made us.
Who we will be now,
    Was crafted by them.
Now we craft for those who follow,
    Now this weight becomes light.
Though their absence gives us sorrow,
    What they were strengthens our flight."

When the last word is spoken, *hertasi* arranged around the chamber pause for three heartbeats, then pull gently on the beaded ropes to set the wind chimes in motion. The chimes alone play while the rafts are sent through, door by door, until finally, the encompassing sound of the final door is heard again.

The dead are gone, but never forgotten.

About the Authors

Jennifer Brozek is a multitalented, award-winning author, editor, and tie-in writer. She is the author of *Never Let Me Sleep* and *The Last Days of Salton Academy*, both of which were finalists for the Bram Stoker Award. Her *BattleTech* tie-in novel, *The Nellus Academy Incident*, won a Scribe Award. Her editing work has netted her a Hugo Award nomination as well as an Australian Shadows Award for *Grants Pass*. Jennifer's short form work has appeared in Apex Publications and in anthologies set in the worlds of Valdemar, *Shadowrun*, *V Wars*, and *Predator*. Jennifer is also the Creative Director of Apocalypse Ink Productions, and was the managing editor of Evil Girlfriend Media and assistant editor for Apex Book Company. She has been a freelance author, editor, and tie-in writer for more than ten years after leaving her high-paying tech job, and she's never been happier. She shares her husband, Jeff, with several cats and often uses him as a sounding board for her story ideas. Visit Jennifer's worlds at jenniferbrozek.com.

Paige L. Christie is originally from Maine and now lives in the North Carolina mountains. She is best known for the Legacies of Arnan fantasy series (#1 *Draigon Weather*). She strives to tell stories that are entertaining and thoughtful and speak especially to women. When she isn't writing, Paige is the director of a nonprofit, runs a wine shop, and teaches belly dancing. She is a proud, founding member of the Blazing Lioness Writers. Find out what she's up to at PaigeLChristie.com

Brigid Collins is a fantasy and science fiction writer living in Michigan. Her short stories have appeared in *Fiction River, Uncollected Anthology Volume 13: Mystical Melodies*, and Mercedes Lackey's *Valdemar* anthologies. Her fantasy series *Songbird River Chronicles* and her dark fairy tale novella *Thorn and Thimble* are available in print and electronic versions on Amazon and Kobo. You can sign up for her newsletter at tinyletter.com/HarmonicStories or check out her website at backwrites.wordpress.com.

Brenda Cooper writes science fiction, fantasy, and the occasional poem. She also works in technology and writes and talks about the future. She has won multiple regional writing awards and her stories have often appeared in Year's Best anthologies. Brenda lives and works in the Pacific Northwest with her wife and multiple border collies and can sometimes be found biking around Seattle.

Hailed as "one of the best writers working today" by bestselling author Dean Wesley Smith, **Dayle A. Dermatis** is the author or coauthor of many novels (including snarky urban fantasies *Ghosted*, *Shaded*, and *Spectered*) and more than a hundred short stories in multiple genres, appearing in such venues as *Fiction River*, *Alfred Hitchcock's Mystery Magazine*, and various anthologies from DAW Books. "Burrowing Owl, Hidden No More" is her sixth story in a Valdemar anthology. She is the mastermind behind the Uncollected Anthology project, and her short fiction has been lauded in year's best anthologies in erotica, mystery, and horror. To find out where she's wandered off to (and to get free fiction!), check out DayleDermatis.com.

Larry Dixon is a renowned fantasy artist and novelist. The husband of Mercedes Lackey, he has collaborated on a number of novels with her, including the Mage Wars

Trilogy and the Owl Trilogy. As a birds-of-prey rehabilitation specialist, Dixon, along with Lackey, has returned several hundred hawks, owls, falcons, and corbies into the wild. Dixon's wildlife rehabilitation led to a minor role in the creation of the digital effects for the giant eagles in the *Lord of the Rings* movies. Dixon took digital photographs of a stuffed golden eagle he had been keeping for its owner. These photographs, along with castings of the beak and talons, were sent to Weta Digital in New Zealand to provide texture mapping for the digital model for Gwaihir and company. His skill at depicting birds of prey has often led to commissions with the United States Military and with Save Our American Raptors, an organization devoted to raptor rehabilitation.

English both by name and nationality, **Charlotte E. English** hasn't permitted emigration to the Netherlands to change her essential Britishness (much). She writes colorful fantasy novels over copious quantities of tea, and rarely misses an opportunity to apologize for something. A lifelong history buff with a degree in Heritage, she loves dressing up, touring historical sites, and eating really good cake. Spanning the spectrum from light to dark, her works include *Modern Magick*, the *Tales of Aylfenhame*, and the *Malykant Mysteries*.

Michele Lang is the author of the *Lady Lazarus* WWII historical fantasy series, and her fantasy, romance, crime, and science fiction short stories have been published by DAW Books, Inc., PM Press, and Running Press among others. Her short story "Sucker's Game" appeared in the Anthony Award-nominated anthology *Jewish Noir*. Michele lives on Long Island with her family and loves writing Valdemar and Elemental Masters stories for Mercedes Lackey anthologies! Learn more about Michele's writing at michelelang.com.

Terry O'Brien is a dual-classed bard/engineer who writes elegant software in several languages and crafts compelling stories and characters in several formats. He currently combines his creative and technical talents behind a camera, in the control room, or at an edit station as a member of multiple audio and video production teams for several clients, employers, and venues. His creative work can be viewed on his website: terryobrien.me.

Fiona Patton was born in Calgary, Alberta, and now lives in rural Ontario with her wife, Tanya Huff, an assortment of cats, and two wonderful dogs. She has written seven fantasy novels published by DAW Books and close to forty short stories. "The More Things Change; The More They Change More" is her 13th story in the Valdemar anthologies, and the 11th to feature the Dann family.

Angela Penrose lives in Seattle with her husband, seven computers and about ten thousand books. She's been a Valdemar fan for decades and wrote her first Valdemar story for the "Modems of the Queen" area on the old GEnie network back in the 1980s. In addition to fantasy, she writes SF and mystery, sometimes in combinations. She's had stories published in *Loosed Upon the World, Fiction River, The Year's Best Crime and Mystery Stories 2016,* and of course the previous Valdemar anthologies *Choices* and *Seasons.* Find links to all her work at angelapenrosewriter.blogspot.com.

Kristin Schwengel lives near Milwaukee, Wisconsin, with her husband, along with the obligatory writer's cat (named Gandalf, of course), a Darwinian garden in which only the strong survive, and a growing collection of knitting and spinning supplies. Her writing has appeared in several previous Valdemar anthologies, among others. This is the second story featuring Herald Rinton and the Karsite-born Mindhealer Mirideh, and Kristin hopes to write several more exploring their perspective on the events of the Winds and Storms trilogies.

Anthea Sharp grew up on fairy tales and computer games and has melded the two in her *USA Today*-bestselling

Feyland series, where a high-tech game opens a gateway to the treacherous Realm of Faerie. In addition to the GameLit fun of *Feyland*, she writes Victorian spacepunk set in a universe where the British Empire spans the galaxy, and Dark Elf romantic fantasy resonant with fairy tale magic. Her short fiction has appeared in multiple Valdemar anthologies, *The Future Chronicles*, and *Fiction River*, among others. She lives in sunny Southern California but would rather be traveling the globe. Her newest release, *Into the Darkwood*, sweeps readers away into the magical land of Elfhame, where a mortal girl and a Dark Elf prince are driven by prophecy into a battle to save their world. Find out more at antheasharp.com.

Stephanie D. Shaver lives in Southern California, where she is gainfully employed by Blizzard Entertainment. When she's not doing things for them, she's probably writing or catching up on sleep. You can find more at sdshaver.com, along with occasional ramblings on life and pictures of food she's making for herself and her family.

A lover of local history and fantastical possibilities, **Louisa Swann** spins tales that span multiple genres, including historical fantasy, science fiction, mystery, and her newest love: steampunk. Her short stories have appeared in Mercedes Lackey's Elemental Masters and Valdemar anthologies (which she's thrilled to participate in!); Esther Friesner's *Chicks and Balances*; and several *Fiction River* anthologies, including *No Humans Allowed* and *Reader's Choice*. Her new steampunk/weird west series, *The Peculiar Adventures of Miss Abigail Crumb*, is available at your favorite etailer. Find out more at louisaswann.com or friend her on Facebook @SwannWriter.

Elizabeth Vaughan is the *USA Today*-Bestselling Author of *Warprize*, the first volume of the Chronicles of the Warlands. You can learn more about her writing at writeandrepeat.com.

Elisabeth Waters sold her first story in 1980 to *The Keeper's Price*, the first of the Darkover anthologies. She went on to sell stories to a variety of anthologies. Her first novel, a fantasy called *Changing Fate*, was awarded the 1989 Gryphon Award and published by DAW Books in 1994. Its sequel, *Mending Fate*, was published in 2016. She has also worked as a supernumerary with the San Francisco Opera, where she appeared in *La Gioconda*, *Manon Lescaut*, *Madama Butterfly*, *Khovanshchina*, *Das Rheingold*, *Werther*, and *Idomeneo*.

Phaedra Weldon grew up in the thick, atmospheric land of South Georgia. Most nights, especially those in October, were spent on the back of pickup trucks in the center of cornfields, telling ghost stories, or in friends' homes playing RPGs. She got her start writing in shared worlds (*Eureka!, Star Trek, BattleTech, Shadowrun*) and selling original stories to DAW anthologies before she sold her first urban fantasy series to traditional publishing. Currently, her published series include the Zoe Martinique Investigations, the Eldritch Files, the Witches of Castle Falls and the upcoming paranormal women's fiction series Ravenwood Hills.

About the Editor

Mercedes Lackey is a full-time writer and has published numerous novels and works of short fiction, including the bestselling Heralds of Valdemar series. She is also a professional lyricist and a licensed wild bird rehabilitator. She lives in Oklahoma with her husband and collaborator, artist Larry Dixon, and their flock of parrots.

MERCEDES LACKEY
The Elemental Masters Series

"Putting a fresh face to a well-loved fairytale is not an easy task, but it is one that seems effortless to the prolific Lackey. Beautiful phrasing and a thorough grounding in the dress, mannerisms and history of the period help move the story along gracefully. This is a wonderful example of a new look at an old theme."
—*Publishers Weekly*

"Richly detailed historic backgrounds add flavor and richness to an already strong series that belongs in most fantasy collections. Highly recommended."
—*Library Journal*

The Serpent's Shadow	978-0-7564-0061-3
The Gates of Sleep	978-0-7564-0101-6
Phoenix and Ashes	978-0-7564-0272-3
The Wizard of London	978-0-7564-0363-8
Reserved for the Cat	978-0-7564-0488-8
Unnatural Issue	978-0-7564-0726-1
Home From the Sea	978-0-7564-0771-1
Steadfast	978-0-7564-0946-3
Blood Red	978-0-7564-0985-2
From a High Tower	978-0-7564-1083-4
A Study in Sable	978-0-7564-1161-9
A Scandal in Battersea	978-0-7564-1163-3
The Bartered Brides	978-0-7564-1165-7
The Case of the Spellbound Child	978-0-7564-1212-8
The Bartered Brides	978-0-7564-1165-7
Jolene	978-0-7564-1214-2

To Order Call: 1-800-788-6262
www.dawbooks.com